W9-CNV-499

NEW YORK REVIEW BOOKS

CLASSICS

THE GOLOVLYOV FAMILY

MIKHAIL EVGRAFOVICH SALTYKOV (1826–1889), who wrote under the pseudonym Shchedrin, was born into a family of the landed gentry and, as a young man, entered the civil service in St. Petersburg. In 1847 he began to publish satirical stories, which led to a seven-year term of political exile in the provinces. Returning to St. Petersburg, Saltykov worked as a journalist, eventually becoming editor of the radical monthly *Notes of the Fatherland*. His major works are *The History of a Town* (1869–1870), *The Golovlyov Family* (1876), and *Fables* (1885).

JAMES WOOD was born in Durham, England, in 1965 and attended Cambridge University. He has contributed literary criticism to *The Guardian*, *The New Republic*, and *The New Yorker* and is the author of *The Broken Estate: Essays on Literature and Belief*.

THE GOLOVLYOV FAMILY

Shchedrin

■

Translated by

NATALIE DUDDINGTON

Introduction by

JAMES WOOD

THIS IS A NEW YORK REVIEW BOOK
PUBLISHED BY THE NEW YORK REVIEW OF BOOKS
435 Hudson Street, New York, NY 10014
www.nyrb.com

Library of Congress Cataloging-in-Publication Data

Saltykov, Mikhail Evgrafovich, 1826–1889.
 [Gospoda Golovlevy. English]
 The Golovlyov family / Shchedrin ; translated by Natalie Duddington ;
introduction by James Wood.
     p. cm.
 ISBN 0-940322-57-9 (alk. paper)

 I. Title.
 PG3361.S3 G613 2001
 891.73'3—dc21   00-010981

ISBN 978-0-940322-57-8

Book design by Red Canoe, Deer Lodge, Tennessee
Caroline Kavanagh, Deb Koch
Printed in the United States of America on acid-free paper.
10 9 8 7 6 5

CONTENTS

THE HYPOCRITE MAY serve, among other things, as a deformed ambassador of the truth. By so obviously misrepresenting the truth, he enables us to trace its smothered outlines. In fiction and drama, this traditional hypocrite acts rather like an unreliable narrator. The unreliable narrator is rarely truly unreliable, because his unreliability is manipulated by an author, without whose reliable manipulation we would not be able to take the narrator's measure. As the unreliable narrator is really only a reliably unreliable narrator, so the traditional hypocrite is always reliably hypocritical, which is why we are so unthreatened by—indeed so enjoy the prospect of—Polonius, Tartuffe, Parson Adams, Pecksniff, and others. Such characters are comic and certify our rectitude, giving us pleasure that, whatever we have become, we have not become that kind of person. Though in a curious, unintended way, if we are not careful, such characters may turn us into hypocrites: the content and well-fed audiences watching Molière suggest that this has already happened.

We can see through the traditional hypocrite because his

zeal tends to be a perversion, almost a parody, of a visible moral code. He is nourished by the same food we consume; but, as it were, he eats far too much of it, and has become bullyingly large. Yet what would the hypocrite represent in a world starved of moral nutrition? A world in which the moral code has already been perverted, long before the hypocrite gets to it? Such a character becomes much more menacing than the traditional hypocrite, for there is no longer any truth for him reliably to misrepresent, and our reading of his motives becomes more difficult. He becomes opaque to us precisely because he ceases to be "a hypocrite," and he ceases to be a hypocrite because he is not a liar: there is nothing for him to lie about. Accordingly, he would be more likely to be a tragic than a comic figure, and more likely to be a solipsist or fantasist than a liar. He has merged with his own horrid world; he has no audience.

In his extraordinary novel *The Golovlyov Family*, the Russian writer Shchedrin (the nom de plume of M. E. Saltykov, sometimes known as Saltykov-Shchedrin) depicts just such a character and just such a world. The hypocrite is Porphyry Golovlyov, one of the sons of Arina Petrovna and Vladimir Mikhaylovich Golovlyov, and the novel, called by D. S. Mirsky "certainly the gloomiest in all Russian literature," is set on the Golovlyovs' dismal estate, known as Golovlyovo. The Golovlyovs are minor landowners (a class Shchedrin satirized in many stories and sketches, and from which he himself came), who, supported by the labor of their serfs, squander a privilege of which they are unaware.

Vladimir, the father, spends most of his time in his study, drinking, imitating the songs of starlings, and writing bawdy verse, while the estate is run by his wife, the ferociously continent and cruel Arina Petrovna. She has little but contempt for her three sons, especially the eldest and youngest, Stepan and Pavel. But for her middle son, Porphyry, known from early days to his family as Little Judas or Bloodsucker, she also feels something like fear. Even when the child was a baby, "he liked to behave affectionately to his 'dear friend mamma,' to kiss her unobtrusively on the shoulder and sometimes to tell tales. . . . But even in those early days Arina Petrovna felt as it were suspicious of her son's ingratiating ways. Even at that time the gaze that he fixed at her seemed to her enigmatic, and she could not decide what precisely was in it —venom or filial respect."

Golovlyovo is a house of death. One by one the members of the family try to escape, and one by one they return and die. Of course, they only come home because they are in desperate straits. Thus, having run through a family allowance, Stepan arrives from Moscow, only forty but looking a decade older, "inflamed by drink and rough weather," his eyes bulging and bloodshot: "He looked about him morosely from under his brows; this was due not to any inward discontent, but rather to a vague fear that at any minute he might suddenly drop dead with hunger." Stepan hopes to squeeze a little more life out of the family estate, but the punitive Arina, who has her own survival to think of, rations her indulgence.

Stepan is already dying, in a sense. On the Golovlyov estate, where everyone is barely hanging on to existence, the best means of survival is a kind of shutting down of the moral system, as the body sleeps in very cold weather. Thus, the commonest emotion at Golovlyovo is the moral equivalent of boredom: an empty blindness. Stepan, for instance, is described thus: "He had not a single thought, not a single desire. . . . He wanted nothing, nothing at all." His mother is no less sealed off. She allows Stepan a diet that is just sufficient to keep him from starving, and when she is told that he is ailing, the words do "not reach her ears or make any impression upon her mind." For Arina has the Golovlyov disease: "She had lost all sight of the fact that next door to her, in the office, lived a man related to her by blood."

Likewise, Pavel, who locks himself away and drinks himself

to death, is described as "an apathetic, mutely sullen man whose character was purely negative and never expressed itself in action," and as "the most perfect instance of a man devoid of any characteristics at all." And near the end of the book, when Porphyry's niece, Anninka, also returns to die, she spends the time pacing up and down, "singing in an undertone and trying to tire herself out and, above all, not to think."

Golovlyovo is a place of evil in the sense that Augustine and Calvin understood evil: as nothingness, the absence of goodness. The religious emphasis is proper, for in this vacated world, the man who briefly prospers, Little Judas, is above all a brilliant manipulator of religious hypocrisy. He fills the abyss with a diabolic version of traditional religion. Once Stepan, Vladimir, and Pavel have died (the latter is "comforted" by the unctuous Porphyry, but has enough life in him to shout from his deathbed, "Go away, you bloodsucker!"), Porphyry comes alive, and takes control of the estate.

Porphyry is Shchedrin's great creation. His vivacity as a character proceeds, in part, from a paradox, which is that he is interesting in proportion to his banality. Traditionally, the great fictional hypocrites are generally interesting as liars are interesting. But Porphyry does not really lie to himself, for the truth is nowhere to be found in his world. He speaks the "truths" (as he sees them) that are all around him, and they are the most dismal, banal, lying platitudes. Shchedrin is explicit about this at one point. The hypocrites of French drama, he writes, are "conscious hypocrites, that is, they know it themselves and are aware that other people know it too." Porphyry, he writes, "was a hypocrite of a purely Russian sort, that is, simply a man devoid of all moral standards, knowing no truth other than the copy-book precepts. He was pettifogging, deceitful, loquacious, boundlessly ignorant, and afraid of the devil. All these qualities are merely negative and can supply no stable material for real hypocrisy."

Porphyry grinds down his mother and his servants with endless banalities. His usual technique is to invoke God: "What would God say?" His sure idea of God's providence is used to justify his cruelty, his swindling, his meanness, and his theft. There is a vivid and comic scene as his brother Pavel is dying. Porphyry arrives in a coach-and-four; immediately his mother thinks to herself, "The Fox must have scented a carcass." Porphyry enters the house with his two sons, Volodenka and Petenka (Volodenka mimicking his father's pieties, "folding his hands, rolling his eyes and moving his lips"). Seeing his mother unhappy, Porphyry says to her: "You are despondent, I see! It's wrong, dear! Oh, it's very wrong! You should ask yourself, 'And what would God say to that?' Why, He would say, 'Here I arrange everything for the best in My wisdom, and she repines!'" He continues:

> As a brother—I am grieved. More than once, in fact, I may have wept. I am grieving over my brother, grieving deeply.... I shed tears, but then I think: "And what about God? Doesn't God know better than we do?" One considers this and feels cheered. That's what everyone ought to do.... Look at me. See how well I'm bearing up!

Still, Porphyry is afraid. He spends much of his time crossing himself, or praying before his icons. In true Golovlyov fashion, he prays not for anything positive, but negatively, to be saved from the devil. (It is a nice implicit joke that Porphyry is afraid of the devil but is in fact the devil.) "He could go on praying and performing all the necessary movements, and at the same time be looking out of the window to see if anyone went to the cellar without permission." Porphyry uses religious platitudes to protect himself from anything that would threaten his survival; religious hypocrisy is his moral camouflage.

One of the most horrifying events in the novel occurs when Porphyry's son Petenka comes home to beg for money. He has gambled away three thousand rubles belonging to his regiment, and if he cannot pay them back, he will be sent off to Siberia. Petenka enters his father's study; Porphyry is kneeling, with uplifted arms. He keeps his son waiting for half an hour on purpose, and when Petenka finally explains that he has lost money, Porphyry replies, "amiably": "Well, return it!" When Petenka tells him that he doesn't have that kind of money, Porphyry warns him not to "mix me up in your dirty affairs. Let us go and have breakfast instead. We'll drink tea and sit quietly and perhaps talk of something, only, for Christ's sake, not this." Bitterly, Petenka says to his father, "I am the only son you have left," and his father replies: "God took from Job all he had, my dear, and yet he did not repine, but only said, 'God has given, God has taken away—God's will be done.' So that's the way, my boy."

Hypocrisy is a familiar subject in Russian literature—Gogol's landowners, Dostoevsky's governors, Chekhov's doctor in "Ward 6"—and within it, religious hypocrisy has a special place. The traditional hypocrite may, in his extremism, unwittingly strengthen the visible moral code. But religion, which is itself an extremism, must be weakened by the hypocrite's misuse of it. Religion, after all, unlike ordinary morality, is a devotion—one professes it—so the Christian hypocrite commits an enhanced crime: hypocrisy about which one should certainly not be hypocritical. Thus he may awaken in people the conclusion that religion is itself a hypocrisy: since religion is itself already a profession of morality, it may seem that religion is the source of its hypocritical profession.

Morality is misused by the traditional hypocrite; but religion is only used by the religious hypocrite. Heresy lurks in the distinction. Outside Russian literature, Fielding's Parson Adams, though a benign creature, tends to discredit the Christianity which enables his hypocrisy. And Stendhal, depicting the hypocritical priests of The Red and the Black, means to provoke heresy. So too, in a gentler way, does

Chekhov, the son of a terrible religious hypocrite, when, in his story "In the Ravine," he makes fun of a priest who pompously comforts a woman who has just lost her baby while pointing at her with "a fork with a pickled mushroom at the end."

When he began to write *The Golovlyov Family*, in the latter half of the 1870s, Shchedrin, who was known as Russia's greatest satirist, had already mocked religious hypocrisy in his *Fables*, a collection of Aesopian tales about feeble governors, greedy landowners, imbecilic bureaucrats, and cruel priests. In "A Village Fire," a widow loses her only son to the flames, and the priest, like Porphyry, accuses her of grieving too much. "Why this plaint?" he asks her, "with kindly reproach." The priest tells her the story of Job and reminds her that Job did not complain, "but still more loved the Lord who had created him." Later in the story, when the daughter of the village's landowner tells her mother of the widow's suffering, the landowner, like Porphyry, invokes destiny: "It's dreadful for her; but how worked up you are, Vera! . . . That will never do, my love. There's a Purpose in all things—we must always remember!"

At times *The Golovlyov Family* seems less a novel than a satirical onslaught. Its relentlessness has the exhaustiveness not of a search for the truth so much as the prosecution of a case. Its characters are vivid blots of essence, carriers of the same single vice. Indeed, Shchedrin would seem to enjoy shocking the reader by annulling the novel's traditional task, that of the patient exploration, and elucidation, of private motives and reasons as they are played out in relation to a common condition. Instead, he gives us his sealed monsters, people whom we cannot explore since they are shut off from the moral world. Shchedrin knows how terrible, how—given the conventions of the novel—shocking it is to witness Stepan's homecoming, which is a cruel inversion of the parable of the Prodigal Son: "All understood that the man before them was an unloved son who had come to the place he hated, that he had come for good and that his only escape from it would be to be carried, feet foremost, to the church-yard. And all felt both sorry for him and uneasy." All except Stepan's mother, of course.

Shchedrin knows that it is both a kind of affront to de-cency and to the decency of the novel itself to present a fam-ily reunion in such inhuman terms, and his narration, at points throughout the book, registers the offense. Usually, Shchedrin breaks in to tell us what we should think about each charac-ter, acting as an omniscient satirist. But at other times, he writes as if from one of the character's minds. When Stepan returns, Arina, Pavel, and Porphyry hold a family conference to discuss his fate. Arina tells Porphyry and Pavel that she has decided to allow Stepan the meanest of allowances. Shchedrin writes: "Although Porphyry Vladimiritch had re-fused to act as a judge, he was so struck by his mother's gen-erosity that he felt it his duty to point out to her the dangerous consequences to which the proposed measure might lead." Since the reader can see that there is nothing "generous" about Arina, the novel's narration, at this point, is ironic, af-fecting to think of Arina as Porphyry might think of his mother. Yet we know that Porphyry can never be trusted, and that Porphyry never thinks well of anyone. What does it mean, then, to be told that he thought his mother generous? Is it pos-sible that the moral sense has been so polluted in Porphyry that, even though he hates his mother, he credits his own hypocritical lies, his own devious fawning and playacting, and actually believes his mother to be generous at this moment? Or, more simply, is it just that Porphyry truly thinks that Arina's terms are too good for Stepan, that, in effect, Porphyry hates his brother more than his mother? Shchedrin's devilish twist is that he has left us alone: we do not know.

This technique, antinovelistic in its essence, nonetheless grants Shchedrin a peculiar novelistic power of his own. He uses it to bring us closer to the characters, letting us, if only for a minute, inhabit the wilderness of their souls. The method is especially effective when used with Porphyry, for we are made to share in his self-deceptions. Here Shchedrin's narration is genuinely "unreliable," and unreliable about an already unreliable man. At one devastating moment in the novel, Shchedrin writes of Porphyry: "He had lost all connections with the outside world. He received no books, no newspapers, no letters. One of his sons, Volodenka, had committed suicide; to his other son, Petenka, he wrote very little, and only when he sent him money." The reader starts at this: the last time Volodenka was mentioned by Shchedrin, he was a little boy, mimicking his father. This is the first time we have heard anything about his committing suicide. But again, if we see the sentence as, in effect, issuing from Porphyry's mind, it is just the heartless way that he would think of his dead son—as an unimportant memory, hardly worth mentioning.

The closer Shchedrin brings us to Porphyry, the more unknowable he actually becomes. In this sense, Porphyry is a modernist prototype: the character who lacks an audience, the alienated actor. The hypocrite who does not know he is one, and can never really be told that he is one by anyone around him, is something of a revolutionary fictional character, for he has no "true" knowable self, no "stable ego," to use D. H. Lawrence's phrase. Around the turn of the twentieth century, Knut Hamsun, a novelist strongly influenced by Dostoevsky and the Russian novel, would invent a new kind of character: the lunatic heroes of his novels *Hunger* and *Mysteries* go around telling falsely incriminating stories about themselves and acting badly when they have no obvious reason to. It is difficult to know when they are lying and not lying, and impossible to understand their motives. They too are unknowable, even though they are, in a sense, antihypocrites, so deeply in revolt against the pieties of Lutheranism that they have become parodically impious. They broadcast their self-invented sinfulness in the streets, though no one is really listening. The line from Dostoevsky, through Shchedrin, and on to Hamsun, is visible. In this regard, *The Golovlyov Family*, this strange, raucous book, whose characters both suffer from and aspire to the condition of nothingness, a book which is at times broad satire, at times Gothic horror, and at times an antinovel, becomes more modern the older it gets.

—JAMES WOOD

THE
GOLOVLYOV
FAMILY

1

THE FAMILY TRIBUNAL

ONE DAY WHEN Anton Vassilyev, the bailiff of a distant estate, had finished telling his lady, Arina Petrovna Golovlyov, about his journey to Moscow to collect the tax from her serfs living there, and she had given him leave to go, he lingered as though he had something else to report and hesitated to do so.

Arina Petrovna, who could read her people's smallest gestures and, indeed, their inmost thoughts, at once scented trouble.

"What is it?" she asked, looking at the bailiff intently.

"That's all," Anton Vassilyev tried to prevaricate.

"None of your fibs—there's something more! I see it from your eyes!"

Anton Vassilyev could not make up his mind to speak, and shifted from one foot to the other.

"Now, what else have you to tell me?" Arina Petrovna cried peremptorily. "Speak! Don't wriggle . . . you turncoat!"

Arina Petrovna liked to give nicknames to members of her domestic and administrative personnel. She called Anton

Vassilyev a turncoat not because he had really been caught in some act of perfidy, but because he could not be trusted to hold his tongue. The estate he managed had a big trading center, a village with a number of pothouses. Anton Vassilyev loved to sit there drinking tea and boasting of his lady's omnipotence—and in doing so inadvertently said too much. And as Arina Petrovna always had various lawsuits on foot, her bailiff's chatter often disclosed the lady's stratagems before they could be put to the test.

"There is something, that's true..." Anton Vassilyev muttered at last.

"What? What is it?" Arina Petrovna asked in excitement. Being a woman of imperious character and great creative faculties she instantly imagined all sorts of things that could be said or done against her, and was at once so filled with the idea that she turned pale and jumped up from her chair.

"Stepan Vladimiritch has sold his Moscow house...." the bailiff announced deliberately.

"Yes?"

"He has sold it."

"Why? How? Don't mumble, speak!"

"For debts, I expect! They don't sell one up for behaving properly, do they?"

"So it was the police sold it? The magistrates?"

"It must have been. They say the house went for eight thousand at the auction."

Arina Petrovna sank heavily into her chair and stared at the window. For the first minute she seemed stunned by the news. Had she been told that Stepan Vladimiritch had committed murder, that the Golovlyov peasants had rebelled and refused to work for her, that serfdom had been abolished—she would have been less impressed. Her lips moved, her eyes looked into the distance but saw nothing. She did not even notice that the girl Dunyashka had just made a dash past the window covering something with her apron, but suddenly, seeing her mistress, whirled round and slowly turned back (at another time such behavior would have led to a regular inquisition). At last, however, Arina Petrovna recovered and said:

"That's a nice thing to do!"

Several more minutes of ominous silence followed.

"And so you say the police sold it for eight thousand?"

"Yes, madam."

"Selling his mother's blessing—the scoundrel!"

Arina Petrovna felt that the news she had just heard required some immediate decision on her part, but she could think of nothing because her mind wandered in entirely opposite directions. On the one hand, she thought: "The police sold it! But it could not have all happened in a minute! They must have taken an inventory, made a valuation, announced the auction. They sold it for eight thousand, though only two years ago she had with her own hands given twelve thousand rubles in hard cash for that very house! Had she known, she might have bought it herself for eight thousand at the auction!" On the other hand, she kept thinking, "The police sold it for eight thousand! His mother's gift! The scoundrel! He has let his mother's blessing go for eight thousand!"

"Who told you?" she asked at last, coming to the conclusion that the house had been sold, and so the hope of acquiring it cheaply was lost to her for ever.

"Ivan Mihailitch, the innkeeper."

"And why didn't he warn me in time?"

"I expect he was afeard."

"Afeard! I'll teach him to be afeard! Send to Moscow for him, and as soon as he comes take him to the recruiting office to be made a soldier. Afeard, indeed!"

Serfdom still existed, though the end of it was in sight. Anton Vassilyev had often received most peculiar orders from his mistress, but the present one was so unexpected that he felt positively uncomfortable. He could not help recalling his nickname of "Turncoat." Ivan Mihailitch was a steady, prosperous peasant, and it seemed inconceivable that he should get into trouble. Besides, he was his friend—and now the man was to be sent for a recruit simply because he, Anton Vassilyev, could not hold his tongue.

"Forgive . . . Ivan Mihailitch, I mean!" he tried to intercede.

"Out with you . . . you conniver!" Arina Petrovna shouted at him in such a voice that he did not think of persisting in his defense of Ivan Mihailitch.

But before I go on with my story I will ask the reader to make a closer acquaintance with Arina Petrovna and her family.

Arina Petrovna was a woman of about sixty, still vigorous and used to having her own way. Her manner was formidable; she ruled over the vast Golovlyov estate autocratically, giving account to no one; she lived quietly and economically, almost stingily, making no friends with her neighbors; she was on good terms with the local authorities, and required of her children such obedience that she expected them before doing anything to ask themselves, "And what would mamma say?" Altogether she had an independent, indomitable, and rather domineering character, partly owing to the fact that not a single member of the Golovlyov family was capable of offering her any opposition. Her husband was a frivolous man, generally a little drunk (Arina Petrovna readily said of herself that she was neither a wife nor a widow); some of her children were in Government service in Petersburg, others had taken after their father and, being in disfavor, were not allowed to take any part in family affairs. Early in life Arina Petrovna had come to feel isolated, and had indeed completely lost the habit of family life, though the word "family" was always on her lips and ostensibly the only motive of her actions was the anxiety to provide for it.

The head of the family, Vladimir Mihailitch Golovlyov, had been known from his youth up for a shiftless and trouble-some man, and Arina Petrovna, an exceptionally serious-minded and business-like woman, had never been in sympathy with him. He led an idle and useless life, and spent most of his time shut up in his study imitating the singing of star-lings, the crowing of cocks, etc., and composing so-called "free verses." In moments of confidence he boasted that he had been a friend of Barkov and that the latter had actually given him his death-bed blessing. Arina Petrovna took from the first a dislike to her husband's verses, calling them "filthy buffoonery"; and since Vladimir Mihailitch's chief object in marrying was to provide himself with a ready audience for his verses, dissensions were not long in coming. Gradually growing more intense and bitter, they ended on the part of the wife in a complete and contemptuous indifference to her clownish husband, and on the part of the husband in a sincere hatred for the wife—a hatred in which, however, there was a considerable element of fear. The husband called the wife "a termagant" and a devil, and the wife called the husband "a windmill" and a "stringless balalaika." They lived together for forty years on such terms, and it never occurred to either of them that there was anything unnatural in their life.

Vladimir Mihailitch did not grow less troublesome as time passed, but on the contrary became more provoking. In addi-tion to his poetical exercises in Barkov's style he took to drinking and waylaying maid-servants in the corridor. At first Arina Petrovna was disgusted and upset by her husband's new diversion (though she suffered more from the affront to her authority than from jealousy as such), but afterwards she dismissed it from her mind and merely watched that the hussies should not bring any vodka to the master. Having said to herself once and for all that her husband was no help to her, she devoted all her energies to one object—increasing her estate, and in the forty years of her married life she succeeded in increasing it tenfold. With astonishing patience she kept keen watch on the estates far and near, ascertained, on the quiet, how their owners stood with the Trustees' Council, and appeared at auctions like a bolt from the blue. In the whirl of this fantastic pursuit of possessions Vladimir Mihailitch retreated further and further into the background and at last became quite a recluse. At the time when our story begins he was a decrepit old man who hardly ever left his bed, and on the rare occasions when he did so it was solely in order to thrust his head through the half-open door of his wife's room and shout, "You devil!"—and disappear again.

Arina Petrovna was scarcely more happy in her children. Her nature was too independent; she was too much of a bachelor, so to speak, to regard children as anything but a burden. She only breathed freely when she was alone with her accounts and plans of acquisition, when no one interrupted her business conversations with bailiffs, foremen, housekeepers, etc. Children were to her merely a part of the preordained framework of life, against which she would have thought it wrong to rebel though it did not stir a single chord of her inner being, which was entirely taken up with the numberless details of practical life. She had four children: three sons and a daughter. Of her eldest son and of her daughter she did not even like to speak; she was more or less indifferent to her youngest son, and only for the second, Porphyry, she had some feeling, though it was more akin to fear than affection.

Her eldest son, Stepan Vladimiritch, with whom the present story is chiefly concerned, was known in his family under the names of Styopka the dolt, and Styopka the rascal. He had very early fallen into disfavor, and had from a child been something between a pariah and a clown in the family. Unfortunately he was a gifted boy who absorbed quickly and readily the impressions of his environment. He inherited from his father his inexhaustible naughtiness, and from his mother the capacity for quickly discerning people's weak points. Owing to his first characteristics he soon became his father's favorite—which made his mother dislike him all the more. Often, while Arina Petrovna was out on business, the father and the son withdrew to the study adorned with a portrait of Barkov, read libertine verses and gossiped chiefly about "the termagant," i.e. Arina Petrovna. But the termagant scented as it were what they were doing: she quietly drove up to the house, tiptoed to the study door and listened to the lively talk. Styopka the dolt was severely whipped there and then, but it had no effect; he was insensitive both to beatings and to admonitions, and in half an hour's time was at his pranks again. He either cut the maid Anyutka's kerchief to pieces or put some flies into sleeping Vassyutka's mouth, or found his way into the kitchen and stole a pie (Arina Petrovna kept her children on short commons for the sake of economy), though, it is true, he immediately shared it with his brothers.

"You ought to be killed!" Arina Petrovna repeated to him constantly. "I'll kill you and won't have to answer for it! The Tsar wouldn't punish me for it!"

This constant humiliation had its effect on the boy's slack, easygoing nature. Instead of making him embittered or rebellious, it developed a servile character, a desire to please even at the loss of personal dignity, and a complete lack of forethought and of any sense of proportion. Such people fall easy prey to any influence, and may become anything: drunkards, beggars, clowns, and even criminals.

At the age of twenty Stepan Golovlyov finished the course of studies in one of the Moscow gymnasiums and entered the University. He had a poor time of it as a student. In the first place, his mother gave him just enough money not to starve; secondly, he had not the slightest inclination to work, and suffered from the curse of an artistic temperament that expressed itself chiefly in a talent for mimicking; thirdly, he had a craving for company, and could not bear to be by himself for a moment. And so he took up the easy part of a hanger-on and *piqueassiette*; his readiness to fall in with every prank soon made him popular with the richer students. While admitting him to their society, however, they made it plain that he was not their equal, but was merely a sort of clown, and that was, indeed, what most people thought of him. Having once taken this line he sunk lower and lower, and by the end of the fourth year became a kind of professional jester. Nevertheless, owing to his faculty of taking in and remembering all that he heard he passed his examinations successfully and obtained his degree.

When he appeared before his mother with a diploma, Arina Petrovna merely shrugged her shoulders and said, "Queer!" She kept him for a month in the country and then sent him off to Petersburg with an allowance of a hundred paper rubles* a month. He wandered from one Government office to another. He had no powerful friends, and not the slightest desire to make his way by his own efforts. The young man's idle mind had so lost all habit of concentration that even such bureaucratic tasks as reports and résumés were too much for him. Golovlyov struggled on in Petersburg for four years, and at last had to confess to himself that he had no hope of ever rising beyond an office clerk. In answer to his complaints Arina Petrovna wrote him a wrathful letter beginning with the words, "I was certain of it all along," and ending with an order to come to Moscow. There, at a council of her favorite serfs, it was decided to find a post for Styopka the dolt at the Law Courts, and to put him in charge of an attorney who had always acted for the Golovlyov family. History does not say what Stepan Vladimiritch did at the Courts and how he behaved, but in three years' time he was no longer

---

*A paper ruble at that time (about 1845) was worth less than a third of a silver ruble. —Translator's note.

there. Then Arina Petrovna decided on an extreme measure: she "chucked her son a piece" which was at the same time to figure as "his mother's blessing": she bought him a house in Moscow, paying twelve thousand rubles for it.

For the first time in his life Stepan Golovlyov breathed freely. The house was likely to bring in a thousand silver rubles a year, and by comparison with the past this sum seemed to him quite a fortune. He kissed his mother's hand with real feeling ("Mind now, you dolt, don't expect anything more of me!" Arina Petrovna said as he did so) and promised to prove worthy of the favor bestowed on him. But, alas! he was so unused to handling money, he knew so little of practical life, that the fabulous thousand rubles a year lasted him a very short time. In some four or five years he was completely bankrupt and was only too glad to volunteer for the army when fresh reserves were being called up.* His regiment, however, had only marched as far as Harkov when peace was made, and Golovlyov returned to Moscow once more. He wore a rather shabby soldier's uniform and top-boots, and had a hundred rubles in his pocket. He tried to speculate with that money, that is, he gambled at cards and soon lost it all. Then he began visiting the rich peasants of his mother who had homes in Moscow: he dined with one, begged for a quarter of a pound of tobacco from another, borrowed a trifle from the third. But at last a moment came when he found himself, so to speak, up against a wall. He was nearly forty and he had to admit that he could not stand a homeless life any more. The only thing that remained for him was—Golovlyovo.

Arina Petrovna's second child was her daughter Anna, whom she did not like to mention either.

The fact was that Arina Petrovna had had plans about Anna, but instead of justifying her hopes the girl created a

---

*During the Crimean War. —Translator's note.

scandal that all the district talked of. When Anna had left school Arina Petrovna settled her in the country, hoping to make of her an unpaid secretary and book-keeper, but Anna ran away from home one night with the cornet Ulanov and married him instead.

"They married without their parents' blessing just like dogs!" Arina Petrovna complained. "Thank Heaven that at least the man put a wedding-ring on her finger! Any other one would have simply taken his pleasure and made off! You might whistle for him!"

Arina Petrovna acted as resolutely in her daughter's case as in the case of the bad son: she "chucked her a piece." She gave her five thousand rubles and a village with thirty serfs and a dilapidated house in which every window was drafty and every floor-board creaked. In a couple of years the young people spent their money and the cornet disappeared, leaving Anna with twin daughters: Anninka and Lubinka. Three months later Anna died, and Arina Petrovna had, willy-nilly, to give a home to the orphans; she put the babies in the lodge of her house and appointed a one-eyed old woman, Palashka, to look after them.

"God has many mercies," she said; "the orphans' food won't cost so very much, and they will be a comfort to me in my old age! God has taken away one daughter and given me two." At the same time she wrote to her son Porphyry Vladimiritch, "Your sister died as shamefully as she lived, throwing her two brats on to my shoulders."

It is only fair to observe, cynical as the remark may seem, that her gifts to Stepan and to Anna were of no financial detriment to Arina Petrovna, and that they served, indeed, indirectly to increase the Golovlyov property by decreasing the number of its owners. For Arina Petrovna was a woman of principle, and having once "chucked a piece" to the bad children, considered all her duties towards them at an end. It never entered her head that she might one day have to apportion something to her orphaned grand-daughters. She merely tried to squeeze as much as possible out of the small estate she had given to their mother, investing the money in the Trustees' Council and saying as she did so: "Here I am saving money for the orphans, and I don't charge anything for the keep and the care of them! God will repay me, maybe, for what I spend on them!"

Arina Petrovna's younger children, Porphyry and Pavel, lived in Petersburg: the first was in the Civil Service and the second in the Army. Porphyry was married, Pavel a bachelor.

Porphyry Vladimiritch was known in the family under three names: "Iudushka,"* "bloodsucker," and "candid boy"; all three had been given him in childhood by Styopka the dolt. From babyhood he liked to behave affectionately to his "dear friend mamma," to kiss her unobtrusively on the shoulder and sometimes to tell tales. He used to open quietly the door of his mother's room, steal noiselessly into a corner, and sit down, never taking his eyes off her while she was writing or making up accounts. But even in those early days Arina Petrovna felt as it were suspicious of her son's ingratiating ways. Even at that time the gaze that he fixed at her seemed to her enigmatic, and she could not decide what precisely was in it—venom or filial respect.

"I can't make out that look in his eyes," she said to herself sometimes; "it's just as though he were trying to lay a snare for me. Such a venomous, deceitful look!"

She recalled the significant details of what happened just before Porphyry was born. There lived in their house at the time a certain pious old man known as "Porphyry the crazy saint," who had the gift of prophecy; she always consulted him when she wanted to know something about the future. When she asked this old man how soon she was to be confined and whether she would have a son or a daughter, he

---

*Little Judas. —Translator's note.

13

made no direct answer but crowed three times like a cock and then muttered:

"A young cock, a young cock, his claw sharp as a saw; he threatens the hen, crowing now and again; the hen cries 'cluck-cluck,' but too late for her luck"

—that was all. But three days later (that was it—he crowed three times!) she gave birth to a son (that was it—a young cock!), who was christened Porphyry, in honor of the holy old man.

The first half of the prophecy had come true, but what could be the meaning of the mysterious words,

"The hen cries 'cluck-cluck,' but too late for her luck"?

Arina Petrovna wondered about it as she glanced from under her hand at Porphyry sitting in his corner and gazing at her with his enigmatic expression.

The boy sat there quietly and modestly, looking at her so intently that tears came into his wide-open eyes. It was as though he guessed the doubts stirring in his mother's mind and behaved so that his meekness should disarm the most watchful suspicion. At the risk of annoying his mother he always thrust himself forward, saying as it were, "Look at me! I don't conceal anything. I am all obedience and devotion, not only for fear but for conscience' sake." And convinced as she was that the wretched boy was merely making up to her while he set a trap for her with his eyes, her heart could not resist such overwhelming devotion. In spite of herself her hand sought out the best piece on the dish to give it to her affectionate son, although the very appearance of that son raised a vague uneasy foreboding in her mind.

Pavel was a complete contrast to his brother Porphyry. He was the most perfect instance of a man devoid of any characteristics at all. As a boy he did not show the slightest inclination for study, or games, or other children's company, but liked to be by himself, away from people. He would tuck himself into a corner and sit there, pouting, indulging in flights of fancy. He would pretend that he had had too much oatmeal to eat and his legs had grown so thin that he could not do his lessons. Or that he was not Pavel, a gentleman's son, but Davidka the shepherd, and that he had a wart on his forehead like Davidka and was cracking a whip instead of doing lessons. Arina Petrovna would look at him for a while and her heart would boil within her.

"Why do you sit there sulking?" she could not resist shouting at him. "Fancy harboring spite at your age! You never think of coming to your mother and saying, 'Kiss me, mamma darling.'"

Pavel left his corner and slowly walked up to his mother as though someone were pushing him in the back.

"Mamma," he repeated in a bass voice, unnatural in a child, "kiss me, darling."

"Off with you, you...sneak! You think that if you sit tucked away in a corner you'll deceive me, but I see right through you, my dear! I see all your plans and designs as plain as can be."

Pavel walked back as slowly and hid in his corner again.

Years passed, and Pavel Vladimiritch gradually developed into an apathetic, mutely sullen man whose character was purely negative and never expressed itself in action. He may have been kind but he showed no kindness to anyone; he may have had brains but he never did anything intelligent. He was hospitable but no one appreciated his hospitality; he readily spent money but it never did any good or gave any pleasure to anyone; he never wronged anyone but no one gave him credit for it; he was honest but no one was ever heard to say, "How honorably Pavel Golovlyov behaved on such and such an occasion." He was often rude to his mother and at the same time feared her like fire. I repeat again, he was sullen but there was nothing but inertia behind his sullenness.

When both brothers were grown up the difference in their character expressed itself most clearly in their attitude to their mother. Iudushka regularly sent her every week a long epistle in which he informed her at length about all the particulars of Petersburg life and assured her in choice expressions of his disinterested filial affection. Pavel wrote seldom and shortly, sometimes quite enigmatically, and it seemed as though every word were extracted from him with pincers.

"I have received such and such a sum, on such and such a date, precious friend mamma, from your agent, the peasant Yerofeyev," Porphyry Vladimiritch would inform his mother, "and for sending the above sum to be spent on my keep, in accordance with your gracious wish, dear mamma, I express my heartfelt gratitude and with sincere filial devotion kiss your hands. The only thing that causes me grief and anxiety is the fear lest you overtax your precious health by your unremitting solicitude in providing not only for our needs but even for our whims. I do not know what my brother thinks, but I . . ." and so on. On the same occasion Pavel would write: "Dearest parent, I have received such and such a sum on such and such a date, and according to my reckoning it is six and a half rubles short of my allowance, for which I respectfully beg you to excuse me." When Arina Petrovna reprimanded her children for spending too much (this happened frequently though she had no serious cause for it), Porphyry always received her remarks with meekness and wrote: "I know, dear friend mamma, that you are carrying burdens beyond your strength for the sake of us, your unworthy children; I know that we very often behave in a way that does not justify your motherly care of us, and that, worst of all, owing to a natural human frailty, we actually forget this, for which I make my sincere filial apologies, hoping in time to free myself from this vice and to be circumspect in the use of money which you send for my keep and other expenses, precious friend mamma." But Pavel answered as follows: "Dearest parent! Though you have not yet paid any of my debts, I make no objections to your reprimanding me as a spendthrift, of which I earnestly beg you to be assured." The two brothers responded differently to Arina Petrovna's letter with the news of their sister Anna's death. Porphyry wrote: "I am stricken with grief at the news that Anna Vladimirovna, my beloved sister and dear companion of my childhood, has departed this life, and my grief is all the greater at the thought that you, dear friend mamma, have a fresh cross laid upon you in the persons of the two baby orphans. As though it were not enough that you, our general benefactress, should deny yourself in everything and without sparing your health, devote all your strength to providing your family not merely with necessaries, but with luxuries as well! Really, one cannot help repining sometimes, though it is a sin to do so. And in my opinion the only refuge for you in your present trouble, dearest, is to recall as often as possible what Christ Himself had to endure."

Pavel wrote: "I have received the news of my sister dying a victim. I hope, however, that the Almighty will give her rest in His mansions, though this is uncertain."

Arina Petrovna read again and again her sons' letters, trying to guess which of them would prove to be her enemy. She read Porphyry's letter, and it seemed to her that he was the villain.

"Just think how he writes! What twists and turns he gives to his tongue!" she exclaimed. "It's not for nothing Styopka the dolt has nicknamed him Judas! There's not a word of truth in what he says! It's all lies—'dear friend mamma,' and about my burdens, and about the cross.... He does not feel any of it, really!"

Then she took up Pavel's letter, and again she fancied that he was the villain.

"He may be stupid, but see how he sticks pins into his mother! 'Of which I earnestly beg you to be assured . . .' That's a nice thing to say! I'll teach him 'earnestly to be assured!' I'll chuck him a piece as I did to Styopka the dolt, then he'll know what I think of his 'assurances'!"

And in conclusion a truly tragic wail escaped from the mother's breast:

"Whom am I saving all this wealth for? Whom am I providing for, going short of sleep and of food? Whom is it all for?"

Such was the position of the Golovlyov family at the moment when the bailiff Anton Vassilyev told Arina Petrovna that Styopka the dolt had squandered the piece that had been chucked him. The low price for which it had been sold made it appear in her eyes more than ever as "a mother's blessing."

Arina Petrovna sat in her bedroom, unable to recover her mental balance. Something seemed to stir within her but she could not make out what it was. The most experienced psychologist could not have determined whether there was in it an admixture of sudden pity for the man who was after all her son, or whether she was suffering merely from a crude feeling of the affront to her authority: all her feelings and sensations were mixed up and they changed with bewildering rapidity. At last the fear that she would once more be burdened with the "hateful boy" stood out against the confused mass of her other thoughts.

"That wretch Anna saddled me with her brats and now there's the dolt" . . . she reflected.

She sat still for some hours staring at the window and not saying a word. They brought her dinner, which she hardly touched; they came to say, "Please give the master some vodka," and she flung them the store-room key without looking. After dinner she went to the icon room, ordering all the sanctuary lamps to be lit, and gave word for the bath-house to be heated. All these were unmistakable symptoms that the mistress was angry, and so everything in the house grew still, died down as it were. The maids walked on tiptoe; the house-keeper, Akulina, rushed about like one distracted: she was to have made jam that afternoon, and now the time had come, the fruit had been cleaned, but there were no orders from the mistress; Matvey the gardener came to ask if the peaches were to be picked, but the maids said "Hush" so impressively that he hastened to retire.

Having said her prayers and washed in the bath-house, Arina Petrovna felt more at peace and sent for Anton Vassilyev once more.

"Well, and what is the dolt doing?" she asked.

"Moscow is big—it would take more than a year to go all round it!"

"But he has to eat and drink, hasn't he?"

"He feeds with our peasants. With some he has dinner, from others he begs ten kopecks for tobacco."

"And who said they might give it him?"

"Why, madam, the peasants don't mind! They give alms to strangers, and is it likely they would refuse their own master?"

"I'll teach them . . . the almsgivers! I'll send the dolt to your village, and let you all keep him at your own expense."

"As you please, madam."

"What? What did you say?"

"I said, 'It is as you please, madam. If you say so we'll keep him.'"

"Keep him. . . . I should think so! Don't you be too free with your tongue!"

There was a silence. But it was not for nothing Anton Vassilyev had been nicknamed by his mistress a turncoat. He could not keep quiet and began fidgeting, longing to tell her something more.

"He is a sharp one!" he said at last. "They say he had a hundred rubles when he returned from the campaign. A hundred rubles is not much, but one could live on it for a time. . . ."

"Well?"

"But he thought he would mend his fortunes, if you please, and do a bit of business. . . ."

"Speak plainly, now!"

"He took the money to the German club. He thought he would find a fool and win from him at cards, but he ran up against a clever one instead. He tried to steal away, but they stopped him in the hall, it appears, and took all his money from him."

"I suppose he came in for a thrashing too?"

"He did. The next day he came to Ivan Mihailov and told him all about it. And the funny thing is, he was laughing . . . quite cheerful, as though something good had happened to him!"

"He doesn't care! If only he doesn't come before my eyes. . . ."

"I expect he will, though."

"What! Why, I won't let him in at the door!"

"He is sure to come," Anton Vassilyev repeated. "Ivan Mihailitch told me that he said: 'It's all up with me, I'll have to go to the old woman to eat dry bread!' And to tell you the truth, madam, there's nowhere else for him to go. He can't go visiting his peasants in Moscow for ever. He needs clothes too, and a home. . . ."

This was precisely what Arina Petrovna feared; this was the very thing that had loomed before her, causing her vague uneasiness. Yes, he will come, he has nowhere else to go—there's no escaping it! He would be here, always before her, the odious creature she had cursed and forgotten! Why, then, had she "chucked him a piece"? She thought that having received "his due" he would disappear for ever—but here he was coming back! He would come, he would make claims, he would be an eyesore to everyone in his tatters. And she would have to do what he asked because he was an impudent, violent man. There was no keeping him under lock and key;

he was capable of appearing in rags before strangers, of making a row, of running to the neighbors and telling them all the secret history of the Golovlyov family. Could she perhaps banish him to the Suzdal monastery? But there was no telling whether that monastery actually existed, and whether it really was there for the purpose of sparing aggrieved parents the sight of their obstreperous children. People talked of the penitentiaries . . . but how could one take a burly man of forty to a penitentiary?

In short, Arina Petrovna was quite overwhelmed at the thought of the troubles that threatened her peaceful existence with the arrival of Styopka the dolt.

"I'll send him to your village, keep him yourself!" she threatened the bailiff. "Not at the village expense, but at your own!"

"What for, madam? What have I done?"

"What for? Because you croak. Caw, caw! 'He is sure to come!' . . . Out of my sight . . . you crow!"

Anton Vassilyev turned round to go, but Arina Petrovna stopped him again.

"Stop! Wait! So it's certain that he is making tracks for Golovlyovo?" she asked.

"As though I would deceive you, madam! Sure enough he said, 'I'll go to the old woman to eat dry bread.'"

"I'll show him what sort of bread the old woman has for him!"

"Ah, madam, he won't be with you for long!"

"Why not?"

"He coughs a lot . . . he keeps clutching at his left side. He hasn't long to live!"

"Men like that, my good man, live all the longer! He'll outlive us all. He'll go on coughing and coughing—it's nothing to a long-legged horse like him! Well, we shall see. You go now! I have to see to things."

Arina Petrovna spent the whole evening thinking and

determined at last to call together a family council to settle the dolt's future. Constitutional measures were not in her character, but this time she decided to forgo the traditions of autocracy so that public opinion should not hold her personally responsible for the decision. But she had no doubts as to the result of the family council, and so it was with a light heart that she sat down to write to Porphyry and Pavel ordering them to come immediately to Golovlyovo.

While all this was going on, the cause of the trouble, Styopka the dolt, was already on his way from Moscow to Golovlyovo. He booked a seat in one of the so-called diligences in which petty tradesmen and peasants living in town used to travel in the old days—and still do in some places when going for a visit to their native village. The diligence went in the direction of Vladimir, and the kind-hearted innkeeper Ivan Mihailitch paid Stepan's fare and bought him food on the journey.

"That's what you must do, Stepan Vladimiritch," he said to him: "step out of the diligence at the cross-roads and go on to your mamma's on foot, dressed as you are!"

"That's it, that's it!" Stepan Vladimiritch agreed. "It's not much to walk from the cross-roads—only ten miles! I'll do it in no time. I'll come before her just as I am, covered with dust and dirt!"

"When your mamma sees your clothes maybe she'll have pity on you!"

"Of course she will! She is sure to! My mother is a kind old creature."

Stepan Golovlyov was not yet forty, but he looked at least fifty. Life had played such havoc with him that there was no trace of a gentleman born left in him, nor the slightest indication of his having once been to a university and enjoyed the benefits of a liberal education. Disproportionately tall, with long ape-like arms and narrow chest, he was thin from under-feeding, dirty, and unkempt. His face was bloated, his grayish hair and beard disheveled, his protruding eyes were inflamed by drink and rough weather, his voice was loud but hoarse as though he had a cold. He was wearing a shabby gray military jacket, fearfully soiled; the braid had been torn off and sold. On his feet he had rusty-looking boots, much patched and down at the heel. Through the opening of his jacket one could see a shirt that was almost black and seemed covered with soot; with true army cynicism he called it a flea-shirt. He looked about him morosely from under his brows; this was due not to any inward discontent, but rather to a vague fear that any minute he might suddenly drop dead with hunger.

He talked unceasingly, disconnectedly, jumping from sub-ject to subject; he talked when Ivan Mihailitch listened and when he dropped asleep to the music of his voice. Stepan Vladimiritch was fearfully uncomfortable in the diligence. As there were four people in it, he had to sit with his feet tucked under him, and after some two or three miles this gave him cruel pains in the knees. But he talked constantly in spite of the pain. Clouds of dust flew in at the side-windows, slanting rays of the sun sometimes found their way in and suddenly lit up the inside of the carriage as with a bright flame—and he talked on and on.

"Yes, brother, I have had the devil of a life," he said; "it's time I had a rest! After all, I am not likely to eat her out of house and home, and surely she can find a crust to spare for me! What do you think, Ivan Mihailitch?"

"Your mother has plenty to spare."

"But not for me—that's what you mean, don't you? Yes, my dear, she has tons of money, but she grudges a copper if it's for me. She has always hated me, the old hag! What for? But she can do nothing to me now—you can't draw blood out of a stone! I don't care what I do! If she tries to drive me away,

I won't go! If she doesn't give me any food, I'll help myself! I have served my country, brother, and now it's everybody's duty to help me. One thing I fear, she won't give me any tobacco—and that's damnable!"

"Yes, I am afraid you'll have to say good-bye to tobacco."

"I'll tackle the bailiff, then—perhaps the bald-headed old devil might give some to his master."

"He might, of course. But what if your mamma forbids him?"

"Well, then, I shall be done for. The only luxury left me of all my former magnificence is tobacco! When I had money, brother, I used to smoke a quarter of Zhukov's tobacco a day!"

"You will have to say good-bye to vodka also."

"That's damnable too. Vodka is good for my health—it loosens my cough. You know, brother, as we were marching to Sebastopol, we had had nearly three gallons each before we came as far as Serpuhov!"

"I expect you were quite fuddled?"

"I don't remember. I believe we were. I got as far as Harkov, brother, but for the life of me I don't remember anything. I only remember we marched through villages and through towns and that a government contractor made a speech to us in Tula. He shed tears, the scoundrel! Yes, our Mother Russia had had the devil of a time! Contractors, receivers, profiteers —it's a wonder the country survived!"

"And your mamma managed to make some profit out of the war, too. More than half of the recruits from our estate are missing, and the Government, they say, is giving the owners a blank certificate for each of the men they had sent. And those certificates are worth four hundred rubles each."

"Yes, my mother is a clever woman! She ought to have been a statesman instead of sitting at Golovlyovo making jam! Do you know what? She was unfair to me, she wronged me, and yet I respect her! She is devilishly clever—that's the chief thing! If it had not been for her, where should we have been now? We should have had nothing except Golovlyovo—a hundred serfs and a half! And see what the devil of a lot she has added to it!"

"Your brothers will be very well off."

"They will. But I shall have nothing—that's certain. Yes, my dear fellow, I am ruined root and branch! And my brothers will be rich, the little Bloodsucker especially. He will worm himself in anywhere with his blarney. But in time he will make an end of the old hag: he will suck the estate and the capital out of her—I have a sharp nose for that sort of thing! Now, my brother Pavel is a right sort of man! He'll send me some tobacco on the quiet—you'll see! As soon as I come to Golovlyovo I'll send a missive to him: that's how things are with me, dear brother—do me a favor! Ah! If I were rich now!"

"What would you do?"

"To begin with, I'd shower gold on you."

"But why on me? Think of yourself, I am content as it is, thanks to your mother."

"Oh no, brother, don't say that! I would make you commander-in-chief over all the estates! Yes, my friend, you have given food and shelter to an old soldier—I am grateful to you. If it hadn't been for you I should be trudging on foot to my ancestral home! I would make you a free man at once and open all my treasures before you—eat, drink, and be merry! Why, what did you think of me, my boy?"

"No, sir, you leave me out of it. What else would you do if you were rich?"

"Then I would at once take a mopsy. When we were at Kursk we went to have a service sung to Our Lady, and I saw a girl . . . ah! a nice little bit of goods! Would you believe it, she couldn't stand still a minute!"

"But perhaps she wouldn't want to be your mopsy?"

"And what is money for? What is filthy lucre for? If one hundred thousand isn't enough, take two! If I have money, brother, I don't stick at anything so long as I have my pleasure! To tell you the truth I did offer her three rubles through the sergeant at the time—but she wanted five, the viper!"

"And I suppose you didn't happen to have five?"

"I don't know what to say, brother. I tell you, it's as though I had dreamt it all. Perhaps she did come to me after all, but I have forgotten. The whole of our march, the two months of it—I remember nothing! This has never happened to you, has it?"

But Ivan Mihailitch was silent. Stepan Vladimiritch looked at him carefully and found that his companion's head was swaying rhythmically: at times, when his nose almost touched his knees, he started violently and then began nodding again.

"There now!" Golovlyov said. "Rocked to sleep! Want to go bye-byes! You've grown too fat, brother, with your teas and innkeeper's fare! And I can't sleep! Sleep doesn't come to me and there's nothing for it! I wonder what trick I could play now? The fruit of the vine perhaps...."

Golovlyov glanced round him and made sure that all his companions were asleep. The tradesman who sat next to him kept knocking his head against the bar, but he was fast asleep all the same. His face was shiny as though covered with varnish and a number of flies were settled round his mouth.

"If one were to dispatch all these flies into his gullet now, wouldn't he have a fit!" a happy thought occurred to Golovlyov suddenly. He began stealthily moving his hand to carry out his intention, but half-way he remembered something and stopped.

"No, no more pranks—enough! Slumber in peace, my friends! And meanwhile I'll ... where did he stow away the bottle? Ah, here it is, the darling! Come here, now! O Lord, sa-ave Thy people!" he sang in an undertone, taking the bottle out of a hempen bag fixed to the side of the carriage and putting its mouth to his lips. "There, that's splendid! It's warmed me up. Shall I have some more? No, this will do ... it's another fifteen miles to the station. I'll have time enough to drink my fill.... Or shall I have some more now? Ah, damnation take this vodka! If I see a bottle I can't resist it. Drink is bad for me, but drink I must, for I can't sleep! If only the damned stuff would finish me off!"

Taking a few more gulps from the bottle he put it back into the bag and began filling his pipe.

"Excellent," he said. "I've had a drink and now we'll have a smoke! The old hag won't give me any tobacco—he is right there. I wonder if she'll give me anything to eat? I expect she'll send me her leavings! Ah me! I had money—and I have none! I was a man—and there's nothing left of me. That's how it is in this world; to-day you have enough to eat and to drink, you live for your pleasure and enjoy your pipe, and to-morrow—man where art thou? But I ought to have a bite of something. I soak up drink like a leaky tub, and I never have a square meal. And doctors say liquor is only good for one if there's appropriate nutriment to go with it, as Bishop Smaragd put it when we were marching through Oboyan. Was it Oboyan? The devil only knows, perhaps it was Kromy. That's not the point though, the thing is to find some food. I seem to remember he put a sausage and three French loaves in his bag. Too stingy to buy caviar, of course! Just look how he sleeps! What tunes he plays with his nose! I expect he put the food under his seat."

He fumbled round him and could find nothing.

"Ivan Mihailitch! hey, Ivan Mihailitch!" he called.

Ivan Mihailitch woke up and did not seem to understand for a moment how he came to sit opposite his master.

"I was just beginning to doze off!" he said at last.

"Never mind, brother, sleep on! I only meant to ask, where is our provision bag?"

"Hungry? But you must have a drink first."

"There's something in that! Where have you put the bottle?"

Having had a drink Stepan Vladimiritch tackled the sausage.

27

It proved to be hard as stone, salty as salt itself, and encased in such tough skin that one had to use the sharp point of the knife to pierce it.

"Sturgeon would be just the thing now," he said.

"You must excuse me, sir, I forgot all about it. I remembered it in the morning, and told my wife to be sure and remind me about sturgeon—and then it completely slipped my mind!"

"Doesn't matter, sausage will do. We ate worse things than that on the march. You know, papa told me of an Englishman who betted that he would eat a dead cat—and he did!"

"You don't say so! He ate it?"

"He did. But he was sick afterwards. Rum cured him. He drank two bottles at a gulp and was as fit as a fiddle. And another Englishman betted that he would eat nothing but sugar for a whole year."

"Did he win?"

"No, he popped off just two days before the year was out. But why don't you have a sip yourself?"

"I've never taken vodka in my life."

"You fill yourself up with tea? That's wrong, brother; that's why you are growing a belly. One must be careful with tea: you must drink a cup and cover it over with a glass of vodka. Tea tightens the cough and vodka loosens it. Isn't that so?"

"I don't know; you scholarly people know best."

"That's right. When we were on the march we had no time to bother about teas and coffees. But vodka is a splendid thing: you screw open the flask, pour some out, drink and have done. They drove us along much too fast—so fast that I hadn't washed for ten days on end!"

"You have had a hard time of it, sir."

"Not so hard as all that, but it's no joke marching along the high road! It wasn't so bad going to the front—people gave us things, treated us to dinners, and there was plenty of vodka. But on the way back they weren't treating us any more."

28

Golovlyov worked hard chewing the sausage and at last succeeded in swallowing a piece.

"It's a bit salty, that sausage," he said. "But I am not particular! My mother isn't going to provide me with dainty fare, either: a plateful of cabbage soup and a bowl of porridge, and that's all."

"It mayn't be so bad! Perhaps she will treat you to a piece of pie on holidays."

"No tea, no tobacco, no vodka—you are right there. They say she has taken to playing cards lately—perhaps that will help me. She might call me in to have a game and give me some tea. But as for the rest—good-bye to all that!"

They stopped at a station for four hours to feed the horses. Golovlyov had finished the bottle and was very hungry. The passengers had gone into the house to have dinner.

After wandering about the yard, peeping into the back garden and the horses' trough, scaring the pigeons and even trying to go to sleep, Stepan Vladimiritch came to the conclusion that the best thing for him was to follow the other passengers into the station house. A bowl of cabbage soup was steaming on the table and a big piece of meat that Ivan Mihailitch was cutting up into small bits lay on a wooden trencher at the side. Golovlyov sat down at a distance and lighted his pipe, not knowing what to do about his dinner.

"Good appetite to you, gentlemen!" he said at last. "The soup is rather good, I fancy."

"It isn't bad," Ivan Mihailitch answered. "Why don't you have some, sir?"

"No, I merely mentioned it; I am not hungry."

"Not hungry, indeed! You have only had a piece of sausage, and the cursed stuff does nothing but blow out your belly. Have some soup! I'll ask them to serve you separately, and you have a good meal! Lay the table for the gentleman apart, my good woman—that's right!"

The passengers sat down to their food in silence and

exchanged a knowing look. Golovlyov guessed that they saw through him, though during the journey he acted with some impudence the part of a master, calling Ivan Mihailitch his treasurer. He frowned, letting out clouds of tobacco smoke from his mouth. He would have liked to refuse the dinner, but the demands of hunger were so insistent that he greedily pounced on the bowl of soup put before him and instantly emptied it. As soon as he had had enough his self-confidence returned, and he said, turning to Ivan Mihailitch as though nothing were the matter:

"Well, my dear treasurer, you settle up for me, and I'll go to the hay-loft to have a snooze."

He waddled to the hay-loft, and as this time his stomach was full, he slept like a top. At five o'clock he was up and about. Seeing that the horses were standing by the empty trough rubbing their heads against the side, he roused the driver:

"Snoring away, the rascal!" he shouted. "We are in a hurry and he is having pleasant dreams!"

He went on in this way till they reached the cross-roads to Golovlyovo. Only then Stepan Vladimiritch sobered a little. His courage obviously began to fail him and he grew silent. Now it was Ivan Mihailitch who cheered him, persuading him above all things to part with his pipe.

"As you come near the estate, sir, throw it among the nettles; you'll find it afterwards!"

At last the horses that were to take Ivan Mihailitch further on were ready. The moment of parting came.

"Good-bye, brother," said Golovlyov in a faltering voice, kissing Ivan Mihailitch; "she will be the death of me!"

"It won't be so bad; don't you be too frightened!"

"She will be the death of me!" Stepan Vladimiritch repeated with such conviction that Ivan Mihailitch lowered his eyes.

Then Golovlyov sharply turned towards the by-road,

and strolled along leaning on a gnarled stick he had just cut from a tree.

Ivan Mihailitch followed him with his eyes and then ran after him.

"I'll tell you what, sir," he said, catching him up. "When I was cleaning your coat this morning I saw a three-ruble note in the side-pocket—mind you don't drop it inadvertently."

Stepan Vladimiritch hesitated, not knowing how he ought to act in the circumstances. At last he stretched out his hand to Ivan Mihailitch and said with tears in his eyes:

"I see.... A tip to an old soldier ... thank you! But as for the rest ... she will be the death of me, my dear! Remember my words—she will!"

Golovlyov finally turned into the by-road, and in another five minutes his gray military cap could be seen a long way off appearing and disappearing among the thick green bushes. The hour was still early—a little after five; coils of golden morning mist floated over the path, and the rays of the sun, just risen above the horizon, barely filtered through it; the air was filled with the scent of pines, mushrooms, and wild berries; the road wound across a low-lying plain teeming with flocks of birds. But Stepan Vladimiritch noticed nothing: all his frivolity suddenly left him and he walked as though going to the Last Judgment. One thought filled his whole being: another three or four hours and there will be no going further. He recalled his former life at Golovlyovo and he fancied that the doors of a damp vault were opening before him; the moment he stepped over the threshold they would bang to— and all would be over. He recalled other details that had no direct relation to him but certainly threw light on the Golovlyovo ways. There was his uncle Mihail Petrovitch (in common parlance "rowdy Mishka"), who was also in disfavor and had been sent by his grandfather Pyotr Ivanitch into exile at Golovlyovo, where he lived in the servants' hall and ate from the same bowl with the dog Tresorka. There was Auntie

Vera Mihailovna, who was kept at Golovlyovo by her brother Vladimir Mihailitch out of charity and died "from abstinence" because Arina Petrovna reproached her with every mouthful she swallowed at dinner and with every log of wood burned for warming her room. Something very similar was in store for him. An endless series of hopeless days leading to a kind of gray, yawning abyss appeared before his imagination and he instinctively closed his eyes. Henceforth he would be alone with the spiteful old woman—not even spiteful but petrified in an apathetic tyranny. This woman would be the death of him, not through tormenting but through forgetting him. There would be no one to speak to, there would be nowhere to escape—she would be everywhere, authoritative, contemptuous, paralyzing. The thought of this inevitable future filled him with such anguish that he stopped beside a tree and beat his head against it time after time. It was as though his whole life of idleness and silly fooling flashed suddenly before his mind's eye. He was going to Golovlyovo, he knew what awaited him there and yet he was going, he could not help going there. There was nowhere else for him to go. The humblest of men could do something, could manage to earn their living—he alone could do nothing. This thought seemed to have struck him for the first time. He had occasionally thought of the future and imagined all sorts of possibilities, but he always pictured for himself a life of idle comfort and never of work. And now he was faced with retribution for the irretrievable folly of his past. A bitter retribution, expressed in one ominous phrase: "She will be the death of me!"

It was about nine in the morning when the white belfry of the Golovlyovo church showed from behind the forest.

Stepan Vladimiritch turned pale, his hands trembled; he took off his cap and crossed himself. He recalled the Parable of the Prodigal Son returning home, but he grasped at once that so far as he was concerned the idea was a snare and a delusion. At last he caught sight of the boundary post close to the road and found himself on the Golovlyov land, that hostile land that had brought him forth and nurtured him unloved, let him out into the world with no one to care for him and now received him back into its bosom, as hostile as ever. The sun stood high in the sky scorching pitilessly the endless Golovlyovo fields. But he turned paler and was beginning to shiver.

He reached the churchyard at last, and there his courage left him completely. His mother's house looked out from behind the trees so peacefully that one could not believe there was anything happening there; but it had on him the effect of Medusa's head. He fancied it was his coffin. "Coffin! Coffin! Coffin!" he repeated unconsciously.

He did not venture to go straight to the house, but called first at the priest's and asked him to inform Arina Petrovna of his arrival, and to ask whether she would receive him.

The priest's wife was much concerned when she saw him and at once set to making an omelet for him; village boys crowded round him, looking at their master with surprise; peasants took off their caps as they passed him, glancing at him rather enigmatically; an old house-serf actually ran up and asked to kiss his hand. All understood that the man before them was an unloved son who had come to the place he hated, that he had come for good and that his only escape from it would be to be carried, feet foremost, to the churchyard. And all felt both sorry for him and uneasy.

At last the priest returned and said that "Stepan Vladi-miritch's mamma was ready to receive him." Ten minutes later he was there. Arina Petrovna met him sternly and solemnly, measured him from head to foot with an icy stare, but did not indulge in any useless reproaches. She did not admit him into the house but saw him on the backdoor steps and gave orders that the young master should be taken by the other entrance to see his father. The old man, white like a corpse and wearing a white nightcap, lay dozing on his bed covered with a white quilt. He woke up when Stepan Vladimiritch came in and broke into idiotic laughter:

"Aha, my boy, you've been caught in the old hag's clutches!" he called out when his son kissed his hand. Then he crowed like a cock, laughed again, and repeated several times: "She'll eat you up! she'll eat you up!"

"She will," Stepan Vladimiritch repeated in his mind.

His forebodings came true. He had a room assigned to him in the lodge where the estate office was. They brought him there some underclothes of homespun linen and his father's old dressing-gown, which he put on straightaway. The doors of the sepulchral vault opened, let him in—and slammed to.

There followed a succession of dull, hideous days, swallowed up one after another in the gray, yawning abyss of time. Arina Petrovna refused to see him, and he was not admitted to his father. Three days after his arrival the bailiff Finogey Ipatitch announced to him the "settlement" his mother had made: he was to receive board and lodging and one pound of Faller's tobacco a month. Stepan Vladimiritch listened to his mother's decision and merely remarked:

"Just think, the old creature has nosed it out that Zhukov's tobacco costs two rubles and Faller's one ruble ninety kopecks—so she is saving ten kopecks a month on that! I suppose she wants it for almsgiving at my expense."

The symptoms of moral sobering he had shown while he walked to Golovlyovo along that country road vanished once more; his frivolity reasserted itself, and he resigned himself to "mamma's settlement." The hopeless, desperate future that had for a moment flashed before his mind filling him with terror grew more and more misty every day and at last completely ceased to exist. The grim and bare present claimed him—claimed him so impudently and insistently that his whole being and all his thoughts were taken up with it. And what room, indeed, could there be for any thoughts of the future when the whole course of his life had been irrevocably settled in its minutest details in Arina Petrovna's mind?

For days on end he paced up and down his room, his pipe in his mouth, humming bits of songs and unexpectedly passing from church tunes to jaunty ones. When the foreman happened to be at the office Stepan Vladimiritch came in to him and reckoned out what Arina Petrovna's income was.

"Whatever does she do with such a heap of money!" he exclaimed in surprise when he arrived at the figure of more than eighty thousand paper rubles. "I know she doesn't give my brothers overmuch; she herself lives stingily and feeds my father on salted goose.... She must put it in the bank, there's nothing else for it!"

Sometimes Finogey Ipatitch himself came to the office bringing the peasants' tax, and then the money that caused Stepan Vladimiritch such heart-burning was placed in bundles on the table.

"Here's a pile of money for you!" he exclaimed. "And she will swallow it all! No chance of her sparing a bundle for her son—saying, 'There, my son, thou art in trouble, take this for your vodka and tobacco!'"

Then followed endless and extremely candid conversations with Yakov the foreman of how one could soften Arina Petrovna's heart and make her dote on him.

"I met a man in Moscow," Golovlyov related, "and, would you believe it, that man knew a magic word. When his mother refused to give him any money he just said that word, and she would at once go into convulsions—her arms and legs and her whole body!"

"I expect he cast a sort of evil spell on her," Yakov surmised.

"Well, you can call it what you like, but it's perfectly true that there is such a magic word. And another man told me, you must take a living frog and put it in the dead of night into an ant-heap; by the morning the ants will have eaten it all, and only one little bone will be left; take that bone—and, so long as you carry it in your pocket, you may ask whatever you like of any woman—she can refuse you nothing."

"Well, we can do that straightaway if you like."

"Ah, brother, but the point is you must first lay a curse upon yourself! If it hadn't been for that, the old hag would have been crawling on all fours before me by now."

Hours were spent in such conversations, but they could not hit upon any magical remedy. One had either to lay a curse upon oneself first or sell one's soul to the devil. So there was nothing for it but to accept "mamma's settlement," improving it slightly by certain arbitrary requisitions from the estate officials. Stepan Vladimiritch laid a tribute on everyone of them in the form of tobacco, tea, and sugar. He was extremely badly fed. He was generally given the remnants of his mother's dinner; and, as Arina Petrovna was moderate to the point of stinginess, there was little left for him. He found it particularly trying because, since vodka had become a forbidden fruit for him, he developed an excellent appetite. He was hungry from morning to night and thought of nothing but food. He watched for the time when Arina Petrovna was asleep, and ran to the kitchen and the servants' hall looking for something to eat. Sometimes he sat by the open window waiting for someone to drive past. If one of the Golovlyovo peasants turned up he stopped him and imposed a tribute of an egg or a scone.

At their first meeting Arina Petrovna drew for him briefly but clearly the whole program of his existence. "Live here for the present," she said, "there's a corner for you at the office, you shall have food from my table, but as for the rest you must excuse me, my dear! I never went in for dainty fare and I am not likely to provide it for you. Your brothers will come presently, they'll decide between them what's to be done about you, and I'll do what they suggest. I don't want to take a sin upon my conscience—as your brothers decide, so it shall be."

He was eagerly waiting for his brothers now. But he did not think at all of the effect their arrival might have upon his future (he seems to have decided that it was no use thinking of it), and merely wondered whether his brother Pavel would bring some tobacco and how much.

"And maybe he'll stump up some money," he added in his mind. "Porphyry the bloodsucker will not give me any, but Pavel. . . . If I say to him, 'Give something to an old soldier for vodka'—he'll give it to me. He is sure to."

He did not notice how the time passed—he spent it in absolute idleness but he hardly seemed to mind that. He was only bored in the evenings because the foreman went home at eight o'clock, and Arina Petrovna did not allow him any candles, saying that he could pace up and down his room just as well in the dark. But he soon grew accustomed to it and indeed came to like the darkness; his imagination worked in it more intensely, carrying him far away from the hateful Golovlyovo. The only thing that troubled him was a strange sensation in his heart and the peculiar way it fluttered, especially when he went to bed. Sometimes he jumped out of bed feeling almost stunned and ran about the room clutching at his left side.

"Ah, if only I could drop down dead!" he thought. "No it's not likely! And yet perhaps . . ."

But when one morning the foreman mysteriously informed him that his brothers had arrived in the night, he was startled and changed color. Something childish suddenly woke up in him, he wanted to make haste and run to the house to see where his brothers were sleeping, what they were wearing and whether they had traveling-bags like the one he had seen at an Army captain's; he wanted to hear them talk to mamma, to spy out what they would have for dinner. In short, he wanted once more to take part in the life that was so obstinately excluding him, to fall at his mother's feet and beg her forgiveness, and then perhaps, in the joy of reconciliation, eat the fatted calf. All was still quiet in the house, but he had already been to the kitchen and found out from the cook what had been ordered for dinner—for the first course, a small pot of fresh cabbage soup and yesterday's broth warmed up, for the second, salted goose and four cutlets, for the third, roast mutton and four woodcocks, and for pudding, raspberry pie and cream.

"Yesterday's soup, salt goose, and mutton is for the outcast, brother," he said to the cook. "And I don't suppose they'll give me any pie, either."

"That will be as your mother pleases, sir."

"Ah, me! And there was a time when I used to eat snipe, brother, I did! I once had a bet with Lieutenant Gremkin that I would eat fifteen snipe at one go—and I won! Only after that I couldn't bear to look at snipe for a month."

"And now you wouldn't mind having some again."

"She won't give me any! And yet why should she grudge it? Snipe is a free bird, one hasn't to feed it or to look after it—it lives at its own expense! Neither snipe nor mutton costs her anything, but there you are—the old hag knows that snipe is tastier than mutton, so she won't give me any! I might rot here before she gave it me! And what is there for lunch?"

"Liver, mushrooms in sour cream, and custard-cakes."

"You might at least send me a custard-cake—do your best, brother, will you?"

"I'll do what I can. I'll tell you what, sir: when your brothers sit down to lunch, send the foreman here, he'll bring you a couple of cakes in the breast of his coat."

Stepan Vladimiritch spent the morning waiting for his brothers, but they did not come. At last, about eleven o'clock, the foreman brought the two promised cakes and reported that the gentlemen had just finished lunch and locked themselves up with Arina Petrovna in her bedroom.

Arina Petrovna met her sons solemnly, overwhelmed by sorrow. Two maids were supporting her by the arms; wisps of gray hair escaped from under her white bonnet, her head was bent and lolled from side to side, her legs seemed giving way under her. She liked to play before her children the part of a venerable and stricken mother, and on such occasions she shuffled along painfully and required maids to support her by the arms. Styopka the dolt used to call these solemn receptions "Bishop's Mass," his mother "A lady Bishop," and the two maids "The Bishop's staff-bearers." But as it was past one o'clock in the night the meeting passed off almost in silence. Without speaking she gave the children her hand to kiss, kissed and blessed them, and when Porphyry Vladimiritch expressed his readiness to spend the rest of the night, if need be, chatting to his dear friend mamma, she said, with a wave of her hand, "Go and rest after your journey, this is no time for conversation, we'll talk to-morrow."

Next morning the two sons went to kiss their papa's hand, but papa did not let them. He was lying in his bed with his eyes closed, and when his children came in he shouted:

"So you have come to judge the sinner? Out of here, you pharisees! Clear out!"

Nevertheless Porphyry Vladimiritch came out of his father's study greatly moved and with tears in his eyes, while Pavel Vladimiritch, like a "truly insensitive idiot," merely picked his nose.

"He is in a bad way, kind friend mamma! In a very bad way!" Porphyry Vladimiritch exclaimed, throwing himself on his mother's breast.

"Why, is he very weak to-day?"

"So weak, so weak, one can see he hasn't long to live!"

"Oh, he'll last a bit longer!"

"No, dear mamma, no! I know that there has never been much joy in your life, but when I think of all these blows falling upon you at once I wonder how you have the strength to endure your trials!"

"Well, my dear, one has to endure if such is God's will. You know what it says in the Bible, 'Bear ye one another's burdens'—and He in His Fatherly providence has chosen me to bear my family's burdens!"

Arina Petrovna closed her eyes; it was so delightful to think of everyone living carefree, everything provided for them, while she alone knew no rest from morning to night bearing other people's burdens.

"Yes, my dear," she said after a moment's pause, "it's not easy for me in my old age! I have done my bit and provided for my children; it's time I had a rest. Four thousand serfs is no joke, you know. Fancy managing such a property at my age! You've got to keep an eye on everyone, to be always on the watch, always on the run! Take these bailiffs and stewards now: they may stand before you, cap in hand, but never you mind—they keep one eye on you and the other on the main chance! You can't trust them. Well, and what about you," she broke off suddenly, turning to Pavel—"picking your nose?"

"And how do I come in?" Pavel Vladimiritch snarled back, interrupted in his engrossing occupation.

"How do you come in? Why, he is your father after all, you might feel sorry for him!"

"What if he is? There's nothing out of the way with him . . . he is just the same. He's been like that for ten years. You are always down on me!"

"Why should I be down on you, my dear? I am your mother! Look at Porphyry now—he is sorry for me, and shows his affection as a good son should. But you won't even look at me properly, you keep scowling as though I weren't your mother but your enemy! Mind you don't bite me!"

"But what have I done?"

"Wait! Keep still a minute, let your mother have a word! Do you remember what the commandment says: 'Honor your

father and your mother—that it may be well with thee...'
You evidently don't want it to be well with you!"

Pavel Vladimiritch looked at his mother with a puzzled
expression and said nothing.

"You see, you are silent!" Arina Petrovna went on, "you
feel your conscience isn't clear. Well, God forgive you! In
honor of the occasion we'll pass it over. God sees everything,
my dear, and I... I've seen through you for years and years!
Ah, my children, my children! You will think of your mother
when she is lying in her grave—but it will be too late then."

"Mamma!" Porphyry Vladimiritch interposed, "please
don't have those black thoughts!"

"Everyone must die, my dear," Arina Petrovna pro-
nounced sententiously; "these aren't black thoughts but truly
pious ones! My health is failing, my children, failing fast!
Nothing of my old self is left—I am just a weak old woman.
Those wretched maids of mine have noticed it too and don't
care a fig for what I say! You should just hear the way
they answer me back! The only thing they are afraid of is
my saying I'll complain to the young masters; that shuts
them up sometimes."

Tea was served, then lunch, and all the time Arina Petrovna kept complaining and pitying herself. After lunch she
invited her sons to her bedroom.

As soon as the door was locked she approached the subject
for the sake of which the family council had been called.

"The dolt has turned up, you know!" she began.

"So we have heard, mamma," Porphyry Vladimiritch
answered with what sounded like irony, but might have
been merely the complacence of a man who had just had a
good meal.

"He arrived quite pleased with himself as though he had
done the right thing. He might have been saying to himself: 'I
can play the giddy goat as much as I like, my old mother will
always provide for me!' How spitefully he has behaved to me

all these years! What I have suffered from his nasty clownish tricks, let alone other things! What trouble I had to get him taken into Civil Service—and it's all like water off a duck's back! At last I grew desperate and thought to myself, if he doesn't want to look after himself, surely I can't be expected to wear myself out for the sake of the long-legged dolt! I'll chuck him a piece, I thought; perhaps if he has some money of his own he'll sober down a bit! And I did. I looked out a house for him, I put down with my own hands twelve thousand rubles in hard cash for it! And what happened? In less than three years he's come to sponge on me again! It's sheer mockery! How much longer am I to stand this?"

Porphyry cast his eyes up to the ceiling and sadly shook his head as though to say, "Oh, dear, dear! Fancy worrying dear mamma so much! Had everyone behaved nicely and lived in peace and quiet, nothing of this would have happened and mamma would not have been angry.... Oh, dear, dear!" But Arina Petrovna was not the sort of woman to put up with any interruption in the flow of her thoughts, and she did not like Porphyry's movement.

"Don't you be in a hurry to wag your head!" she said. "You must hear me first! How do you suppose I felt when I heard he let his mother's blessing go to the dogs like a bone with no more meat on it? I went, so to speak, without food and sleep for his sake, and that's how he behaved! Just as though he had bought some trinket at the market, and when he grew tired of it chucked it out of the window! His mother's blessing—just think of it!"

"Oh, mamma, it's such a dreadful thing to do..." Porphyry Vladimiritch began, but Arina Petrovna stopped him again.

"Stop! Wait! You can speak your mind when I tell you to! And if only he had warned me, the scoundrel! If he had said, 'I am sorry, mamma, this is how it happened...I couldn't help myself'—had I known in time I would have bought the house for next to nothing myself! If an undeserving son could not make good use of it, let the deserving children have it! That house would bring in 15 percent a year without the slightest trouble. Had he warned me I might have chucked him another thousand rubles by way of almsgiving! But not a bit of it—here I was, with no shadow of suspicion in my mind, and he had already settled it all. I paid twelve thousand rubles for the house with my own hands, and he let it go for eight thousand by auction!"

"And the worst of it is, mamma, that he dealt so meanly with your blessing to him!" Porphyry Petrovitch interposed hastily, as though afraid that his mother would interrupt him again.

"There's that too, my dear, and there's something else as well. I didn't come by my money easily; it wasn't by quips and cranks but by the sweat of my brow that I made my fortune. How do you suppose I grew rich? When I married your papa, all he had was Golovlyovo with a hundred-and-one serfs and a few outlying hamlets with twenty serfs in one place and thirty in another—some hundred-and-fifty souls altogether, and, as to me, I had nothing at all, and see what a fortune I have made! Four thousand serfs—there's no hiding it! I might like to take them into my grave with me, but it can't be done. Well, do you suppose that it was easy for me to come by those four thousand souls? No, my dear friend, it was so hard, so hard, that at times I could not sleep at night for thinking how to manage the business so that nobody had wind of it till the moment came. And there was the constant fear of being cut out or of spending too much! What haven't I been through! Cold and sleet and ice and spring floods—I had a taste of it all. It's only of late years I have treated myself to a coach, but in the early days they would just bring a peasant cart for me, tie some kind of awning over it, harness a pair of horses, and off I would go, trit-trot to Moscow! And as I jolted along I kept worrying, what if somebody else snatched the bargain! In Moscow I used to put up at an inn in the Rogozh-sky, in dirt and stench—I have been through it all, my dears. To save ten kopecks on a cab I trudged all the way on foot from Rogozhsky to the Solianka! Even the house-porters wondered at me. 'You are young, lady,' they said, 'and you have means, and yet you put yourself to such trouble!' But I bore it all in silence. And all the money I had on that first oc-casion was thirty thousand paper rubles. I had sold your papa's far-off hamlets, with about a hundred souls—and with that sum I set out to buy a thousand souls. No joke, this! I had a service sung at the Iversky shrine and went to try my luck. And would you believe it, it was as though Our Lady had seen my bitter tears. She allowed me to buy the estate! It was marvelous—as soon as I offered thirty thou-sand, not counting the Crown mortgage, I seemed to have cut short the auction! They had been wrangling and shouting, but they all left off bidding—you could have heard a pin drop. The auctioneer got up and congratulated me and I couldn't understand a word he said! Ivan Mihailitch, the attorney, was there. He came up to me and said, 'Congratulations on your purchase, madam!' and I simply stood like a post! And to think of the Lord's mercy—if someone had seen my dis-tracted state and shouted just out of mischief, 'Thirty-five thousand,' I might easily have bidden forty in my madness! And where could I have got it?"

Arina Petrovna had more than once told her children the history of her first steps along the path of wealth, but it evi-dently had not yet lost for them the charm of novelty. Por-phyry listened to his mother, smiling, sighing, looking up to heaven or casting his eyes down, according to the incidents she was relating. Pavel opened his eyes wide like a child who is being told a familiar story of which he can never grow weary.

"I expect you think your mother's fortune cost her noth-ing!" Arina Petrovna continued. "No, my dears, you can't even have a pimple on your nose for nothing. After my first purchase I was laid up with fever for six weeks! So think what it means to me, after all my sufferings, to see my hard-earned money flung on the rubbish-heap!"

There was a minute's silence. Porphyry was ready to rend his garments, but feared that in the country there might be no one to mend them. Pavel sank back into apathy as soon as the "fairy tale" was over and his face assumed its former indifferent expression.

"So this is what I have called you for," Arina Petrovna began again; "you must judge between me and him, that wretch! As you decide, so it shall be. If you find him guilty, that means he is to blame; if you find me guilty, I shall be to blame. Only I am not going to let that villain get the better of me!" she added quite unexpectedly.

Porphyry Vladimiritch felt that his chance had come and gave full rein to his eloquence. Like a true "bloodsucker," however, he did not go straight for the main point but began in a roundabout way.

"If you will allow me, dear friend mamma, to express my opinion," he said, "here it is in two words: Children must obey their parents, must follow their guidance without question and take care of them in their old age—that's all. What are children, dear mamma? Children are loving creatures that belong entirely to their parents—from their very selves to the last rag they have on. Parents may therefore judge their children, but the children their parents—never! The children's duty is to revere and not to judge. You say, 'Judge between him and me.' That is generous of you, dear mamma, splendid! But can we even think of such a thing without fear—we, upon whom you have showered benefits from the very day we were born? Say what you like, it would be blasphemy for us to judge you! It would be such blasphemy, such blasphemy."

"Stay! Wait a minute! If you say you must not judge me, then decide in my favor and condemn him!" Arina Petrovna interrupted. She had listened attentively, but could not make out what the "bloodsucker" was driving at.

"No, mamma darling, I can't do that either! Or, rather, I daren't do it and have no right to: I cannot judge at all—can neither condemn nor justify. You are our mother; you alone know how to treat us, your children. If we have deserved it—reward us, if we have erred—punish us. Our duty is to obey and not to criticize. Even if in your parental anger you happened to overstep the limits of justice, we daren't repine, for the ways of Providence are hidden from us. Who knows? Perhaps that is as it should be! It's the same in this case: our brother Stepan has behaved badly, in fact shockingly, but you alone are capable of determining the degree of retribution he deserves for his misdeeds!"

"So you refuse to help me? Settle your troubles as best you can, dear mamma, you say?"

"Oh, mamma, mamma! It's too bad of you! Aie-aie-aie! I was saying let Stepan's fate be what you please to decide; and you . . . ah, what black thoughts you suspect in me!"

"Very well. And what do you say?" Arina Petrovna turned to Pavel.

"What does it matter? You won't listen to me, anyway," Pavel began as though half-awake, but suddenly he took courage and went on: "Of course he is guilty . . . tear him to pieces, pound him in a mortar. . . . It's a settled thing. . . . What's it to me?"

After muttering these incoherent words he paused, staring at his mother open-mouthed as though unable to believe that he really had said them.

"I'll talk to you later, my dear," Arina Petrovna interrupted him coldly. "I see you want to follow in Styopka's footsteps. . . . Mind you don't make a mistake my friend. You may live to regret it—but it will be too late!"

"But why? I haven't said anything! . . . I say, Do what you like! What is there . . . disrespectful in this?" Pavel capitulated.

"Presently, my dear, I'll talk to you presently! You imagine that because you are an officer there's no way of bringing you to heel? But there is, my boy, and very much so! So, then, you both refuse to judge between us?"

"I, dear mamma...."

"And I too. It's all one to me. For aught I care you can cut him to pieces...."

"Be quiet, for Christ's sake, you...bad son!" Arina Petrovna knew that she had a right to call him a scoundrel, but refrained "in honor of the occasion." "Well, if you refuse, I must judge him myself. And this is my decision: I'll try kindness on him once more. I shall give him papa's Vologda property; shall have a small house built there and let him live there like a kind of pensioner, getting his keep from the peasants."

Although Porphyry Vladimiritch had refused to act as a judge, he was so struck by his mother's generosity that he felt it his duty to point out to her the dangerous consequences to which the proposed measure might lead.

"Mamma!" he exclaimed, "you are more than generous! You have been treated in ... the vilest, meanest way imaginable ... and suddenly you forgive and forget all! It's magnificent! But excuse me ... I am afraid for you, dear! I don't know what you'll think of me, but if I were you ... I wouldn't do it!"

"Why not?"

"I don't know... Perhaps because there isn't in me any of that generosity... any of that maternal feeling, so to speak.... But I keep wondering, What if my brother with his natural depravity treats your second gift the same as the first?"

Arina Petrovna had already thought of this, but she had another consideration in her mind, which she now had to put into words:

"The Vologda estate is part of your father's family property," she said through her teeth; "sooner or later we should have to give him a share of that."

"I understand that, dear friend mamma. . . ."

"And if you understand it, you must understand too that after giving him the Vologda village we can make him sign a declaration that he has received his share of his father's property and is content with that?"

"I understand that too, mamma darling. You made a great mistake that time through your kindness! You ought to have done it when you bought the house for him—you ought then to have made him sign away his claims on papa's property!"

"There's nothing for it, I didn't think of it."

"In his delight he would have signed anything you liked! And you, in your kindness. . . . Oh, what a mistake you made! What a mistake! What a mistake!"

"Much good your cackling is! You should have cried out at the time. You want to put it all down to your mother now, but when it comes to settling matters you wash your hands of the whole thing! That isn't the point though: I dare say I can get his signature out of him now just as easily. I don't suppose your papa will die just yet, and meanwhile the dolt must eat and drink. If he refuses to sign away his claim we can always turn him out—let him wait for papa's death! But I still want to know, why do you object to my giving him the Vologda property?"

"He'll squander it, dear! He had his house sold for debt, and it will be the same with the estate!"

"If he does he will have only himself to blame!"

"He will come to you again, you know."

"Fiddlesticks! Certainly not! I won't let him in! I won't give him a crust of bread or a drop of water, the hateful creature! People wouldn't blame me for it, and God wouldn't punish me. Why, losing a house, and then an estate . . . am I his serf that I should all my life provide for him alone? I have other children, I should think!"

"But, all the same, he would come to you. He is so impudent, you know, mother darling!"

"I tell you, I won't let him in at the door! Why do you repeat like a parrot, 'He'll come, he'll come'? I won't let him in!"

Arina Petrovna paused and sat staring at the window. She herself was vaguely aware that the Vologda property meant only a temporary release from the "hateful creature," that he would be sure to squander it and come to her again, and that *as a mother* she *could not* refuse him a home; but the thought that her enemy would remain with her for ever, that even shut up in the office he would still perpetually haunt her imagination, was so unbearable that she could not help shuddering at it.

"Never!" she cried out at last, banging her fist on the table and jumping up from her chair.

Porphyry Vladimiritch looked at his dear friend mamma, shaking his head dolefully.

"Why, mamma, you are angry!" he said at last in a voice so playfully caressing that one might think he meant to tickle his mamma.

"You'd have me dance with delight, I suppose?"

"A-ah! And what does it say in the Gospel about patience? Possess your soul in patience, it says! In patience—that's the way! Do you suppose God doesn't see it all? He does, dear friend mamma! We may sit here suspecting nothing, planning this and that while He up there has made up His mind already and said, 'I think I'll send her a trial.' A-a-ah! And I thought you were a good girl, mamma!"

But Arina Petrovna understood very well that the "bloodsucker" was merely setting her a snare and grew angrier than ever.

"Do you want to make fun of me?" she shouted at him. "Your mother talks to you seriously and you play the fool! It's no use throwing dust in my eyes! Tell me, what's in your mind? Do you want to saddle me with him for good and leave him at Golovlyovo?"

"Quite so, mamma, if you graciously consent. Leave him as he is and make him sign away his chains."

"Yes.... I see ... I knew you would suggest it. Very well. Suppose I do what you say. I can't endure having the hateful creature always about me—but evidently no one cares about my feelings. I bore my cross when I was young, and now that I am old there's all the more reason I shouldn't try to shirk it. Suppose I do it; let us talk of something else now. So long as your papa and I are alive he will live in Golovlyovo; he won't starve. But when we are dead?"

"Mamma darling! why such black thoughts?"

"Black or white, one must think them. We aren't young. When we are done for, what will become of him?"

"Mamma! surely you can trust us, your children! Think in what principles you have brought us up."

And Porphyry Vladimiritch cast at her one of the enigmatic glances that always made her uncomfortable.

"It's a trap!" said a voice in her heart.

"Why, mamma, I would be all the more happy to help a poor man! A rich one doesn't need anything, bless him. He has enough as it is. But a poor man—do you know what Christ said about the poor?"

Porphyry Vladimiritch got up and kissed his mother's hand.

"Mamma, allow me to give my brother two pounds of tobacco!"

Arina Petrovna made no answer. She was looking at him and thinking: Is he really so heartless that he could turn his own brother out into the street?

"Well, let it be your way! If he is to live at Golovlyovo, so be it!" she said at last. "You have caught me in your net. You began by saying, 'Do as you please, mamma,' and in the end you make me dance to your tune. But listen to me now! I hate him, he's been nothing but a worry and a disgrace to me all his life, and he has ended by making a mock of my maternal gift to him—but all the same, if you turn him out or force him to work for wages, you shan't have my blessing! You shan't! Go to him now, both of you. I expect he's strained his goggle-eyes looking out for you."

Her sons went out of the room; Arina Petrovna got up and watched them walk across the courtyard, not speaking a word to each other. Porphyry kept taking off his cap and crossing himself—at the church, showing white in the distance, at the wayside shrine, and at the post with the mug for alms stuck to it. Pavel's eyes seemed riveted to his new boots, the tips of which shone like mirrors in the sun.

"For whom have I been saving it all, going without food and sleep? Whom is it all for?" she wailed suddenly.

The brothers went away; Golovlyovo was quiet once more. Arina Petrovna resumed her work with redoubled energy; the cook could no longer be heard chopping meat in the kitchen, but instead there was increased activity in the office, in the granaries, store-rooms, cellars, etc. Summer the Harvester was drawing to an end; they were jam-making, pickling, salting; winter supplies were arriving from everywhere, cart-loads of the women's tax-in-kind were being brought in from all the villages: dried mushrooms, berries, eggs, vegetables, etc. All this was measured, received, and joined to the stores of former years. It was not for nothing that the lady of Golovlyovo had a row of cellars, store-rooms, and granaries built; they were all crammed full, and some of the provisions had gone bad so that one could not go near them for the putrid smell. All the stores were sorted at the end of the summer, and those of doubtful quality were sent to the servants' kitchen.

"Those cucumbers are still good, they only look a bit slimy at the top and smell a little; the servants may as well have a treat!" Arina Petrovna said, giving orders to put aside this or that barrel.

Stepan Vladimiritch had taken to his new life remarkably well. At times he desperately wanted "to get drunk as a fiddler," and generally, "to let himself go" (he actually had the money to do so, as we shall see later), but he denied himself manfully, as though calculating that the "right moment" had not yet come. He was busy every minute now, for he took the most active and lively part in the laying in of stores, disinterestedly rejoicing or grieving at every achievement or setback of his mother's domestic management. In a fever of excitement he made his way from the office to the cellars, hatless and wearing only his dressing-gown, hiding from his mother behind trees and all kinds of outhouses that lumbered the courtyard. Arina Petrovna had seen him more than once, all the same, and her maternal heart strongly urged her to give "the dolt" a good scolding, but on second thoughts she decided to take no notice of him. With feverish impatience he watched them unloading carts, bringing jars, barrels, and tubs from the storehouses, and sorting out the goods which eventually disappeared in the yawning abyss of the cellars and store-rooms. As a rule he was well pleased.

"They brought two cart-loads of pickled mushrooms from Dubrovino to-day—you never saw such mushrooms!" he told the foreman delightedly. "Why, we were afraid we shouldn't have any for the winter! We have to thank the Dubrovino people for this! Well done, Dubrovino! They've got us out of a scrape!"

Or:

"To-day my mother sent them to catch carp in the pond— ah, splendid fish. Some are more than a foot long! I expect we shall be eating carp all this week."

Sometimes, however, he was grieved:

"The cucumbers are no good this year, brother! They are rough and spotty! No decent cucumbers, and that's the end of it! I expect we shall be eating last year's, and this year's will be given to the servants—there's nothing for it."

But on the whole he disapproved of Arina Petrovna's system of housekeeping.

"What a lot of stuff she lets rot, brother, it's simply dreadful! They took no end of things out of the store-rooms to-day: salt meat, fish, cucumbers—she had it all sent to the servants' kitchen! Now, is there sense in that? Is that the way to manage things? There's plenty of fresh provisions, but she won't touch them till all the old rotten stuff has been eaten!"

Arina Petrovna's confidence that there would be no difficulty in making Styopka the dolt sign any document you pleased was fully justified. He signed all the papers sent him by his mother without raising the slightest objection, and boasted to Yakov the foreman in the evening:

"I've been signing papers to-day, brother—resigning my claims to the estate! I am cleaned out now. I haven't a penny to bless myself with and am not likely to have in the future. I've put the old woman's mind at rest."

He parted with his brothers amicably and was delighted at having a supply of tobacco. He could not resist of course calling Porphyry "bloodsucker" and "little Judas," but these expressions were absolutely drowned in a flood of chatter in which one could not trace a single consecutive thought. As they were going away, his brothers actually gave him some money, and Porphyry said as he did so:

"Suppose now you want a little drop of oil for the sanctuary lamp, or a nice wax taper to put before an icon—the money is here ready to hand! So that's that, brother! Live quietly and peaceably and mamma will be pleased with you. You will be comfortable, and we shall all be happy. Mother is kind, my friend!"

"She may be kind," Stepan Vladimiritch assented, "but she feeds me on putrid meat!"

"And whose fault is that? Who despised his mother's blessing? It's your own fault, you squandered your property! And what lovely property it was—profitable, splendid property! If you had lived quietly and modestly, you would be eating nice roast beef now and delicious veal, and you could have some sauce with it too, if you were so minded. And you would have had plenty of everything—best potatoes, and good firm cabbage and tender peas. . . . Isn't it so, brother?"

Had Arina Petrovna heard this speech she could not have refrained from saying, "He is at it again!" But luckily for Styopka the dolt his sense of hearing did not retain other people's words. Iudushka could talk as much as he liked and be certain that not a single word of his would reach its destination.

In short, Stepan Vladimiritch parted with his brothers in a friendly way, and with some complacency showed Yakov the foreman two twenty-five ruble notes that he had found in his hand after saying good-bye to them.

"That will last me a long time, brother," he said. "We have tobacco, we are well provided with tea and sugar, vodka is the only thing lacking—and we can have vodka too if we like! But I won't have it just yet—I haven't time, I must run to the cellar. If I don't keep an eye on them they'll make off with the stuff in no time! And you know, brother, the old hag did see me as I crept along the kitchen wall one day! She was standing at the window, and I expect she thought as she looked at me, 'No wonder I am short of cucumbers—that's what it is!' "

October came at last; it poured with rain; the road was impassable with black mud. Stepan Vladimiritch could not go out because all he had on his feet were his father's old slippers, and on his shoulders, his father's shabby dressing-gown. He sat in his room all day gazing through the double glass of the window at the row of peasant huts sunk in mud. None the worse for the summer's hard work, people were flitting to and fro like black dots in the gray autumn fog. Their present work was no less hard, but it was carried on in different surroundings; the joyous brilliance of the summer was replaced by continual twilight. The corn-kilns were smoking past midnight; the patter of flails resounded dully throughout the neighborhood. In the Golovlyovo barns they were threshing also, and it was said in the office that they would have to go on till Lent to finish the tremendous quantity of corn there was. Everything looked dull and sleepy, everything weighed on the spirit. The office doors were no longer wide open, as in the summer, and inside a bluish steam rose from the wet sheepskins.

It is hard to say what impression was produced on Stepan Vladimiritch's mind by the picture of the busy autumn in the country, or indeed whether he grasped that in the squelching mud under a constant downpour of rain people were working as hard as they had done in the summer; but there is no doubt that the gray tearful autumn sky depressed him. It seemed to be hanging just overhead, threatening to drown him in the yawning gulfs of mud. He had nothing to do except sit at the window and watch the heavy masses of clouds. In the morning as soon as it was light the horizon was completely covered by them. The clouds stood there as though spell-bound: an hour, two hours, three hours passed and they were still in the same place, without the slightest change in their shape or color. That cloud there, lower and darker than the others (looking like a cassocked priest with outstretched arms), that showed clearly against the whitish mass of the clouds above it, had essentially the same shape at midday. True, the right arm had grown a little shorter, while the left stretched out hideously, pouring down rain at such a rate that a dark, almost black streak showed against the already dark background of the sky. There was another cloud further off. It had hung like a huge shaggy mass over the Naglovka village, threatening as it were to strangle it—and at midday it hung in the same shape in the same spot, stretching down its paws as though ready to jump down on it. Clouds, clouds, and clouds —all day long. About five in the afternoon there came a change; the horizon grew more and more misty, and finally disappeared altogether. The clouds were the first to go, hidden by a uniform veil of blackness; then the forest and Naglovka were lost, then the church, the wayside shrine, the nearest village, and the orchard. The eye that closely followed these mysterious disappearances could still descry the Golovlyovo house that stood at a distance of less than a hundred yards. It was quite dark indoors; no lights were yet lit in the office, and there was nothing for it but to walk up and down the room, up and down, up and down, endlessly. A sickly languor lay heavy on Stepan Vladimiritch's mind; in spite of his idleness his whole body felt unreasonably, unendurably tired; one fretting, gnawing thought obsessed him; that thought was—"This is my grave, my grave, my grave!" Those black dots flitting by the village threshing-yards against a dark background of mud were not obsessed by that thought; they would not sink under the burden of weariness and dejection: even if not actually waging war against heaven, they were at any rate struggling, planning, defending, contriving something. Stepan Vladimiritch never asked himself whether that for the sake of which they labored night and day was worth defending and struggling for, but he understood that those nameless dots were infinitely superior to him because he could not even struggle, because he had nothing to defend and to plan. He spent his evenings at the office because Arina Petrovna still refused to allow him any candles. He asked her several times through the bailiff to give him top-boots and a sheepskin; the answer was that leather boots had not been provided for him but that when the frosts came he would receive a pair of felt snow-boots. Arina Petrovna evidently intended to carry out her plan to the letter and do no more than keep him from starving. At first he railed against his mother, but afterwards he seemed to forget about her; he tried as it were to remember something and then he gave up trying. The very light of the candles at the office grew irksome to him and he shut himself in his room to be alone with the darkness. He had only one resource left him now—a resource that attracted him irresistibly, though he was still afraid of it. That resource was—to get drunk and forget. To forget completely and irretrievably, to sink into the gulf of oblivion so deeply that one could never rise to the surface again. Everything helped to drive him to this; the disorderly habits of his past, his enforced idleness in the present, his sick body tortured by a stifling cough, unendurable attacks of sudden breathlessness and continually increasing pains in the heart. At last he could stand it no longer.

"You must procure me a bottle of vodka to-night, brother," he said one day to the foreman in a voice that boded nothing good.

The first bottle was followed by a succession of others—and from that time onwards he unfailingly got drunk every night. At nine o'clock, when the lights were put out in the office and men went home to their lairs, he put on the table the bottle of vodka and a slice of bread thickly covered with salt. He did not begin on the vodka at once but gradually stole up to it as it were. Everything around him was dead asleep; only mice scratched behind the wall-paper that had come unstuck, and the clock in the office ticked insistently. Taking off his dressing-gown, with nothing but his shirt on he scurried up and down the heated room; sometimes he stopped, came up to the table fumbling for the bottle, and then began walking again. He drank the first glasses making traditional drinkers' jokes and voluptuously sipping the burning liquid; but gradually his tongue began babbling something incoherent, his heart beat faster, and his head was on fire. His dulled mind struggled to create images, his deadened memory strove to break through into the realm of the past; but the images were senseless and disconnected, and the past did not respond with a single recollection, sweet or bitter, as though a thick wall had risen once for all before that which had been and was now. All there was before him was the present in the shape of a tightly locked prison in which the idea of space and of time disappeared without a trace. The room, the stove, three windows, a creaky wooden bed with a thin hard mattress on it, the table with the bottle of vodka—this was the horizon beyond which his mind could not penetrate. But as the contents of the bottle diminished and his head was more and more on fire, even this limited consciousness of the present became too much for him. His muttering, which at first had some semblance of rational speech, grew utterly meaningless; in the effort to make out the outlines of the darkness that filled the room the pupils of his eyes dilated enormously; at last the darkness disappeared and was replaced by space filled with phosphorescent brilliance. It was a dead, endless void, sinister and luminous, without a single sound of life. It followed at his heels, tracking every step he took. There were no doors, no windows—nothing but the boundless garish void. He felt frightened; he wanted to stifle his consciousness of the outside world so completely that even this void should cease to exist. A few more efforts and his purpose was attained. His stumbling legs carried his body, numb to all sensation; the muttering was replaced by a shout; his very existence seemed to cease. He was in that strange torpid state when all signs of conscious life are absent and yet another kind of life, following its own course, is unquestionably going on. Groan after groan broke forth from his breast without in the least disturbing his sleep; the disease carried on its work of destruction without causing, apparently, any physical pain.

He woke up when it was light, and anguish, disgust, and hatred woke up in him. It was a mute, unreasoning hatred— hatred of something vague and indefinite. His inflamed eyes dwelt senselessly first on one object, then on another, gazing at it long and attentively; his arms and legs trembled; his heart seemed to sink and fall, and then beat so violently that his hand instinctively clutched at his chest. He had not a single thought, not a single desire. The stove was in front of him, and his mind was so occupied with taking it in that it was impervious to any other impression. Then the window replaced the stove; window, window, window . . . He wanted nothing, nothing at all. He filled his pipe, lighted it mechanically and let it drop out of his hands before he had finished smoking; his tongue was muttering something, but evidently just from habit. The best thing was to sit still and stare at one point without speaking. It would have been good to have a drop of vodka at such a moment to raise his temperature so that he could, if only for a short time, feel alive; but in the daytime he could not procure vodka at any price. He had to wait for the night to snatch once more those blissful moments when the ground slipped from under his feet, and instead of the hated four walls of his room a boundless luminous void opened before his eyes.

Arina Petrovna had not the faintest idea of how the dolt was spending his time. The sudden glimpse of feeling that showed for a moment in her conversation with Porphyry vanished so rapidly that she did not even notice it. Her behavior was not the result of a deliberate policy; she had simply forgotten Stepan's existence. She had lost all sight of the fact that next door to her, in the office, lived a man related to her by blood, a man who was perhaps pining away in his longing for a wider life. Once she adopted a certain routine she followed it almost mechanically, and she believed that other people ought to do the same. It never occurred to her that the way of filling one's life varied according to a number of circumstances over which one had no control, and that some people (including herself) loved the particular way in which their life was filled, while others had it forced upon them and hated it. And so, although the bailiff reported to her more than once that Stepan Vladimiritch did not seem well, it did not reach her ears or make any impression upon her mind. At most she answered with a stereotyped phrase:

"Never you fear, he'll get over it and survive us both!

What can ail a long-legged horse like him? He coughs! Why, some men cough for thirty years on end and grow fat on it!"

But when she was informed one morning that during the night Stepan Vladimiritch had disappeared from Golovlyovo, she suddenly came to her senses. She instantly sent the whole household in search of him and personally conducted the inquiry, beginning with an examination of the room in which "the bad son" lived. The first thing that struck her was the bottle on the table with a little vodka still left in it; in the excitement they had not thought of hiding it.

"What's this?" she asked, as though not understanding.

"I expect he...amused himself!" the bailiff answered with some hesitation.

"Who fetched it?" she began, but on second thoughts she controlled her anger and went on with her examination.

The room was so grimy, dusty, and filthy that even Arina Petrovna, who had no standards of comfort, felt ashamed. The ceiling was black, the wall-paper had cracked and hung in tatters in many places, the window-sills were dark under a thick layer of ashes, the pillows lay on the slimy floor, a crumpled sheet, gray with dirt, was thrown on the bed. The double frame in one of the windows had been wrenched out and the window was half-open: "the bad son" had evidently gone out that way. Arina Petrovna instinctively glanced out of the window and was more alarmed than ever! It was the beginning of November but the autumn was mild that year and the frosts had not come yet. The fields and the roads were wet, black, impassable. How could he have walked through it? Where had he gone? She recalled that he had only a dressing-gown on and slippers, one of which had been found by the window, and that, as ill luck would have it, it had never stopped raining all night.

"It's a long time since I've paid you a visit, good people!" she said, sniffing the air that smelt of a hideous mixture of cheap vodka, coarse tobacco, and wet sheepskins.

All that day, while the men were searching the forest, she stood by the window gazing into the bare distance with dull attention. All this fuss for the sake of "the dolt"! It all seemed to her like an absurd dream. She had said at the time that he ought to be sent to the Vologda estate—but no, that cursed Iudushka had wheedled her into leaving him at Golovlyovo—and now she was in a nice predicament! He could have lived there as he liked, out of her sight, and God bless him! She would have done her duty; he squandered one piece of property, she chucked him another! And had he squandered the second, he would have had to go without, that's all! God Himself can't provide for a bottomless pit! All would have been peace and quiet, and now—just think of the trick he's played! We have to go whistling for him in the forest! And it will be something to be thankful for if they bring him home alive—it doesn't take a drunken man long to put his head through a noose! He'd take a rope, catch it on a branch, twist it round his neck—and that's the end of him! His mother had gone without food and sleep for his sake, and he, if you please, could think of nothing better than to go and hang himself. And it isn't as though he had had a bad time, had been starved or made to work—he did nothing but slouch up and down his room like one crazy, and eat and drink! "Another man couldn't have thanked his mother enough, but this one had the bright idea to hang himself—very nice and considerate of you, my dear son!"

Arina Petrovna's surmises about the dolt's violent death were not justified, however. Towards evening a covered cart, drawn by a pair of peasant horses, came into sight; it brought the fugitive to the office. He was half insensible, covered with cuts and bruises, and his face was blue and swollen. It appeared that in the night he had walked as far as Dubrovino, a distance of fifteen miles from Golovlyovo.

He slept for the next twenty-four hours and then woke up. He began pacing up and down the room as usual, but he did not touch his pipe, as though forgetting about it, and did not say a word in answer to all the questions put to him. Arina Petrovna was so moved that she almost had him transferred from the office to the house; on second thoughts, however, she left him where he was and merely gave orders that his room should be swept and scrubbed, bed linen changed, curtains hung on the windows, etc. The following evening, when she was told that Stepan Vladimiritch had woken up, she sent for him to come to tea at the house and actually found some kind notes in her voice in speaking to him.

"Why ever did you go running away from your mother like that?" she began. "You caused me much anxiety, you know. It's a good thing your father did not hear of it—it would have been dreadful for him in his condition."

But Stepan Vladimiritch seemed indifferent to his mother's kindness, and stared with fixed, glassy eyes at the tallow candle as though watching the deposit of grease gradually forming round the wick.

"Ah, you silly, silly boy!" Arina Petrovna went on still more kindly. "You might have thought how people would talk of your mother because of you! I have no end of ill-wishers and goodness only knows what gossip there will be! They'll say I didn't feed or clothe you . . . ah, you silly boy!"

There was the same silence and the same fixed senseless stare.

"And what made you suddenly discontented, living at your mother's? You have clothes to your back, enough to eat, thank God. You are warm and comfortable. . . . What else can you want? You are bored, but there's nothing for it, my dear— this isn't town! We have no balls and entertainments here— we all sit in our nooks and have a dull time of it. I too might like to dance and sing, but just look out of the window—in this wet one can't do as much as go to church!"

Arina Petrovna paused, expecting the dolt to make at least

some inarticulate sound; but he seemed turned to stone. She was beginning to lose her temper but controlled herself.

"And if you were dissatisfied about anything—perhaps you were short of food, or of linen—why couldn't you have told your mother straight out? 'Order some liver or some curd-cakes for me, mamma,' you should have said.—Do you imagine your mother would have refused you that? Or take vodka now—suppose you had wanted a drink, why, have it, bless you! A glass, two glasses—as though your mother would grudge it you! But see what you did—you weren't ashamed to ask from the serfs and you couldn't bring yourself to speak to your mother!"

But all those soft words were in vain: Stepan Vladimiritch was not moved in the least (Arina Petrovna had hoped that he might kiss her hand), showed no signs of repentance and indeed did not seem to have heard anything she said.

From that day he grew completely silent. For days together he walked about his room, unconscious of any fatigue, frowning morosely and moving his lips. Sometimes he stopped as though wishing to say something but unable to find the words. Apparently he had not lost the power of thinking, but his mind had so feeble a grasp of what passed before it that it retained nothing; that was why he did not even feel impatient at not being able to find the right words. As for Arina Petrovna, she believed that he would certainly set the estate on fire.

"He is silent all day long!" she said. "But he must be thinking of something, the dolt, while he is silent! Remember my words: he'll set fire to the place!"

But the dolt simply did not think at all. He seemed to have sunk into a hopeless darkness in which there was no room either for reality or for fancy. His brain was working at something, but that something had no relation either to the present or to the future. It was as though a black cloud enveloped him from head to foot and he did nothing but watch it, following its imaginary curves, and at times with a shudder trying as it were to ward it off. This mysterious cloud swallowed up both the outer and the inner world for him.

In December of the same year Porphyry Vladimiritch received the following letter from Arina Petrovna:

> Yesterday morning a new trial befell us with which the Lord has visited us; my son and your brother, Stepan, passed away. He had been perfectly well the evening before and had even taken supper, but in the morning he was found dead in his bed—so fleeting is this life of ours! And what grieves my maternal heart most is that he left this world of vanity without any ministration in order to fly into the realm of the unknown.
>
> Let this be a lesson to us all: those who neglect their family duties must always expect such an end. Adversity in this life, premature death and eternal torments in the life to come—all spring from this source. For however clever and exalted we may be, if we do not respect our parents the latter will be sure to turn our cleverness and achievements to nothing. Such are the rules which every person living in this world must learn by heart, while the serfs are bound to revere their masters also.
>
> In spite of this, however, being my son, Stepan has received all the honors due to the departed. I sent to Moscow for the pall, and the funeral service was performed by the Father Archimandrite whom you know, together with other priests. Masses and requiem services are being said to this day, as the Christian custom is. I am sorry for my son's death, but I dare not repine, and I don't advise you to either, my children. For who can tell? We may be repining while his soul is having an enjoyable time on high!

2

GOOD RELATIVES

IT WAS A hot midday in July. Everything seemed dead
on the Dubrovino estate. Not only those enjoying leisure but
even laboring people had gone to some shady corner and lain
down to rest. The dogs sprawled under the huge willow-
tree in the middle of the front courtyard, and one could hear
them snap their teeth catching flies, half-asleep. The very
trees seemed exhausted and stood drooping and motionless.
All the windows, both in the manor-house and in the servants' quarters, were wide open. Heat was pouring down like
a fiery wave; the ground, covered with short, scorched grass,
was blazing hot; a blinding haze of golden light made it difficult to distinguish objects in the distance. The house which
had once been painted gray but was now white, the small
flower-garden in front, the birch copse across the road, the
pond, the village and the rye-fields adjoining it—all was veiled
with the luminous mist. The air was thick with smells of
all kinds, including the fragrance of the flowering limes and
the stench of the cattle-yard. Not a sound was heard except

the rattle of the cook's knives in the kitchen, foretelling the invariable kvass soup and mince-meat for dinner.

Noiseless anxiety pervaded the house. An old lady and two young girls tense with expectation sat in the dining-room without touching their knitting that lay neglected on the table. In the maids' room two women were preparing compresses and mustard plasters, and the rhythmic jingle of the spoons broke the stillness like the chirrup of a cricket. Barefooted girls cautiously ran along the corridor on their way from the first floor to the maids' room and back again. At times a shout came from upstairs: "What about the mustard plasters? Have you dropped asleep, eh?"—and a girl dashed out of the maids' room.

At last heavy footsteps were heard creaking on the stairs, and the regimental doctor came into the dining-room. He was a tall, broad-shouldered man, with firm, ruddy cheeks that seemed bursting with health. He had a clear voice, a firm step, bright and cheerful eyes, full soft lips and a frank, open expression. He was a *bon-vivant* in the full sense of the term, in spite of being fifty; he had never yet found any amount of food or drink too much for him, and was not likely to do so for years to come. He was smartly dressed in a white piqué summer uniform with bright embossed buttons. He came in smacking his lips and clicking his tongue.

"I'll tell you what, my dear! Bring us some vodka and something to eat!" he said, stopping at the door leading into the corridor.

"Well, how is he?" the old lady asked anxiously.

"God's mercy is infinite, Arina Petrovna," the doctor answered.

"How do you mean? So then . . ."

"Quite so. He'll last another two or three days and that's all."

The doctor made a significant gesture and hummed in an undertone: "*Headlong, headlong, headlong he will fly.*"

"But how is that? The doctors have been treating him all this time—and all of a sudden ..."

"What doctors?"

"Our local doctor and the one from town."

"Doctors, indeed! Had they applied a good seton a month ago he would have lived."

"Can really nothing be done now?"

"I tell you, God's mercy is infinite, and I can add nothing to that."

"But perhaps it will have effect?"

"What do you mean?"

"Perhaps the medicine will have effect?"

"Perhaps it will."

A woman in a black dress and a black kerchief brought in a tray with a decanter of vodka and two plates—one with sausage and the other with caviar. Conversation stopped when she came in. The doctor poured out a glass, looked at it against the light, and clicked his tongue.

"Your health, madam!" he said, turning to Arina Petrovna and swallowing the vodka.

"Thank you, my dear."

"This is just what Pavel Vladimiritch is dying of in the prime of life—this vodka!" the doctor said, screwing up his face pleasantly and sticking his fork into a piece of sausage.

"Yes, many people come to grief through it."

"Not to everyone is it vouchsafed to receive this—that's why. But to me it is, so I'll have another glass! Your health, ma'am!"

"Do have some. There's no harm in it for you!"

"No, there isn't. My lungs and kidneys and liver and spleen are all in order! Oh yes, I meant to ask," he said, turning to the woman in black who stood at the door as though listening to the conversation, "what is there for dinner to-day?"

"Kvass soup, mince rolls, and roast chickens," the woman answered with a sour smile.

"Have you any salt fish?"

"Of course we have, sir! There's sturgeon, and other fish. . . . Plenty of it."

"Then tell them to make us some cold soup with sturgeon for dinner . . . a good slice with some fat on it, you know! What is your name—Ulita, isn't it?"

"Yes, sir, that's what I am called."

"Well, be quick then, Ulita, there's a good girl!"

Ulita went out. There was a gloomy silence. Arina Petrovna got up from the chair and looked out of the door to see if Ulita had really gone.

"Have you spoken to him about the orphans, Andrey Osipitch?" she asked the doctor.

"I have."

"What does he say?"

"It's the same story. 'As soon as I recover,' he says, 'I'll certainly make my will and write the IOUs.' "

A still more gloomy silence followed. The girls took their embroidery from the table and, with trembling fingers, made stitch after stitch; Arina Petrovna sighed dejectedly; the doctor paced up and down the room whistling, "*Headlong, headlong . . .*"

"You should have put it to him more plainly!"

"What could be plainer? I said he would be a scoundrel if he didn't provide for the orphans. Yes, you did put your foot into it! Had you called me in a month ago I would have made him a seton and done my best about the will too. . . . And now it will all go to Iudushka, the lawful heir . . . sure to!"

"Whatever shall we do, grandmamma!" the older of the two girls said almost through her tears. "How can uncle treat us like this?"

"I don't know, my dear, I don't know. I don't know what's to become of me either. To-day I am here, and to-morrow—I don't know where. . . . It may please God I should sleep in a barn or in a peasant's hut!"

"Goodness, how stupid uncle is!" the younger sister exclaimed.

"You should have a rein over your tongue, young lady!" the doctor remarked, and, turning to Arina Petrovna, added: "But what about yourself? You should try and persuade him!"

"No, no, no! He won't listen! He won't even see me! The other day I came into his room, and he said: 'You've come to give me the last ministrations, I suppose?'"

"I expect it's mostly Ulita's doing. . . . She sets him against you."

"She does! That's just what she does! And she reports everything to Porphyry! They say he has horses harnessed all day so as to be in time at his brother's death-bed! And, would you believe it, the other day she made an inventory of everything—furniture, crockery, clothes. 'In case anything is lost,' she said. She wants to make out that we are thieves, if you please!"

"You should treat her in the military fashion. . . . Make her 'fly headlong,' you know. . . ."

But before the doctor had had time to develop his idea a maid ran breathless into the room, crying in a frightened voice:

"Come to the master, please! The master calls for the doctor!"

The family that is being described here is already known to us. The old lady is no other than Arina Petrovna Golovlyov; the dying owner of Dubrovino is her son, Pavel Vladimiritch; the two girls, Anninka and Lubinka, are her grand-daughters, the children of Anna Vladimirovna, to whom she had once "chucked a piece." Not more than ten years had passed since we last saw them, but the position had changed so much that not a trace remained of the artificial bonds which made the Golovlyov family appear something like an impregnable fortress.

The family stronghold erected by Arina Petrovna's indefatigable hands had crumbled away so imperceptibly that she herself, not knowing how it happened, had been an accomplice and, indeed, an active agent in the process of destruction, the prime mover in which was, of course, Porphyry "the bloodsucker."

The scolding and autocratic Arina Petrovna, owner of the Golovlyov estates, had become a modest hanger-on in the house of her younger son—an idle hanger-on with no voice in the domestic management. Her head was bowed, her back was bent, her eyes had lost their luster, she walked with flagging steps, and her movements were no longer impetuous. Having nothing to do she learned knitting in her old age, but she was not very successful with that either, because her thoughts were always far away. Where was her mind wandering? She herself could not always tell, but it was certainly far from her knitting-needles. She would sit and knit for a few minutes, and then suddenly her hands dropped, her head leaned on the back of the chair, and she began recalling the past. She sat lost in her memories till a drowsy stupor possessed her aging body. Sometimes she got up and walked about the rooms looking for something, peeping at the corners, like a woman who had carried keys all her life and cannot think why and how she has lost them.

The first blow to Arina Petrovna's autocracy was dealt by the abolition of serfdom or, rather, by the preparations that preceded it. At first there were rumors, then meetings of the gentry presenting addresses to the Tsar, then provincial committees, then organizing committees—all this worried her and threw her mind into a turmoil. Arina Petrovna's fertile imagination kept dwelling on endless trifles. Suddenly she would wonder, "What am I to call Agashka now? Agafyushka, I suppose ... or perhaps I'll have to address her as Agafya

Fyodorovna?" Or she would picture herself wandering through the empty house while all the servants had collected in the kitchen, guzzling away! When they were tired of eating they chucked the food under the table! Or she would imagine that she peeped into the pantry and saw two maids gorging themselves! She was just going to scold them, but the words stuck in her throat. "How can one say anything to them, now that they are free? I expect there's no way of bringing them to justice!"

These were trifles, but she gradually came to build up from them a fantastic world that engrossed her mind and paralyzed her powers of action. Arina Petrovna suddenly let go the reins of government, and for two years did nothing but exclaim from morning to night:

"If only they'd settle it—at least we'd know where we are. But those endless parleys! It's neither one thing nor the other!"

It was at that time that Vladimir Mihailitch died—just when the work of the Committees was in full swing. He died at peace with himself and everyone, having renounced Barkov and all his works. His last words were:

"I thank my God that He did not let me appear before Him side by side with the serfs!"

These words sank deep into Arina Petrovna's impressionable mind, and her husband's death, together with her fantastic fears for the future, gave as it were a tinge of hopelessness to the life at Golovlyovo. It was as though the old Golovlyovo house and all that lived in it were going to die all together.

From a few complaints in his mother's letters Porphyry Vladimiritch intuitively guessed the turmoil that reigned in her thoughts. Arina Petrovna no longer reprimanded or sermonized him in her letters, but chiefly expressed her trust in God's mercy, "which in these credulous times doesn't fail even the serfs, but especially those who, owing to their wealth, have been the staunchest support of the Church and adorned it." Iudushka instinctively grasped that if mamma began to put her trust in God something must be amiss in her life. And he took advantage of this with his usual sly cleverness.

Just before the emancipation he paid an unexpected visit to Golovlyovo and found Arina Petrovna depressed and almost exhausted.

"Well, what's happening? What are they saying in Petersburg?" was the first thing she asked after they had greeted each other.

Porphyry looked down and said nothing.

"Now, just consider my position!" Arina Petrovna went on, understanding from her son's silence that nothing good was to be expected. "I have thirty of those sluts sitting in the maids' room—what am I to do with them? If they are left for me to keep—how am I to feed them? Now I have potatoes and cabbage and bread in plenty, and so we manage to live. If there are no potatoes, I order cabbage soup; if there's no cabbage, we eke it out with cucumbers. But then I shall have to run for everything to the market and pay in cash, buy and fetch everything—how am I to provide for all that horde?"

Porphyry looked his dear friend mamma in the eyes and smiled bitterly in token of his sympathy.

"And if they just let them loose, saying 'Run along, dears, wherever your legs carry you,' well, then . . . I don't know. I simply don't know what will come of it!"

Porphyry grinned as though the idea of what would come of it struck him as very comical.

"No, don't you laugh, my friend! It's very serious, very serious indeed. The only hope is that the Lord may make them more reasonable, and then . . . Take me, for instance: After all, I too count for something; they must provide for me somehow, but how is it to be done? You know the way we've been brought up—just taught to dance and to sing and to receive visitors, so what shall I do without my sluts? Serving meals, or clearing away or cooking—I can do nothing of that, dear!"

"God is merciful, mamma!"

"He was merciful, my dear, but He is no longer! While we were good, the King of Heaven was good to us; but we have grown bad—and there it is! You know sometimes I wonder if I'd better give it all up while there's still time. Really! I'll build myself a hut near papa's grave, and live there in peace and quiet!"

Porphyry Vladimiritch pricked up his ears; his mouth watered.

"But who will see to the estate then?" he asked cautiously, as though throwing out a bait.

"Well, there's nothing for it; you'll have to see to it yourselves! Thank God, I've provided for you well enough. Why should I be the only one to labor?"

Arina Petrovna stopped short and raised her head. She suddenly caught sight of Iudushka's face all aglow with a kind of rapacious light, an oily smile on his slobbering lips.

"I believe you are preparing to bury me!" she observed dryly. "Isn't it too soon, my dear? Mind you make no mistake!"

So on the first occasion it all came to nothing. But some conversations, once begun, can never end: In a few hours' time Arina Petrovna returned to the subject once more.

"I shall go to St. Sergius's shrine," she said, "divide the property between you, buy myself a little house close to the Monastery and settle there."

Taught by experience, Porphyry Vladimiritch said nothing.

"Last year, while your father was still alive," Arina Petrovna went on, "I was sitting one day in my bedroom alone, and suddenly I heard someone whispering to me: 'Go to the Saint! Go to the Saint! Go to the Saint!'—three times. I looked round—there was no one! So I thought, why, this must have been a vision! Well, I said, if my faith has found favor with the Lord, I am ready. And as soon as I said it the room was filled with such a fragrance, you can't imagine! Of course I gave word to pack at once, and by the evening I was on my way."

Arina Petrovna actually had tears in her eyes. Iudushka took advantage of this to kiss her hand, and even ventured to put his arm round her waist.

"There, now you are a good girl!" he said. "Ah, how nice it is, dearest, to be on good terms with God! You address God with prayers and He sends you His help. That's the way, dear friend mamma!"

"Wait, I haven't told you all. I arrived at the Monastery the next evening and went straight to church. The Vigil service was going on; the singing, the lights, the fragrance from the censers—I simply did not know if I was in heaven or on earth! After church I went to see Father Iona, and said to him: 'Why was the service so particularly beautiful to-night, your reverence?' And he said: 'Why, madam, Father Avvacum had a vision during the service! Just as he raised his arms in prayer he saw a light in the cupola overhead and a dove looking at him!' And after that I made up my mind that whatever years may be allotted to me, I'll spend the end of my life by St. Sergius's shrine."

"But who will take care of us? Who will look after your children? Ah, mamma, mamma!"

"Oh, you are grown up, you can look after yourselves. And I . . . I'll go with Annushka's orphans to the Saint and live there under his wing! And if one of them too feels a desire to serve God—the Hotkov Convent is next door! I'll buy myself a cottage and have a kitchen garden with potatoes and cabbage in it—I shall have plenty of everything."

This idle conversation went on for several days in succession; several times Arina Petrovna put forward extremely daring plans, took them back and made them again, and at last brought matters to such a pitch that she could retreat no longer. Not more than six months after Iudushka's visit the position was as follows: Arina Petrovna had not gone to St. Sergius's or retired to a hut beside her husband's grave, but she had divided the estate between her sons, keeping only the capital for herself. Porphyry was given a better share of the estate than Pavel.

Arina Petrovna remained at Golovlyovo as before, but of course there was a little family comedy in the usual style. Iudushka shed tears and begged his dear friend mamma to manage his estate as though it were her own, using the income from it at her discretion—"and I shall be content with anything you can spare me, however little it is." Pavel, on the contrary, thanked his mother coldly ("he looked as though he'd bite"), immediately retired from the Army ("never asked his mother's blessing but just bolted out like one crazy") and settled at Dubrovino.

Then a kind of blindness came upon Arina Petrovna. The hidden image of "Porphyry the bloodsucker," that in the old days she divined with wonderful clearness, was suddenly clouded over as it were. The only fact she seemed to grasp was that, in spite of the division of the estate and the emancipation of the serfs, she was living at Golovlyovo as before, giving no account of her doings to anyone. Her other son was living next door to her, but what a difference! Porphyry had trusted himself and his family entirely to his mother's discretion, while Pavel never asked her advice about anything, and spoke through his teeth when he met her!

The more clouded her reason, the greater was her zeal for her affectionate son's welfare. Porphyry asked nothing from her, but she went out of her way to meet his wishes. She began to find fault with the shape of the Golovlyovo property. In one spot somebody else's land cut into it—it would be a good thing to buy that land; in another place one could fix up a nice little farm, but there was not enough meadow—and close by there was a meadow for sale, a lovely meadow! Arina Petrovna was carried away, both as a mother and as a business woman who wants to display her abilities at their best before her affectionate son. But Porphyry Vladimiritch put on a shell of impenetrability. In vain Arina Petrovna tempted him with the possible purchases: To all her suggestions to buy this or that wood or meadow he invariably answered: "I am quite content with what you have kindly given me, dear friend mamma."

Such answers merely egged her on. Carried away by her business plans on the one hand, and on the other by a desire to spite "that rascal Pavel," who lived close by but would have nothing to do with her, she lost all conception of her real position at Golovlyovo. The old fever for acquisition possessed her once more, though she was no longer acquiring for herself but for her favorite son. The Golovlyov estate increased, spread, and flourished.

And at the very moment when Arina Petrovna's capital had dwindled down so that it was almost impossible to live on the interest from it, Iudushka sent her, together with a most respectful letter, a whole bundle of book-keeping forms which were to guide her in the future in drawing up the yearly accounts. Alongside the main branches of farming the accounts were to include income from gooseberries, raspberries, mushrooms, etc. A special form was drawn up for each item, somewhat as follows:

The number of raspberry bushes in the year 18**	—	
Freshly planted in that year	—	
Amount of berries collected from all the bushes	lb	oz
Of that amount		
Used by you, dear mamma	lb	oz
Used for jam for the household of his excellency		
Porphyry Vladimiritch Golovlyov	lb	oz
Given to boy X as a reward for good conduct	lb	oz
Sold to the peasants as a treat	lb	oz
Rotted for lack of customers and for other reasons	lb	oz

And so on, and so on.

Note.—If the present year's harvest should be smaller than last year's, the cause of it must be set forth, such as drought, rain, hail, etc.

Arina Petrovna simply gasped. To begin with, she was astounded by Iudushka's meanness: she had never dreamed that gooseberries could be regarded as an item in the book-keeping at Golovlyovo—and he seemed to be particularly keen on it; secondly, she understood perfectly well that all these schedules meant a death-blow to her autocratic rule.

The end of it was that after a long controversy by post Arina Petrovna, insulted and indignant, moved to Dubrovino, and Porphyry Vladimiritch retired from the service and settled at Golovlyovo.

From that time onward a succession of colorless days of enforced idleness followed for the old woman. Though he was a man of no marked characteristics, Pavel Vladimiritch was invariably disagreeable with his mother. He received her tolerably well, that is, he promised to keep her and his orphaned nieces, but on two conditions: first, she was not to go to his rooms upstairs; and, secondly, she was to have no voice in the household management.

Arina Petrovna was particularly distressed by this second condition. Pavel Vladimiritch's estate was run by Ulita the housekeeper, a spiteful woman, known to have carried on a secret correspondence with Porphyry the bloodsucker, and by Kiryushka, a former valet of Arina Petrovna's husband, a man who knew nothing about agriculture, and sermonized his master every day like a true flunkey. Both pilfered mercilessly. Arina Petrovina's heart ached at the sight of the robbery that went on, and she longed to open her son's eyes on the subject of tea, sugar, butter. Enormous quantities of it all were used, and many a time Ulita, utterly unabashed, hid handfuls of sugar in her pocket before the very eyes of her old mistress. Arina Petrovna saw it all, but had to remain a silent witness of the robbery. The moment she opened her mouth to say something Pavel Vladimiritch stopped her:

"Mamma!" he said, "some one person must give orders in the house. It isn't my idea—everybody acts on it. I know that my orders are stupid—well, let them be stupid! And your orders are clever—very well! You are clever, very clever, and yet Iudushka has turned you out of your home."

To crown it all, Arina Petrovna made an awful discovery: Pavel Vladimiritch drank. The passion for drink gained on him gradually, owing to his solitary life in the country, and at last reached such a pitch that it was bound to lead to the fatal end. When his mother first settled in the house he seemed a little ashamed of himself; he often came downstairs to talk to his mother. Noticing that his speech was confused, Arina Petrovna put it down to his stupidity. She did not like his coming to talk to her, and considered these conversations a great infliction. And, indeed, he did nothing but grumble in an absurd kind of way. It was either that there had been no rain for weeks, and then it came on in floods, or that there was a plague of beetles ruining all the trees in the orchard, or that the moles had dug up all the meadows. All this provided an endless source of complaints. He would come downstairs, sit down opposite his mother and begin:

"There are clouds all round—Golovlyovo is not far off. The bloodsucker had a splendid downpour yesterday, and we had no rain at all! The clouds go wandering all round, but not a drop on my land!"

Or:

"Just see how it's coming down! The rye has come into flower, and it does nothing but pour! Half the hay is rotten already, but it never seems to stop! Golovlyovo isn't far off, one would have thought, but the bloodsucker finished his hay-making ages ago while we have to sit and wait! We'll have to feed the cattle on rotten hay in the winter."

Arina Petrovna listened to the stupid talk in silence, but sometimes her patience gave way and she said:

"Your being idle won't improve matters."

No sooner had she said it than Pavel Vladimiritch flew into a fury.

"And what would you have me do? Transfer the rain to Golovlyovo, or what?"

"No, but generally speaking..."

"No, you tell me, what do you think I ought to do? Not 'generally speaking' but straight out.... Should I change the climate to please you? Look at Golovlyovo now: they needed rain, and it rained; they don't want it, and it doesn't rain! So, of course, everything is growing there. And with us it's the other way about! We shall see how you'll talk when we have nothing to eat!"

"Well, that must be God's will...."

"You should say then straight out that it's God's will! But your 'speaking generally' isn't much of an explanation!"

Sometimes he went so far as to find his estate a burden.

"Why ever did Dubrovino fall to my share?" he grumbled. "There's nothing in it!"

"What's wrong with Dubrovino, now? The soil is excellent, there's plenty of everything.... What has come into your head suddenly?"

"What has come into my head is that at the time we live in one ought to have no property at all! Money—that's another matter! You take money, put it in your pocket and make off with it. But this landed property..."

"But what is there so special about the time we live in? Why can't you have property nowadays?"

"What is there so special about it? You don't read newspapers and I do. There are lawyers now all over the place—think of that! If a lawyer hears you have property he'll start hauling you round the law-courts!"

"But how can he do that if you have proper documents?"

"He'll do it right enough, you may be sure. Or perhaps that bloodsucker there will hire a lawyer and he'll send me summons after summons!"

"What next! The land is yours by right."

"That's just because it's mine by right that he'll send me a summons. If it hadn't been, they would have taken it away from me without any summons, but now they'll summon me. A friend of mine, Gorlopyatov, had an uncle who died, and he, like a donkey, accepted his legacy. The legacy turned out to be worth a farthing, but the debts were a hundred thousand: IOUs, and forged ones at that! So the law has been at him for the last three years: First they took his uncle's estate from him, and then sold his own by auction. That's what landed property is!"

"Is there really such a law?"

"If there were no law they wouldn't have sold him up. There are all sorts of laws. If a man has no conscience he can take advantage of any law; but if he has a conscience the law is a closed book to him. He can go searching for it if he likes!"

Arina Petrovna always gave way in these discussions. More than once she was tempted to shout, "Out of my sight, you scoundrel!" but on second thoughts she refrained. Sometimes she complained to herself:

"Oh, Lord, how could I have borne such awful children? One is a regular bloodsucker, and the other a kind of a natural! For whose sake have I been saving it all, going short of food and of sleep? Whom did I do it for?"

As Pavel Vladimiritch grew more addicted to drink his conversations became more fantastic and, so to speak, startling. Arina Petrovna noticed at last that something was wrong. For instance, every morning a decanter full of vodka was put in the sideboard in the dining-room, but by dinner-time there was not a drop left in it. Or, as she sat in the drawing-room, she heard mysterious creakings in the dining-room close to the sideboard; when she called out, "Who is there?" she heard someone walking quickly but cautiously upstairs.

"Good heavens, I believe he drinks!" she said to Ulita one day.

"He does," she replied, smiling sarcastically.

Seeing that his mother had guessed his secret, Pavel Vladimiritch gave up all ceremony. One fine morning the decanter disappeared from the dining-room altogether. To Arina Petrovna's question what had become of it Ulita replied:

"The master said it was to be kept upstairs; it will be more convenient for him there."

And indeed, upstairs the decanters followed one another with remarkable rapidity. Shutting himself up in his room, Pavel Vladimiritch came to hate other people's company, and created a special fantastic world for himself. It was a kind of stupid melodramatic novel with himself and the "bloodsucker" for chief characters. He was not fully aware how deep was his hatred for Porphyry. He hated him with his every thought, with every fiber of his being, hated him continually, every minute. The vile image of Iudushka vividly came before his eyes, his ears rang with Iudushka's lachrymosely hypocritical twaddle, permeated with a kind of dry, almost abstract malice for everything that had life in it and failed to conform to the code of traditional hypocrisy. Pavel Vladimiritch recalled the past as he drank. He recalled all the insults and humiliations he had to endure because of Iudushka's claim to be the most important person in the family. He recalled particularly clearly the division of their property, counting every penny, comparing every bit of land—and hating his brother. Heated by vodka, his imagination drew before him a series of dramatic situations in which all his wrongs were avenged, and not Iudushka but he was inflicting the injuries. He imagined, for instance, that he had won two hundred thousand in a lottery and came to give the news to Porphyry, whose face was positively contorted with envy (a scene with conversations followed). Or it was a case of his grandfather dying (another scene with conversations, though there was no grandfather in reality), leaving him a million and nothing at all to the "bloodsucker." Or he pictured himself inventing a means to become invisible and playing such nasty tricks on Porphyry that the man simply groaned. His imagination was inexhaustible in inventing those tricks, and the rooms upstairs rang with his inane laughter, to the delight of Ulita, who hastened to inform Porphyry Vladimiritch of what was going on.

He hated Iudushka, and at the same time feared him. He knew that Iudushka's eyes cast a poisonous spell, that his voice crept like a snake into one's mind and paralyzed one's will—and so he resolutely refused to meet him. Sometimes the "bloodsucker" came to Dubrovino to kiss dear friend mamma's hand (he had driven her out of the house, but he was as respectful as ever), and then Pavel Vladimiritch locked himself up in his rooms upstairs and sat there while Iudushka chatted with mamma.

Thus the days passed until at last Pavel Vladimiritch was faced with a fatal disease.

The doctor spent the night at the house merely as a matter of form and left for town early in the morning. Before going he said plainly that the invalid could not last more than a couple of days, and that it was too late to think of his making any will, because he could not even sign his name properly.

"He'll sign something unintelligible, and you may have no end of trouble with the law," he added. "Iudushka greatly respects his mamma, of course, but he'll be sure to say it's forgery, and if mamma is made to take a trip to Siberia, he will merely have a service sung to bless her on her way."

All the morning Arina Petrovna walked about like one dazed. She tried to pray—perhaps God would give her some guidance—but she could not think of prayer, and her tongue would not obey her. She began: "*Have mercy upon me, O*

God, after Thy great goodness," and suddenly found herself saying, *"from evil."*

"Cleanse me! Cleanse me!" she repeated mechanically, but her mind wandered: it peeped upstairs, looked in at the cellar ("What a lot of stores there was in the autumn, and now they've pilfered it all!"), recalled something from the far-away past. It was all in a kind of twilight, and in that twilight people, many people, stirring busily, providing for the future. *"Blessed is the man ... blessed is the man ... like incense ... teach me ... teach me ..."* At last her tongue refused to move; her eyes gazed at the icons, seeing nothing—her mouth was open, her hands were folded at her waist, and she stood motionless as though turned to stone.

Finally she sat down and wept. Tears poured from her lusterless eyes down her old withered cheeks, lingering in the folds of the wrinkled skin and dropping on to the greasy collar of her old cotton blouse. A feeling of bitterness possessed her, hopeless and at the same time impotently rebellious. Her old age, her feebleness, her helpless position—all seemed to point to death as the only way to peace. But there was her past with its sense of power, freedom and plenty, and the memories of that past held her in their grasp, dragging her down to the earth. "I wish I could die" flitted through her mind, but it was immediately replaced by "I want to live!" She had no thought of Iudushka or of the dying Pavel—they had both ceased to exist for her, as it were. She was not thinking of anyone, she was not accusing or being indignant with anyone; she forgot whether she had any capital and whether it was sufficient to provide for her old age. Anguish, mortal anguish possessed her. "I am wretched! I am miserable!"—that was the only explanation she could have given of her tears. Those tears dated far back: they accumulated drop by drop from the moment she had left Golovlyovo and settled at Dubrovino. She had been prepared for what awaited her there, she had expected and foreseen it all; but somehow she had never grasped that what she had been expecting would have an end. And that end had come—an end full of misery and desperate loneliness. All her life she had been arranging something, wearing herself out for the sake of it, and now it proved to be a phantom. All her life the word "family" had been on her tongue; it was in the name of the "family" that she rewarded some and punished others; it was for the sake of the family that she had exposed herself to privations and suffering, that she had warped her whole life—and now it turned out that she had no family after all!

"Good God, can it be the same with everybody?" she kept thinking.

She sat leaning her head on her hand and turning her face wet with tears towards the sun, that rose higher and higher in the sky, as though saying to it "See!" She did not groan or curse, but merely sobbed quietly, choking with tears; her very soul was on fire with the thought:

"I have no one! No one, no one!"

At last she had no more tears to shed. She washed her face and walked aimlessly into the dining-room, where the girls assailed her with fresh complaints that struck her as particularly trying.

"Whatever is going to happen, grandmamma? Shall we really be left penniless?" Anninka grumbled.

"How stupid uncle is!" Lubinka echoed her.

About midday Arina Petrovna decided to go in to her dying son. She cautiously climbed up the stairs, making hardly any sound, and fumbled for the door leading to his rooms. They were in semi-darkness; the windows were covered with green curtains, and the light barely filtered through them; the stagnant air was filled with an unpleasant mixture of different smells, including the smell of fruit, of plasters, of lamp oil, and the odors that unmistakably suggest disease and death. There were only two rooms. Ulita sat in the first picking fruit and furiously blowing away clouds of flies that swarmed over the heaps of gooseberries and impudently settled on her nose and lips. Through the half-opened door of the next room came a continual sound of a dry, barking cough, interrupted occasionally by painful expectoration. Arina Petrovna stopped irresolutely, looking into the semi-darkness and waiting to see what Ulita was going to do in view of her coming. But Ulita never stirred, evidently convinced that any attempt to influence the invalid would be fruitless. Only her lips moved angrily, and Arina Petrovna thought she heard her whisper, "The devil!"

"You had better go downstairs, my dear," Arina Petrovna said to Ulita.

"What next?" she snarled back.

"I want to speak to Pavel Vladimiritch. Go!"

"Why, madam, how can I leave him? If anything happened there would be no one to attend to him."

"What is it?" a hollow voice said from the bedroom.

"Tell Ulita to go away, my dear. I want to speak to you." This time Arina Petrovna was so insistent that she carried her point. She crossed herself, and went into the invalid's room. His bed stood alongside the inner wall, furthest away from the windows. Covered with a white quilt he lay on his back, almost unconsciously smoking a cigarette. In spite of the smoke, flies were attacking him so fiercely that he was all the time waving them off his face first with one hand, then with the other. His arms were so weak, so lacking in muscle, that they clearly showed the outline of the bone, almost equally narrow from the wrist to the shoulder. His head was buried in the pillow with a kind of hopelessness; his face and his whole body were burning with fever. His large, sunken, round eyes wandered as though searching for something; his nose had grown longer and sharper, his mouth was half-open. He did not cough, but his breath was so labored that the whole of his vital energy seemed centered in his chest.

"Well, how do you feel to-day?" Arina Petrovna asked, sinking into the armchair at his feet.

"Fairly well.... To-morrow... that is, to-day... When was it the doctor came?"

"He was here to-day."

"Well, that means to-morrow...."

The invalid stirred uneasily, as though trying to remember a word.

"You'll be able to get up?" Arina Petrovna prompted him. "God grant you may, my dear."

Both were silent for a minute. Arina Petrovna wanted to say something, but in order to do so she had to keep up a conversation, and this was precisely what she could never do when alone with Pavel Vladimiritch.

"Iudushka ... still living?" the invalid asked at last.

"What could ail him! He is living right enough."

"I expect he is thinking, 'My brother Pavel is going to die, and by the grace of God I'll come into another estate.'"

"We shall all die some day and everyone's property will go to one's lawful heirs."

"But not to the bloodsucker! I'd rather chuck it to the dogs than leave it to him!"

Here was an excellent opportunity: Pavel Vladimiritch had broached the subject himself. Arina Petrovna took advantage of it at once.

"You ought to give it a thought, my dear," she said casually, without looking at her son, but examining her hands against the light as though they were the chief object of her attention.

"What do you mean?"

"Why, if you don't wish your estate to go to your brother..."

The invalid said nothing, but his eyes dilated unnaturally and his face grew hotter and hotter.

"You might consider, my dear, that you have two orphaned nieces—they are not provided for at all, really. And there's your mother too!" Arina Petrovna went on.

"You've let all your money go to Iudushka, have you?"

"What's done is done. . . . I know I have myself to blame. . . . But, after all, it was no great sin. . . . I thought, as he was my son. . . . And you needn't bring it up against your mother."

There was a pause.

"Well? Won't you say something?"

"And how soon do you intend to bury me?"

"Not to bury you, but still. . . . Other Christians too. . . . Everyone isn't going to die at once, but as a general thing . . ."

"As a general thing, that's it! You always talk 'in general.' Do you suppose I don't see?"

"What do you see, my dear?"

"Why, I see you think I am a fool! Very well, granted I am a fool, let me be one! Why do you come to a fool? Don't you come, don't you worry yourself!"

"I don't worry. I was speaking generally . . . that there's a limit to every man's life."

"Well, wait for it!"

Arina Petrovna bowed her head and pondered. She saw very well that hers was a bad case, but she was in such misery at the thought of her hopeless future that in spite of all the evidence she could not give up further attempts as useless.

"I don't know what you hate me for," she brought out at last.

"Not at all. . . . I don't. . . . Not in the least! On the contrary. . . . Why, you have been so . . . impartial to us all!"

He spoke in gasps, struggling for breath; there was a kind of sobbing and yet triumphant laughter in his voice; his eyes sparkled; his arms and legs stirred restlessly.

"Maybe I have really done you some wrong—then forgive me for Christ's sake."

Arina Petrovna got up and bowed, touching the ground with her hand. Pavel Vladimiritch closed his eyes and made no answer.

"It's true that in your present condition . . . you certainly can't make any arrangements about the estate. . . . Porphyry is the legitimate heir; well, let him have the land. But what about your moveable property, about the capital?" Arina Petrovna ventured to ask point-blank.

Pavel Vladimiritch started but made no answer. Quite possibly, hearing the word "capital," he thought not of Arina Petrovna's innuendoes but of its soon being September: "It will be time to receive the interest. . . . Sixty-seven thousand six hundred multiplied by five and divided by two—how much will that be?"

"You imagine, perhaps, that I wish for your death, but I assure you I don't, my dear! So long as you live, there's nothing to trouble an old woman like me. There's nothing I want. I am warm and comfortable here, I have plenty to eat, and if I want something specially nice I can always have it. I am merely saying that it is a custom with Christians, while waiting for the life to come . . ."

Arina Petrovna paused, trying to find a suitable phrase.

"To make provision for their relatives," she ended, looking out of the window.

Pavel Vladimiritch lay motionless, coughing quietly and not showing any sign of whether he was listening to his mother. He was evidently bored by her moralizing.

"You might give away the capital in your lifetime," Arina Petrovna said, as though throwing out a casual suggestion, and again began examining her hands against the light.

The invalid started slightly, but Arina Petrovna failed to notice it and went on:

"It is perfectly lawful to transfer capital, my dear. For it's a thing that may be gained or lost: it's here one day and gone the next. And no one can require you to account for it. You can give it to whomever you like."

Pavel Vladimiritch suddenly gave a malicious laugh.

"I expect you remembered Palotchkin's story," he hissed.

"He too *gave away* his money to his wife, and she ran away with her lover!"

"I have no lovers, my dear!"

"Then you'll run away without a lover . . . with the capital!"

"So that's what you think of me!"

"I don't think of you at all. . . . You have always said to everyone I was a fool—well, I am a fool. Let me be one! A fine idea, that—to give you my money! And what about myself? Would you have me go into a monastery to save my soul and watch you from there spending my money?"

He said it all in one breath, angry and excited, and was completely exhausted. For at least a quarter of an hour afterwards he coughed so violently that it was surprising to see this miserable wreck of a man have so much vigor still left in him. At last he got his breath and closed his eyes.

Arina Petrovna looked about her distractedly. Up to that moment she somehow could not believe it, but now she was finally convinced that every fresh attempt to argue with the dying man would merely bring the day of Iudushka's triumph nearer. She seemed to see Iudushka everywhere. She saw him following his brother's coffin, giving him a Judas's kiss while two nasty little tears dropped from his eyes. She saw the coffin being lowered into the ground. "Good-bye, brother!" Iudushka would exclaim, twitching his lips, rolling his eyes, and trying to put a note of sorrow into his voice, and then say half-turning to Ulita: "Don't forget to bring home the fromenty, and mind you put it on a nice clean table-cloth. . . . We must have it at the memorial dinner." Then there would be the funeral dinner, during which Iudushka would talk to the priest without stopping about his deceased brother's virtues, his praises being fully confirmed by the priest.

"Ah, brother, you would not stay with us!" he would exclaim, getting up from the table and asking for the priest's blessing. At last everyone, thank God, would have had enough to eat and taken his after-dinner nap. Iudushka—the master now—would be walking about the rooms, checking the inventory and glancing suspiciously at his mother whenever he felt doubtful about anything.

All these inevitable scenes of the future passed vividly before Arina Petrovna's eyes; the sound of Iudushka's unctuous and piercing voice addressed to her seemed to ring in her ears:

"Do you remember, mamma, my brother had some nice little golden studs . . . such pretty ones; he used to wear them on holidays? . . . I can't think what can have become of those studs!"

No sooner had Arina Petrovna come downstairs than a coach-and-four appeared on the hill by the Dubrovino church. Porphyry Golovlyov was solemnly sitting in the back seat with his hat off, crossing himself at the church; opposite him sat his two sons Volòdenka and Pètenka. Arina Petrovna's heart sank. "The Fox must have scented a carcass," she thought. The young ladies, too, felt alarmed, and clung helplessly to their grandmother. There was a commotion in the house that had only a minute before been so quiet: doors banged, people ran to and fro, there were shouts of "The master is coming!" "The master is coming!" and the whole population of the place rushed out on to the front steps. Some were crossing themselves, others simply stood in an expectant attitude; everyone apparently was aware that what had so far been going on at Dubrovino was merely temporary, but that now they were in for the real thing, with a real master at the head. Many of the old people, former house-serfs, had been receiving a monthly allowance of provisions; many fed their cows on the "old" master's hay, had their own kitchen gardens, and altogether had an easy time of it; so that, naturally, all were anxious to know whether the "new" master would leave things as they were or introduce his own Golovlyovo ways.

Iudushka had meanwhile driven up to the house, and from the greeting accorded to him concluded that his brother's end was approaching rapidly. In leisurely fashion he stepped out of the carriage, waved away the servants, who had rushed to kiss his hand, folded his hands devoutly, and slowly walked up the steps whispering a prayer. His face expressed both sorrow and an unswerving submission to destiny. As a man he sorrowed—as a Christian he did not dare to repine. He was praying for grace but, above all, hoping for the best and bowing before the will of Providence. His sons walked behind him, side by side. Volòdenka was mimicking his father, folding his hands, rolling his eyes and moving his lips; Pètenka was thoroughly enjoying his brother's performance. A crowd of servants followed them in silence.

Iudushka kissed his mamma's hand, then her lips, then her hand again, patted the "dear friend" on the waist and said, sadly shaking his head:

"You are despondent, I see! It's wrong, dear! Oh, it's very wrong! You should ask yourself, 'And what would God say to that?' Why, He would say, 'Here I arrange everything for the best in My wisdom, and she repines!' Ah, mamma, mamma!"

Then he kissed both his nieces, and with the same bewitching familiarity in his voice said to them:

"You in tears too, grasshoppers! Now, I will have none of this! Smile at once, if you please, and that's the end of it!"

And he stamped, or rather pretended to stamp, while letting them see it was only a gracious jest.

"Look at me," he went on. "As a brother—I am grieved. More than once, in fact, I may have wept. I am grieving over my brother, grieving deeply. . . . I shed tears, but then I think: 'And what about God? Doesn't God know better than we do?' One considers this and feels cheered. That's what everyone ought to do. You, mamma, and you, dear nieces, and everyone . . . everyone," he added, turning to the servants, "look at me. See how well I'm bearing up!"

And with the same bewitching playfulness he showed how he was bearing up, that is, he drew himself up and took a step forward, puffing out his chest. Everyone smiled but rather sourly, as though saying to himself, "The spider has begun on his web!"

Having finished the performance in the hall, Iudushka passed to the drawing-room and kissed his mother's hand again.

"So that's how it is, dear friend mamma!" he said, settling down on the sofa. "Here's my brother Pavel now . . ."

"Yes, Pavel too . . ." Arina Petrovna echoed quietly.

"Yes, yes, yes. It seems much too soon, much too soon. You know, mamma, though I try to keep up my courage, in my heart I too . . . grieve for my brother very, very much. He has always disliked me, I know. Who knows, perhaps that's why God is punishing him."

"You might forget it at a moment like this. You shouldn't think of your old quarrels now. . . ."

"I forgot them long ago, mamma! I merely mentioned, by the way, that Pavel never did care for me—I don't know why. I tried all I could. I did my best to get round him. 'Brother darling,' I called him, but it wasn't a bit of good. He simply wouldn't let me come near him! And, all unseen to us, God has judged it best to shorten his days."

"I tell you, you mustn't think of the past. The man is at his last gasp."

"Yes, mamma, death is a great mystery. You know not the day or the hour—that's the kind of mystery it is. Here he'd been making all sorts of plans; he thought he was so ex-alted there was no reaching up to him—and all of a sudden God contraverted all his ideas in one moment. He might be only too glad now to cover up his sins—but no, they are all written down in the Book of Life. And what is written in that book is not easily scratched out, mamma!"

"But you may be sure repentance is accepted."

"I hope so, I sincerely hope so. My brother never cared for me but I wish him well. I wish well to everyone. To those who hate me and injure me—to all, in fact. He was unfair to me, and so God sent him this illness. It was God's doing, not mine. And does he suffer much, mamma?"

"No, not so very.... The doctor has given us hope, in fact," Arina Petrovna lied.

"There, that's splendid now! Don't you grieve, dear mamma, he may get over it yet. Here we are sorrowing for him and repining against the Creator, and perhaps he is sitting up in bed quietly and thanking God for his recovery."

Iudushka was so pleased with the idea that he positively simpered.

"I have come to stay with you for a few days, mamma," he went on, as though announcing a pleasant surprise. "I have to, you know.... It's a family matter. Anything may happen, and, after all, as a brother I can comfort him and give advice and make arrangements. You'll allow me, won't you?"

"It's not for me to give permissions—I too am only a guest here."

"I'll tell you what then, dear. As it's Friday to-day, will you order a Lenten dinner for me, if you would be so kind? Say, a little salt fish and a few mushrooms and a bit of cabbage. I don't want much, you know. And meanwhile I'll do my duty as a brother and go upstairs to the invalid. Who knows, I may succeed. I may do something for his soul if not for his body. And it seems to me in his condition the soul is of more importance. The body can be mended with tonics and compresses, mamma, but the soul needs a more serious remedy."

Arina Petrovna did not object. The thought that "the end" was inevitable took possession of her so completely that she watched in a kind of stupefaction all that was happening around her. She saw Iudushka get up from the sofa and shuffle along, clearing his throat and bending his back. (He liked to pretend to be an invalid on occasion; he fancied he looked more venerable.) She understood that his sudden appearance upstairs was bound to upset the sick man and perhaps hasten his death, but she was overcome with such weariness after the emotions of the day that she felt as though she were in a dream.

While all this was going on Pavel Vladimiritch was in a state of indescribable agitation. He lay quite alone upstairs and heard some unusual commotion in the house. There was something mysterious about the banging of doors and the footsteps in the passage. He called, shouting at the top of his voice for several minutes, but, seeing that shouts were useless, he mustered all his strength and, sitting up in bed, listened intently. The running about and loud conversation of many voices were followed by a deadly stillness. Something unknown and terrible seemed to close in upon him; the daylight hardly penetrated through the window curtains, and the sanctuary lamp burning before the icon in the corner made the dusk that filled the room appear darker and more dense. Pavel fixed his gaze on that mysterious corner as though something in the depths of it had struck him for the first time. The icon in its gilded setting lit up by the direct rays of the lamp stood out of the darkness with a startling vividness like some living thing; a circle of light flickered on the ceiling, bright one instant and faint the next, as the lamp flared up or burned low. Everything below was in semi-darkness and shadows flitted across it. On the wall next to the lighted corner hung a dressing-gown that seemed to move as the patches of light and shadow passed over it. Pavel Vladimiritch gazed and gazed at it, and it suddenly seemed to him that everything was astir in that corner. Solitude, helplessness, deadly stillness, and shadows swarming in the midst of it! He fancied that those shadows were gliding, gliding towards him. . . . In indescribable terror he stared, open-eyed and open-mouthed, at the mysterious corner; he could not scream and only moaned. His hoarse, spasmodic groans sounded like a bark. He did not hear the creaking of the stairs nor the cautious, shuffling footsteps in the room next to his—and suddenly Iudushka's hated figure appeared by his bedside. He imagined that it had come out of there, out of the darkness stirring so mysteriously before his eyes, that there were more shadows there . . . endless shadows coming towards him.

"What have you come for? Where from? Who let you in?" he cried, sinking helplessly on to his pillow.

Iudushka was standing at his bedside, looking intently at him and sorrowfully shaking his head.

"Are you in great pain?" he asked, in a voice as unctuous as he was able to make it.

Pavel Vladimiritch said nothing, and stared at him senselessly, as though trying to understand. Iudushka meanwhile went up to the icon, knelt down feelingly, bowed three times to the ground, and, getting up, came to the bedside once more.

"Well, brother, get up. God has sent us blessings!" he said in such a joyful voice, settling down in the armchair, that one might think he had the "blessings" in his pocket.

Pavel Vladimiritch understood at last that this was no shadow but the bloodsucker in the flesh, and he seemed to shrink together suddenly, as though in a shivering fit. Iudushka's eyes had a bright, brotherly expression, but the sick man knew very well that there was a snare in them which would clutch him by the throat in a minute.

"Ah, brother, you don't look pretty, you know!" Iudushka went on with his brotherly jokes. "Come, try and take yourself in hand! See if you can't get up and run! Trit-trot, trit-trot—let mamma see what a fine fellow you are! Make a good show!"

"Go away, you bloodsucker!" the sick man cried desperately.

"A-ah, brother, brother! I have come to you with comfort and affection, and you . . . what a word you used. Oh, how very wrong! I wonder you could bring yourself to say such a thing to your own brother. It's a shame, my dear, a real shame. Wait a bit, I'll straighten your pillow for you." Iudushka got up and dug his finger into the pillow. "That's right," he went on, "that's splendid now. You can lie as snug as you please— no need to straighten it for the next twenty-four hours."

"Go away . . . you."

"Ah, how illness has spoiled you! Your temper has grown quite sour. 'Go away,' you keep on saying, but how can I go? If you want a drink, I am here to give it you. The icon lamp there isn't burning properly, I'll put it right and add a nice little drop of oil to it. You'll lie and I'll sit by you in peace and quiet. We'll never notice the time pass."

"Go away, you bloodsucker!"

"Here you are abusing me, but I will pray for you. I know that it isn't you who are saying this but your illness. I am used to forgiving people, my dear boy. I forgive everyone. To-day, for instance, as I was coming to you, I met a peasant in the road, and he said something. Well, Christ be with him! He defiled his own tongue, that's all. And I . . . I wasn't in the least angry with him. Why, I actually made the sign of the cross over him—really!"

"I suppose you had robbed . . . that peasant?"

"Who? I? No, my friend, I don't rob people. Highwaymen do that, but I always adhere to the law. I caught his horse in my meadow, and so I said: 'Come to the magistrate, my dear man. If the magistrate says you may graze your horses on other people's meadows, so be it. But if he says you mustn't, there is nothing for it, you have to pay a fine.' I always adhere to the law, my dear boy, always."

"You Judas . . . you ruined your mother."

"You may be angry if you like, but I will say again that you are not talking sensibly. And if I weren't a Christian I might . . . bring it up against you."

"You did ruin her . . . you took every penny from her."

"Stop now, do. I will pray for you, that may calm you."

Iudushka controlled himself, but he was so stung by the dying man's abuse that his lips were white and twitching. Hypocrisy was, however, so much a part of his nature that he simply could not stop acting the part he had chosen. With the last words he actually did kneel down, and spent a quarter of an hour raising his arms to heaven and whispering. Having done this he returned to the dying man's side, with a calm, almost bright expression on his face.

"You know, brother, I have come to talk to you of a serious matter," he said, settling down in the armchair. "Here you are abusing me, but I am thinking of your soul. Tell me, please, when did you last partake of the Holy Sacrament?"

"Good heavens, this is too awful.... Take him away. Ulita! Agashka! Who is there?" the invalid moaned.

"There, there, calm yourself, my dear. I know you don't like talking of it. Yes, brother, you have always been a bad Christian, and you remain one to this day. But oh, what a good thing it would be to think of your soul at a moment like this! Our soul, you know...ah, how careful one must be about it, my friend! You know what the Church prescribes? Bring thanksgivings and supplications, it says.... And another thing, we pray for a Christian end to our life, painless, peaceful, and unashamed. That's what it ought to be, my dear. You should send for the priest, and with sincere penitence.... Very well, very well, I won't. But it would be a good thing, you know."

Pavel Vladimiritch was purple in the face, and almost choking; if at that moment he could have smashed his head he would certainly have done so.

"About the estate too. Perhaps you have made some arrangement?" Iudushka continued. "It's a dear little estate you have here, there's no gainsaying it. The land is even better than at Golovlyovo, the soil is more sandy. And there's your capital, too. Of course I know nothing about it. I merely know that you let your peasants redeem their land, but I have never been interested to inquire about the details. To-day, for instance, I was saying to myself as I drove here: 'I expect my brother Pavel has some capital.' But if he has, I thought, he is sure to have made some arrangement about it."

The sick man turned away, sighing deeply.

"You haven't? Well, that's all the better, my friend. Let the law decide—it's fairer so. The property won't go to strangers in any case but to your own relatives. Take me now: my health is as frail as can be. I have one foot in the grave, and yet I think, why should I make a will if the law can settle it all for me? And what a good thing that is, my dear! There can be no quarrels or envy or intrigues—it's the law."

It was terrible. Pavel Vladimiritch fancied he had been buried alive and lay fettered by lethargy, unable to stir a limb, while he listened to the bloodsucker jeering at his corpse.

"Go away, for Christ's sake go!" he began imploring his tormentor at last.

"There, there, calm yourself, I'll go. I know you dislike me. . . . It's a shame, my friend, a very great shame, to dislike your own brother. But I am fond of you. I always say to my children, 'Though my brother Pavel has wronged me, I love him all the same.' So, then, you haven't made a will? Well, that's excellent, my friend. But sometimes even in one's lifetime the capital may be filched away, expecially if one lives by oneself, with no relatives. Well, I'll see to it. Yes? What? I've bored you? Very well, so be it, I'll go. Let me just say a prayer."

He stood up, folded his hands, and whispered hurriedly to himself.

"Good-bye, dear, don't worry. Have a nice little sleep, and perhaps, God willing, you'll be better. And meanwhile I'll have a chat with mamma, and maybe we'll think of something. I have asked them to cook a Lenten dinner for me, brother. . . . A bit of salt fish, a few mushrooms, a bit of cabbage. . . . You must excuse me. What is it? Am I boring you again? Ah, brother, brother! Very well, very well, I am going. The chief thing, my dear, is not to worry, not to excite yourself. Sleep peacefully. Hrr . . . hrr." . . . He jokingly pretended to snore, deciding to go away at last.

"Bloodsucker!" The shriek that followed him was so piercing that it made even Iudushka feel hot.

While Porphyry Vladimiritch was having his chat upstairs Arina Petrovna collected the young people round her downstairs (partly with the object of finding something out from them) and engaged them in conversation.

"Well, and how are you getting on?" she turned to her eldest grandson Pètenka.

"Fairly well, grandmamma. I shall get my commission next year."

"Will you? You promised it last year, and the year before. I can't make it out. Are your examinations so hard or what?"

"He failed at the last exams in 'First Principles,' grandmamma. The priest asked him, 'What is God?' and he said, 'God is a spirit—and a spirit . . . and to the Holy Spirit.' "

"You poor boy! However could you? Why, even my orphans here know it!"

"I should think so! God is a spirit, invisible . . ." Anninka hastened to show off her knowledge.

"No one has seen Him anywhere," Lubinka interrupted her.

"All merciful, omniscient, omnipotent, omnipresent," Anninka continued.

" 'Whither shall I go then from Thy Spirit; or whither shall I go then from Thy presence: if I climb up into heaven Thou art there; if I go down to hell Thou art there also.' "

"You too should have answered like this, and you'd have had your epaulettes by now. And what do you think of doing, Volodya?"

Volodya turned crimson and said nothing.

"You are another such, I see! Ah, children, children! You

look bright enough, and yet learning seems too much for you! And it isn't as though your father spoiled you. . . . How does he treat you now?"

"Just the same, grandmamma."

"Does he thrash you? I heard he had given that up."

"Not so much, but still . . . the worst of it is, he pesters one so. . . ."

"I don't understand that. How can one's father pester one?"

"He does, grandmamma, very much so. We mayn't go out without permission, mayn't take anything. . . . Beastly!"

"Well, you should ask permission—it wouldn't hurt you to do it!"

"Not we! If one says anything to him there is simply no end to it. 'Wait and see, more haste less speed,' and all the rest of it. . . . His talk is so boring, grandmamma!"

"You know, grandmamma, he listens behind the door to what we are saying! The other day Pètenka caught him at it."

"You naughty boy! And what did he do?"

"Nothing. I said to him, 'It's not the thing to listen behind doors, papa. One might easily smash your nose, you know,' and he merely said, 'There, there! There's no harm in it. I am like a thief in the night, my boy!' "

"The other day he picked up an apple in the orchard, grandmamma, and put it in his cupboard—and I went and ate it. There was such a to-do! He searched for it all over the place, cross-questioned all the servants. . . ."

"Has he grown so stingy, or what?"

"No, it isn't that he is stingy but . . . he is always after such trifles. He hides away bits of paper, looks for windfalls."

"He says Mass in his study every morning, and afterwards gives us a bit of the church bread . . . stale as stale could be! But we played a trick on him one day: we found out where he keeps the church bread, cut a hole in the bottom, scraped out the soft part and put in a lump of butter!"

"Well, I must say you are a pair of dare-devils!"

"No, just imagine his surprise the next day! Church bread with butter in it!"

"I expect you caught it badly?"

"Oh no.... He merely kept spitting all day and saying, as though to himself, 'The blackguards!' But of course we pretended that it wasn't meant for us. You know, grandmamma, he is afraid of you!"

"Why should he be afraid of me? I am not a scarecrow!"

"He is afraid—that's true. He thinks you will curse him. He is simply terrified of those curses."

Arina Petrovna pondered. "And what if I really do ... curse him?" came into her mind. "Suppose I say suddenly: 'I curse you!'" This idea was replaced by one of more practical importance: "What is Iudushka doing? What tricks is he playing upstairs? I expect he is simply turning himself inside out!" At last a happy thought struck her:

"Volodya, darling," she said, "you are light on your feet, how would it be for you to walk up quietly and listen to what's going on *there*?"

"With pleasure, grandmamma."

Volodya tiptoed to the door and disappeared behind it.

"How is it you thought of paying us a visit to-day?" Arina Petrovna began, questioning Pètenka.

"We had long been meaning to come, grandmamma, and this morning Ulita sent a messenger to say that the doctor had been and that uncle is sure to die to-day or to-morrow."

"Well, and have you had any conversation ... about the legacy?"

"We talk of nothing but legacies, grandmamma! He keeps telling us of how things were in the old days before grandpapa's time.... He actually remembers Goryushkino! 'If Auntie Varvara Mihailovna had had no children Goryushkino would have been ours!' he says, 'and goodness only knows by whom she had those children, but we should not judge others. We see a mote in our neighbor's eye and don't notice a beam in our own. . . . That's how it is,' he says."

"What a man! Auntie was married—even if there had been anything, the husband made it right!"

"But he does say it, grandmamma. He repeats it every time we drive past Goryushkino. 'My grandmother Natalya Vladimirovna came from Goryushkino,' he says; 'it ought by all rights to have remained in the Golovlyov family, but papa went and gave it as dowry to his sister. What melons used to grow at Goryushkino!' he says. 'Twenty pounds in weight—that's the kind of melons they were.' "

"Twenty pounds indeed! I have never heard of such. And what are his plans about Dubrovino?"

"Oh, the same sort of thing—melons and pumpkins . . . such silly things, you know. Though the last few days he kept asking: 'And how much capital do you think, children, my brother Pavel has?' He reckoned it all out long ago, grandmamma . . . what the redemption money came to, and when the estate was mortgaged, and how much has been paid off. . . . We saw the paper on which he made all these calculations, grandmamma, and we carried it off! We nearly drove him crazy with that paper. . . . He put it in his table, and we moved it to the cupboard; he locked it up in the cupboard, and we found a key to match and put the paper inside one of the church rolls. . . . He went to the bath-house one day and suddenly saw that paper on the shelf there!"

"You have a gay time of it!"

Volòdenka returned; all turned their eyes to him.

"One can't hear properly," he said in a whisper. "I only heard my father saying, 'Painless, peaceful, unashamed,' and uncle replying, 'Go out, you bloodsucker.' "

"And about the will. . . . Have you heard anything?"

"I think they did speak of it, but I couldn't catch it . . . Father closed the door very tight, grandmamma. I could only hear his buzzing. And then uncle shouted suddenly, 'Go away!' So I rushed off."

"I wish he'd give it to the orphans...." Arina Petrovna pondered dejectedly.

"If my father gets it he won't give anything to anybody, grandmamma!" Pètenka assured her. "I think he won't leave us a penny, either!"

"Well, he can't carry it into the grave with him, can he?"

"No, but he will think of some way. It's not for nothing he was talking to the priest the other day. He asked him, 'Suppose one were to build the Tower of Babel, Father—how much would it cost?'"

"Oh, that's nothing.... He may have just asked out of curiosity...."

"No, grandmamma, he really has some sort of scheme. If it's not the Tower of Babel, he'll leave his money to the Athos Monastery, but certainly not to us!"

"And will father have much when uncle dies?" Volodya inquired.

"God alone knows who will die first."

"No, grandmamma, father is quite certain. When we drove past the Dubrovino boundary this morning he took off his cap, crossed himself, and said, 'Thank God, it's going to be our own land once more!'"

"He has settled it already, grandmamma. He saw a copse and said, 'A lovely copse, that, if properly looked after!' Then he saw the meadow, and said, 'A fine meadow! Just see how many haystacks there are! There used to be sheds and stables here.'"

"Yes, yes.... The copse and the meadow—all shall be yours, my dears." Arina Petrovna sighed, "Goodness me, I believe the stairs are creaking."

"Hush, hush, grandmamma. That's he ... like a thief in the night ... eavesdropping."

There was a silence, but it proved to be a false alarm.

Arina Petrovna sighed and whispered to herself. "Ah, children, children." The young men were staring at the girls, as though ready to swallow them; the girls said nothing, they were feeling envious.

"Have you seen Mademoiselle Lotare, *cousine*?" Pètenka asked.

Anninka and Lubinka glanced at each other as though asking whether this was a question on history or geography.

"In the *Belle Hélène* . . . she acts the part of Helen."

"Oh yes . . . Helen . . . and Paris, isn't it? 'Being young and handsome he inflamed the goddesses' hearts?' We know, we know," Lubinka cried joyfully.

"That's it, that's it. The way she does that *cas-ca-ader*, ca-as-cader" . . . wonderful!"

"The doctor this morning kept singing, 'Headlong, headlong, headlong he will fly.' "

"Headlong—that was Lyadova's song. . . . She was a most charming creature. When she died a crowd of two thousand followed her coffin. . . . People thought there would be a revolution."

"Why, I believe you are talking of theaters," Arina Petrovna interposed. "Theaters aren't for them, my dear, the convent is their place."

"You are bent on burying us in a convent, grandmamma," Anninka complained.

"You come to Petersburg instead of the convent, *cousine*. We'll show you everything there."

"They must think pious thoughts, my dear, not be hankering after pleasures," Arina Petrovna went on sententiously.

"We'll take them for a drive to the Sergiev Monastery, grandmamma—that will be pious as well."

The girls' eyes positively glowed, and the tips of their noses turned red when they heard this.

"They say the singing at Sergiev is simply beautiful," Anninka exclaimed.

"You may be sure of that, *cousine*. The way they sing 'Let us put away all earthly care'—even my father couldn't do it so well. And afterwards we'd drive you down the Podya-cheskaya street."

"We'd teach you everything, everything, *cousine*. There are many young ladies like you in Petersburg, you know. You can hear their heels patter-patter down the streets."

"I dare say, you could teach them that," Arina Petrovna interrupted. "Leave them alone, for Christ's sake . . . you teachers! The idea of it! A nice sort of science you'd teach them! When Pavel dies I will go with them to the Hotkov Convent . . . we'll live very nicely there."

"You are still at your ribald talk?" a voice said suddenly at the door.

During the conversation nobody heard Iudushka stealing up like a thief in the night. His head was bowed, his face pale and tear-stained, his hands were folded on his chest, and his lips were whispering. He looked round for an icon, and, finding it, lifted up his heart for a few moments.

"Oh, what a state he is in! Dreadful!" he exclaimed at last, embracing "dear friend mamma."

"So bad as all that?"

"Very, very bad, darling. . . . And do you remember what a fine-looking fellow he used to be?"

"I can't say that I do. . . . He never looked particularly fine."

"Oh, don't say that, mamma! He always looked splendid. . . . I remember so well his leaving the cadet corps—broad-shouldered, well-set-up, the picture of health! Yes, yes . . . that's how it is, dear friend mamma! We are all in God's hands. To-day we are well and strong and want to live, to have a gay time and good things to eat, and to-morrow. . . ."

He made a gesture of despair and shed a tear.

"Did he talk to you, at any rate?"

"Very little, dear; he only said 'Good-bye, brother.' And you know, he feels it, mamma. He feels that he is in a bad way."

"I should think anyone would feel it with a splitting cough like his."

"No, mamma, I don't mean that. I was thinking about prophetic insight; they say some people have it; when a man is going to die he feels it beforehand. But sinners, I understand, are denied this comfort."

"Oh, indeed! Has he said anything about the will?"

"No, mamma. He was going to say something but I stopped him. No, I said, don't let us speak of it. I shall be pleased with anything you like to leave me in your kindness—and if you don't leave me anything I shall pray for your soul just the same. But he does so want to live, mamma. He clings to life—how he clings to it!"

"So does everybody."

"No, mamma, speaking of myself, for instance—if it should please the Lord to call me to Him, I am ready to go any moment."

"It's all very well if you are called to God, but what if it's to Satan?"

The conversation went on in this style till dinner, during dinner and after dinner. Arina Petrovna could hardly sit still with impatience. While Iudushka was holding forth, the thought came more and more often into her mind, "And what if I really . . . curse him?" But Iudushka had no suspicion of the storm raging in his mother's heart. He looked perfectly serene and went on torturing dear friend mamma with his hopeless twaddle.

"I'll curse him. I will. I will." Arina Petrovna was saying to herself more and more decisively.

There was a smell of incense in the rooms, melancholy singing resounded through the house; the doors were wide open, those who wished to take leave of the dead man came and went. While Pavel Vladimiritch lived none took any notice of him; when he died everyone felt sorry for him. They recalled that "he never wronged anyone," "never said a rude

106

word to anybody," "never looked askance at one." These facts, that before had seemed merely negative, suddenly appeared as something positive, and from the desultory, idle talk usual at funerals one could form a picture of a "good master." Many seemed to repent of something, confessing that they had on occasion taken advantage of the dead man's simplicity—but then who could have known that that simplicity would come to so early an end? While it was there to exploit they thought it would last for ever, and all of a sudden.... But were they given another chance, they would have fleeced him just the same: "Don't spare him, lads! No need to mind a fool!" One peasant brought Iudushka three rubles and said: "It's my debt to Pavel Vladimiritch. There was no note of hand—but here's the money."

Iudushka took it, praised the peasant and said that he would give those three rubles towards the oil for an "ever-burning" sanctuary lamp.

"You will be able to see it, my friend, and so will everyone, and the dead man's soul will rejoice. And perhaps he will be able to do something for you there with his prayers. You may not be expecting anything—and suddenly God will send you luck."

Very likely comparison played a certain part in the people's verdict on the dead man's character. Iudushka was not liked. One could get round him, of course, but he was fussy over silly trifles and always pestering people. Few peasants ventured to farm his land, for if they plowed or mowed an inch more ground than was legally theirs he immediately went to law. He ruined many in this way, with no profit to himself (his pettifogging habits were so well known that the court refused his claims almost without going into the case), and the litigation meant expense and loss of time to the peasants. "Buy a neighbor rather than a house," says the proverb —and everyone knew what kind of neighbor the master of Golovlyovo was. It was little comfort that the magistrate decided in one's favor. Iudushka worried one to death with his devilish casuistry. And since spite combined with hypocrisy (and it was not even spite but rather a moral deadness) always inspires a kind of superstitious fear, the new neighbors—to whom Iudushka always suavely referred as "dear neighbors"—timorously bowed down to the waist as they walked past the bloodsucker, who stood by the coffin dressed in black, with his hands folded in prayer and his eyes raised to heaven.

While the dead man was in the house, the whole household walked about on tiptoe, shook their heads, whispered, and kept peeping into the dining-room, where the coffin stood on the table. Iudushka pretended to be at his last gasp, shuffled along the corridor, came in to have a look at the dear dead, shed a tear, straightened the pall, and whispered with the Police Superintendent, who was making the inventory and sealing up chests and cupboards. Pètenka and Volòdenka were busy round the coffin, putting up candles and lighting them, holding the censer, etc. Anninka and Lubinka wept, and through their tears seconded the choristers in high-pitched little voices during the requiems. Women servants in black calico dresses wiped with their aprons their noses, red with crying.

As soon as Pavel Vladimiritch had passed away, Arina Petrovna withdrew into her room and shut herself up there. She had no time for tears because she felt that she had to decide at once what she was to do. She had no intention of staying at Dubrovino.... certainly not. Consequently the only thing that remained to her was to go to Pogorelka, the orphans' little estate—the "piece" she had once chucked to her daughter Anna Vladimirovna.

Having once made up her mind to do this, she felt relieved, as though Iudushka had suddenly lost all power over her. She calmly counted up her 5 percent bonds (it appeared she had fifteen thousand rubles of her own and fifteen thousand that she had saved up for the orphans), and calmly considered how much she must spend to put the Pogorelka house in order. Then she immediately sent for the Pogorelka foreman, gave the necessary orders about hiring carpenters and sending the carts to Dubrovino to fetch her and the girls' luggage, told them to get the chaise ready (she had her own chaise at Dubrovino, and she had proof that it was her own), and began to pack. She was neither hostile nor friendly to Iudushka; she simply felt that she could not bear to have anything to do with him. She no longer enjoyed her food, and ate very little, because she now had to eat what belonged not to Pavel but to Iudushka. Porphyry Vladimiritch looked into her room more than once to have a chat with dear friend mamma (he understood very well that she was making ready to go, though he pretended not to notice it) but Arina Petrovna did not let him in.

"Go along, dear, I haven't time for you," she said.

In three days Arina Petrovna was quite ready to leave. They all went to Mass and attended the burial service. At the burial everything happened exactly as Arina Petrovna had pictured it on the morning of Iudushka's arrival at Dubrovino. He called out, "Good-bye, brother!" when the coffin was lowered into the grave just as she thought he would, and then immediately turned to Ulita and said hastily:

"Be sure to take the fromenty back and put it on a nice clean table-cloth in the dining-room. We'll have to eat it in my brother's memory, you know."

Three priests (including the Father Superintendent) and the deacon had been invited to the dinner, which was served, as the custom is, as soon as they had returned from the funeral. A table apart was set in the hall for the sextons. Arina Petrovna and the girls came to dinner in their traveling-clothes, but again Iudushka pretended not to notice it. Coming up to the hors-d'oeuvres table, Porphyry Vladimiritch asked the Father Superintendent to bless the food and drink, then poured out a glass of vodka for each of the clergy and himself, and said, in a voice full of feeling:

"Eternal memory to the deceased! Ah, brother, brother, you have left us! And one would have thought you were the very man to live long. Oh, you bad, bad brother!"

He crossed himself and drank the vodka, then he crossed himself again and swallowed a piece of caviar, crossed himself again and took a piece of smoked salmon.

"Have some, Father," he begged the Father Superintendent. "It's all my brother's provisions. My brother was fond of good fare. He used to eat well, and he liked other people to have plenty too. Ah, brother, brother, you have forsaken us. Naughty, naughty brother!"

He was so carried away by his eloquence he actually forgot his mother. He only thought of her when he was about to put into his mouth a spoonful of pickled mushrooms.

"Mamma! Darling!" he cried in alarm. "To think of foolish me stuffing myself—how dreadful! Mamma, have some caviar, some mushrooms. Dubrovino is famous for its mushrooms, you know!"

But Arina Petrovna merely nodded without speaking and did not stir. She seemed to be listening to something with interest. It was as though a new light had suddenly dawned before her, and all this comedy to which she had been used from a child and in which she had herself always taken part suddenly struck her as quite new and unexpected.

The dinner began with family altercations. Iudushka insisted that his mother should sit at the head of the table. Arina Petrovna refused.

"No, you are master here, so you must sit where you want to," she said dryly.

"You are the mistress. You are mistress both at Golovlyovo and at Dubrivino—everywhere," Iudushka was persuading her.

"No, you sit there. If, God willing, I have a home of my

own, I'll sit where I like without being asked. But you are master here, so you must take the master's place."

"I'll tell you what we'll do then," Iudushka said with feeling; "we'll leave the place empty. As though my brother were present here invisibly. . . . He is the host and we are his visitors."

They did so. While soup was being served, Iudushka selected a suitable subject and engaged the priests in conversation, addressing himself chiefly to the Father Superintendent.

"Many people nowadays do not believe in immortality . . . but I believe in it," he said.

"Only some desperate characters, I expect," the Father Superintendent responded.

"No, not desperate characters, but there's a science to that effect—that man does it all of himself, you know. . . . He lives and lives—and suddenly he dies."

"There are much too many of these sciences nowadays, they ought to be cut down. People believe in science and don't believe in God. Even peasants have ambitions and want to be learned."

"Yes, Father, you are right. They certainly do have ambitions. Take my neighbors at Naglovka, for instance; they have nothing to eat, but they decided the other day to open a school in the village. Men of learning, indeed!"

"There is a science for everything now. There's a science to give you rain and a science to bring fine weather. In the old days it was simple: people came and had a service sung, and God granted what they asked. If fine weather was needed God sent fine weather; if rain was needed God had rain enough and to spare. God has plenty of everything. But since people took to science it has all come to an end. Everything happens at the wrong season now. When it's sowing-time there's a drought, and when it's hay-making it rains."

"It's the holy truth, what you are saying, Father. In the old days, when people used to pray more, the earth yielded better harvests too. One reaped not as now, four- or fivefold what one had sown, but a hundredfold. I expect my mother remembers those days. Do you remember, mamma?" Iudushka turned to Arina Petrovna, intending to draw her into conversation.

"I haven't heard of it happening in our parts. You were thinking of Canaan perhaps; they did have such harvests there, they say," Arina Petrovna responded dryly.

"Yes, yes, yes," Iudushka said, as though he had not heard his mother's remark. "They don't believe in God, they don't admit immortality... but they want their dinner."

"That's it—all they care for is food and drink," Father Superintendent assented, turning up the sleeves of his cassock to help himself to a piece of the funeral pie.

Everyone began on soup; for a time the only sound heard was the jingle of spoons and the priests snorting as they blew at the hot liquid.

"Or take the Roman Catholics now," Iudushka continued, putting down his spoon, "they don't deny immortality, yet they say that the soul does not go straight to hell or to heaven but finds itself for a time in a kind of intermediate place."

"That too is groundless."

"I am not so sure, Father"... Porphyry Vladimiritch replied thoughtfully. "Speaking from the point of view of..."

"It's no use speaking of idle fancies. How does the Holy Church pray? It prays that the soul may rest in a cool green place where there is neither sorrow nor sighing. How can there be any 'intermediate' place, then?"

Iudushka was not altogether convinced, however, and was just about to reply when Arina Petrovna, who had had enough of this conversation, cut him short.

"There, now, eat your soup, you theologian. I expect it's quite cold," she said, and, to change the subject, asked Father Superintendent, "Have you harvested your rye, Father?"

"Yes, madam, the rye is splendid this year, but the spring crop doesn't seem up to much. The oats hadn't formed the grain properly before they began flopping. There will be neither grain nor straw."

"Everyone is complaining about the oats this year," Arina Petrovna sighed, watching Iudushka scoop out the last of the soup with his spoon.

The next course was served: ham and green peas. Iudushka took advantage of the opportunity to renew the interrupted conversation.

"The Jews now don't eat ham," he said.

"The Jews are a vile race," the Father Superintendent replied—"that's why people jeer at them."

"But the Tatars don't eat pork either. . . . There must be some reason for it."

"The Tatars are a vile people too, that's the reason."

"We don't eat horse-flesh, and Tatars look down on pork. They say that in Paris, during the siege, people ate rats."

"Oh well, that's the French."

So the dinner went on. When carp fried in sour cream was served, Iudushka said:

"Please have some, Father. This carp is something special; my brother was very fond of it."

When asparagus was served Iudushka said:

"Now, this is something like asparagus. In Petersburg one would have to pay a silver ruble for it. My brother looked after it himself. Just look how thick it is, bless it."

Arina Petrovna's heart was boiling within her: an hour had passed and they were only half-way through dinner. Iudushka seemed to dawdle on purpose; he would swallow a few mouthfuls and then put down his knife and fork and talk, then tackle his food again, and again begin talking. How often in the old days Arina Petrovna used to shout at him, "Get on with your dinner, you Satan!" but he had evidently forgotten his mother's admonitions, or perhaps he had not forgotten but did it on purpose, out of revenge, and perhaps it was not even a conscious revenge but just his spiteful nature playing tricks of itself. At last the roast was served, but at the very moment, when all stood up and Father Deacon intoned the prayer for the deceased, there was a scuffle and shouts in the corridor that completely spoiled the effect.

"What's this noise?" Porphyry Vladimiritch cried, "this isn't a public-house, you know."

"Don't shout, if you please. It's me . . . they are carrying out my boxes," Arina Petrovna said, and added with a touch of irony, "Would you like to inspect them?"

Everyone was silent, even Iudushka was at a loss and actually turned pale. He immediately grasped, however, that he must do something to cover up his mother's unpleasant remark, and, turning to Father Superintendent, he began:

"Take woodcock, for instance. In Russia there are lots of them, but in other countries . . ."

"Get on with your dinner, for Christ's sake. We have over fifteen miles to drive, and we must arrive there before dark," Arina Petrovna interrupted him. "Pètenka dear, do go and tell them to hurry with the pudding."

There was a silence of several minutes. Porphyry Vladimiritch quickly finished his piece of woodcock and sat pale and with twitching lips, tapping the floor with his foot.

"You wound me, kind friend mamma. You hurt me very much," he brought out at last, without looking at his mother however.

"You aren't easily wounded I should have thought. And how could I have hurt you so much?"

"I am very, very much hurt. . . . Very much indeed. Going away at such a moment. You have lived here for years and suddenly . . . And then those boxes . . . and talking of inspection . . . It's insulting."

"If you really want to know, I can give you an answer. I lived here so long as my son Pavel was living; he is dead—I am going away. And as to my boxes, Ulita has been spying on me for days at your orders. But I think it is better to tell your mother straight out that she is suspect than to hiss at her like a snake behind another person's back."

"Mamma! Darling! Why, you . . . why, I . . ." Iudushka groaned.

"That will do," Arina Petrovna cut him short, "I have said enough."

"But dear mamma, in what way could I have . . ."

"I tell you I have said enough—leave it at that. Let me go in peace, for Christ's sake. I hear my carriage is ready."

Indeed there was the jingle of bells and the rattle of carriage wheels in the yard. Arina Petrovna was the first to get up from the table; the others got up too.

"Well, now let us sit down for a moment, and then we must be off," she said, going to the drawing-room.

They sat in silence for a few moments; Iudushka meanwhile recovered completely.

"But wouldn't you like to stay at Dubrovino a bit longer, mamma? See how nice it is here," he said, looking at his mother ingratiatingly like a dog that knows it has done wrong.

"No, my dear, I have had enough of it. I don't want to say anything unpleasant to you at parting, but I cannot stay here. There's nothing to hold me here. Father, let us pray."

All stood up and said a prayer, then Arina Petrovna kissed and blessed everyone as good relatives do, and walked to the door treading heavily.

Porphyry Vladimiritch, at the head of all the household, accompanied her to the front steps, but when he saw the carriage he was disturbed by the devil of cupidity. "It's my brother's chaise," the thought flashed through his mind.

"We shall be seeing each other, dear friend mamma," he said, helping his mother into the carriage and casting sidelong glances at it.

"If it be God's will . . . why not."

"Ah, mamma, mamma, you are a naughty girl, you know. Tell them to unharness the horses and come back into your old nest, with God's blessing... really," Iudushka prattled amiably.

Arina Petrovna did not answer. She had quite settled in her place in the carriage and had already made the sign of the cross, but the girls were not quite ready.

Iudushka meanwhile kept glancing at the carriage.

"And what about the carriage, mamma? Will you send it back, or would you like us to fetch it?"

Arina Petrovna positively shook with indignation.

"The carriage is mine," she cried in a voice so strained that everyone felt slightly uncomfortable. "Mine, mine. It's my carriage. I bought it.... I have proofs.... I have witnesses. And you... I'll... well, I'll wait and see... what you'll do next. Children, are you going to be much longer?"

"Why, mamma, I wasn't objecting.... Even if the carriage belonged to Dubrovino..."

"It's my carriage! Mine! It doesn't belong here. Don't you dare to say it does, do you hear?"

"Certainly, mamma.... Well, don't forget us, darling.... Come and see us without ceremony. We'll call on you and you call on us... like good relatives."

"Are you ready? Go," Arina Petrovna cried, hardly able to control herself.

The carriage moved and drove away at a jog-trot.

Iudushka stood on the steps waving his handkerchief, and so long as the carriage was in sight shouted after it: "Like good relatives. We'll call on you and you call on us."

3

THE CASTING UP

IT HAD NEVER entered Arina Petrovna's head that a moment would come when she would be merely an extra mouth to feed, and now it had stolen in upon her just when she saw for the first time in her life that her moral and physical faculties were undermined. Such moments always come unexpectedly. A man's strength may have been giving way for some time, but he still bears up and stands firm when suddenly a last blow is dealt him somewhere out of the blue. It is very difficult to foresee that blow and to understand that it is coming; one has simply to submit to it in silence, for it is the blow which instantly and irrevocably turns an active and energetic person into a complete wreck.

Arina Petrovna's position had been difficult when she broke with Iudushka and settled at Dubrovino, but then she knew at any rate that, although Pavel Vladimiritch was none too pleased at her invasion, he was a man of means and could well afford to keep her. Now the position was quite different. She was the head of a household where every mouthful counted. She knew what that meant, for having passed all her life in the country among the peasants she fully shared the peasant feeling that it was ruinous to have an extra mouth to feed when supplies were scarce.

And yet the first weeks after moving to Pogorelka she kept up her courage, busily settling in the new place, and her administrative insight was as clear as ever. But farming at Pogorelka meant fussing over every little detail and required constant personal supervision. In the first flush of excitement Arina Petrovna thought that it would be simple enough to keep strict account of farthings and pence, but she soon had to confess to herself that this was a mistake. It was simple enough indeed, but she had neither the energy nor the eagerness of her former days. Besides, it was all happening in the autumn when the year's supplies were being gathered in, and the bad weather put a stop to Arina Petrovna's zeal. The infirmities of old age prevented her from going out; long dismal autumn evenings doomed her to idleness. The old woman was restless and worried, but she could do nothing.

She could not help noticing too that all was not well with her grand-daughters. They had suddenly grown bored and dejected. Some vague plans for the future disturbed them—plans in which the thought of work alternated with thoughts of pleasure, of the most innocent kind, of course. Memories of their boarding school, odd bits of reading about devoting one's life to work, and a faint hope of using their school connections in order to find some way into the bright world of real human life, had a share in shaping those plans. Vague as they were, one definite, persistent thought dominated them—to escape at all costs from this hateful Pogorelka. And so one fine morning Anninka and Lubinka informed their grandmother that they could not and would not stay at Pogorelka any longer, it was beyond anything, they never saw anyone except the priest, who for some reason always talked to them about the virgins who had not trimmed their lamps, and altogether they simply couldn't go on like this! The young ladies spoke sharply because they were afraid of their grandmother, and, expecting her to be angry and to oppose them, they assumed quite a truculent manner. But to their surprise Arina Petrovna was not in the least angry at their complaints and did not even indulge in any of the useless moralizing to which weak old age is so prone. Alas! she was no longer the domineering woman who used to say, authoritatively, "I'll go to the Hotkovo Convent and take the girls with me." The change in her was due not wholly to the weakness of old age but partly also to a dawning sense of justice. The last blows of fate had not only humbled her but had thrown a light upon certain aspects of her mental horizon on which her mind had apparently never dwelt before. She understood that there exist in human nature strivings which may be dormant but, once awakened, irresistibly draw one towards the blessed ray of light that one's eyes have long been watching for amidst the hopeless darkness of the present. Having once grasped the legitimacy of such a striving she could no longer oppose it. True, she did try to dissuade the girls, but she did it feebly, half-heartedly; she was anxious about their future, especially as she herself had no connections in so-called society, but she felt it was right and inevitable that they should go away. What would become of them? The question haunted her mind every moment; but then even more formidable questions than that cannot hold back those who long for freedom. And the girls could talk of nothing but escaping from Pogorelka. After some hesitations and delays made out of consideration for their grandmother, they went away.

After their departure the Pogorelka house was plunged into hopeless stillness. Self-centered as Arina Petrovna was by nature, she too felt the soothing effect of other people's nearness. When she had seen off her grand-daughters she felt, perhaps for the first time in her life, that a part of her being had as it were, broken away, and she gained all at once a freedom so limitless that there was nothing but a gaping void before her. To hide this emptiness from herself she immediately gave orders to nail up the reception-rooms and the attic in which the girls had lived. "It will save firewood too," she thought. She kept only two rooms for herself, one of them had a large icon-stand and the other served her as a bedroom, study, and dining-room. For the sake of economy she dismissed the servants, keeping only the old housekeeper Afimyushka, who could hardly walk, and the one-eyed Markovna, a soldier's wife, who acted as cook and laundress. But all these precautions availed but little; the sensation of emptiness soon penetrated into the two rooms in which she had thought to shelter from it. Helpless solitude and dismal idleness were the enemies in whose company she was henceforth doomed to spend her old age. These were soon followed by physical and moral disintegration, all the more relentless because a life in which there was nothing to do offered no resistance to it.

Day followed day with the depressing monotony so characteristic of country life, when one has neither material comfort, nor food for the intellect, nor work. Apart from the external causes that made personal work on the farm impossible for Arina Petrovna, she felt an inner revulsion against the petty cares that fell to her lot at the end of her life. She might perhaps have overcome her aversion had she had a purpose that would make her efforts worth-while—but that was just the point, she had no purpose. Everyone was sick and tired of her, and she was sick and tired of everyone. Drowsy idleness had taken the place of her former feverish activity and the idleness gradually demoralized her will, and developed in her inclinations she had not dreamt of a few months before. The strong and self-possessed woman whom no one ventured even to think of as an old lady had suddenly become a wreck, for whom there was neither past nor future, but only the present moment to be lived through.

She spent the greater part of the day dozing. She would sit down in her armchair in front of a table on which smelly cards were spread out, and doze. Then she would wake up with a start, glance at the window, and without any conscious thought in her mind, gaze for hours at the wide expanse of fields stretching into the distance as far as the eye could see. Pogorelka was a sad-looking place. It had no garden, no shade, no sign of any attempt to make life there comfortable. There was not even a flower-garden. The house had only one story, it seemed crushed down as it were, and was blackened with age and rough weather. The many outbuildings behind it also showed signs of decay, endless fields lay around, and there was not any forest to be seen on the horizon. But as Arina Petrovna had lived all her life in the country, hardly ever leaving it, this poor scenery did not seem dismal to her, it touched her heart, stirring the remains of feeling that still smoldered in it. The best part of her being lived in those bare, boundless fields, and her eyes instinctively turned to them at every moment. She looked intently into the distance, gazing at the villages soaked with rain that showed like black specks on the horizon, at the white churches of the country-side, at the patches of shadow cast by the wandering clouds on the sunlit plain, at the peasant walking between the furrows, and it seemed to her that he never moved at all. But she did not think of anything or, rather, her thoughts were so disconnected that they could dwell on nothing for any length of time. She merely gazed and gazed until the drowsiness of old age began to ring in her ears, covering with a mist the fields, the churches, the villages, and the peasant walking far away.

Sometimes she seemed to recall the past, but it came before her disconnectedly, in fragments. She could not concentrate her attention, that wandered from one distant recollection to another. At times, however, some memory struck her deeply, not a joyful memory—there had been cruelly little joy in her life—but the thought of some bitter, unendurable injury. Something seemed to burn within her, anguish crept into her heart and tears came into her eyes. She began to weep painfully, shedding the scanty tears of pitiful old age that seem to be wrung out under the weight of some night-mare. But while her tears still flowed her unconscious thought went on wandering, imperceptibly drawing her away from the source of her sadness, so that after a few minutes the old woman asked herself in surprise what had happened to her.

She lived without taking any personal part in life, so to speak—lived simply in virtue of some forgotten springs of ac-tion that lay hidden in the wreck and had to be followed up and reckoned with. While those springs were there, life went on its wonted way, compelling her to go through the external actions necessary to keep the ruin from crumbling into dust.

Her days were spent in unconscious drowsiness, but her nights were positively miserable. At night Arina Petrovna was afraid, afraid of thieves, of ghosts, of devils—in short, of everything that her life and education had taught her to fear. There was but little defense against it all, because, with the exception of the two old servants already mentioned, the whole night staff of Pogorelka consisted of a lame peasant Fedoseyushka, who, for two rubles a month, came from the village in the evenings to keep watch over Arina Petrovna's house and generally dozed in the entry, going out occasion-ally to tap his sheet of iron and so show that he was awake. Several workmen and women lived by the cattle-yard, but that was some hundred feet from the house, and it was by no means easy to summon anyone from there.

There is something dreary and depressing about a sleepless night in the country. At nine or at most at ten o'clock all life seems to die down and an awe-inspiring stillness reigns everywhere. There is nothing to do, it is a waste to burn the candles, so there is nothing for it but to go to bed. As soon as the samovar had been taken off the table, Afimyushka, from habit acquired in the times of serfdom, spread a felt mat across the door leading to her mistress's bedroom; after scratching herself and yawning, she lay down on the mat and instantly dropped into a dead sleep. Markovna was busy in the maid's room, muttering to herself and abusing someone, but at last she too had finished, and a minute later could be heard snoring and talking in her sleep. The night-watchman sounded his sheet of iron to make his presence known and no more was heard of him for hours. Arina Petrovna sat before a guttered tallow candle, trying to keep herself awake by playing patience, but as soon as she laid out the cards she was overwhelmed by drowsiness, "Why, I might set the place on fire in my sleep!" she said to herself, deciding to go to bed. But the moment she sank into the feather-bed another trouble was upon her; the sleep that she could hardly struggle against all the evening suddenly forsook her altogether. The room was overheated, warm air poured in from the stove, and the feather-bed made her intolerably hot. Arina Petrovna turned over from side to side. She wanted to call someone but she knew that no one would come. Mysterious silence reigned around—a silence in which a straining ear could distinguish a number of sounds. There was a bang somewhere, or a sudden howl, or someone seemed to walk down the passage, or a breath of wind passed suddenly through the room, actually touching her face. The sanctuary lamp was burning before the icon and its light gave a deceptive appearance to everything—the objects in the room seemed to be mere outlines of themselves. In addition to this uncertain light there was another, coming from the open door of the adjoining room where four or five sanctuary lamps were burning before the icon-stand. That light lay on the floor in a yellow quadrangle, cutting into the semi-darkness of the bedroom but not mingling with it. Flickering, silently moving shadows were everywhere. A mouse scratched behind the wall-paper. "Shh! you wretch!" Arina Petrovna called—and all would be quiet again. Again there would be shadows and a whispering that seemed to come from nowhere. She passed most of the night in wakeful, uneasy drowsiness and dropped really asleep only towards morning. And at six o'clock Arina Petrovna was on her feet again, worn out by the sleepless night.

In addition to all this, two more causes aggravated Arina Petrovna's pitiful existence: scanty food and uncomfortable rooms. She ate little and badly, probably trying to make up in this way for the losses due to her not looking after the estate. The Pogorelka house was old and damp, the room in which Arina Petrovna had shut herself up was never ventilated and was not swept or dusted for weeks on end. Completely help-less, deprived of every comfort and attention, she was gradu-ally sinking into decrepitude.

But the more decrepit she grew, the more eager she was to live; or, to be more exact, it was not so much that she longed for life as that she had no thought of death and wanted to "have a good time." She had been afraid of death before, but now she seemed to have completely forgotten about it. And since her ideal of life differed but little from those of any peasant, the conception of "good living" that lured her was not of a lofty character. All that she had denied herself in the course of her life—good food, rest, other people's society—became a constant object of her thoughts. All the characteris-tics of a typical hanger-on—gluttony, love of idle talk, sneak-ing readiness to please for the sake of a favor—developed in her with astonishing rapidity.

She lived on the servants' cabbage soup and half-putrid salt meat, and kept dreaming of the Golovlyovo stores, of the carp that bred in the Dubrovino ponds, of the mushrooms that grew in plenty in the Golovlyovo woods, of the fowls that were fattened in the Golovlyovo farmyard. "It would be lovely to have soup with goose giblets or mushrooms fried in sour cream," the thought flashed through her mind so vividly that it made her mouth twitch. At night she turned over from side to side, turning cold with fear at every rustle and thought, "At Golovlyovo the bolts are fast, and the watchmen can be trusted, they rattle their clappers all night through— one can sleep as in Christ's bosom!" In the daytime she had hours and hours with no one to speak to, and during that enforced silence the thought crept of itself into her mind: "At Golovlyovo there are plenty of people, one can talk to one's heart's content!" In short, she kept recalling Golovlyovo every moment, and as she did so it became so to speak a point of light where "good living" was centered.

In proportion as her imagination succumbed to the memories of Golovlyovo, her will grew weaker and the bitter injuries of the recent past receded further and further away. Owing to her bringing up and the whole setting of her life, the Russian woman resigns herself much too easily to the part of a dependant, and Arina Petrovna did not escape that fate either, although one would have thought her past ought to have been a warning and a safeguard to her. Had she not made a mistake "at that time" and divided the property between her sons or trusted Iudushka, she would have remained a scolding and exacting old woman who made everyone bow to her will. But since the mistake was irretrievable, the transition from a scolding and arbitrary autocrat to a submissive and ingratiating dependant was merely a question of time. So long as some of her former strength remained, the transition did not express itself outwardly; but as soon as she grasped that she was irrevocably condemned to helpless solitude, all kinds of cowardly impulses crept into her heart and little by little completely demoralized her will that had been weakened already. Iudushka, who on his early visits to Pogorelka had met with an extremely cold reception, suddenly ceased to be hateful to her. The old injuries were unconsciously forgotten, and Arina Petrovna made the first step towards peace.

It began with requests. Messengers from Pogorelka came

to Iudushka seldom at first, and then oftener and oftener. It was either that there were no mushrooms at Pogorelka, or that the cucumbers were spotty because of the rain, or that the turkeys died "because of this freedom"—"and you might, dear friend, tell them to catch some carp for me at Dubrovino, which my son Pavel never refused his old mother." Iudushka frowned but did not venture openly to express his annoyance. He grudged giving the carp but he was afraid above all things that his mother might curse him. He remembered her saying once, "I'll come to Golovlyovo, tell them to open the church, call the priest, and cry, 'I curse you'!"—and this memory restrained him from many of the nasty tricks at which he was a great hand. But, carrying out the wishes of his kind friend mamma, he hinted to his household that every man had a cross laid upon him by Providence and that there was a purpose in this, for if he had no cross to bear, man forgot himself and fell into evil ways.

To his mother he wrote as follows:

> I am sending you as many cucumbers as I am able, kind friend mamma, but as to turkeys, with the exception of those that are being kept for stock, we have nothing but cocks which would be no use to you because of their dimensions and your modest requirements. But perhaps you will do me the favor of coming to Golovlyovo to share my scanty fare, we will then have one of those idle creatures roasted (I call them idle because my cook Matvey caponizes them very cleverly), and we will both have a treat, precious friend mamma.

Since that occasion Arina Petrovna had paid frequent visits to Golovlyovo. She tasted with Iudushka turkeys and ducks, slept to her heart's content, both at night and after dinner, and indulged in endless conversations about nothing in particular, to which Iudushka was prone by nature and she through old age. She did not give up her visits even when the rumor reached her that Iudushka, tired of being a widower, had taken for housekeeper a sexton's daughter called Yevpraxeya. On the contrary, when she heard of this she immediately set out for Golovlyovo, and without waiting to step out of the carriage, called to Iudushka with childish impatience, "Well, well, you old sinner! Show me your beauty, show her!" She enjoyed herself thoroughly that day, because Yevpraxeya waited on her at dinner, made up the bed for her after dinner, and in the evening they all played cards. Iudushka too was pleased at this turn of events—and as a sign of filial gratitude had a pound of caviar put into Arina Petrovna's chaise as she was going home; this was the highest token of respect, for caviar was not home-produce but a bought article. The old woman was so touched that she could not resist saying:

"Thank you very much indeed. God will love you, my dear, for being so good to your old mother. Anyway I shall not be dull now when I return to Pogorelka. I have always been fond of caviar, and now I shall have a treat, thanks to you!"

Five years had passed since Arina Petrovna moved to Pogorelka. Iudushka having once settled on his family estate, never left it. He had grown considerably older, and looked faded and gray, but he cheated, lied, and talked twaddle more than ever because now he had almost always with him "kind friend mamma," who for the sake of creature comforts in her old age became his faithful listener.

It must not be imagined that Iudushka was a hypocrite in the same sense as Tartuffe or any modern French bourgeois who goes off into flights of eloquence on the subject of social morality. No, he was a hypocrite of a purely Russian sort, that is, simply a man devoid of all moral standards, knowing no truth other than the copy-book precepts. He was pettifogging, deceitful, loquacious, boundlessly ignorant, and afraid of the devil. All these qualities are merely negative and can supply no stable material for real hypocrisy.

In France hypocrisy is the outcome of a man's upbringing; it forms part of "good manners" so to speak, and almost always has a distinct political or social coloring. There are religious hypocrites, social morality hypocrites—men who preach on the subject of property, family, State, and even, of recent years, on the subject of "order." If this kind of hypocrisy cannot be described as a conviction, it is in any case a banner around which men who find it profitable to be hypocritical in this rather than in some other way can gather. They are conscious hypocrites, that is, they know it themselves and are aware that other people know it too. For a French bourgeois the universe is nothing but a large theater in which an endless play is going on and one hypocrite gives his cue to another. Hypocrisy sets a standard of decency, of decorum, of good appearance, and, most important of all, hypocrisy acts as a bridle—not of course for those who practice it at the top of the social scale but for those who, without any hypocrisy, throng the bottom of the social cauldron. Hypocrisy restrains society from unbridled passions making the latter a privilege of a very small minority. So long as moral laxity is confined to a small and well-organized group, it is not merely safe but actually helps to maintain the traditions of elegance. Elegance would perish if there did not exist a certain number of *cabinets particuliers* in which it can be cultivated at moments free from the cult of official hypocrisy.

But moral laxity becomes positively dangerous if it is accessible to all, everyone being free to put forward his claims and to prove that they are both natural and legitimate. In that case new social strata are formed which seek either to replace the old or considerably to limit them. The demand for *cabinets particuliers* increases so much that at last the question arises whether it would not be simpler in the future to do without them altogether.

The French ruling classes guard themselves against those undesirable questions and complications by means of systematic hypocrisy which does not remain merely a matter of custom but acquires a legal character, and instead of being simply a social habit becomes a binding law.

The whole of the modern French Theater is, with a few exceptions, founded upon this law of respect for hypocrisy. In the best French plays, i.e. in those which enjoy the greatest popularity, because of the extremely realistic way they reflect the dirty facts of life, the leading characters invariably save up a few moments at the end in order to camouflage the dirt by some grandiloquent sentences, glorifying the sweetness and holiness of virtue. In the course of four acts Adèle may defile her marriage bed in every possible way, but in the fifth she is sure to declare in the hearing of all that the family hearth is the only refuge in which the Frenchwoman can find happiness. Ask yourself, what would happen to Adèle if the authors made the play go on for another five acts—and you may answer with perfect certainty that in the course of the next four acts Adèle would again defile her marriage bed, and in the fifth again address the same statement to the audience. In fact there is no need to make any conjectures—it is enough to go from the Théâtre Français to the Gymnase and from there to the Varieties or the Vaudeville to convince oneself that Adèle everywhere defiles her marriage bed and everywhere ends by declaring that bed to be the only altar at which an honorable Frenchwoman can officiate. This is so ingrained in the national mind that no one even notices the absurd contradiction involved in the situation or sees that the truth of life goes in it hand in hand with hypocrisy, and the two are so intermingled that it is hard to say which has a greater claim to recognition.

We Russians have no strongly biased systems of education. We are not drilled, we are not trained to be champions and propagandists of this or that set of moral principles but are simply allowed to grow as nettles grow by a fence. This is why there are very few hypocrites among us and very many liars, bigots, and babblers. We have no need to be hypocritical for the sake of any fundamental social principles, for we have no such principles and do not take shelter under any one of them. We exist quite freely, i.e. we vegetate, babble, and lie spontaneously, without any principles.

Whether this is a matter for grieving or rejoicing is not for me to say. I think, however, that while hypocrisy may arouse fear and indignation, objectless lying makes one feel bored and disgusted. And so the best thing is not to discuss the advantages or disadvantages of the conscious as compared with the unconscious hypocrisy, but to keep away both from hypocrites and from liars.

And so Iudushka was a sneak, a liar, and a babbling fool rather than a hypocrite. When he retired to the country he found freedom, for nowhere else, in no other sphere of life, could his instincts have such free play as there. At Golovlyovo he never met with any direct opposition or even with any indirect hindrance which might make him feel "I should love to behave shabbily but I am ashamed before other people!" No one's judgment disturbed him, no indiscreet glance troubled him, and so he had no occasion to question his own conduct. His attitude to himself was one of utter slackness. Complete freedom from any moral restraints had attracted him for years, and the only reason why he had not moved to the country before was that he was afraid of idleness. Having spent more than thirty years in the dull atmosphere of a Government office, he had acquired all the habits and instincts of a typical bureaucrat who cannot bear to have a single minute of his life unoccupied with trivialities. But looking at the matter more carefully he came to the conclusion that the world of bureaucratic idling was so mobile that it could without any difficulty be transferred to any sphere one liked. And indeed as soon as he settled at Golovlyovo he immediately invented for himself such a mass of futile occupations that he might be engaged in them for ever without the least danger of ever finishing them. In the morning he sat down to his writing-table and began work; in the first place he checked the accounts of the dairymaid, the housekeeper, and the bailiff first by one method, then by another; secondly, he went in for a very complicated system of book-keeping, both for money and for goods; he entered every farthing and every article in twenty books and reckoned it all up, now losing half a farthing, now making a farthing too much. At last he took up his pen and wrote complaints to the Justice of Peace and to the Peace-mediator. All this did not leave him a moment to spare and had indeed all the appearance of assiduous exhausting work. Iudushka complained not of having nothing to do, but of not having time to do all there was to be done, though he slaved at it all day in his study, wearing his dressing-gown from morning till night. Bundles of accounts carefully sewn together that had not been checked lay about on his desk, including a year's whole accounts from the dairymaid Fyokla; her doings had struck him from the first as suspicious, but he could never find a free moment to go into the matter.

He had lost all connections with the outside world. He received no books, no newspapers, no letters. One of his sons, Volòdenka, had committed suicide; to his other son, Pètenka, he wrote very little, and only when he sent him money. A dense fog of ignorance, superstition, and tiresome futile fussiness surrounded him, but he did not feel the slightest desire to escape from it. He learned that Napoleon III was no longer Emperor a year after the man had died—the Police Superintendent told him of it; but he did not express any special interest at the news and merely crossed himself, whispered "The Kingdom of Heaven be his," and said:

"And how proud he used to be! There was no going near him! This wasn't right for him and that wasn't the thing! Tsars came to pay him respects, princes waited on him! And behold God went and confounded all his fancies in one moment!"

Strictly speaking, he did not know what was going on on his estate, though he did nothing but cast up figures and keep accounts from morning till night. In this respect he had all the characteristics of a typical bureaucrat. Imagine a government official to whom his chief said in a merry moment, "Dear friend, it is essential for my plans that I should know how many potatoes are yearly grown in Russia—so please make the necessary calculations!" Would the man be embarrassed by such a question? Would he, at any rate, ponder about the method he should follow in his inquiry? Not at all, he would act quite simply. Taking a map of Russia he would divide it into perfectly equal squares, find out how many acres were in each square, then ask at the nearest general shop how many potatoes are required to plant an acre of ground and what the average crop is, and then, with God's help and by the aid of the four rules of arithmetic, he would calculate that under favorable conditions Russia can grow so many potatoes and under unfavorable so many. His work would not merely satisfy his chief, but would no doubt be printed in the hundred-and-second volume of some *Proceedings*.

The housekeeper Iudushka had selected was completely in keeping with his surroundings. Yevpraxeya was the daughter of the sexton at St. Nicolas's Church and was in every way a perfect treasure. She was neither clever nor resourceful nor even quick in her movements, but, to make up for it, she was gentle, hard-working, and made no demands whatever. Even after she had "found favor in his eyes" she merely asked whether she might have a drink of cold kvass without asking permission if she were thirsty. Iudushka himself was touched by her disinterestedness, and in addition to kvass gave her two barrels of pickled apples to help herself to without giving him any account on that score.

A lover of beauty would have found nothing specially attractive about her appearance, but it was entirely satisfactory to a man who was not too particular and knew what he wanted. Her broad fair-skinned face with a narrow forehead was framed with thin yellowish hair, she had dull eyes, a straight nose, and an insignificant mouth with the unmeaning elusive smile that one finds on portraits painted by home-grown artists. Altogether there was nothing remarkable about her, except, perhaps, her back, which was so broad and powerful that the least susceptible man instinctively raised his hand to give the girl a good smack between her shoulder-blades. She knew this and did not object, so that when Iudushka patted her for the first time on her fat neck she merely moved her shoulders.

In those dull surroundings day followed day, one exactly like the other, without any change or hope of anything fresh and new.

Arina Petrovna's arrival somewhat enlivened Iudushka's existence, and it is only fair to say that, although at first he frowned at the sight of his mother's carriage in the distance, in time he grew accustomed to her visits and indeed came to like them. They satisfied his passion for empty talk; he managed to indulge in it even when by himself, apropos of various bills and accounts, but to talk twaddle with dear friend mamma was far more pleasant. When they met they talked from morning till night and were never weary of it. They spoke of everything, of what the harvests used to be in the old days and what they were now, of how the landowners used to live before and how they were living at present; of pickled cucumbers not being the same as they used to be—perhaps because salt was better in the old days.

The advantage of these conversations was that they flowed like water and were easily forgotten; consequently they could be renewed endlessly with as much interest as though they were completely new.

Yevpraxeya sat with them while they talked; Arina Petrovna had grown so fond of her that she could not bear her out of her sight. Sometimes, tired of talking, all three sat down to play cards, and sat till late at night playing "fools." They had tried to teach Yevpraxeya dummy-whist, but she could not understand it. The huge Golovlyovo house seemed to come to life on such evenings. Lights showed in all the windows, shadows flitted to and fro, so that a passer-by might think there was some extraordinary merry-making going on. Tea, coffee, and hors-d'oeuvres were on the table all day long. Arina Petrovna's heart grew merry and rejoiced within her, and instead of one day she stayed three or four. And on her way back to Pogorelka she was already inventing a pretext to return as soon as possible to the lure of Golovlyovo's "good living."

It was the end of November; the earth was covered with a white shroud as far as the eye could see. It was night and a snow-storm was raging outside; sharp, cold wind furrowed the snow, instantly heaping it up in mounds, and, striking everything in its way, filled the air with terrific howling. The village, the church, the nearest forest—all disappeared in the whirling mist of snow; a mighty roar arose from the old Golovlyovo garden. But in the house it was warm, light, and cozy. A samovar stood on the dining-table and Arina Petrovna, Iudushka, and Yevpraxeya sat round it. A card-table with some shabby cards on it stood close by. The open doors of the dining-room led to the icon-room on one side, all ablaze with the lights of the sanctuary lamps, and on the other to the master's study, in which there too was a lamp burning before an icon. The stuffy, overheated rooms smelt of lamp oil and charcoal fumes from the samovar. Yevpraxeya sat opposite it, washing the cups and wiping them with a tea-cloth. The samovar was making loud noises; it roared with all its might and then seemed to drop asleep, snoring shrilly. Clouds of steam escaped from under the lid, enveloping the teapot that had been standing on the top of the funnel for the last fifteen minutes. The company were talking.

"Tell me now, how many times have you been made a fool to-day?" Arina Petrovna asked Yevpraxeya.

"I wouldn't have been a fool at all, had I not given in. It's for your pleasure I do it," Yevpraxeya answered.

"What next! I saw what sort of pleasure you felt when I kept dealing you three and five cards at a time. I am not like Porphyry Vladimiritch, you know; he spoils you and deals you only one card at a time, but I have no object in doing that, my dear."

"Why, you cheated!"

"Now that's a thing I never do."

"Whom then did I catch at it? Who wanted to pair off a seven of clubs with an eight of hearts? I saw that myself, you know; I caught you doing it!"

Saying this Yevpraxeya stood up to take the teapot off the samovar and turned her back to Arina Petrovna.

"What a back you have ... bless it!" Arina Petrovna said involuntarily.

"Yes, her back certainly is ..." Iudushka answered mechanically.

"Always talking of my back ... you shameless creatures! What has it done to you?"

Yevpraxeya looked right and left and smiled. Her back was her great asset. That morning even the old cook Savelyitch was absorbed in the contemplation of it and said, "What a back! A regular stove!" And she did not complain of him to Porphyry Vladimiritch.

Tea was poured out and the samovar made less noise.

The snow-storm meanwhile was growing worse and worse, a whole avalanche of snow beat against the window-panes and the wind set up an indescribable wail in the chimney.

"The snow-storm is in good earnest," Arina Petrovna remarked. "It howls like I don't know what."

"Well, let it. It howls, and we are drinking tea—so that's how it is, my friend mamma!" Porphyry Vladimiritch responded.

"It must be dreadful to be caught in the fields by this sort of weather!"

"It may be dreadful for some, but it's right enough for us. Other people are out in the dark and the cold but we are warm and snug indoors. We sit here drinking tea with sugar and lovely cream and fresh lemon. And if we want a drop of rum in it, we can have that too."

"Yes, but if now . . ."

"Allow me, mamma. I am saying: it's very bad out of doors now. No road, no path showing—all covered with snow. And there are wolves too. But here with us it is light and comfortable, and we are not afraid of anything. We sit here as snug as can be, in peace and quiet. If we want to have a game of cards, we can have it; if we want a drink of tea, we can have that too. We won't drink more than we need, but will drink just as much as we should. And why is this? It is because God is kind to us. If it had not been for Him, for the King of Heaven, we might be wandering about the fields now, in the cold and the dark, dressed in some wretched old jerkin tied with a shabby belt, with bark shoes on our feet."

"Bark shoes, indeed! That's too much of a good thing! After all, we are gentlefolk! We wear boots, such as they are."

"But do you know, mamma, why we are gentlefolk? That too is because God is kind to us. If it hadn't been for Him we would be sitting in a peasant hut now, with a lighted splinter instead of a candle, and not even dream of tea or coffee! I'd sit there plaiting bark shoes, you'd be warming up some watery cabbage soup for supper, and Yevpraxeya would be weaving.... And perhaps, to make things worse, the foreman would come and tell me to turn out with my cart and horse...."

"Oh, no foreman would send one out in such weather!"

"There's no telling, dear friend mamma! And what if it were needed for the Army? Maybe there is a war or a revolution somewhere, and the soldiers have to be at the place in time! The Police Superintendent told me the other day that Napoleon III was dead. So you may be sure the French will be at their tricks now! Of course our people will come forward too, and that means that the peasant must turn up with cart and horse! They won't consider whether it's cold or snowing or impassable mud; the peasant must go if he is told to! But they would spare people like you and me, and not send us out."

"There's no doubt of it, God is very good to us."

"That's just what I'm saying! God is everything to us, mamma. He gives us firewood for warmth, and lovely provisions for food—it's all His doing. We fancy that we do it ourselves, buying things with our money, but if we look at it and consider, we see it is all from Him, all from God. And if it were not His will, we should have nothing at all. I should love to have an orange now, for instance; I should eat one myself and treat dear friend mamma to one, and give one to everybody, and I have the money to buy the oranges—I have only to take it out of my pocket and say, 'give me the oranges!' But God says 'Whoa!' and here I am—in a sad plight with no oranges in sight!"

They all laughed.

"It's all very well!" Yevpraxeya remarked. "An uncle of mine was sexton at Pesochnoe, ever such a pious man he was —you'd think God might have done something for him, but one night he was out in the snow-storm and froze to death just the same."

"That's just what I am saying. If God wills it, a man will freeze, and if He doesn't he will remain alive. And about prayer; you see, some prayers are acceptable and some are not. Acceptable prayers reach their destination, and the not acceptable are as good as nothing. Perhaps your uncle's prayers were unacceptable—and so they had no effect."

"I remember in 1824 I went to Moscow—it was just before Pavel was born—I went there in December...."

"Allow me, mamma. I will just finish about prayer. A man prays for everything, because he needs all sorts of things. He needs nice fresh butter, and good firm cabbage and cucumbers, everything, in fact. Sometimes in his weakness he asks even for things he doesn't need. But from on high God can see better. You ask Him for butter, and He gives you cabbage or onions; you are praying for dry and warm weather, and He sends you rain and hail. And we must understand this and not repine. Last September, now, we kept asking God for frost to save winter crops from rotting, but He simply wouldn't give us frost—and our crops rotted, sure enough!"

"Didn't they!" Arina Petrovna echoed sympathetically. "At Novinki the peasants' winter crop is simply done for. They'll have to plow the land again and sow in the spring."

"That's just it! We try to be clever, we plot and scheme, plan to do this and that, and in a single moment God turns all our plans and considerations into dust. You were going to tell us something that happened to you in '24, mamma?"

"Did I? I believe I've forgotten! I expect it was also about the same thing—God's goodness to us. I can't think what it was, my dear."

"Well, God willing, you will think of it some other time. And while the storm is raging outside, you have some jam, dear mamma. These are Golovlyovo cherries! Yevpraxeya made the jam herself."

"I am having some. To tell the truth, cherries are a rare treat for me nowadays. In the old days I enjoyed them often enough, but now... You have fine cherries at Golovlyovo, big juicy ones. At Dubrovino, do what they would, the cherries were never sweet enough. You did put some French vodka into the jam, didn't you, Yevpraxeya?"

"Yes, of course! I did it all just as you told me. And I meant to ask you, when you pickle cucumbers, do you put any cardamom in?"

Arina Petrovna pondered and said, throwing up her hands in perplexity, "I don't remember, my dear. I believe I did put it in. I don't now—my pickling is nothing to speak of nowadays. But I used to put it in.... I am quite sure I did. When I come home I'll search among my recipes and perhaps I'll find it. When I was strong, you know, I took notice of everything—wrote it all down. If I liked something that other people had, I at once asked for the recipe, copied it out and tried it when I came home. I once found out a secret, such a secret—the man refused to part with it for a thousand rubles, do what you would! And I gave twenty-five kopecks to his housekeeper and she told me the whole thing!"

"Yes, mamma, you were a true statesman in your day!"

"I don't know about being a statesman, but I certainly can thank God—I did not squander what I had, but added to it. And here I am eating the fruits of my labor. It was I, you know, planted the cherries at Golovlyovo!"

"And I thank you for it, mamma, thank you very much. Eternal gratitude both for myself and for our descendants—that's what I feel!"

Iudushka got up and kissed mamma's hand.

"And I thank you too for looking after your mother's comfort! Yes, you have fine provisions, very fine!"

"Oh, my provisions are nothing to speak of. Now, yours in the old days, that was something like! Think of all the cellars you had—and not an empty corner in them!"

"I too had good stores, that's true; I liked to have my house in order. And about the cellars being so many, the whole thing was on a bigger scale then, one had ten times as many mouths to feed as now. Take the house-serfs alone—one had to provide for everyone and to feed them all. Cucumbers for one, kvass for another—each had a little and yet it mounted up to a lot altogether."

"Yes, those were good days and there was plenty of everything then. Corn and fruit—all grew abundantly."

"They manured the ground better, that's why."

"No, mamma, it wasn't that. It was God's grace did it. I remember papa brought an apple from the garden one day and everyone marveled—it was too big to go on a plate."

"I can't say I remember that. I know we had good apples, but I don't remember any being the size of a plate. The story of them catching a carp at Dubrovino weighing eighteen pounds—that's true enough."

"Carp and fruit too—all was large then. I remember Ivan the gardener used to grow water-melons that big!"

Iudushka thrust out his arms and pretended he could not make them meet round the imaginary water-melon.

"Yes, water-melons too. I must say, though, water-melons differ from year to year, my dear. Some years they are plentiful and very good; other years they are few and a bad flavor, and sometimes there aren't any at all! And there's another thing to bear in mind—fruit doesn't grow everywhere the same. At Hlebnoe, for instance, Grigory Alexandritch could never grow anything—no berries, no apples, no fruit, in fact, except melons. But his melons were magnificent."

"That means he had God's blessing for melons!"

"Why, of course. Without God's blessing there's no doing anything. There's no getting away from that."

Arina Petrovna had drunk two cups of tea and began glancing at the card-table. Yevpraxeya too was burning with impatience to have a game of "fools." But these plans were disturbed by Arina Petrovna herself, because she suddenly recalled something.

"I have a piece of news for you," she declared. "I received a letter from the girls yesterday."

"So after all this silence they have sent you word at last! They must have been hard put to it; I expect they ask for money."

"No, they don't. Here, what do you think of that!"

Arina Petrovna pulled a letter out of her pocket and gave it to Iudushka, who read as follows:

> Don't send us any more fowls and turkeys, grand-mamma. Don't send us any money either, but put it in the bank. We are not in Moscow, but at Harkov; we have gone on the stage, and in the summer will drive about the fairs. I, Anninka, made my first appearance in *Perichole* and Lubinka in *Pansies*. I was called before the curtain several times, especially after the scene when Perichole comes out slightly tipsy and sings "I am re-a-dy, I am ready, I am re-a-a-a-dy." Lubinka too was a great success. The manager pays me a hundred rubles a month, and I am to have the benefits of one performance at Harkov, and Lubinka receives seventy-five rubles a month and the benefits of a summer performance during the fair. Besides that, we get presents from officers and lawyers. Only, lawyers sometimes give one forged notes, so that one must be careful. And you, dear grandmamma, use everything you like at Pogorelka, we will never go back there and simply cannot understand how anyone can live there. Yesterday we had the first snow and we went driving *troikas* with two lawyers here; one looks just like Plevako—a wonderfully handsome man! He put a glass of champagne on the top of his head and danced the *trepak*—it was lovely, such fun! The other is not much to look at, rather like Yazykov in Petersburg. Would you believe it, he has so upset his imagination with reading *The*

Collection of Best Russian Ballads and Folk Songs and has grown so nervy that he faints in the law-courts. We spend almost every day in this way with lawyers or with officers. We go for drives, have meals in the best restaurants and don't pay anything. Don't save up anything in Pogorelka, grandmamma and help yourself to all there is—bread, and chickens, and mushrooms. We should be very pleased if the capital too . . .

Good-bye! Our friends have come—they want us to go for a drive again. Pet! Charmer! Good-bye!

Anninka.

And I too—Lubinka.

"Tfoo!" Iudushka swore, returning Arina Petrovna the letter.

She sat pondering and said nothing for a few minutes.

"You haven't answered them yet, mamma, have you?"

"Not yet, the letter only arrived yesterday, and I came to you on purpose to show it to you, and here I had almost forgotten it!"

"Don't answer them. Better not."

"But how can I do that? I have to account to them for the estate. Pogorelka is theirs, you know."

Iudushka also pondered; some sinister plan flashed through his mind.

"What troubles me is how they can keep themselves straight in an evil place like that," Arina Petrovna went on. "In this sort of matters, once you make a slip there's no retrieving a girl's honor. You may go and whistle for it!"

"Much they care about it!" Iudushka snapped back.

"Anyway a girl's honor is, one may say, her greatest treasure. Who would marry her if she lost it?"

"Nowadays, mamma, they don't care whether a man is their legal husband. They laugh at what religion teaches us! They walk to a bush, get married under it—and that's that. They call it civil marriage."

Iudushka suddenly recalled that he too was living in sin with a spinster of a clerical family.

"Sometimes, of course, if there is nothing for it," he corrected himself. "If a man is still in his prime, and a widower too. . . . In case of necessity the law may be set aside!"

"Of course! If hard pressed a plover will sing like a nightingale. Even saints sinned when they were driven to it, to say nothing of us, sinners."

"That's just it. Do you know what I would do if I were you?"

"Advise me, dear; tell me."

"I should ask them to give you a deed of trust for Pogorelka."

Arina Petrovna glanced at him in alarm.

"But I have one as it is for managing the estate," she said.

"Not only for managing it, but for selling or mortgaging it—so that you could do what you liked with it in fact . . ."

Arina Petrovna looked down and said nothing.

"Of course it's a matter that wants thinking over. Think about it, mamma!" Iudushka insisted.

But Arina Petrovna was silent. Although in her old age her mind had grown rather dull, she felt distinctly uncomfortable about Iudushka's insinuations. She was afraid of him; she was sorry to lose Golovlyovo with its warmth, comfort, and plenty, but at the same time she fancied it was not for nothing he spoke of a deed of trust and that it was a new snare for her. The atmosphere grew so tense that she wished she had not foolishly shown him the letter. Fortunately, Yevpraxeya came to the rescue.

"Well, are we going to play cards?" she asked.

"Let us, let us!" Arina Petrovna hastened to answer quickly getting up from her seat. But on the way to the card-table another thought struck her.

"Do you know what date it is to-day?" she asked Porphyry Vladimiritch.

"Twenty-third of November, mamma," Iudushka answered with surprise.

"Twenty-third—yes, but do you remember what happened on the twenty-third? I expect you forgot about the requiem?"

Porphyry Vladimiritch turned pale and crossed himself.

"Good heavens! How dreadful!" he exclaimed. "But was it really on the twenty-third? Wait a minute, I'll look in the calendar."

A few minutes later he brought the calendar and found in it a sheet of paper with the words: "November 23. The anniversary of my dear son Vladimir's death. Rest, dear ashes, till the joyous morn! and pray for your papa, who will on that day, without fail, have a Mass and a requiem service said for you."

"There's a nice how do you do!" Porphyry Vladimiritch said. "Ah, Volodya, Volodya! you bad, naughty son! You can't be praying for your papa if God makes him lose his memory like that! What are we to do, mamma?"

"There's nothing so very dreadful in it—you can have the service to-morrow just as well. We'll have the Mass and the requiem, all as it should be. It's all my fault, forgetful old creature that I am! I came here on purpose to remind you, but I forgot all about it on the way."

"Oh, dear, dear! Good thing at least that the sanctuary lamps are lit in the icon-room! It was quite an inspiration on my part. It isn't a holiday to-day—they've simply been left burning since Our Lady's festival—and this morning Yevpraxeya came and asked me, 'Shall I put them out?' And it was just as though something had pushed me—I thought for a moment and said, 'Don't touch them! Let them burn, bless them!' And now I see what it meant!"

"Yes, it's a good thing that the icon-lamps are alight. It's a relief to one's mind, anyway. Where are you going to sit? Will you deal to me, or again give an easy time of it to your fine lady?"

"I don't really know, mamma, whether I ought...."

"Why ever not? Sit down! God will forgive you! You didn't do it intentionally but from forgetfulness. That happens even to the righteous! To-morrow we'll get up with daylight, go to Mass and have a requiem service for him, all in the proper fashion. His soul will be glad that his friends and relatives remember him, and our minds too will be at rest because we shall have done our duty. So there! And you mustn't grieve, my dear—I always say that: you won't bring your son back to life by grieving, and besides, it's a sin against God."

Iudushka was convinced by these words and said, kissing his mamma's hand:

"Ah, mamma, mamma! You have a heart of gold, really! If it weren't for you, where would I be now? I would have been simply lost! Done for!"

Porphyry Vladimiritch gave orders about the following day's ceremony and they all sat down to cards. They played one game, then another. Arina Petrovna grew hot and was indignant with Iudushka for dealing Yevpraxeya only one card at a time. In between the games Iudushka indulged in memories about his dead son.

"And how affectionate he was!" he said. "He would never take anything without permission. If he wanted a piece of paper, he would ask, 'May I take a piece of paper, papa?'—'Take some, dear.' Or: 'Would you be so kind, papa, to have some carp fried in sour cream for lunch to-day?'—'Certainly, dear.' Ah, Volodya, Volodya! You were a good boy in every way, but it was naughty of you to leave your papa!"

A few more games were played; more memories followed.

"And what suddenly came over him I can't make out! He lived nicely and quietly, a joy to his father, all serene— nothing could be better! And suddenly—bang! And just think of the sin of it! Only consider, mamma, what he presumed to do—taking his own life, the gift of our Heavenly Father! And why? What for? What was amiss? Was it for lack of money? I never keep back anyone's salary; not even my enemies can bring this against me. But if you thought you hadn't enough, I couldn't help that, my boy. Papa's money doesn't come to him easily! If you are badly off, you must cut down your needs. You can't always have things sweet and tasty—at times you must have them plain and sour! Yes, my dear boy! Here, your papa was hoping to receive some money this morning, but the steward came and said, 'The Terpenka peasants haven't paid their rent!' Well, there was nothing for it, I wrote a petition to the magistrate. Ah, Volodya, Volodya! You are a naughty boy! You've forsaken your papa, left him alone in the world!"

As the game grew more lively, his reminiscences grew more and more touching.

"And how intelligent he was! I remember he lay ill with measles—he wasn't more than seven at the time—and when his mother came up to him he said, 'Mother, it's only angels that have wings, isn't it?' She said, 'Yes, only angels.' 'Why, then, did papa have wings when he came into the room just now?'"

At last they had a wonderful game: Iudushka was made "a fool" although he had eight cards, including the ace, the king, and the queen of trumps. There was much laughter and teasing, in which Iudushka joined benevolently. Amidst the general merriment Arina Petrovna suddenly grew still and listened.

"Shh! Be quiet! There's someone coming!" she said. Iudushka and Yevpraxeya listened also but could not hear anything.

"I tell you, there's someone coming! There . . . do you hear? The wind blew this way suddenly. . . . Listen! there's someone coming and quite near now!"

All began to listen again, and this time they all heard a distant sound of bells that the wind sometimes brought near and then carried away again. Some five minutes passed and the bell could be heard quite clearly; then there were voices in the yard.

"The young master! Pyotr Porphyryitch has come!" was heard in the hall.

Iudushka, white as a sheet, got up from his chair and stood as though rooted to the spot.

Pètenka walked in somewhat listlessly, kissed his father's hand, then his grandmother's, bowed to Yevpraxeya and sat down. He was a rather good-looking young man of twenty-five, dressed in an officer's traveling uniform. This was all one could say about him, and Iudushka himself hardly knew more than that. The relations between the father and the son could not even be called strained—they were simply non-existent, so to speak. Iudushka knew from his passport that this man was his son, to whom he had on certain dates to send a definite allowance, the amount of which he himself had fixed, and from whom in return he had the right to claim respect and obedience. Pètenka for his part knew that he had a father who could always give him a bad time. He liked coming to Golovlyovo well enough, especially since he had received his commission—not because he enjoyed talking to his father, but because everyone who has no conscious purpose in life instinctively yearns for his native place. This time, however, he obviously came because of some urgent need, and consequently he did not show a single sign of the joyful surprise that generally marks a prodigal son's return to his ancestral home.

Pètenka was disinclined to talk. To his father's exclamations—"This is indeed a surprise! You have played us a trick, my boy! I was wondering who on earth could be driving about this time of night—and here it's you!"—he said nothing, and sometimes smiled a forced smile. To the question, "Whatever made you think of coming?" he answered almost crossly:

"I just thought of it and came, that's all."

"Well, thank you, thank you, for remembering your father,

147

I am delighted to see you! I expect you thought of your old grandmother too?"

"Yes, I did."

"Wait a minute, perhaps you remembered that it was your brother Volòdenka's anniversary to-day?"

"Yes, I thought of that too."

This kind of conversation went on for about half an hour, and one could not make out whether Pètenka meant what he said or spoke at random. And so, patient as Iudushka was about his children's indifference, he could not resist saying at last:

"You aren't particularly amiable, my boy! No one could say you were an affectionate son!"

Had Pètenka said nothing and received his father's remark with meekness, or, better still, had he kissed his papa's hand and said, "Excuse me, kind papa, I am tired after the journey" —all would have been well. But Pètenka behaved most un-graciously.

"I am evidently made that way," he answered rudely, as though to say, "Leave me alone, for heaven's sake!"

Porphyry Vladimiritch felt so hurt, so hurt that he simply could not restrain himself.

"And to think of all the trouble I have taken for your sake!" he said bitterly. "Even as I sit here I never stop think-ing of how to arrange it all neatly and nicely, so that everyone should be snug and comfortable and know no poverty or dis-tress. . . . And you two always tried to keep away from me!"

"How do you mean—'you two'?"

"Well, I'll speak of you only . . . though Volodya was just the same, God rest his soul."

"But I am very grateful to you!"

"I don't see any gratitude in either of you! No gratitude, no affection, nothing!"

"I am not of an affectionate disposition, that's all. But why do you keep speaking of us both? My brother is dead . . ."

"Yes, he is dead, God punished him. God punishes disobedient children. And yet I think of him. He was disobedient, but I still think of him. To-morrow, now, we'll have Mass said for him and a requiem service. He wronged me, but I remember my duty. Good Lord, what are we coming to! A son has no sooner greeted his father than he begins to snort at him! It wasn't like this in my time! Going to Golovlyovo in the old days I used to repeat for the last twenty miles of the journey, 'Remember King David, O Lord, and all his meekness!' But mamma is still here to ask—she'll tell you. And now—I can't make it out, I can't make it out!"

"Nor can I. I have come quietly, kissed your hand in greeting, I am not doing anything to you and sit drinking tea, and if you give me supper, I'll have supper too. Why are you making all this fuss?"

Arina Petrovna sat in her armchair, and it seemed to her as though she were listening to a familiar story that had begun she could not remember how long ago. The book had been closed, one would have thought, and yet it kept opening on exactly the same page as before. She saw quite well, however, that such a meeting between the father and the son boded nothing good and felt called upon to intercede and say a few conciliatory words.

"There, there, you turkey-cocks!" she said, trying to speak playfully. "They have no sooner met than they begin to fight! The way they go for each other, dear me! There will be feathers flying in the air directly! A-ah, how very wrong! You had better sit still, my dears, and talk to each other nicely, and then it will be a pleasure for an old woman like me to listen to you! You must give in, Pètenka! You must always give in to your father, my dear, because he is your father. If sometimes you may think he is hard on you, you must submit cheerfully and respectfully, because you are his son. The bitter may turn into sweet, you know, and you'll be the gainer. And you, Porphyry Vladimiritch, must be considerate. He is

149

your son, and young and used to comfort. He has driven fifty miles over rough roads and snowdrifts: he is tired and cold and sleepy! We have finished tea, so tell them to give us supper and then we'll go to rest. That's the thing to do, my dear! We'll each go to our rooms, say our prayers and feel at peace. With God's help sleep will drive away any bad thoughts we may have had, and to-morrow we'll get up early and pray for the deceased. We'll hear Mass, have a requiem service sung, and then come home and talk. And after having had a rest everyone will tell his story properly. You, Pètenka, will tell us about Petersburg, and you, Porphyry, about your life in the country. And now let us have supper and, with God's blessing—to bed."

This admonition had effect, not because there was anything really convincing in it, but because Iudushka saw that he really had gone too far, and that it was best to end the day peaceably. He got up, kissed his mamma's hand, thanked her for "giving him a lesson," and ordered supper to be served. The meal passed in gloomy silence.

The dining-room was deserted; all had retired. The house was gradually growing quiet; dead stillness crept from room to room, reaching at last the stronghold in which the routine life of the day persisted longest—that is, the master's study. Iudushka finished the allotted number of genuflexions he had long been counting before the icons and went to bed also.

He lay in bed, but he could not go to sleep. He was aware that his son's arrival betokened something unusual, and all kinds of trivial admonitions were already springing up in his mind. The advantage of these admonitions was that they fitted any occasion and did not express any coherent train of thought. They required no grammatical form, no rules of syntax. They accumulated in the mind in the shape of disconnected aphorisms and slipped off the tongue of themselves just as they came. Whenever something out of the ordinary happened, these aphorisms simply seethed in

Iudushka's mind and not even sleep could calm the turmoil of his thoughts.

Iudushka could not go to sleep: an oppressive mass of empty words seemed to crowd around him. Strictly speaking, Pètenka's mysterious arrival did not particularly trouble him, for he was always ready for *everything*. He knew that *nothing* could catch him unawares or cause him to make the slightest deviation from the stale and meaningless precepts that entangled him from head to foot as in a net. Sorrow and joy, love and hate, did not exist for him: the whole world was in his eyes merely something dead that simply provided one with an opportunity for an endless flow of talk. There was cause for real sorrow when Volodya committed suicide, but Iudushka remained unmoved. It was a very sad affair that lasted for two years. For two whole years Volodya had tried to bear up; at first he was proud and determined not to ask his father's help: then he weakened and began to beg, to argue, to threaten. . . . And he always received in answer some ready-made precept that was like a stone given to a hungry man. It is hard to say whether Iudushka understood that it was stone and not bread, but in any case he had nothing else to offer and he gave his stone as the only gift he could provide. When Volodya shot himself, he wrote down the date of his death in the calendar and promised to have Mass and a requiem service sung for him every year on November 23rd. And when, in spite of all, some inner voice seemed vaguely to mutter to him at times that solving family quarrels by means of suicide was, to say the least of it, a rather doubtful procedure, he immediately produced a whole series of ready-made aphorisms, such as "God punishes disobedient children," "Pride goes before a fall," etc.—and put his mind at rest.

It was the same thing now. There was no doubt that something bad had happened to Pètenka, but he, Porphyry Golovlyov, must at all costs rise above any such eventualities. You don't gather grapes from thistles; as you made your

bed so you must lie on it; you called the tune, now you must
pay the piper; yes, that was it—this was precisely what he
would say the next day, whatever his son might tell him. But
what if Pètenka, like Volodya, refused to take a stone instead
of bread? What if he too.... Iudushka banished the thought
as coming from the evil one. He turned over from side to
side trying to go to sleep, but sleep he could not. As soon as
he began to drop off, he suddenly found himself saying: "It's
no use crying for the moon," "you must cut your coat according to your cloth...now I...and you, you see...you are
in too great a hurry, and you know the proverb—Hurry is
no use except for catching fleas." Empty words seemed to be
all round him, creeping up to him, closing in upon him.
Iudushka could not sleep under the burden of trite phrases in
which he hoped to take refuge the next day.

Pètenka could not sleep either, though he was tired
enough after the journey. He had something on his mind, and
that could only be settled here at Golovlyovo, but he did not
know how to tackle the business. To tell the truth, Pètenka
knew very well that his case was hopeless, that the visit to
Golovlyovo would merely mean fresh unpleasantness, but
there is in every man an obscure instinct of self-preservation
that overrules his conscious mind and eggs him on to try every
possible means of escape. And so Pètenka came, but instead
of bracing himself to endure it all, he very near quarreled
with his father from the first. What would come of his visit?
Would the miracle of turning stone into bread take place?

Would it not have been simpler to have taken a revolver
and said, holding it to his temple: "Gentlemen, I am not worthy to wear your uniform! I have squandered the regiment's
money and so I pass a stern but just sentence upon myself!"—bang! And all would have been over. "The *deceased*
lieutenant Golovlyov is struck off the lists"—Yes, that would
have been decisive and...picturesque. His comrades would
have said: "You are unlucky, you have been carried away,

but you were a *noble* character!" But instead of acting in that way he had let things drag on till everyone came to know what he had done—and he had been let off for a certain number of days to find the money he owed and then leave the regiment. It was with this purpose—which meant a shameful end to the career he had just begun—that he came to Golovlyovo, perfectly sure of receiving a stone instead of bread!

But perhaps something would come of it. Things do happen sometimes.... The Golovlyovo of to-day might vanish suddenly and a new Golovlyovo appear in its place in which he ... Not that his father might die ... why should he?—but simply ... there might be a change.... And perhaps his grandmother would come to the rescue—she had money of course! When she heard that he was in trouble she might suddenly give it to him! Take it, and go, she would say, hurry back before your time is up! And he would dash along, hurrying the drivers and just managing to get to the station in time—and arrive at his regiment two hours before he was due! "Well done, Golovlyov!" his comrades would say. "Your hand, noble young man, and let us forget the past!" And he would not merely stay on in his regiment but be made a first-lieutenant and then a captain, and an aide-de-camp (he had already been the regiment's treasurer), and at last, on the day of the regimental jubilee....

Ah, if only the night would pass! To-morrow ... well, to-morrow, come what may! But what he would have to listen to! What wouldn't his father say to him! Though why to-morrow? He still had another day before him.... He had stipulated for two days on purpose that he might have time to persuade his father, to touch his heart.... Touch his heart, indeed! Not much chance of that, damn it....

At this point his thoughts grew completely muddled and faded away one after another into the fog of sleep. A quarter of an hour later Golovlyovo was plunged in profound slumber.

The whole household was up early the next morning. All went to church except Pètenka, who stayed at home under the pretext of being tired after the journey. After hearing Mass and the requiem service they came home. Pètenka went up as usual to kiss his father's hand, but Iudushka gave him his hand sideways and everyone noticed that he did not even bless his son. They had tea and ate the traditional fromenty; Iudushka walked about gloomily, shuffling his feet; he avoided conversation, kept sighing and folding his hands in sign of inward prayer, and did not even glance at his son. Pètenka looked uncomfortable and smoked cigarette after cigarette in silence. Instead of improving during the night, the strained atmosphere of the day before grew so much worse that Arina Petrovna was alarmed and decided to find out from Yevpraxeya whether anything had happened.

"What's the matter with them that they look at each other like enemies all the morning?" she asked.

"How should I know! I don't ask them questions."

"Is it because of you, I wonder? Perhaps my grandson is after you?"

"Why should he be? Simply, he waylaid me in the passage this morning, and Porphyry Vladimiritch saw it!"

"H'm, so that's what it is!"

And indeed in spite of his desperate position Pètenka had behaved with his usual frivolity. He too admired Yevpraxeya's powerful back and decided to tell her so. It was with this purpose, really, that he stayed away from church, hoping that Yevpraxeya, as the housekeeper, would remain at home also. When all was quiet in the house he threw his coat over his shoulders and hid in the passage. Two or three minutes later the door from the passage to the maids' room opened with a bang and Yevpraxeya appeared at the end of the passage holding a tray with a freshly baked bread-ring for breakfast. But Pètenka had hardly had time to give her a good slap between her shoulder-blades and say, "My word, that's something like a back!" when the dining-room door opened and his father's figure appeared in the doorway.

"If you have come here to play your nasty tricks, you scoundrel, I'll have you thrown down the stairs!" Iudushka said in a voice of indescribable malice.

Pètenka, of course, disappeared instantly. He understood well enough that the morning's mishap was not likely to improve his chances, and so he decided to say nothing that day, putting off the explanation till the morrow. But in the meantime he did nothing to allay his father's irritation and behaved in the most thoughtless and foolish way imaginable. He smoked continuously, regardless of the fact that his father ostentatiously waved away the clouds of smoke with which he filled the room. Then he kept throwing idiotically tender glances at Yevpraxeya, who answered them with a kind of wry smile—and Iudushka noticed that too.

The day dragged on. Arina Petrovna tried to have a game of "fools" with Yevpraxeya, but it was not a success. No one felt inclined to play or talk and even the usual trivialities did not come into their minds, though they each had such a rich store of them. Dinner came at last, but at dinner too all were silent. After dinner Arina Petrovna thought of going back to Pogorelka, but Iudushka was positively alarmed at his kind friend mamma's intention.

"Why, bless you! Would you leave me alone with this . . . bad son?" he exclaimed. "No, no, no! You mustn't think of it! I won't let you go!"

"But what is it? What has happened? Tell me!" she asked.

"Nothing has happened yet, but you'll see. . . . No, please don't leave me! I'd rather you were here when. . . . It's not for nothing he has come! So if anything happens, you be witness!"

Arina Petrovna shook her head and decided to stay. After dinner Porphyry Vladimiritch went to have a nap, having first sent Yevpraxeya to the village priest's. Arina Petrovna also went to her room and dozed in an armchair. Pètenka thought this an opportune moment to try his luck with grandmamma and went in to her.

"What is it, have you come to have a game of 'fools' with the old woman?" Arina Petrovna asked.

"No, grandmamma, I have come on business."

"Well, tell me what it is."

After hesitating for a moment Pètenka blurted out suddenly: "I've gambled away government money, grandmamma."

The shock made Arina Petrovna see dark.

"Much?" she asked in a frightened voice, looking at him with a fixed stare.

"Three thousand."

A moment's silence followed; Arina Petrovna glanced anxiously from side to side as though hoping for help to arrive.

"And do you know that you may have to go to Siberia for that?" she brought out at last.

"I know."

"Ah, you poor boy!"

"I was wondering if you could lend me the money, grandmamma. . . . I would give you good interest for it."

Arina Petrovna was quite frightened.

"What are you talking about!" she said in a flurry. "I only have enough money left for my funeral and the requiems! I couldn't keep myself if it weren't for my grand-daughters and these visits to my son. No, no, no! Leave me in peace, I beg you! You know, you had better ask your papa."

"One might as well draw blood from a stone! I was reckoning on you, grandmamma!"

"Good heavens! Why, I should have been only too glad, but I have no money to speak of. I have none to spare. Try your father, and mind you speak affectionately and respectfully—say: 'This is how it is, papa: being young and foolish I got into trouble. . . .' Make light of it, smile, kiss his hand, go on your knees and shed a few tears—he likes that—and he'll untie his purse-strings for his dear son."

"You think I'd better try? Wait a minute! What if you were to say to him, grandmamma, 'If you don't give the money, I'll curse you!' He has always been afraid of your cursing him."

"Come, come, why should I curse him! You can ask him without my doing that. Beg him, dear! After all, it won't hurt you to go down on your knees to him—he is your father! And he too will see.... Do as I tell you, really!"

Pètenka walked about the room with his arms akimbo, though thinking things over; at last he stopped and said:

"No, it's no use. He won't give it me anyway. I might crack my head beating it against the ground, and still he wouldn't give it me. He might, if you threatened to curse him.... Well, what am I to do, grandmamma?"

"I really don't know. Try—you may soften him. But how could you do anything so desperate? It's no joke gambling away government money! Had anyone put you up to it?"

"I just went and did it, that's all. Well, if you have no money of your own, give me some of my cousins'!"

"My dear, think what you are saying! How can I give you the orphans' money? No, please spare me, I beg you! Don't talk to me about it, for Christ's sake!"

"So you won't? It's a pity. I would give you good interest on it. Would you like to have 5 percent a month? No? Well, then, a 100 percent at the end of the year!"

"Don't you tempt me!" Arina Petrovna waved him off. "Leave me alone, for Christ's sake! Your papa might hear and think that I put you up to it! Oh, dear, dear! I was going to have a rest and had just dozed off in fact, and here he comes to an old woman like me with such a business!"

"Oh, very well. I'll go away. So you cannot? Excellent. Like good relatives! For the sake of three thousand your grandson will have to go to Siberia. Don't forget to have a service sung to bless me on the way!"

Pètenka banged the door and went out of the room. One of

his frivolous hopes had failed him—what was he to do now? The only thing that remained was to make a clean breast of it to his father. And maybe . . . perhaps something . . .

"I'll go at once and make an end of it!" he said to himself. "Or no . . . no, why should I do it to-day? Something might turn up . . . though what could it be? Yes, better wait till to-morrow. . . . Anyway I have to-day. Yes, let it be to-morrow! I'll speak to him and go away."

He decided on that: the next day was to settle it all.

After his explanation with his grandmother time dragged on more slowly than ever. Arina Petrovna became subdued after learning the reason of Pètenka's visit. Iudushka tried to draw her out, but seeing that she had something on her mind, relapsed into silence. Pètenka too did nothing but smoke. At supper Porphyry Vladimiritch turned to him with the question:

"Will you tell us, at last, why you have honored us with your visit?"

"I'll tell you to-morrow," Pètenka answered sullenly.

Pètenka got up early after an almost sleepless night. The same double-edged thought pursued him—the thought that began with the hope, "Maybe he'll give it me!" and invariably ended with the question, "Why ever have I come here?" It may be that he did not understand his father, but he certainly did not know of a single feeling, of a single weakness in him on which one might play in order to attain one's object. He merely felt that in his father's presence he was face to face with something slippery and incalculable. Not knowing at which end to begin or how to put anything to him made Pètenka uneasy, if not actually frightened. It had been so since his childhood. As far back as he could remember it had always seemed better to abandon a plan altogether than to submit it to his father's decision. It was the same thing now. How was he to begin? What should he say? Oh, why had he come!

He felt wretched. But since he had only a few hours left he knew that something had to be done. Screwing up his courage he buttoned his coat, and, whispering something to himself on the way, walked with a fairly firm step to his father's study.

Iudushka was at his prayers. He was pious and readily devoted several hours a day to prayer. But he prayed not because he loved God or hoped to enter into communion with Him through prayer, but because he was afraid of the devil and hoped that God would save him from evil. He knew a number of prayers and had thoroughly mastered the technique of praying—that is to say, he knew when to move his lips and look up to heaven, when to fold his hands and when to raise them, when to show feeling and when to stand sedately, crossing himself occasionally. His eyes and nose turned red and watered at appropriate moments indicated by devotional practice. But prayer did not regenerate him, did not purify his feelings or bring in a single ray of light into his dull existence. He could go on praying and performing all the necessary movements, and at the same time be looking out of the window to see if anyone went to the cellar without permission, etc. Prayer was for him a thing apart sufficient unto itself and not in the least connected with life as a whole.

When Pètenka came in, Porphyry Vladimiritch was kneeling, with uplifted arms. He did not change his position but merely waved one hand to show that it was not yet time. Pètenka settled down to wait in the dining-room where the table was already set for breakfast. The half-hour he spent there seemed to him an eternity, especially as he was convinced that his father kept him waiting on purpose. The assumed courage with which he had armed himself gradually gave way to vexation. At first he sat still, then walked up and down the room, and at last began to whistle a tune. As he did so, the study door opened slightly and Iudushka's angry voice said:

"Those who want to whistle may go and do it in the stables."

A few minutes afterwards Porphyry Vladimiritch came out, all in black and wearing a clean shirt, as though for some solemn occasion. His face had a serene and gentle expression, breathing of joy and humility as though he had just had some holy experience. He went up to his son, blessed and kissed him.

"Good morning, dear," he said.

"Good morning!"

"How did you sleep? Was your bed comfortable? Did any bugs or fleas disturb you?"

"Thank you. I slept."

"Well, if you slept, thanks be to God. One doesn't sleep anywhere so sweetly as under the parental roof. I know it from my own experience; I might be ever so comfortable in Petersburg, but I never slept there as sweetly as at Golovlyovo. It's like being rocked in a cradle. Well, what shall we do: have breakfast first, or have you something to say to me now?"

"No, let us talk first. I have to leave in six hours from now, and you may need time to think things over."

"Very well. But I tell you straight, my boy, I never think things over. I always have my answer ready. If you ask for what is right—have it, I never refuse what is right. It may be hard for me sometimes, and more than I can manage, but if I am asked to do what is right, I cannot refuse—it isn't my nature. But if you ask for what is wrong, you must take no for an answer. I may be sorry for you, but I'll refuse! There are no subterfuges about me, my boy! I am a plain man. Well, come to the study, you'll talk and I'll listen. Let's hear what you have to say!"

When they came into the study Porphyry Vladimiritch left the door slightly ajar, and instead of sitting down or offering his son a chair, began walking up and down the room. He seemed to know by instinct that it would be a ticklish business and that it was far more convenient to discuss such matters while moving about. It was easier to conceal one's expression and to cut short the explanation if it took too unpleasant a turn. And the door left ajar made it possible to call in witnesses, for mamma and Yevpraxeya would be sure to come into the dining-room directly.

"I have gambled away government money, papa," Pètenka said dully, without any preliminaries.

Iudushka was silent and one could only see that his lips twitched. Then he began to whisper to himself as was his wont.

"I lost three thousand," Pètenka explained, "and if I don't return the money the day after to-morrow the consequences may be very unpleasant for me."

"Well, return it!" Porphyry Vladimiritch said amiably.

The father and the son made a few tours of the room in silence. Pètenka wanted to explain further but felt a spasm in his throat.

"But where am I to get the money?" he brought out at last.

"I don't know your resources, my dear. You must have reckoned on something when you were gambling with government money and you must pay out of that."

"You know perfectly well that in such cases one doesn't do any reckoning."

"I know nothing about it, my dear. I have never played cards—except for a game of 'fools' with mamma, just to amuse the old lady. And don't you mix me up in your dirty affairs. Let us go and have breakfast instead. We'll drink tea and sit quietly and perhaps talk of something, only, for Christ's sake, not of this."

Iudushka made for the door, intending to slip into the dining-room, but Pètenka stopped him.

"But excuse me," he said. "I must find some way out of this fix!"

Iudushka smiled and looked Pètenka in the face.

"You must, dear!" he agreed.

"Then help me!"

"Ah, that's a different matter. You certainly must find some way out—you are right there—but how are you to do it is none of my business!"

"But why don't you want to help me?"

"In the first place because I have no money to cover up your dirty affairs, and secondly because it simply has nothing to do with me. You've got yourself into a scrape and you must get yourself out of it. You've made your bed and you must lie on it. That's how it is, my dear. I have begun by telling you, you know, that if you ask for what is right..."

"I know, I know. You have plenty of words for all occasions."

"Wait with your impertinence, let me finish. I'll prove to you in a minute that they are not mere words.... And so, I have said to you just now: if you ask for what is right and proper—very well, my dear, I am always ready to satisfy you! But if you come with an absurd request—you must excuse me, my boy! I have no money for your nasty affairs, no, no, no! And I shall not have any, let me tell you! Don't you dare to say that these are 'mere words'—you'll see, they come very near to deeds!"

"But just think what will happen to me!"

"It will all be as God wills!" Iudushka answered, slightly raising his hands and glancing sideways at the icon.

The father and the son made a few more tours round the room. Iudushka walked reluctantly, as though complaining that his son held him prisoner. Pètenka walked behind, with his arms akimbo, biting his mustache and smiling nervously.

"I am the only son you have left," he said. "Don't forget that."

"God took from Job all he had, my dear, and yet he did not

repine, but only said, 'God has given, God has taken away—God's will be done.' So that's the way, my boy."

"It was God took Job's children, but with you it's your own doing. Volodya . . ."

"I think you are beginning to talk nonsense."

"No, it isn't nonsense, it's the truth. Everybody knows that Volodya . . ."

"No, no, no! I won't listen to your absurdities. I've had enough. You have said what you had to say. I have given you my answer. And now let us go and have breakfast. We'll sit and talk, then have a meal and a drink to set you off on your journey—and God speed to you. You see how kind God is to you! The snow-storm has stopped and the roads are better. You'll drive along at your ease, jigety-jig, and find yourself at the station in no time."

"But listen, I beg you! If there's a spark of feeling in you . . ."

"No, no, no! We won't speak of it! Let us go to the dining-room: I expect mamma wants her cup of tea. It doesn't do to keep an old lady waiting."

Iudushka turned sharply and almost ran to the door.

"You may go or stay, but I won't leave this conversation!" Pètenka called after him. "It will be worse for you if we talk before other people!"

Iudushka turned back and faced his son.

"What do you want of me, you scoundrel? Speak out!" he asked in a trembling voice.

"I want you to pay the money I lost at cards."

"Never."

"So this is your last word?"

"Do you see this?" Iudushka exclaimed solemnly, pointing to the icon in the corner, "do you see? This is my father's blessing. . . . Here, before it, I tell you . . . never!"

And he walked out of his study with a resolute step.

"Murderer!" his son shouted after him.

Arina Petrovna was already at the table and Yevpraxeya was making tea. The old woman was silent and thoughtful, and seemed, as it were, ashamed of Pètenka. Iudushka went up as usual to kiss her hand and she blessed him, also as usual. Then followed the usual questions about her health and the kind of night she had had, and the usual monosyllabic answers.

She had been depressed since the day before. From the moment that Pètenka asked her for money and reminded her of "the curse" a kind of restlessness gained possession of her; she was haunted by the thought, "And what if I do curse him?" When she heard in the morning that there was an explanation going on in the study, she asked Yevpraxeya:

"Go and listen quietly at the door to what they are saying!" But although Yevpraxeya did listen she was too stupid to understand anything.

"They are just talking! They are not shouting much!" she announced, coming back.

Arina Petrovna could contain herself no longer and went into the dining-room, where the samovar had been brought meanwhile. But the explanation was coming to an end; she only heard Pètenka raising his voice and Porphyry Vladimiritch buzzing in reply.

" 'Buzzing,' that's just the word," the thought came into her mind. "He buzzed just like this in the old days, and to think I didn't understand at the time!"

At last both the father and the son came into the dining-room. Pètenka was red and breathed heavily; his eyes were wide-open, his hair disheveled, and small beads of perspiration stood out on his forehead. Iudushka looked pale and angry, he wanted to appear unconcerned, but in spite of all his efforts his lower lip was trembling. He could hardly manage to utter his usual morning greeting to dear friend mamma.

All took their places round the table; Pètenka sat down at some distance, leaning on the back of his chair and crossing his legs; as he lighted a cigarette he glanced ironically at his father.

"It's a fine day, mamma," Iudushka began, "after all the confusion of yesterday it was enough for God to will it—and all is still and serene. Isn't that so, dear?"

"I don't know, I haven't been out to-day."

"We are seeing off our dear guest, so it's a good thing," Iudushka went on. "I got up very early this morning and looked out of the window—and all was as still and peaceful outside as though God's angel had flown past and quieted all that turmoil with his wing!"

But no one made any answer to Iudushka's pleasant words; Yevpraxeya was noisily drinking tea out of the saucer, blowing and snorting; Arina Petrovna looked into her cup and said nothing; Pètenka was rocking his chair and looking at his father so sarcastically and defiantly that one might think he was ready to burst with laughter.

"Even if Pètenka doesn't drive fast," Porphyry Vladimiritch went on, "he'll reach the station easily enough before the evening. Our horses are our own, they are quite fresh, and if they have a couple of hours' rest at Muravyovo they'll rush him there in no time. And then, phew! the train will go puff-puff-puff! But it's really too bad of you, Pètenka! I wish you'd stay with us for a bit—do! It would be company for us, and see how you would pick up here in one week!"

But Pètenka went on rocking his chair and looking at his father.

"Why do you keep looking at me?" Iudushka boiled over at last, "do you see any patterns on me, or what?"

"I am waiting to see what you'll be doing next."

"No use your waiting, my boy! It will be as I have said. I won't go back on my word."

A moment's silence followed and then an audible whisper: "Judas!"

Porphyry Vladimiritch unquestionably heard it (he actually

turned pale) but he pretended that the exclamation did not refer to him.

"Ah, children, children!" he said. "One is sorry for you and would like to pet you and be affectionate, but there is no doing it—it evidently isn't meant to be. You turn away from your parents, you have your own friends and comrades who are dearer to you than your father and mother. Well, there is nothing for it! If one thinks of it, one has to give in. You are young, and the young naturally like to be with those of their own age and not with a grumbling old man. And so one has to be humble and not repine. All one asks of the Heavenly Father is, 'Work Thy will, O Lord'!"

"Murderer!" Pètenka whispered again so audibly that Arina Petrovna looked at him in alarm. It was as though the shadow of Styopka the dolt suddenly flitted before her eyes.

"Whom do you mean?" Iudushka asked, shaking with emotion.

"Oh, someone I know."

"I see. You'd better be clear about that! Heaven only knows what's in your mind: you may be referring to someone in the room!"

All were silent; their tea was untouched. Iudushka also leaned against the back of his chair, rocking himself nervously. Pètenka, seeing that all hope was lost, felt something like mortal anguish and no longer cared what he did. The father and the son looked into each other's eyes with an indescribable smile. In spite of all his self-control Porphyry Vladimiritch could restrain himself no longer.

"You had better go before any harm is done!" he said at last. "Yes!"

"I'll go right enough."

"Why wait? I see you want to pick a quarrel, and I don't want to quarrel with anybody. We live here in peace and quiet, with no quarrels or dissensions; your old granny is sitting here—you might consider her, at any rate. What have you come here for, I should like to know?"

"I have told you."

"Oh, if that was all, you needn't have troubled. Go away, my boy! Hey, who is there? Tell them to harness the horses for the young master! And pack a nice roast chicken and some caviar, and something else . . . say, a few eggs . . . wrap it up in paper. You'll have something to eat at the station, my boy, while they are feeding the horses. God speed to you!"

"No, I am not going yet. I'll go to the church first and ask to have a requiem sung for the murdered servant of God, Vladimir."

"You mean, for the suicide."

"No, he was murdered."

The father and the son stared at each other; they both seemed ready to jump up from their seats. But Iudushka made a superhuman effort and turned his chair towards the table.

"Extraordinary!" he said in a choking voice. "Ex-tra-or-di-na-ry!"

"Yes, murdered," Pètenka insisted rudely.

"Who was it murdered him, then?" Iudushka inquired, still hoping, apparently, that his son would think better of it.

But Pètenka was not in the least abashed and said point-blank,

"You!"

"I?"

Porphyry Vladimiritch was beyond himself with amazement. He stood up hastily and, turning towards the icon, began to pray.

"You! you! you!" Pètenka repeated.

"There, now, thank God, I feel easier after saying a prayer!" Iudushka declared, sitting down to the table again. "Well, wait a minute! As your father I needn't go into any explanations with you, but so be it! So you think it was I killed Volòdenka?"

"Yes, you!"

"Well, I don't think it was so at all. I think he shot himself. I was at the time here, at Golovlyovo, and he was in Petersburg. So how could I have come into it? How could I have killed him at a distance of five hundred miles?"

"Do you really pretend not to understand?"

"I don't understand . . . God is my witness, I don't."

"And who was it had left Volodya penniless? Who had stopped his allowance? Who was it?"

"Tut-tut-tut! But why had he married against his father's wish?"

"Why, but you gave him permission!"

"Who? I? What next! I never gave it! N-never!"

"Well, you acted here too in your usual way. With you a word means ten different things: try and guess what it is!"

"I never gave him permission! He wrote to me at the time, 'I want to marry Lidochka, papa.' You understand: I *want*, not *I ask your permission*. Well, so I answered, 'if you *want* to marry, do so, I can't prevent you.' That was all."

"That was all!" Pètenka mimicked him. "And isn't that a permission?"

"That's just the point, it isn't. What did I say? I said 'I cannot prevent you'—that's all. But whether I allowed him to marry is a different matter. He didn't ask my permission, he wrote straightaway, 'I *want* to marry Lidochka, papa'—so I too said nothing about permission. If you *want* to marry—do, bless you! Marry Lidochka or anyone you like—I can't stop you."

"But you can leave one to starve! You should have said then: 'I don't like your intention and so, though I don't put any obstacles in your way, I warn you that you must not reckon on any money from me.' That would have been clear, at any rate."

"Oh no, I could never demean myself to that. Bullying a grown-up son—never! My rule is not to hinder anyone. If he wants to marry—let him! But as to the consequences—that's another matter. He ought to have foreseen them himself—that's what God has given us brains for. But I don't interfere with other people's business, my boy. I don't interfere with their business and I don't ask them to interfere with mine, I don't—in fact I forbid them to! Do you hear, you bad, disrespectful son?—I forbid it!"

"Forbid as much as you like, you can't stop everybody's mouth."

"And it's not as though he repented or understood that he had wronged his father! He did a foolish thing—very well, why couldn't he repent and ask my pardon? Why couldn't he say, 'Forgive me, darling papa, for having grieved you'? But not he! not a bit of it!"

"But he did write to you; he explained he had nothing to live on, that he couldn't stand it any longer...."

"One doesn't have explanations with one's father. One asks a father's forgiveness—that's all."

"He did that too. He was so wretched that he did ask your forgiveness. He did everything—everything he could!"

"Well, even so he was to blame. He asked my pardon once, saw that papa did not forgive him—he should have asked again!"

"Oh, you!..."

Pètenka suddenly stopped rocking his chair, turned to the table and leaned both hands on it.

"And here am I..." he said almost inaudibly.

His face began to work.

"And here am I..." he repeated, breaking into hysterical sobs.

"And whose fault is it...."

But Iudushka had not time to finish his moralizing because at that moment something utterly unexpected happened. During the altercation that has just been described both the father and the son seemed to have forgotten Arina

Petrovna. But she remained by no means an indifferent spectator of the family scene. On the contrary, one might have suspected at the first glance that something rather unusual was taking place in her and that perhaps the moment had come when all that her own life had meant appeared suddenly in its grim truth before her mind's eye. Her face grew more alive, her eyes gleamed and opened wider, her lips moved as though trying to utter something. And suddenly, at the very moment when Pètenka broke into hysterical sobs, she rose heavily from her easy-chair, stretched out her arm towards Iudushka, and a loud cry broke from her:

"I cu-u-r-rse you!"

4

THE NIECE

IUDUSHKA DID NOT give Pètenka any money after all, though as a good father he had some roast chicken, veal, and pies put into his sledge as he left. Then, in spite of the wind and the frost, he came out on the front steps to see his son off, inquired if he was comfortable, if his legs were well wrapped up, and, returning to the house, made several times the sign of the cross over the window, sending a blessing to the sledge that took Pètenka away. In short, he carried out all the ritual properly, as a father should.

"Ah, Pètenka," he said, "you are a bad, naughty son! To think of the mess you have got yourself in.... Oh, oh, oh! You could have lived with no cares or troubles, in peace and quiet with your papa and your old granny, one would have thought—but no! that wasn't good enough! 'I have a mind of my own, I can do what I like!' And that's what your own mind has brought you to! Dreadful!"

But not a single muscle of his wooden face stirred as he said it, not a single note of his voice suggested anything like a call to the prodigal son. And indeed no one heard his words, for the only person in the room was Arina Petrovna, who after the shock she had just experienced seemed to have suddenly lost all her vital energy and sat by the samovar with her mouth open, hearing and seeing nothing.

Life went on as before, full of idle fussing and endless talk. . . .

Contrary to Pètenka's expectations, Porphyry Vladimir-itch bore his mother's curse rather calmly and did not depart by a hair's-breadth from the decisions that were, so to speak, always ready-made in his mind. It is true he turned slightly pale and rushed to his mother with a cry:

"Mamma! darling! What are you saying! Calm yourself, dear! God willing, everything will come right!"

But these words were an expression of anxiety on his mother's account rather than on his own. Arina Petrovna's outburst was so sudden that Iudushka had not even thought of pretending to be frightened. Only the day before mamma had been kind to him, joked and played "fools" with Yev-praxeya—so that evidently it was just a momentary aberration and there was nothing "real" and intentional about it. He certainly had been very much afraid of his mother's curse, but he pictured it quite differently. His idle fancy had drawn for him the whole *mis-en-scène* of it: icons, lighted candles, mamma standing in the middle of the room with a dark, terrible face . . . cursing him! Then there was thunder, the candles went out, the veil was rent in twain, darkness covered the earth, and the wrathful face of Jehovah appeared in the flicker of lightnings amidst the clouds above. But since nothing of the kind had happened, it must have been just a whim on mamma's part, a sudden fancy—nothing more. And there was no occasion for her to curse him "in earnest" because of late there had not been even a pretext for any dissension between them. Much water had flowed by since he had expressed doubts about the chaise really belonging to her (Iudushka admitted to himself that *then* he had been to

blame and deserved cursing): Arina Petrovna had become resigned and Iudushka thought of nothing but dear friend
mamma's comfort.

"The old lady is getting weak, very weak! She forgets herself at times!" he reassured himself. "The dear thing sits
down to play 'fools'—and in another moment she's dozed off
already!"

It is only fair to say that he felt really anxious about Arina
Petrovna's health. He was not yet prepared to lose her; he had
not thought it all out or made the necessary calculations:
what capital mamma had on leaving Dubrovino, what the interest on it would be, how much of it she was likely to have
spent and how much to have added to the capital. In short,
there was a number of trifles he had not seen to, and that always made him feel at a disadvantage.

"She has a strong constitution!" he comforted himself.
"But she will not get through all her money; how could she!
When she divided the property she had a good capital. She
might have passed on some of it to the orphans—but no, she
wouldn't give much to them! She is sure to have money!"

But there was as yet nothing serious about these musings
and they left no permanent trace on his mind. He had so
many trifles to see to every day that he had no wish to increase his burden so long as there was no imperative need for
it. Porphyry Vladimiritch kept putting things off, and only after the sudden episode with the curse he grasped that it was
time to begin.

The catastrophe came sooner than he had thought, however. The day after Pètenka's departure Arina Petrovna went
to Pogorelka and did not return to Golovlyovo any more.
She spent a month in complete solitude, shut up in her room,
hardly exchanging a word with her servants. After getting up
in the morning she sat down, from habit, at her writing-table,
and, also from habit, began to play patience, but hardly ever
finished a game and sat perfectly still, her eyes fixed on the

window. The subtlest interpreter of the inmost secrets of the human heart could not have discovered what she was thinking or whether she was thinking at all. It seemed as though she were trying to recall something—for instance, to recall how she came to be there, within those four walls—and could not. Alarmed by her silence Afimyushka peeped into the room, rearranged the cushions with which she was propped up, tried to talk to her but received monosyllabic and impatient answers. Porphyry Vladimiritch paid two or three visits to Pogorelka; he invited mamma to Golovlyovo trying to inflame her imagination by the prospect of pickled mushrooms, delicious carp, and the other allurements he had to offer, but she merely smiled enigmatically at all his proposals.

One morning she wanted to get up as usual, and could not. She was not conscious of any pain, did not complain of anything, but simply could not get up. She was not in the least disturbed by that circumstance, as though it were the most usual thing in the world. Only the day before she had sat at the table and was able to walk—and now she lay in bed "unwell." She felt more comfortable in bed. But Afimyushka was alarmed and without saying anything to her mistress sent a messenger to Porphyry Vladimiritch.

Iudushka arrived early the following day. Arina Petrovna was considerably worse. He questioned the servants minutely as to what mamma had eaten and whether she had had too much, but was told that Arina Petrovna had scarcely touched food for the last month and refused it altogether since the day before. Iudushka was duly grieved and, before going in to mamma, warmed himself by the stove in the maids' room, like a good son, so as not to bring cold air into the invalid's room. And meanwhile he at once began to make arrangements: he had quite an uncanny flair for death. He asked if the priest was at home, so that one could send for him at once in case of emergency, inquired where mamma's chest with papers stood and whether it was locked, and, having satisfied himself about the essentials, called the cook and ordered dinner.

"I don't want much!" he said. "Have you a fowl to spare? Well, make me a little chicken broth! Perhaps you have some salt meat—cook a little piece for me. Then a little roast beef or something—and that will be plenty!"

Arina Petrovna lay on her back with her mouth open, breathing heavily. Her eyes were wide open; one arm had strayed from under the hareskin coverlet and remained poised in the air. She had evidently been listening to the sounds of her son's arrival and perhaps she could hear the orders he was giving. The window curtains were down so that the room was in semi-darkness. The wicks in two of the sanctuary lamps had burned down and one could hear them crackle as they touched the water. The air was bad; the overheated stove, the burning oil of the lamps and the odors of the sick-room made the place unendurably stuffy. Porphyry Vladimiritch in his felt boots glided like a snake towards his mother's bed; his tall, lean figure stirred mysteriously in the twilight. Arina Petrovna's eyes followed him with alarm or perhaps with surprise as she huddled herself together under her coverlet.

"It's me, mamma," he said. "Why, you seem quite out of sorts to-day! Aie-aie-aie! No wonder I couldn't sleep last night: I kept fidgeting and thinking to myself I must go and see how my friends at Pogorelka are getting on! As soon as I got up this morning I ordered a carriage-and-pair—and here I am!"

Porphyry Vladimiritch tittered amiably, but Arina Petrovna made no answer and seemed to shrink together more and more under her coverlet.

"God willing you'll soon be well, mamma!" Iudushka went on. "The chief thing is not to give in! Pull yourself together and take a brisk little walk round the room! Like this!"

Porphyry Vladimiritch got up from his chair and showed her what a brisk little walk meant.

"Wait a minute, let me draw the curtain and have a look at

you! Why, you look splendid, dear! All you have to do is to cheer up and say your prayers and make yourself smart—and you can go to a dance straightaway! Here, I have brought some holy water for you—drink some!"

Porphyry Vladimiritch pulled a bottle out of his pocket, found a wine-glass on the table, poured out some of the water and gave it to the invalid. Arina Petrovna tried to raise her head but could not.

"Send for the girls . . ." she moaned.

"There, now you are asking for the girls! Ah, mamma, mamma! Fancy your giving in so suddenly! You shouldn't lose your courage because you are a bit out of sorts! We'll do it all, we'll send a message to the girls, all in proper time! There's no hurry, you know; there are many years before us yet! And very fine years too! When summer comes, we'll go to the forest together to look for mushrooms, for juicy strawberries and wild raspberries! Or we'll drive to Dubrovino to catch carp: we'll have the old piebald harnessed and go trit-trot in the long droshki, jogging along comfortably!"

"Send for the girls . . ." Arina Petrovna repeated miserably.

"They'll come right enough. . . . Have patience, we'll call everyone, we shall all be here. We shall gather round you—you'll be the mother-hen and we the chicks. . . . Chuck-chuck-chuck! You shall have all you want if you are a good girl. But it's not like a good girl to be ill! That's very naughty of you. . . . Aie-aie-aie! You should set us an example and that's what you go and do! It isn't nice of you, dear! Not nice at all!"

But though Porphyry Vladimiritch did his best to cheer up dear friend mamma with his little jokes, she grew weaker every hour. They sent to the town for a doctor, and as the invalid seemed distressed, and kept asking for the girls, Iudushka wrote a letter to Anninka and Lubinka comparing their conduct with his own and calling himself a Christian and them—ungrateful. The doctor came in the night but it was too late.

Arina Petrovna had crumpled up, as the saying is, in one day. About four in the morning the last agony began, and at six Porphyry Vladimiritch was kneeling by his mother's bedside wailing:

"Mamma! dearest! bless me!"

But Arina Petrovna did not hear. Her wide-open eyes gazed dully into space as though she were trying to understand something and could not.

Iudushka did not understand either. He did not understand that the grave opening before his eyes took away his last link with the world of the living, the last creature with whom he could share the dust that filled him, and that henceforth that dust, finding no outlet, would gather till in the end it choked him.

With his usual fussiness he busied himself with the numberless details of the funeral. He had requiem services sung, ordered requiem Masses to be said for forty days, talked to the priest, shuffled along from one room to another, peeped into the dining-room where the dead woman lay, crossed himself, raised his eyes to heaven and, getting up at night, walked noiselessly to the door to listen to the monotonous reading of the psalms. He was pleasantly surprised to find that all this did not involve him in any extra expense because Arina Petrovna had in her lifetime put away a special sum for her funeral, indicating in great detail how much was to be spent and in what way.

After burying his mother Porphyry Vladimiritch immediately began putting her affairs in order. Sorting out her papers he found at least ten different wills (in one of them she called him "disrespectful"), but they had all been written when Arina Petrovna was still a great lady and had never been put into legal form. Iudushka was very much pleased that there was no need for him to prevaricate in declaring himself the only lawful heir of his mother's property. This property consisted of fifteen thousand rubles and a few possessions, including the famous chaise that had once very nearly caused a quarrel between mother and son. Arina Petrovna carefully kept her accounts separate from those of the girls, so that one could see at a glance what belonged to her and what to them. Iudushka proved his claims as heir, sealed the papers dealing with the orphans' estate and gave to the servants his mother's scanty wardrobe. He sent to Golovlyovo the chaise and two cows which had been put down by Arina Petrovna in the inventory under the heading "mine," and after the last requiem service went home.

"Wait for the owners," he said to the servants who had gathered in the porch to see him off. "If they come—they are welcome; if they don't, it's their own affair. I, for my part, have done all I could; I have put their accounts in order without concealing or omitting anything—all I did was in the sight of all. My mother's capital belongs to me by law; the chaise and the two cows which I sent to Golovlyovo are also legally mine. Maybe something of mine has been left here, but I don't mind that; God himself tells us to give alms to orphans. I am sorry to lose mamma, she was a kind, thoughtful old lady! Here she had thought of you, her servants, and left you her wardrobe. Ah, mamma, mamma! It wasn't nice of you, darling, to have left us! But since it pleased God that this should be, we must submit to His holy Will. So long as your soul is at rest, it doesn't matter about us!"

The first grave was soon followed by a second. It was hard to tell what Porphyry Vladimiritch really felt about his son's fate. He received no papers and no letters from anyone so that he could not know anything about Pètenka's trial, and it was doubtful whether he wished to know. Speaking generally, he was a man whose chief concern was to avoid worry and who had so deeply sunk into the mire of petty cares of the most contemptible self-preservation that his existence left behind it no trace of any kind. There are plenty of such people in the world; they all live isolated lives not knowing how to attach themselves to anything, and not wishing to do so; they simply live from day to day and disappear at last like rain-bubbles bursting in the water. They have no friends because friendship implies common interests; they have no ties with their colleagues in the service because their souls are too dead even for the deadly world of bureaucratic red tape. For thirty years on end Porphyry Vladimiritch had fussed about in a government office; one fine morning he disappeared and no one noticed it.

And so he was the last to learn the fate that had over-taken his son, after the news had spread among his servants. But even then he pretended not to know anything about it, so that when Yevpraxeya ventured to mention Pètenka one day Iudushka waved his hands at her and said:

"No, no, no! I don't know, I haven't heard, and I don't wish to hear! I don't want to know his dirty affairs."

But he did have to learn the news at last. A letter came from Pètenka saying that he was about to leave for one of the distant provinces and asking whether papa would still send him his allowance. For a whole day after this Porphyry Vladimiritch was obviously perplexed; he kept going from room to room, peeping into the icon-room, crossing himself, and sighing. Towards evening, however, he faced the task and wrote as follows:

My Criminal Son, Pyotr!

As a loyal subject whose duty it is to respect the law I ought to leave your letter unanswered. But as a father who shares human weaknesses I cannot, from a feeling of compassion, refuse good advice to a child who through his own fault has hurled himself into a whirlpool of evils. And so, here is, in short, my opinion on the sub-ject. The punishment you are undergoing is severe but entirely deserved by you—this is the first and the main idea, which you must never lose sight of in your new life. As to your habits of self-indulgence you must forget the very thought of them, for in your position it will only be a provocation to you and cause you to repine. You have already tasted the bitter fruits of conceit—try now to taste the fruits of humility, especially as there is nothing else left for you in the future. Do not murmur against your punishment, for the authorities are not even punishing you, but merely providing you with the means of reforming your character. You must be grateful for this and do your best to expiate your deed— you must be continually thinking of that and not of luxurious living, in which I never indulge, though I haven't offended against the law. Listen to the voice of reason and become a new man, completely new and regenerate, being content with what your superiors think fit, in their kindness, to give towards your keep. And I for my part will pray the Giver of all blessings to grant you humility and fortitude, and on the very day that I am writing these lines I went to church and prayed ardently about it. I bless you on your new path and remain

Your indignant but still
loving father
Porhpyry Golovlyov

History does not say whether this letter ever reached Pètenka: a month after he had been sent to Siberia, Porphyry Vladimir-itch was officially informed that his son did not arrive at his destination but was taken ill and died in a hospital on the way.

Iudushka was alone in the world now; but in the heat of the moment he failed to grasp that after this new loss he was cut adrift altogether and had nothing left him but his own empty talk. This happened soon after Arina Petrovna's death, when he was completely engrossed in accounts and calculations. He went through her papers, counting every penny and tracing its connections with the orphans' pennies—not wishing, as he said, to lose what was his own or to take what did not belong to him. Throughout all this fussing it never even occurred to him to ask why he was doing it all, and who would enjoy the fruits of his labor? From morning to night he toiled at his writing-table criticizing his mother's arrangements or indulging in flights of fancy; he was so busy that he gradually came to neglect the accounts of his own estate.

Everything in the house sank into silence. The servants who had always preferred to spend the time in their own quarters abandoned the house almost altogether, and when they did go in, walked about on tiptoe and spoke in whispers. There seemed to be a sense of doom about that house and its master; something that unconsciously inspired a kind of superstitious fear. The gloom that hung over Iudushka's existence was destined to grow darker and darker every day.

In Lent, when the theaters were closed, Anninka came to Golovlyovo and said that Lubinka could not come with her because she had signed a contract some time before for the whole of Lent and was to give concerts at Romny, Izyum, Kremenchug, etc., singing all her music-hall repertoire.

Anninka had matured considerably during her short career as an actress. She was no longer the naïve, anemic, and rather listless girl who used to wander about aimlessly from room to room at Dubrovino and at Pogorelka, swaying her body clumsily and singing to herself. Her character was quite formed now; she had free and easy manners and one could unmistakably tell from the first glance that she was never at a loss for a word. Her appearance too had changed and gave quite a pleasant surprise to Porphyry Vladimiritch. He saw before him a tall, well-built woman with a handsome rosy face, prominent gray eyes, a high well-developed bosom, and a lovely ash-blond plait of hair that came down heavily on to her neck—a woman who was evidently fully conscious of being the *Belle Hélène*, after whom all the officers were fated to sigh. She arrived at Golovlyovo in the early morning and immediately withdrew to a separate room, appearing at breakfast in a magnificent silk gown with a rustling train which she skillfully steered between the dining-room chairs. Although Iudushka loved his God above all things, this did not prevent him from having a taste for good-looking women especially if they were rather big. And so he first of all blessed Anninka, then kissed her deliberately on both cheeks and in so doing cast such a strange sidelong glance at her bosom that Anninka smiled to herself.

They sat down to breakfast; Anninka raised both arms and stretched herself.

"It's fearfully dull here, uncle!" she began, yawning slightly.

"There now! You haven't had time to turn round and you say it's dull! Stay with us for a bit, then we shall see: you may find it gay after all," answered Porphyry Vladimiritch with an oily glitter in his eyes.

"No, it isn't interesting! What is there here? Snow all round, no neighbors.... You have a regiment quartered near you, haven't you?"

"We have, and we have neighbors too, though, to tell the truth, it doesn't interest me. But perhaps if..."

Porphyry Vladimiritch glanced at her and did not finish his sentence; he merely cleared his throat. Perhaps he broke off on purpose, wishing to rouse her feminine curiosity; in any case the same, hardly perceptible smile flitted over her face. She leaned on the table and looked with some attention at Yevpraxeya who was wiping the glasses. Her cheeks were flushed and she kept glancing at Anninka from under her brows with her large, dull eyes.

"This is my new housekeeper...an excellent worker!" Porphyry Vladimiritch remarked.

Anninka nodded slightly and began humming: "*Ah! ah!*

que j'aime ... que j'aime ... que j'aime ... les mili-mili-mili-taires," unconsciously wriggling her hips as she did so.

There was a silence. Iudushka, meekly casting down his eyes, slowly sipped his tea.

"Fearfully dull!" Anninka yawned again.

"Dull again! That's all you have to say! Wait, live with us for a bit. . . . We'll have the sledge ready for you presently—you can go sleighing to your heart's content."

"Uncle, why didn't you go into the hussars?"

"Because, my dear, every man has his own task appointed him by God. One is to be a hussar, another—a government official, a third—a tradesman, a fourth . . . !"

"Oh, yes, a fourth, a fifth, a sixth—I had forgotten! And it's God who arranges it all, doesn't He?"

"Yes, He does! This is nothing to laugh at, my dear. You know what it says in the Gospel: if it be not God's will . . ."

"That's about the hair? Yes, I know that too. But the trouble is, everyone wears false hair now, and I think no provision was made for that. By the way, uncle, see what lovely hair I have! Isn't it splendid?"

Porphyry Vladimiritch walked up to her (on tiptoe for some reason) and held her plait in his hand. Yevpraxeya bent forward and not letting go her saucer of tea asked, holding a piece of sugar between her teeth:

"A chillon, I expect?"

"No, not a chignon but my own hair. I'll let it down to show you some day, uncle!"

"Yes, beautiful hair!" Iudushka praised it almost slobbering in an unpleasant smirk; but remembering that one ought really to scorn such temptations he added: "ah, you grasshopper! you think of nothing but beautiful hair and fine dresses and you don't ask about what really matters!"

"Oh yes, about grandmamma! She died, didn't she?"

"She passed away, my dear! And what a beautiful death

it was! So peaceful, so quiet that no one heard her go. That was indeed a Christian end to her earthly life! She thought of everyone, blessed us all, called for a priest, took the sacrament . . . and she felt so completely, so completely at rest! She herself said so, the darling—and suddenly she began to sigh. She sighed once and twice and three times—and behold she was no more!"

Iudushka got up, turned to the icon, folded his hands and said a prayer. Tears actually came into his eyes: he had told such a touching lie! But Anninka was evidently not of the sentimental sort. True, she pondered for a moment but it was for quite a different reason.

"Do you remember, uncle," she said, "how she used to give my sister and me sour milk to drink when we were little? Not these last years . . . she was very good then . . . but when she was still rich?"

"Come, come, you mustn't think of old scores! They gave you sour milk, but see what a fine girl you've grown, bless you! Will you go to her grave?"

"Very well, let us."

"Only do you know what: you'd better purify yourself first!"

"How do you mean . . . purify myself?"

"Well, after all, you know . . . you are an actress. Do you imagine your grandmamma was happy about it? So before going to the grave you'd better hear Mass and be purified! I'll order early Mass to-morrow and then you can go after that."

Absurd as Iudushka's suggestion was, Anninka was disconcerted for a moment. But then she frowned angrily and said sharply:

"No, I'll go as I am . . . straightaway."

"I don't know, just as you like. But my advice is, let us hear Mass to-morrow, then have breakfast, then order a pair of horses and a covered sledge and drive there together. You would be purified and your grandmother's soul . . ."

"How absurd you are, uncle! You talk extraordinary nonsense and insist on it too!"

"Oh, you don't like it, do you? Well, you must forgive me —I am a plain-spoken man! I don't like lies. I tell the truth to other people and am ready to hear it from others. It sometimes goes against the grain, it tastes bitter—but yet one has to hear it. One ought to hear it, because it is the truth! Yes, my dear! Stay with us a bit, live in our way—and you will see for yourself that it's better than going from fair to fair with a guitar."

"What are you talking about! With a guitar!"

"Well, it's all the same. With a tambourine, perhaps. But you were first to insult me, calling me absurd, and it's only right that an old man like me should tell you the truth."

"Very well, let it be the truth, we won't talk of it. Tell me, please, did grandmother leave any property?"

"Of course! But the lawful heir was there to receive it."

"That is you ... well, so much the better. Is she buried here, at Golovlyovo?"

"No, in her parish, near Pogorelka. It was her own wish."

"I'll go then. May I hire some horses here, uncle?"

"Why hire? We have horses of our own. You are not a stranger, you know! You are my niece ..." Porphyry Vladimiritch said, smiling like a good relative. "A covered sledge ... a pair of horses. I am not a poor man, thank heaven! And hadn't I better come with you? We would go to the grave and then call at Pogorelka. We'd look round and think things over and have a good talk about it all.... You have a nice little estate, you know; it has excellent points!"

"No, I'd better go by myself.... Why should you trouble. By the way, Pètenka, too, is dead, isn't he?"

"He is dead, dear, yes, Pètenka is dead too. On the one hand I am sorry for him, so sorry I could weep, but on the other— it's his own fault. He had always been disrespectful to his father—and so God punished him! And what God has arranged in His wisdom, it isn't for us to change."

"Naturally, we cannot change it. But I keep thinking, uncle, how is it you aren't afraid to live?"

"And why should I be afraid? See, how much grace I have round me?" Iudushka moved his hand, pointing to the icons. "There is grace here, and in my study, and my icon-room is a perfect paradise! You see how many defenders I have."

"But even so. . . . You are always alone . . . it's dreadful!"

"And if I feel nervous I kneel down and pray—and that puts me right at once. And what is there to fear? in the day-time it's light, and in the night I have sanctuary lamps burn-ing in every room. From the outside it looks as though there were a dance in the house. A dance, indeed! Our defenders and God's holy saints—that's all my company!"

"Do you know, Pètenka wrote to us before his death."

"Well, you are his relatives! It's a good thing that at least he hadn't lost all family feeling."

"Yes, he wrote to us. After the trial, when he had been sentenced. He wrote that he had lost three thousand rubles at cards and that you wouldn't give him the money. You are rich, uncle, aren't you?"

"It is easy to count money in other people's pockets, my dear. Sometimes we imagine that a man is simply rolling in gold, but if one looks into it, he has only enough to buy lamp oil and a votive candle—and even that isn't his but God's!"

"Well, in that case we are richer than you. We subscribed something, and made our gentlemen friends subscribe—we collected six hundred rubles altogether and sent him."

"What 'gentlemen friends'?"

"Why, uncle! We are actresses, you know! You have just been suggesting I should 'purify myself'!"

"I don't like it when you talk like that!"

"Well, there's nothing for it. You may like it or not but what's done can't be undone. According to you, this too is from God!"

"Don't blaspheme, whatever you do. You may talk as you

like but . . . I forbid you to blaspheme! Where did you send the money?"

"I don't remember. To some little town. . . . He gave us the address."

"That's strange. If he had that money, I should have received it after his death! He could not have spent it all at once! I don't know, I haven't received anything. I expect those wretched warders and guards pocketed it!"

"Oh, we are not asking it back—I merely mentioned it by the way. But say what you will, uncle, it's dreadful that a man should perish because of three thousand rubles!"

"But then it isn't because of three thousand. We only fancy that it is, and keep repeating 'three thousand, three thousand!' But God . . ."

Iudushka had just warmed up to the subject and was going to explain in detail how God . . . Providence . . . unseen ways . . . and all the rest of it. But Anninka yawned unceremoniously and said:

"It's fearfully dull here, uncle!"

This time Porphyry Vladimiritch was really offended and grew silent. They walked up and down the dining-room side by side for some time; Anninka yawned and Porphyry Vladimiritch crossed himself in every corner. At last they were told that the sledge was ready and there followed the usual comedy of seeing off one of the family. Porphyry Vladimiritch put on his coat, came out on to the front steps, kissed Anninka, shouted at the servants "mind you wrap up her feet properly" or "are you sure you've taken the fromenty? Don't you forget it!" And he made a sign of the cross in the air.

Anninka went to her grandmother's grave, asked the priest to hold a requiem service, and when the choristers mournfully intoned "eternal memory," she wept. It was melancholy scenery all round. The church beside which Arina Petrovna was buried was a poor one; the plaster had peeled off the walls in many places showing big patches of the brickwork underneath; the bell had a dull, muffled sound; the priest's vestments were shabby; the churchyard was covered with deep snow that had to be shoveled away before one could reach Arina Petrovna's grave; there was no tombstone yet, but only a plain white cross on which nothing was even written. The church stood in a solitary position, with no village near it; the priest's, the deacon's, and the sexton's cottages blackened with age were huddled together beside it, and a desolate snowy desert stretched all round, with some kind of dry reeds showing in places on the surface. A strong March wind was blowing, tearing at the priest's vestments and carrying away the sounds of the singing.

"Who would have thought, madam, that the richest landowner in the district has found rest under this humble cross, beside our poor church!" said the priest when the requiem was over.

At these words Anninka wept again. She recalled the line "a coffin stands on the festive board" and her tears flowed and flowed. Then she went to the priest's cottage, had a talk to his wife, drank some tea, again recalled "and all behold pale death"—and cried long and bitterly.

No word had been sent to Pogorelka about her arrival and the house had not been heated. Without taking off her fur coat Anninka walked through the rooms and only stopped for a minute in her grandmother's bedroom and in the icon-room. Arina Petrovna's bedstead still had a heap of greasy feather-beds on it and a few pillows without pillow-cases. Bits of paper were scattered on the writing-table; the floor had not been swept, and everything was covered with a thick layer of dust. Anninka sat down in her grandmother's armchair and sank into thought. At first memories of her past came before her mind; they were replaced by images of the present. The memories were fragmentary and flitted rapidly by; the images of the present had greater vividness. It was not long since she had longed for freedom and thought Pogorelka a hateful place—and now her heart was suddenly filled with a painful longing to live in the place she had hated. It was dull, uncomfortable, unattractive, but it was quiet, so quiet that everything might have been dead around her. There was plenty of air and space: the fields stretched into the distance and she felt she wanted to run there—to run without purpose, without looking back, simply so as to breathe more deeply and to feel one's breast aglow. And *there*, in the half-nomadic surroundings which she had just left and to which she *had* to return—what awaited her? And what had she brought away from there? Memories of smelly hotels, of continual noise coming from the dining- and the billiard-rooms, of unkempt and unwashed waiters, of rehearsals on a drafty, half-dark stage among the painted scenery that one could not touch without disgust, in the cold and the damp . . . that was all! And then officers, lawyers, cynical speeches, empty bottles, wine-stained table-cloths, clouds of smoke, and noise, noise, noise! The way they talked to her! The shameless way they touched her! Especially that man with red eyelids, a big mustache, a voice hoarse with drinking, and a smell of the stables. . . . Oh, what he said to her! Anninka actually shuddered at the memory and closed her eyes. Recovering herself she heaved a sigh and walked into the icon-room. Very few icons remained in the stand—only those which unquestionably belonged to her mother. Iudushka, as Arina Petrovna's heir, had taken to Golovlyovo all those that were hers. The empty spaces left in the icon-stand looked like blind eyes. There were no sanctuary lamps either—Iudushka had taken them all; only a bit of a yellow wax candle stuck desolately in its metal holder.

"He wanted to take the stand as well and kept asking if it was part of your mother's dowry."

"Well, he might as well have taken it. Tell me, Afimyushka—was grandmamma very bad before she died?"

"Not very, she had scarcely two days in bed. She seemed

just to pine away. She wasn't ill properly, or anything. She hardly spoke at all, except that she asked for you and your sister once or twice."

"Then it was Porphyry Vladimiritch took away the icons?"

"Yes, he did. He said they were his mamma's icons. He took the chaise too and two cows. He must have seen from your grandmother's papers that they weren't yours but hers. He wanted to grab one horse too but Fedulitch wouldn't let him. 'It's our horse,' he said, 'it has always belonged to Pogorelka'—so he didn't venture to take it."

Anninka walked about the yard, peeped into the outbuildings, the threshing-yard, and the cattle-shed. Her "working capital"—some twenty lean cows and three horses—stood there in a bog of manure. She asked for some bread, saying, "I'll pay," and gave a piece to every cow. Then the dairymaid invited her into the cottage where a jar of milk had been placed on the table and a new-born calf was housed in the corner by the stove behind a low wooden partition. Anninka drank some milk and running up to the calf kissed it impulsively. But she at once wiped her lips in disgust, saying that the calf had a horrid face, all wet and slimy. At last she pulled out three yellow notes from her purse, gave them to the old servants and made ready to go.

"What are you going to do?" she asked old Fedulitch before she stepped into the sledge. Being the bailiff, he escorted the young mistress, his arms folded on his chest.

"What is there to do! We'll just live," Fedulitch answered. Anninka felt sad again; she fancied there was a note of irony in his words. She stood still for a minute and said with a sigh:

"Well, good-bye!"

"And we had thought you'd come back and live with us!" Fedulitch said.

"No . . . what's the good! Never mind . . . you stay on!"

Tears flowed from her eyes again, and everyone else wept too. It was all so strange: she thought there was nothing she regretted here, nothing she could even recall affectionately and yet she was crying. And the others too: nothing had been said beyond the most commonplace questions and answers, and yet all suddenly felt sad, "sorry." They helped her into the sledge, wrapped her up, and sighed deeply, all of them.

"Good luck to you!" she heard behind her when the sledge moved.

As she drove past the churchyard she told the driver to stop and walked all by herself along the path that had been cleared to the grave. It was almost dark and lights had been lit in the church cottages. She did not cry but stood clutching with one hand at the memorial cross, rocking herself to and fro. She was not thinking of anything in particular, she could not have put any definite thought into words, but she felt wretched, utterly wretched, not at the thought of her grandmother, but of herself. She stood there, unconsciously bending to and fro for some fifteen minutes, and suddenly she pictured Lubinka, who at that very moment perhaps was trilling away in merry company somewhere at Kremenchug:

> "Ah! ah! que j'aime, que j'aime!
> Que j'aime les mili-mili-mili-taires!"

She almost collapsed. Running to the sledge she stepped into it and told the coachman to drive as fast as he could to Golovlyovo.

Anninka returned to her uncle depressed and quiet. This did not prevent her however from feeling hungry (in the excitement her uncle had not given her even a chicken to take with her) and she was very glad to find the table laid for tea. Porphyry Vladimiritch of course immediately opened a conversation:

"Well, have you been there?"

"Yes, I have."

"And you prayed at the grave? Had a requiem sung?"

"Yes, I had."

"So the priest was at home?"

"Of course he was. How else could I have had a requiem?"

"Yes, yes. . . . And the two servitors? Did they sing 'eternal memory'?"

"They did."

"Yes. Eternal memory to her, bless her! She was a solicitous old lady, fond of her family."

Iudushka got up, turned to the icons and said a prayer.

"Well, and how did you find things at Pogorelka? All well?"

"I really don't know. Everything seems to be in its place."

"That's just it—'seems'! It always 'seems,' but when you look into the matter, this is rotten, that is awry. . . . That's how we get our notions of other people's wealth: it 'seems' to us they must be rich. Though I must say you have a nice little estate; mamma's settled you very comfortably and spent indeed a good deal of her own money on it. . . . Well, it's only right to help orphans!"

Listening to these praises Anninka could not resist teasing her charitable uncle.

"And why did you take two cows from Pogorelka, uncle?" she asked.

"Cows? Which cows? Do you mean Tchernavka and Privedenka? Why, dear, they belonged to mamma."

"And you are her lawful heir? Well, keep them! Would you like me to send you the calf as well?"

"There, there! Now you are in a temper! But you should talk seriously. Whose cows were they, do you think?"

"How should I know! They were at Pogorelka."

"But I do know; I have proofs that they were mamma's cows. I found an inventory in her own handwriting and it distinctly said there 'mine.'"

"Oh, don't let's go into it. It's not worth talking about."

"Now there's a horse at Pogorelka—a white-faced one—

and about that horse, I can't be certain. I believe it's mamma's but I don't know. And what I don't know I cannot speak of."

"Let's leave the subject, uncle."

"No, why leave it? I am a straightforward man, my dear—I like to have everything plain and above-board! And why not speak of it? No one likes to lose what's his: you don't like it, nor do I—so we must talk it over. And if we do talk, I'll tell you straight out: I don't want what is other people's but I am not going to give away what's mine! And so, though you are not strangers to me, I . . ."

"You took even the icons!" Anninka could not resist saying again.

"I took the icons and everything that belongs to me as the lawful heir."

"The icon-stand seems all in holes now. . . ."

"Well, there's nothing for it! You must pray before it as it is. God wants your prayers and not the icon-stand. If you approach Him in all sincerity, your prayers will reach Him however poor the icon. But if you merely wag your tongue while you look round and smile and curtsey—not even good icons will save you!"

Nevertheless Iudushka stood up and thanked God for his own "good" icons.

"And if you don't like the old icon-stand, have a new one made. Or put other icons in the place of those I've taken. It was mamma had bought and fixed them up, and it's for you to provide new ones!"

This way of looking at the matter seemed to him so simple and reasonable that he positively tittered.

"Tell me, please, what have I to do now?" Anninka asked.

"Wait a bit. Rest first, make yourself comfortable and have a good sleep, and then we'll consider it and talk it over and see what can be done. Perhaps between us we'll think of something."

"We are of age, aren't we?"

"Yes, you are. You can do what you like with yourselves and with your property."

"Thank heaven for that, anyway."

"My congratulations!"

Porphyry Vladimiritch went up to kiss her.

"How strange you are, uncle! You are always kissing!"

"Why shouldn't I kiss you? You are not a stranger—you are my niece! I behave like a good relative, dear! I don't mind what I do for my relatives! They may be third or fourth cousins—it's all one to me. . . ."

"You'd better tell me what ought I to do. I have to go to the town, haven't I, and see to things?"

"We'll go to the town and see to everything—all in good time. But first you must stay with us for a bit and rest. You are not at an hotel, thank heaven, but at your own uncle's. There is plenty to eat, and tea to drink and jam if you want something sweet. And if there's any dish you don't like—ask for another! Ask, insist! If you don't want cabbage soup, tell them to bring you some broth. Cutlets, ducklings, sucking pigs. . . . Get hold of Yevpraxeya! By the way, Yevpraxeya, I have just boasted of sucking pigs but I don't really know—have we any?"

Yevpraxeya, who was at that moment holding a saucer of hot tea in front of her mouth, sniffed affirmatively.

"There, you see, we have sucking pigs as well. That means you may ask for whatever you fancy! So that's that!"

Iudushka stretched towards Anninka again and, like a good relative, patted her slightly on the knee, letting his hand rest there for a moment, no doubt by accident. Anninka instinctively drew away.

"But I have to go, you know!" she said.

"That's just what I am saying. We'll talk it over and consider it all, and then we'll go. We'll go with God's blessing, having said our prayers, and not like a shot out of a pop-gun!

The longest way round is the shortest way home, you know! If there's a fire, one has to hurry, but thank heaven, our house isn't burning! Lubinka, now, has to hurry to the fair, but you needn't. Oh, I was going to ask you: will you live at Pogorelka now?"

"No, there's nothing for me to do at Pogorelka."

"That's just what I was going to say. Come and settle with me! We'll get along very nicely—have a splendid time, in fact!"

Iudushka looked at Anninka with such oily eyes as he said this that she felt uncomfortable.

"No, uncle, I couldn't settle with you. It's too dull here."

"Ah, you silly, silly child! You think of nothing but that! 'Dull, dull' you say, but you can't really tell why it should be dull. If one is busy and knows how to control oneself, one is never bored, my dear. I, for instance, simply do not see how the time goes. On week-days there's work: one has to go and have a look at that and a peep at this, to have a word with one and a chat with another—and the day is gone! And on holidays one goes to church. You must do the same! Live with us—you'll find something to do; and if not—play 'fools' with Yevpraxeya, or order a sledge and drive about to your heart's content! And when summer comes we'll go mushrooming, have tea on the grass in the forest!"

"No, uncle, it's no use your offering it me."

"Really, you had better stay!"

"No. But I tell you what: I am tired after the journey, so may I go to bed?"

"Oh, yes, you may go bye-byes! I have a nice little bed ready for you, and everything is arranged for you properly. If you want to go bye-byes—sleep, bless you! But do think it over: it would be far better for you to stay with us at Golovlyovo!"

Anninka spent a restless night. She was still possessed by the nervous uneasiness that had come over her at Pogorelka. There are moments when a person who has so far merely *existed* suddenly begins to understand that he really *lives* and that there is some canker in his life. He does not as a rule clearly see how and why it formed and generally ascribes its presence to wrong causes: but he does not really care about the causes—it is sufficient for him that the canker is there. Such a sudden revelation is equally painful to everyone, but its subsequent effects vary according to the person's temperament. It regenerates some people, inspiring them with the resolution to begin a new life, on a new basis: in others it merely causes temporary distress, leading to no change for the better but making them more miserable for the moment than those whose awakened conscience looks forward to a brighter future as a result of their new resolutions.

Anninka was not one of those who are regenerated through understanding the evil of their lives; but, being an intelligent girl, she saw perfectly well that there was all the difference in the world between the vague dreams of earning her own living that had led her to leave Pogorelka in the first instance and her position as a provincial actress. Instead of a quiet, hard-working life she had let herself in for a feverish existence full of continual merry-making, cynical talk, and endless hustle that led nowhere. Instead of hardships and privations which she had once been ready to accept she had found a comparative comfort and even luxury, that she now could not recall without blushing. And all this change had somehow happened quite imperceptibly: it was as though she had been going to some good place but by mistake had opened a wrong door. Her dreams had certainly been very modest. How often, sitting in her attic at Pogorelka, she pictured herself as a serious, hard-working girl, longing to improve her mind, bravely enduring privations and poverty for the sake of the ideal (though the word "ideal" probably had no definite meaning for her): but as soon as she took up the broad path of independence she found herself in surroundings which shattered her dreams at once. Serious work does not come to one of itself: determined effort is needed to find it, and previous training, which, even if imperfect, helps one at any rate to look in the right direction. Anninka was not fitted for such work either by temperament or by education. Easily excited, she was not one to devote herself to a thing whole-heartedly, and her educational equipment was insufficient to qualify her for any serious profession. Her education had been of the genteel and artistic type, a mixture, so to speak of the boarding school and the comic opera. It included, in chaotic disorder, the problem about a hundred flying geese, the *pas de chale*, the preaching of Pierre of Picardy, the escapades of Helen of Troy, Derzhavin's ode to Felitsa, and the feelings of gratitude to the directors and patrons of young ladies' schools. This bewildering hotch-potch (apart from which she might justly describe herself as a *tabula rasa*) was not likely to serve as a starting-point for practical life. It fostered not a love of work but a love of gaiety, a desire to be popular in society, to listen to gallantries, and, generally speaking, to plunge into the rushing and sparkling whirl of the so-called life.

Had she been more introspective when, at Pogorelka, she made her first plans for earning her living, regarding it as a kind of deliverance from Egyptian captivity, she would have detected that she dreamed not so much of work as of being surrounded by congenial people and spending time in contin-ual conversation. Of course the people of her dreams were in-telligent and their talk was serious and high-minded, but anyway it was the festive side of life that was in the fore-ground. The poor surroundings were clean and tidy, the pri-vations meant simply absence of luxury. And so when her hopes of work ended in her being offered an engagement as a comic-opera singer in a provincial theater, she did not take long to make up her mind. She hastily polished up her school information about Helen's relations to Menelaus, looked up a few biographical details about Potyomkin and decided that this was quite enough for acting the *Belle Hélène* and the *Grand-Duchess of Gerolstein* in provincial towns and at fairs. To appease her conscience she recalled how a student whom she met at Moscow kept talking of "holy art": she made these words her motto all the more readily because they lent a certain seemliness to her action and provided her with an excuse for entering a path to which she was instinctively and overwhelmingly attracted.

Her life as an actress threw her off her balance. With no friends, no training, and no conscious purpose in life, eager for excitement, glamour, and adulation, she soon found herself caught in a kind of whirl with innumerable people round her, succeeding one another at random. These people differed so widely in character and convictions, that her reasons for being friends with this one or that one could not have been the same, and yet they all formed her circle—which proved that, strictly speaking, there could be no question of "reasons" about it at all. It was clear that her life had become a kind of inn, at the gates of which anyone might knock if he felt young, gay, and well off. Obviously it was not a question of *selecting* a congenial set of people but of keeping in with any set to escape solitude. In truth her "holy art" had landed her in a cesspool but she lived in such a giddy whirl that she failed to see it. The waiters' unwashed faces, the dirty stage, the noise, stench, and babble at the inns and hotels, and her admirers' impudence could not sober her. She failed to notice that she was always in men's company and that some impassable barrier had arisen between her and women of definite social standing.

Her visit to Golovlyovo did sober her for a moment.

Something had been gnawing at her ever since the morning, almost from the moment she arrived. Being an impressionable girl she quickly assimilated new experiences and no less quickly adapted herself to every situation. And so as soon as she arrived at Golovlyovo she felt that she was "a young lady." She recalled that she had something of her own: her house, her family graves; she wanted to see her old surroundings once more and to breathe again the atmosphere that she had only a short time before been so eager to leave behind. But this feeling was bound to disappear at the first contact with the Golovlyovo life. She was like a person who comes with a friendly expression on his face into the company of people he had not seen for some time and suddenly notices that they all regard his friendliness in a rather peculiar way. Iudushka's nasty sidelong glance at her bust at once reminded her that she had a past which was not easily left behind. When, after the naïve questions of Pogorelka servants, the priest's and his wife's meaning sighs and Iudushka's admonitions, she was at last left alone and considered at leisure the impressions of the day, she saw quite clearly that the "young lady" had gone for ever; that henceforth she was nothing but an actress of a miserable provincial theater, and that in Russia an actress was regarded as little better than a woman of the streets.

So far she had lived as in a dream. She appeared half-naked in the *Belle Hélène*, acted the drunken Perichole, sang shameless couplets in the *Grand-Duchess of Gerolstein*, and was positively sorry that *l'amour* and *la chose* were not shown on the stage, picturing to herself how seductively and with what *chic* she would wriggle her hips and maneuver her train. But it had never occurred to her to think what she was doing. She had only been anxious to do everything "prettily" and "with *chic*," and to please the officers of the local regiment. She had never asked herself what it all meant, and what kind of sensations her wrigglings produced in the officers. They formed the most important section of the audience and she knew that her success depended upon them. They intruded behind the scenes, knocked without ceremony at her dressing-room door while she was half-dressed, called her by pet-names—and she regarded it all as a mere form, as an inevitable part of her trade, and merely asked herself whether she behaved "prettily" in those surroundings. She had never yet felt that either her soul or her body was public property. But now when for a moment she became a "young lady" once more, she was suddenly overwhelmed with disgust. It was as though she had been stripped in the presence of all and felt all over her body the vile breaths smelling of drink and of the stables, the touch of moist hands and slobbering lips: it seemed to her that eyes clouded with animal lust wandered senselessly over the curves of her naked figure, demanding, as it were, an answer from her: What is *la chose*?

Where was she to turn? Where could she leave the burden of her past? This question throbbed in her mind, not finding and indeed not even seeking an answer. After all, it was all a kind of dream: the life she had been leading was a dream and her awakening just now was a dream too. She was depressed, overwrought—that was all. It would pass. One has happy moments and bitter ones—that's how it always is. Both joy and bitterness glide over the surface of life without in the least changing its established routine. In order to change that, a great many efforts are needed as well as courage, both moral and physical. It is almost the same thing as suicide. A man may be cursing his life, he may feel certain that death means freedom for him, and yet the instrument of death trembles in his hand, the knife glides over his throat, the pistol aimed at the forehead goes off lower down and disfigures him. It is the same thing here, only still more difficult. Here too one has to destroy one's former life, but in doing so one must remain alive. The "non-being" achieved in ordinary suicide by a momentary pull at the trigger, in the special case of suicide that is called "regeneration," is achieved through strenuous, almost ascetic self-discipline. And the end is "non-being" just the same, because an existence consisting of nothing but efforts at self-control, abstentions, and privations cannot be called life. Those whose will is weak, who are demoralized by easy living, feel giddy at the very prospect of such "regeneration," and instinctively turning away and shutting their eyes follow the beaten track once more, ashamed of their own cowardice and full of self-reproach.

Ah, a life of work is a great thing! But only people of character, or those who are doomed to labor as a kind of curse for original sin, take to it. They alone are not afraid of it: the first, because they understand the meaning of work and its possibilities, and are able to find enjoyment in it; the second, because for them work is a natural duty that becomes a habit.

It never entered Anninka's head to settle at Pogorelka or at Golovlyovo, and matters were much simplified for her by the fact that she had business obligations which she was instinctively determined to keep. She had been given a holiday and she had planned her time beforehand, fixing a day for leaving Golovlyovo. People of weak character find the external forms of life of great help in bearing its burdens. In cases of difficulty they instinctively cling to those forms, finding in them a justification for themselves. That was precisely what Anninka did: she decided to leave Golovlyovo as soon as possible, and, if her uncle pestered her too much, to say to him that she had to be back at the appointed time.

Waking up next morning she walked through all the rooms of the huge Golovlyovo house. Everything seemed alien and comfortless, everywhere there was a sense of death and desolation. The thought of settling in this house for good quite frightened her. "Not for anything!" she repeated to herself with strange emotion, "never!"

Porphyry Vladimiritch greeted her that morning with his usual graciousness, which made it hard to tell whether he meant to be affectionate or had evil designs upon one.

"Well, Miss Hurry-scurry, have you had a good night? Where are you hurrying off to now?" he asked jokingly.

"It's quite true I must hurry, uncle: I am on my holiday, you know, and must be back in time."

"You mean—at your buffoonery again? I won't let you go!"

"You may let me or not. I'll go just the same."

Iudushka sadly shook his head.

"And what would your grandmamma have said?" he asked in a tone of kind reproach.

"Grandmamma knew. And what queer expressions you use, uncle! Yesterday it was going with a guitar about the fairs, to-day you talk of buffoonery. I won't have you talk like this, do you hear?"

"Aha! the truth isn't to your taste, is it? And I, now, love the truth! I think, if it's the truth . . ."

"No, no, no, I don't want it! I don't want either truth or untruth from you! Do you hear? I won't have you talk like that!"

"There, there! We've lost our temper! You'd better come and have breakfast, grasshopper! I expect the samovar has long been snoring and snorting on the table."

By his jokes and laughter Porphyry Vladimiritch wanted to correct the impression left on Anninka by the word "buffoonery," and, in token of peace, tried to put his arm round her waist: but Anninka thought it all so silly and contemptible that she drew away.

"I tell you seriously, uncle, that I must hurry."

"Come and let us have a drink of tea first, and then we'll talk."

"But why must we drink tea first? Why can't we talk now?"

"Because you mustn't ask questions! Because everything must be done at the proper time. First one thing, then another. First we'll drink tea and chatter, and then talk business. There's plenty of time."

There was no answering this kind of argument and Anninka had to give in. They sat down to breakfast: Iudushka wasted time in a most provoking way, taking tiny sips of tea, crossing himself, chatting about dear mamma, and so on.

"Well, now let us talk," he said at last. "How long do you think of staying?"

"I can't stay more than a week. I have to go to Moscow on my way."

"A week, my dear, is a long time: one may do a great deal in a week, or very little—according to how one tackles it."

"We had better do a great deal, uncle."

"That's just what I am saying. One may do a great deal, or very little. Sometimes one wants to do a great deal but it comes to very little; and sometimes one doesn't seem to be doing much but suddenly finds that with God's help one had finished all there was to do. Here now you are hurrying away, you say you have to go to Moscow, but if one asked you why—you couldn't say yourself. But I think you had better see to your affairs instead of going to Moscow."

"I must go to Moscow because I want to see if I can get an engagement there. And as to my affairs, you have just said yourself that one can do a great deal in a week."

"That depends on how you tackle the business, my dear. If you tackle it properly, it will all go smoothly and evenly, but if you don't, there will be hitches and delays."

"Then please direct me, uncle!"

"That's just it. When you need me, then 'please direct me, uncle,' and when you don't, then you are bored with your uncle and want to run away from him! Isn't that so?"

"But only tell me what I have to do!"

"Wait a bit. So what I am saying is this: when you need your uncle he is a pet and a dear and a darling, and when you don't—you turn your back on him! It never enters your head to ask him: 'What do you think, uncle darling—may I go to Moscow?'"

"How strange you are, uncle! It's essential for me to go to Moscow, and suppose you say I mustn't?"

"If I say you mustn't, you have to stay! It wouldn't be a stranger saying this but your own uncle—you might do as he tells you. Ah, my dear, my dear! It's a good thing anyway that you have an uncle—someone to pity you and to pull you up. Think of those who have no one! No one to pity them, no one to admonish them—they grow up all alone! No wonder things happen to them . . . all sorts of things happen in life, my dear."

Anninka was on the point of answering but she understood it would be merely adding fuel to the fire and said nothing. She sat and looked hopelessly at Porphyry Vladimiritch talking away.

"I have long been meaning to say to you"—Iudushka went on: "I don't like it, I don't like it at all, the way you go about those fairs! You were annoyed at my talking about guitars, but still . . ."

"But it's not enough to say you don't like it! You must point a way out."

"Live with me—that's a way out."

"Oh no . . . not that . . . certainly not!"

"Why?"

"Because there's nothing here for me to do. What is there to do here? Get up in the morning and have breakfast. At breakfast, think that lunch will be served presently. At lunch—that there will be dinner: at dinner, wonder how soon there will be tea again. And then supper and to bed . . . I should die here!"

"Everyone lives in that way, my dear. First they have breakfast, then those who are used to it take lunch—though I, for instance, am not used to it and don't take lunch: then they have dinner, then evening tea and at last go to bed. Surely there is nothing either ridiculous or reprehensible in it! If, now, I . . ."

"There's nothing reprehensible, only it doesn't suit me."

"If, now, I injured somebody, or spoke evil, or passed judgment upon people—then indeed I might blame myself for it. But there's no harm in having tea, lunch, and dinner.... Why, bless you! You yourself, clever as you are, can't do without food!"

"Yes, it is all very well, but it's not my way of looking at it."

"You mustn't be thinking of yourself always—think of your elders! 'My way,' 'not my way'—you shouldn't talk like that! You should ask whether it's God's way—that would be right and sensible. If, now, at Golovlyovo we didn't live in God's way, if we trespassed against God, if we sinned, repined, were envious or did any other wrong, then indeed we should be to blame and deserve censure. Only, you would first have to prove that we really were offending God. It's no use simply saying that you don't like it. Take me, for instance —there are lots of things I don't like. I don't like the way you talk to me and sniff at my hospitality—and yet I sit here and say nothing! I think to myself perhaps I'll bring it home to her by keeping quiet—perhaps she may come to her senses of herself. Perhaps while I am answering your sallies with jokes and laughter, your guardian angel may set you on your right path! It's on your account I am grieved, not on my own. Ah, my dear, it is very, very wrong of you! And it isn't as though I had said something bad to you, or taken advantage of you or done you some wrong—that would have been different. Though it is God's command that we should put up with admonitions from our elders, had I offended you I would have merited your being cross with me. But here I am, as quiet as can be, not saying anything, and only thinking how to arrange things for the best, to everybody's joy and comfort—and you turn up your nose at all my kindness! You shouldn't say anything that comes into your head, my dear, but first think and pray, and ask God to enlighten you! And then if..."

Porphyry Vladimiritch held forth in this way for a long time without stopping. Words followed one another endlessly in a sticky stream. Anninka looked at him with a vague fear, wondering that he did not choke. But he never told her after all what she was to do in view of Arina Petrovna's death. She tried to ask him the same question at dinner and at tea, but every time Iudushka began some rigmarole that had nothing to do with it, and Anninka was sorry she had started the conversation. Her only thought was "When will it end?"

After dinner Porphyry Vladimiritch went to have a nap, and Anninka was left alone with Yevpraxeya. She felt a sudden desire to get into conversation with her uncle's housekeeper. She wanted to know how it was Yevpraxeya was not afraid of living at Golovlyovo and what gave her the strength to withstand the torrents of empty words that flowed from her uncle's mouth from morning till night.

"Are you bored at Golovlyovo?" she asked.

"Why should I be bored? I am not a lady."

"But still . . . you are always alone . . . you have no amusements or distractions of any kind, nothing."

"I am not one for amusements. If I am dull, I look out of the window. When I lived at my father's I hadn't much fun either."

"Still, I should have thought you had a better time at home. You had friends, went to see each other, played games . . ."

"Of course."

"And with my uncle. . . . He talks of such dull things and at such length! Does he always do it?"

"Always, he talks like that all day long."

"Doesn't it bore you?"

"Oh, I don't mind. I don't listen, you know."

"But you cannot always do that. He might notice it and be offended."

"And how can he tell? I look at him while he talks. I look, and meanwhile think my own thoughts."

"What do you think about?"

"All sorts of things. If it's time to pickle cucumbers, I

think about cucumbers: if we have to send to town for something, I think about that. Anything that's wanted in the house—I think of it all."

"So, although you are living together, you are really quite alone?"

"Yes, almost alone. Sometimes he fancies a game of 'fools' in the evening—well, then we play. And even then he suddenly stops in the middle of the game, puts down the cards, and begins talking. And I sit and look at him. It was better when Arina Petrovna was living. He was afraid to talk too much before her: the old lady pulled him up now and again. But now it's beyond anything, he just lets himself go!"

"And you see, Yevpraxeya, that frightens one! It's terrible when a man talks and doesn't know why he talks and what he is saying and if he is ever going to stop. It is frightening, isn't it? It makes one uncomfortable, you know."

Yevpraxeya looked at her as though some wonderful thought had dawned on her for the first time.

"You are not the only one," she said—"many people here dislike him for it."

"Indeed!"

"Yes. Take the footmen now—not one can stay with us for any time; we change them almost every month. And bailiffs too. And all because of that."

"He bores them?"

"He wears them out. Drunkards, now, don't mind living here, because they don't listen. You might blow a trumpet for aught they care—it's as good as though they had a pot over their heads. But the trouble is, master doesn't like drunkards."

"Well, there you are! And he is persuading me to settle at Golovlyovo."

"Well, miss, it might be a good thing! Perhaps he'd draw in his horns a bit then!"

"No, thank you! I wouldn't have the patience, you know, to look into his eyes."

"Of course not! You are a lady—you can do as you please! Though I expect you too have to play second fiddle sometimes."

"And very often too!"

"I thought so. And another thing I wanted to ask you: do you enjoy being an actress?"

"I earn my living—that's something."

"And is it true, Porphyry Vladimiritch told me, that strangers can put their arms round an actress when they like?"

Anninka flushed crimson.

"Porphyry Vladimiritch doesn't understand," she answered irritably. "That's why he talks such nonsense. He can't tell stage acting from real life."

"Well, I don't know. . . . It's not for nothing that he too, Porphyry Vladimiritch, I mean . . . He fairly licked his chops when he saw you! 'Dear niece' he says, like a good one, but his shameless eyes are all agog."

"Yevpraxeya! Why do you talk nonsense?"

"I? It's nothing to do with me! If you stay with us, you'll see for yourself. But I don't care. If I am turned out I'll go back to my father. It really is dull here; you are right there."

"You needn't think that I could possibly stay here. But about its being dull at Golovlyovo—that's a fact. And the longer you live here, the more bored you'll be."

Yevpraxeya pondered a little, then yawned and said:

"When I lived at my father's I was thin as a rake, and now see what a size I am! Being bored seems to do me good."

"But you won't be able to stand it long all the same. Remember my words, you won't."

This was the end of the conversation. Fortunately Porphyry Vladimiritch had not heard it, or he would have found a fresh and fruitful subject that would have given a new turn to his endless moralizing.

Porphyry Vladimiritch went on tormenting Anninka for two more days. He kept saying: "Wait and see! More haste

less speed! Pray first and then act!" and so on. She was quite
worn out. At last on the fifth day he made up his mind to go
to the town, though here too he found an opportunity for torturing his niece. After she had put on her fur coat and was in
the hall ready to go, he dawdled for a whole hour as though
on purpose. He washed, dressed, smacked his legs, crossed
himself, walked about, sat down, gave orders such as "So
that's that, my man!" or "Well, mind what you do . . . see that
nothing goes wrong!" Altogether he behaved as though he
were leaving Golovlyovo for ever and not for a few hours.
Having tired out everyone—both the people and the horses
that waited for an hour and a half with the carriage—he found
at last that his throat was dry with talking of nothing in particular, and decided to go.

They finished all they had to do in the town while the
horses had a feed of oats at the inn. Porphyry Vladimiritch
presented a paper showing that the orphans' capital on the
day of Arina Petrovna's death amounted to nearly twenty
thousand rubles in 5 percent bonds. The petition for handing
over the estate and the capital to the owners, accompanied by
documents proving that they were of age, was granted forth-
with. The same evening Anninka signed all the papers and in-
ventories drawn up by Porphyry Vladimiritch and breathed
freely at last.

She was in a perfect fever during the days that followed.
She wanted to leave Golovlyovo at once, but her uncle met
all her attempts to do so with jokes which in spite of their
kindly tone revealed such stupid obstinacy that no human
power could override it.

"You have said yourself that you would stay a week—so
you must stay!" he said. "Why shouldn't you? You haven't to
pay for lodgings—we are only too glad to have you! And if
you want a drink of tea, or a meal—you can have anything
you fancy!"

"But I really must go, uncle!" Anninka pleaded.

"You are anxious to go, but I won't give you the horses!" Iudushka joked, "and if I don't give you the horses you are my prisoner! When the week is over, I won't say a word against your going. We'll hear Mass, take dinner, and a drink of tea to set you on the way, have a talk and a good look at each other —and then God speed to you! And I'll tell you what! Hadn't you better go to your grandmamma's grave once more?—say good-bye to her—and perhaps she'll give you good advice from the other side?"

"I might," Anninka agreed.

"I'll tell you, then, what we'll do: on Wednesday we'll go to Mass quite early, then have dinner to set you on the way, and then my horses will take you to Pogorelka, and from there you can go to Dvoriki with the Pogorelka horses. You are a landowner yourself! You have horses of your own!"

She had to submit. Vulgarity is a tremendous power; those who are unused to it are always caught by it unawares: while they look about them in amazement they find themselves in its clutches. It has probably happened to everyone to stop one's nose and hold one's breath while walking past an open drain; a similar effort is necessary when one enters the domain of vulgarity and empty talk. A man must dull his sight, hearing, taste and smell, and turn utterly insensible; only then will he escape being choked with the miasma of vulgarity. Anninka grasped this rather late in the day; in any case she decided to leave her deliverance from Golovlyovo to the natural course of events. Iudushka so completely subdued her by his unanswerable twaddle that she dared not draw away when he embraced her and like a good uncle stroked her back saying: "There, now you are a good girl!" She could not help shuddering when she felt his bony and slightly shaky hand creeping down her back, but the thought "What if he doesn't let me go at the end of the week!" restrained her from expressing her disgust. Luckily for her Iudushka was by no means squeamish, and though he may have noticed her impatient movements, he said nothing. His theory of the relations between the sexes could evidently be expressed by the proverb: "You may love me, you may not, but behave as though you do."

The eagerly awaited day of her departure came at last. Anninka got up about six o'clock, but Iudushka had been first. He had already finished his morning devotions and, waiting for the first sound of the church bell, slouched about the rooms in his slippers and an old jacket, peeping round the corners, listening behind doors, and so on. He was obviously agitated and gave a kind of sidelong glance at Anninka when he met her. It was quite light out of doors but the weather was bad. The sky was completely covered with dark clouds; sleet was coming down; there were pools in the black-looking road—a sure sign of the snow being waterlogged; a strong south wind was blowing, bringing rain and thaw; the trees had lost their covering of snow, and their bare tops waved helplessly in the wind; the outbuildings looked black and clammy. Porphyry Vladimiritch took Anninka to the window and pointed to this scene of spring rejuvenation.

"I wonder if you ought to go," he said. "Hadn't you better stay?"

"Oh no, no!" she cried in alarm. "It . . . it will clear up!"

"I don't think so. If you leave at one you are not likely to be at Pogorelka before seven. And you can't travel in the dark when the roads are like this—you'll have to stay the night at Pogorelka anyway."

"Oh no, I'll travel in the night, I'll go straightaway. . . . I am brave, uncle, you know! And why should I wait till one o'clock? Uncle darling! let me go at once!"

"And what will your grandmamma say? She will say: 'Here's a nice grandchild! She came, hopped about, and didn't even ask for my blessing!'"

Porphyry Vladimiritch paused. He shifted his feet and kept glancing at Anninka and looking down again. He was evidently making up his mind to say something.

"Wait a minute, I'll show you something!" he ventured at last, and pulling out of his pocket a folded sheet of notepaper gave it to Anninka. "There, read this."

Anninka read:

"I was praying to-day and asking kind God to leave me my Anninka. And kind God said to me: 'Take Anninka by her plump little waist and press her to your heart.'"

"Yes?" he asked, turning slightly pale.

"Ugh, uncle, how horrid!" she answered, looking at him in bewilderment.

Porphyry Vladimiritch turned paler still, and saying through his teeth, "So it's hussars we want!" crossed himself and shuffled out of the room.

Half an hour later, however, he returned perfectly unconcerned and was joking with Anninka as before.

"Well then, will you call at Voplino on your way?" he asked. "Want to say good-bye to your old granny? Do, my dear! It is very nice of you to have thought of grandmamma. One must never forget one's relatives and especially those who were ready to give their very life for one!"

They heard Mass and had a requiem sung, ate some fromenty in church and some more at home when they sat down to breakfast. As though to spite Anninka, Porphyry Vladimiritch sipped his tea slower than usual and talking between every two gulps, dragged out his words in a most provoking manner. By ten o'clock, however, breakfast was over and Anninka begged:

"Uncle, may I go now?"

"And dinner! A meal to set you on the way? Did you imagine your uncle would let you go away hungry? What next! Certainly not! It's unheard of in our family! Why, mamma would have forbidden me the house had she known that I let my own niece go on a journey without giving her dinner!"

Anninka had to submit again. . . . An hour and a half passed but there was no trace of any preparations for dinner. All had gone out; Yevpraxeya could be seen flitting across the yard between the cellar and the store-room, rattling her keys; Porphyry Vladimiritch talked to the bailiff, wearing him out with senseless orders, slapping himself on the legs and altogether doing his best to while away the time. Anninka walked up and down the dining-room, glancing at the clock, counting her steps and then the seconds: one, two, three.... At times she looked out of the window and saw that the pools were growing bigger and bigger.

At last there was a rattle of spoons, knives, and plates; Stepan the footman came into the dining-room and spread the table-cloth. But it looked as though he too had been infected by Iudushka's deadness. He handled the plates as slowly as could be, blew into the glasses and held them against the light. It was just one o'clock when they sat down to dinner.

"Well, here you are going away!" said Porphyry Vladimiritch, opening a conversation suitable to the occasion.

There was a plate of soup before him but he did not touch it; he was looking at Anninka so tenderly that the tip of his nose turned red. Anninka was hastily swallowing spoonful after spoonful. He also took up his spoon and put it into his soup, but immediately put it down again.

"You must excuse an old man like me," he buzzed. "You have eaten your soup post-haste, and I make a long job of it. I don't like treating God's gift in an offhand fashion. Bread has been given us for our nourishment, and we waste it—see what a lot of crumbs you've made! And altogether I like doing everything properly and without hurry—it's more sound. Maybe it annoys you that I don't jump over hoops—or what do you call it?—at dinner; well, there is nothing for it! Be cross if you like! You'll be cross for a bit, and then forgive me. You won't always be young, you know, or always be jumping over hoops, you too will gain experience some day— and then you'll say: 'Perhaps my uncle was right, after all!' That's how it is, my dear. Now you may be thinking as you listen to me 'Horrid uncle! old grumbler!' But when you'll have lived to be my age you'll sing a different tune; you will say: 'Nice uncle! he gave me good advice!' "

Porphyry Vladimiritch crossed himself and swallowed two spoonfuls of soup. Having done this he left the spoon in the plate and leaned back in his chair as a sign that he had more to say.

"Bloodsucker!" was on Anninka's tongue. But she controlled herself and, quickly pouring out a glass of water, drank it at one gulp. Iudushka seemed to scent what was going on in her.

"Oh, you don't like it, do you? Well, even if you don't you should listen to your uncle! I have long been meaning to talk to you about your always being in a hurry, but I haven't had the leisure to do so. I don't like this hurry: it shows rashness, a lack of thought. That time for instance, there was really no occasion for you to leave your grandmamma—she was so grieved—and what was it all for?"

"Oh, why recall it, uncle! What is done is done. It isn't nice of you."

"Wait! Nice or not nice, my point is that even when a thing is done it can be undone. Not only we, sinners, change our actions but God Himself does it: He sends us rain one day, and fine weather the next. Come, now! The stage isn't anything very precious you know. Come! Give it up!"

"No, uncle, don't talk of it, I beg you."

"And another thing I want to tell you: I don't like your rashness, but I dislike even more the light way you treat your elders' remarks. Your uncle wishes your good, and you say, 'Leave it alone!' Your uncle is kind and affectionate to you, and you turn up your nose at him! But do you know who has given you your uncle? Tell me, now, who has given him to you?"

Anninka looked at him in perplexity.

"God has given you your uncle—that's who! God! If it had not been for God, you would have been alone in the world and wouldn't have known what to do and what petition to send in, and to whom, and what would come of it. You would have been as good as lost; people would have been rude to you, taken advantage of you or simply laughed at you! But since you have an uncle, we have, with God's help, settled your whole business in a single day. We went to the town, called at the trustees' office, filed a petition and received a reply. So that's what it means to have an uncle, my dear!"

"But I am grateful to you, uncle!"

"And if you are grateful to your uncle, don't turn up your nose at him but do as he tells you. Your uncle wishes you well, though you fancy sometimes . . ."

Anninka was hardly able to control herself. There was one means to put an end to her uncle's admonitions: to pretend that theoretically at least she accepted his invitation to stay at Golovlyovo.

"Very well, uncle," she said, "I'll think about it. I understand of course that it isn't quite the thing to live alone, away from my relations. . . . But in any case I cannot decide anything at the moment. I must think it over."

"There, now—you see it at last. But what is there to think about? Let's give word to unharness the horses and take your luggage out of the sledge—that's all!"

"No, uncle, you forget that I have a sister!"

There was no telling whether Porphyry Vladimiritch was convinced by this argument; he may have acted the whole scene merely for appearance' sake without being at all certain if he really wanted Anninka to stay at Golovlyovo, or if it was just a momentary whim on his part. In any case, after this the dinner went on more smoothly. Anninka agreed with everything he said and gave answers that afforded no opportunity for moralizing. Nevertheless, it was half-past two when the meal was over. Anninka jumped up from the table as out of a steam-bath and ran up to her uncle to say good-bye to him.

Ten minutes later Iudushka in his fur coat and bearskin

boots was seeing her off at the front door and personally supervising her departure.

"Drive carefully down the hill, do you hear! And mind you don't upset the sledge on the Senkino slope!" he ordered the coachman.

At last Anninka was wrapped up and the sledge cover was fastened.

"Hadn't you better stay?" Iudushka called after her, wishing to show to the assembled servants that everything was as it should be between good relatives. "At any rate, will you come and see me? What do you say?"

Knowing that she was already free, Anninka suddenly felt mischievous. She leaned out of the sledge and answered deliberately:

"No, uncle, I will not come! It's terrifying to be with you!"

Iudushka pretended not to have heard but his lips turned white.

Anninka was too glad to have escaped from the Golovlyovo captivity to give a thought to the man whom she was leaving behind in that captivity for ever, and whose last link with the world of the living was severed by her departure. She was only thinking of herself: she had escaped and was happy. This sensation of freedom was so strong that when she visited her grandmother's grave again she showed no trace of the nervous sensibility she had felt on her first visit there. She calmly heard the requiem, bowed before the grave without tears, and readily accepted the priest's invitation to take a cup of tea in his cottage.

The priest lived in very poor surroundings. The only sitting-room in the house was dismally bare; a dozen stained wooden chairs upholstered in shabby horse-hair were ranged round the walls; there was a sofa of the same kind with a curved back that looked like the puffed-out chest of an old-fashioned general; a deal table covered with a dirty cloth, with parish registers, an ink-pot and pen lying on it, stood between the windows; in the east corner there was an icon-stand with a sanctuary lamp burning before it; two boxes covered with faded gray cloth stood underneath. There were no wall-papers; several faded daguerreotypes of bishops hung in the middle of one wall. The room had a peculiar smell, as though it had served for years as a cemetery for flies and cockroaches. The priest himself, though still a young man, seemed to have faded in these surroundings. His thin, fair hair hung down in straight wisps like the branches of a weeping-willow; his eyes, that had once been blue, had a dejected look, his voice trembled, his beard was scanty; his cotton cassock was too loose for him but did not meet properly in front. His young wife, worn out with yearly child-bearing, looked even more exhausted than her husband.

And yet Anninka could not help noticing that, poor, downtrodden, and half-starved as those people were, they regarded her with compassion as a lost lamb rather than as an ordinary parishioner.

"Have you been staying with your uncle?" the priest began, carefully taking a cup of tea from the tray that his wife handed him.

"Yes, I have spent a week there."

"Porphyry Vladimiritch is the biggest landowner in all our neighborhood now—the most important man here. But he doesn't seem to have much luck. He lost first one of his sons, then the other, and then his mother died too. It's strange he hasn't persuaded you to settle at Golovlyovo."

"He did offer it me but I wouldn't stay."

"Why not?"

"It's better to be free, you know."

"Freedom of course is a good thing, madam, though it too has its dangers. And considering that you are Porphyry

Vladimiritch's nearest relative and heiress to his estate, one would have thought you could restrict your freedom a bit."

"No, Father, I prefer to work for my living. It is more satisfactory, somehow, to feel independent."

The priest looked at her dully, as though wanting to ask: "Come, do you know what working for one's living means?" but he was too shy. He merely pulled his cassock round him nervously.

"And what salary do you receive as an actress?" his wife asked.

The priest was quite alarmed and gave a warning look to his wife. He thought Anninka would be offended. But she was not, and answered quite simply.

"Now I receive a hundred and fifty rubles a month, and my sister a hundred. And we have benefit performances too. We earn something like six thousand a year between us."

"And why is your sister paid less? Isn't she as good as you?" the priest's wife went on questioning.

"No, it isn't that—her style is different. I have a voice and can sing—the public prefers this, and my sister's voice is rather weak, so she acts in vaudevilles."

"So it's the same thing as in the church, then: some are priests and others deacons and others mere choristers?"

"We share our income though; we decided from the first to go halves."

"Like good sisters? That's excellent. How much does it come to, husband? Six thousand rubles divided by months— what will that be?"

"Five hundred rubles a month, or two hundred and fifty each."

"That's a lot of money! We wouldn't get through it in a year. And another thing I wanted to ask you: is it true that men treat actresses as though they weren't real women?"

The priest was so flustered that he let go the skirts of his cassock; but seeing that Anninka took the question quite calmly he thought, "Well, she must be a tough one"—and calmed down.

"How do you mean—not real women?"

"Why, people say, men kiss them and put their arms round them . . . and, even if they don't want to, they must put up with it."

"They don't kiss but only pretend to. And there can be no question of wanting or not wanting, because it's all done according to stage directions: one just does what is written in the play."

"It may be in the play, and yet . . . Some slobbering creature too loathsome to look at will thrust his mug at you, and you've got to offer him your lips."

Anninka could not help blushing; she suddenly pictured the bold Captain Papkov's slobbering face that certainly did "thrust" itself upon her, and, alas! not even according to stage directions.

"You have quite a wrong idea of what happens on the stage," she said rather dryly.

"Of course we've never been to a theater, and yet I expect things aren't always nice there. My husband and I often talk of you; we are sorry for you, very sorry."

Anninka said nothing; the priest sat tugging at his beard as though making up his mind to put in his word too.

"Of course, madam, every occupation has its pleasant and its unpleasant side," he brought out at last, "but, in his weakness, man takes delight in the first and tries to forget the second. Why forget? Just so as to avoid, madam, having before him this last reminder of duty and virtuous life."

And he added, with a sigh:

"And above all, madam, one must preserve one's treasure!" The priest looked at Anninka admonishingly; his wife shook her head dejectedly, as though saying "Not likely!"

"And it seems rather doubtful if one can preserve that treasure, being an actress," the priest went on.

Anninka did not know what to say to this. She began to fancy that these simple-hearted people's talk about "the treasure" was exactly on a par with the officers' conversations about *la chose*. It was evident to her that here too, as at her uncle's, she was regarded as something out of the ordinary, to be pitied, perhaps, but to be kept at a distance for fear of soiling oneself.

"Why is your church so poor, Father?" she asked, to change the subject.

"There is no reason for it to be rich—that's why. All the landowners are away on government service, and the peasants haven't the means. And there are only two hundred of them in the parish."

"Our bell is too bad, really!" the priest's wife sighed.

"The bell, and everything else too. Our bell weighs only about five hundredweight, and it's split into the bargain. It makes a queer kind of noise instead of ringing—quite unseemly, indeed. Arina Petrovna of blessed memory had promised to give us a new one and, had she lived, I am sure we should have had it."

"You should tell my uncle that grandmamma promised it."

"I did tell him, madam, and, to do him justice, he heard my request quite favorably. But he could give me no satisfactory answer; he had not heard anything from his mother about it, he said. It appears that she had never mentioned it to him. But if he had heard, he would certainly have carried out her wish, he said."

"Not heard, indeed!" the priest's wife said. "All the neighborhood knows it and he hadn't heard!"

"So that's how things are with us. We used to live in hopes, at least, but now we have no hope. Sometimes I have nothing for celebrating Mass: no wheaten bread, no wine. And our own circumstances I won't even mention."

Anninka was on the point of getting up and saying goodbye when a new tray appeared on the table with a bottle of madeira and two plates: one with mushrooms and another with bits of caviar.

"Please stay and have some, I beg you!"

Anninka obeyed and hastily swallowed two mushrooms, refusing the madeira.

"There's another thing I wanted to ask you," the priest's wife was saying, "there's a girl in our parish who has been in service with an actress in Petersburg. She says it's a fine life being an actress, only one has to have a special ticket* renewed each month . . . is that true?"

Anninka looked at her open-eyed, not understanding her.

"That's to have more freedom," the priest explained, "only, I think what she says isn't true. On the contrary, I have heard that many actresses are rewarded with a government pension."

Anninka saw that the further into the wood, the thicker the trees, and got up to say good-bye.

"And we had thought you'd give up the stage now!" the priest's wife went on.

"Why should I?"

"Oh, well, you are a lady, you know. Now you have come of age, you have an estate of your own—what could be better!"

"No, I am not going to live here."

"And we did so hope you would! We kept saying to each other: Our young ladies are sure to settle at Pogorelka. It is very nice here in the summer: one can go mushrooming in the woods."

"We have plenty of mushrooms even in a dry summer," the priest seconded her.

At last Anninka left them. The first thing she said when she came to Pogorelka was to ask for horses. "Please make haste!" But Fedulitch merely shrugged his shoulders.

"Horses, indeed! We haven't fed them yet," he grumbled.

---

*The reference is to the "yellow ticket" held by prostitutes. —Translator's note.

"But why ever not? Oh dear! It's as though you had all determined to stop me going!"

"Of course we have! Naturally. Anyone can see that you can't travel at night in the thaw. You'd get stuck in the water-logged snow—so we thought you'd be better indoors."

Arina Petrovna's rooms had been heated. The bed was made and the samovar was puffing on the writing-table; Afimyushka had scraped together the remnants of tea left at the bottom of an old-fashioned tea-caddy after Arina Petrovna's death. While the tea was infusing Fedulitch with his arms crossed stood in the doorway facing the young lady; Markovna and the dairymaid stood on either side of him in attitudes that suggested they were ready at the least sign from her to run to the ends of the earth.

"It's your grandmamma's tea," Fedulitch began the conversation, "there was some left at the bottom when she died. Porphyry Vladimiritch wanted to take the caddy but I didn't agree. Maybe the young ladies will come, I said and want some tea before they have had time to buy some of their own. Well, he didn't mind, in fact he joked about it: 'You'll drink it yourself, you old rascal,' he said, 'see that you bring the tea-caddy to Golovlyovo when it's empty!' I expect he'll send for it to-morrow."

"You should have given it to him there and then."

"Why should I? He's plenty of tea as it is. Now at any rate we can have a drink after you've finished. By the way, miss, are you going to hand us over to Porphyry Vladimiritch?"

"Certainly not."

"Good. We weren't going to agree to it, you know. We thought we'd all give notice if you pass us on to him."

"Why is that? Is my uncle such a terror?"

"No, but he does wear one out with his talk. His words are enough to rot a man."

Anninka could not help smiling. There really was something putrid about Iudushka's long-winded sententiousness. It was like an open, festering sore.

"Well, and what have you decided to do about yourself, miss?" Fedulitch went on.

"How do you mean, what have I to decide?" Anninka asked somewhat uneasily, foreseeing that she would once more have to listen to arguments about "the treasure."

"But surely you won't remain an actress now?"

"Yes, I will . . . that is, I haven't thought about it yet. But what harm is there in my earning my living as best I can?"

"There's nothing good in going about the fairs with a tambourine, cheering up the drunkards! You are a lady, you know."

Anninka said nothing and merely frowned. Her mind throbbed painfully with the question, "Good heavens, when shall I get away from here?"

"Of course you know best what to do with yourself, but we had thought you'd return to us. The house is warm and roomy—you could play rounders in it! Your grandmamma had arranged it all very nicely. If you are bored, you can go for a sledge drive, and in the summer there's mushrooming!"

"We have all sorts of mushrooms here, and no end of them!" Afimyushka lisped alluringly.

Anninka leaned both arms on the table trying not to listen.

"A girl from these parts," Fedulitch insisted mercilessly "had been a servant in Petersburg—and she told us that all actresses have to have a ticket. They have to show it at the police station every month!"

Anninka went hot all over: she seemed to have been listening to these words all day.

"Fedulitch!" she cried out. "What have I done to you? Is it that you enjoy insulting me?"

She had had enough. There was a lump in her throat—one word more, and she would break down.

5

ILLICIT FAMILY JOYS

NOT LONG BEFORE the catastrophe with Pètenka, Arina Petrovna noticed on one of her visits to Golovlyovo that Yevpraxeya looked a little bigger. Brought up in the times of serfdom Arina Petrovna had a keen eye for that sort of thing, for in those days the maid-servants' pregnancy used to lead to a thorough and rather interesting investigation and was regarded almost as a source of income. She had no sooner fixed her gaze on Yevpraxeya's waist than the latter flushed crimson and turned away without a word, fully conscious of her guilt.

"Come, come, my beauty, look at me! Are you with child?" the experienced old lady asked the erring damsel: but there was no reproach in her voice, on the contrary she spoke jestingly, almost gaily, as though she suddenly felt a breath of the good old times.

Yevpraxeya said nothing, looking both shy and complacent, but her cheeks grew redder and redder under Arina Petrovna's inquiring glance.

"I noticed yesterday you kept huddling yourself together—so that's it! You thought you'd go about wagging your tail like a good one, did you? No, my dear, you won't take me in! I see all your girl's tricks three miles off! Now, what wind brought you this? When? Make a clean breast of it! Speak!"

A thorough interrogation followed. When did she notice the first symptoms? Had she a midwife in view? Did Porphyry Vladimiritch know of the joy in store for him? Was Yevpraxeya taking care of herself? Did she lift anything heavy? etc. It appeared that Yevpraxeya was in the fifth month of pregnancy; that she had no midwife in view; that she had told Porphyry Vladimiritch but he said nothing and merely whispered to himself, folding his hands and looking at the icon as a sign that all was from God and He, the King of Heaven, would provide for everything; that one day Yevpraxeya had foolishly lifted a samovar and immediately felt as though something had snapped inside her.

"Well, you are a pair, I must say!" Arina Petrovna said with concern when she had heard it all. "I see I shall have to take the thing in hand myself. Just fancy, the fifth month and they haven't thought of a midwife! You should have seen Ulita, anyway, you silly!"

"I had thought of it, but master doesn't like Ulita."

"Nonsense, my dear, nonsense! He may have something against Ulita but that's another matter—this isn't the time to think of it! and besides it isn't as though we had to make love to her! No, there's nothing for it, I shall have to see to it myself!"

Arina Petrovna felt like being sorry for herself and saying that even in her old age she had to carry other people's burdens, but the subject of the conversation was so fascinating that she smacked her lips and went on:

"Well, my beauty, now you are in for it! You've enjoyed the sowing, now try the harvesting! You just try it, my dear! I brought up three sons and a daughter, and buried five as babies, so I know! Those wretched men do give us a time of it!" she added emphatically.

Suddenly she had a new idea.

"Good heavens! I believe it was on the eve of a fast, too! Wait a minute, I'll reckon it out!"

They began counting on their fingers, they counted once, twice, three times—it proved to be precisely on the eve of a fast.

"Well, there it is! That's our holy hermit! I'll tease him about it presently! Our man of prayer has made a nice mess of it! I won't let him off! You may be sure of that!" the old woman joked.

And indeed that very day at tea Arina Petrovna made fun of Iudushka in Yevpraxeya's presence.

"Well, my humble Christian, you have played a fine trick! Or perhaps your madam really did catch it in the wind? I must say you have surprised me, my boy!"

At first Iudushka felt squeamish about his mother's jokes, but seeing that Arina Petrovna spoke "like a good mother" and "in all kindness" he gradually cheered up.

"You are a naughty one, mamma! You really are!" he joked in his turn. But, as was his wont, he would not commit himself on the vital subject.

"Naughty, indeed! We must talk of it seriously. This is no light matter. It's a holy thing—that's what it is! Though it isn't as it should be, yet.... Yes, we must certainly think it over and very carefully too! What's your idea—do you want her to be confined at home, or will you take her to the town?"

"I don't know, mamma, I know nothing about it, dear!" Porphyry Vladimiritch said evasively. "You really are naughty, you know!"

"Well, then, you wait, my girl! You and I will have a good talk about it presently and settle all we have to do. Those wretched men think of nothing but their pleasure and we women have to pay the bill!"

Having made her discovery, Arina Petrovna felt like a duck in water. She talked to Yevpraxeya for the whole evening and couldn't have enough of the subject. Her cheeks were flushed, and her eyes sparkled like a girl's.

"Have you thought what this means, my dear? It's . . . holy, you know!" she insisted. "For though it isn't all as it should be, it's the real thing all the same. . . . But mind! if, heaven forbid, it was on a fast day, I'll simply give you no peace!"

Ulita was taken into their councils. At first they discussed the practical side of the matter—whether Yevpraxeya should have an enema or have her stomach rubbed with ointment. Then they turned to their favorite subject once more and began reckoning on their fingers—and each time they made out that the child must have been begotten on a fast day. Yevpraxeya flushed red as a poppy but did not deny the charge and merely pleaded that she had no choice in the matter.

"It's nothing to do with me," she said, "it's as the master pleases. If it's his orders, how can I go against him?"

"There, there, you little fraud, it's no use wagging your tail!" Arina Petrovna joked. "I expect you were only too glad. . . ."

In short, the women thoroughly enjoyed the whole business. Arina Petrovna recalled a number of incidents from her own past and of course proceeded to relate them. At first she told about her own confinements—of the awful time she had with Styopka the dolt, of driving to Moscow in time for the Dubrovino auction when she was expecting Pavel and nearly dying in consequence, and so on, and so on. All her pregnancies were in some way remarkable; the only child that gave her no trouble was Iudushka.

"I felt no discomfort whatever," she said; "I used to sit and wonder to myself if I really was with child. And when my time came I lay down on the bed for a minute and suddenly I was delivered, I don't know myself how! It was the easiest confinement I have ever had! By far the easiest!"

Then followed stories about the serf girls. Some of them she had "caught" herself, others she had tracked down by confidential servants, chiefly by Ulita. The old woman's memory preserved all the details with astonishing clearness. Spying out the maids' love affairs was the only thing that stirred a living chord of romance in the whole of her colorless past, completely absorbed as it was with accumulating possessions, big and little.

It was something like the *belles-lettres* section in a dull magazine in which the reader expects to find articles about fogs and the place of Ovid's tomb—and suddenly comes across "*A jaunty troika flies along....*" The simple-hearted romances of the maids' room generally ended cruelly indeed, inhumanly: the guilty girl was married off into some distant village, always to a peasant, a widower with a large family; the guilty man was sent into the army or made to work in the cattle-yard. But the memory of these endings had somehow faded (generally speaking, cultured people's memory is very lenient with regard to their conduct in the past) while the actual process of tracking out the "love intrigue" still had all the vividness of reality. And no wonder! In its time it was followed with the same absorbing interest as some serial novel of the present day, in which the author, instead of crowning at once the hero and heroine's mutual attraction, puts a full stop after the most heart-rending passage and writes "To be continued."

"I had no end of trouble with them!" Arina Petrovna related. "Some of them tried to carry it off, up and doing till the last minute—hoping to deceive me! But there was no taking me in, my dear, I have been through it all myself!" she added almost sternly, as though threatening someone.

Then followed stories of pregnancies of a "political" nature so to speak, in which Arina Petrovna figured no longer as an avenger but as a helper and conniver.

Thus, for instance, her papa, Pyotr Ivanitch, a decrepit old man of seventy, had a mistress who suddenly proved to be with child, and, for various important reasons, the fact had to be concealed from him. As ill luck would have it, Arina Petrovna was at that time on bad terms with her brother Pyotr Petrovitch, who, also for some ulterior motives, was interested in the matter and wanted to open the old man's eyes to his favorite's character.

"And would you believe it, we managed it all almost before papa's eyes! He was asleep in his room, the dear man, and we were at it quite close to him! Speaking in whispers, walking on tiptoe! I stopped her mouth with my own hands to stifle her cries, and I cleared away the soiled linen, and when her son was born—such a pretty, healthy baby he was!—I took a cab and carried him off to the Foundling Hospital! When my brother heard of it a week later he simply gasped: 'Well, my sister is a caution,' he said."

There was another "political" pregnancy: it happened to Arina Petrovna's sister-in-law, Varvara Mihailovna. Her husband was away fighting the Turks, and she went and got herself into trouble. She rushed like mad to Golovlyovo: "Save me, sister!"

"We were on bad terms at that time, but I showed no sign of it: I received her properly, reassured and comforted her, and, under the pretext of her being on a visit to me, managed the whole thing so neatly that her husband knew nothing as long as he lived!"

Thus ran Arina Petrovna's tales and, it must be confessed, few story-tellers find such attentive listeners as hers were. Yevpraxeya hung on every word, as though some wonderful fairy tale were being enacted before her eyes; as to Ulita, she had taken part in most of the stories and now merely smacked her lips in acquiescence.

Ulita too had blossomed out and was enjoying herself. Her life had been an anxious one. From early youth she had been consumed with servile ambitions and dreamed of nothing but pleasing her masters and bullying her fellow-servants and yet she had had no luck. No sooner had she placed her foot on the higher rung of the ladder than some unseen power hurled her down into the bottomless pit once more. She was endowed to perfection with all the qualities of a useful servant: she was spiteful, had an evil tongue and was always ready for any perfidy, but she was so inordinately anxious to please everyone that all her malice came to nothing. In the old days Arina Petrovna willingly made use of her when it was a case of a secret inquiry in the maids' room or some other shady business, but she never valued her services or admitted her to any position of importance. In consequence, Ulita went in for complaints and slander, but no one took any notice of it, for everyone knew that she was a spiteful girl, cursing one into hell one moment and cringing and fawning on one the next at the least encouragement. And so she struggled on, trying to make her way in life and achieving nothing, till at last the abolition of serfdom put an end to her servile ambitions.

Something did happen in her youth that had distinctly raised her hopes. During one of his visits to Golovlyovo Porphyry Vladimiritch had an affair with her and the rumor said she bore him a child—which caused Arina Petrovna to be angry with him for years. History does not say whether their relations continued during his subsequent visits to his parental home, but in any case Ulita's hopes were dashed to the ground in a most provoking way when Porphyry Vladimiritch settled at Golovlyovo altogether. As soon as he arrived she rushed to him bearing tales in which Arina Petrovna was accused almost of cheating; but though "the master" graciously listened to the gossip, he looked at Ulita coldly and failed to remember her "services" in the past. Offended and deceived in her hopes Ulita migrated to Dubrovino where Pavel Vladimiritch, out of hatred for his brother, welcomed her and made her his housekeeper. Her fortunes seemed to have mended for a time. Pavel Vladimiritch sat in his room upstairs drinking glass after glass, and she spent her days running round the cellars and the store-rooms rattling her keys, talking loudly, and intriguing against Arina Petrovna whose life she did her best to poison.

But Ulita was too fond of perfidy to enjoy her good luck in peace. Pavel Vladimiritch was drinking so hard that one might feel distinctly hopeful about the results. Porphyry Vladimiritch understood that in the circumstances Ulita was a perfect treasure—and again beckoned to her. She received orders from Golovlyovo not to leave the victim for a moment, not to contradict him in anything, not even in his hatred for his brother, and do all she could to prevent Arina Petrovna's interference. It was one of those family crimes that Iudushka did not plot and plan deliberately, but committed, as it were, instinctively, as a matter of course. Needless to say Ulita carried out her orders to the letter. Pavel Vladimiritch had always hated his brother, but the more he did so the less able he was to listen to anything Arina Petrovna said about "making arrangements." Every gesture, every word of the dying man was immediately reported at Golovlyovo, so that Iudushka could with full knowledge of the case determine the moment when he ought to appear on the scene as the master of the situation he had created. And he made full use of it, coming to Dubrovino just when it fell into his hands of itself, so to speak.

Iudushka rewarded Ulita for this service by giving her a woolen dress, but he did not admit her to any intimacy. Once more Ulita was hurled headlong from giddy heights to the bottomless pit, and this time it looked as though nobody in the world would ever beckon to her again.

As a special favor for her "having looked after his dear brother in his last hours" Iudushka assigned to her a corner in the cottage where some of the deserving former serfs lived after serfdom had been abolished. There Ulita gave up all her ambitions at last, and when Porphyry Vladimiritch picked out Yevpraxeya, so far from being disagreeable about it, she was the first to come and pay her respects to the "master's madam" and to kiss her on the shoulder.

And suddenly, at the very moment when she felt completely forgotten and forsaken, her luck turned again: Yevpraxeya was with child. They remembered that somewhere in the servants' cottage lived a woman '"with hands of gold" and beckoned to her. True, it was not the master himself who "beckoned" but at any rate he had made no difficulties about it. The first thing that Ulita did on coming into the house was to take the samovar out of Yevpraxeya's hands and, bending slightly sideways, jauntily carry it into the dining-room where Porphyry Vladimiritch was sitting. And "the master" did not say a word. She fancied that he actually smiled when on another occasion, also with a samovar in her hands, she met him in the passage and called to him from a distance: "Stand out of the way, sir—I'll burn you."

When Arina Petrovna called her to the family council, Ulita was very punctilious and would not sit down. But when Arina Petrovna ordered her in a friendly voice, "Sit down now! No need to play your tricks—the Tsar has made us all equal! Sit down!" she did sit down, very humbly at first and then quite at her ease.

That woman too had her reminiscences. Many unsavory memories had been stored in her mind since the days of serfdom. Besides carrying out delicate commissions and nosing out the maids' love affairs, Ulita used to act as leech and apothecary in the Golovlyovo household. The number of mustard plasters, poultices, and especially enemas she had administered in her life! She had done it for the old master Vladimir Mihailitch, for Arina Petrovna, and for every one of the young masters—and had preserved most grateful memories about it. And now there was an almost unlimited scope for these memories. . . .

The Golovlyovo house seemed to have mysteriously come to life. Arina Petrovna constantly came from Pogorelka to see her "good son," and preparations to which as yet no name was given were actively being made under her supervision. After the evening tea the three women retired to Yevpraxeya's room, treated themselves to home-made jam, played "fools" and till late at night indulged in reminiscences which sometimes made the young woman flush crimson. The least incident provided an occasion for fresh stories. Yevpraxeya put out some raspberry jam—Arina Petrovna recalled how, when she was carrying her daughter Sonya she could not endure the very smell of raspberries.

"The moment they brought it into the house I could smell it was there! I simply screamed, 'Take the damned stuff away, take it away!' And after my confinement I didn't mind, and came to like it again!"

Yevpraxeya served some caviar—Arina Petrovna recalled an incident à propos of that.

"Caviar, now—a most peculiar thing happened to me about it! I hadn't been married more than a month or two— and suddenly I felt I simply must have some caviar! I kept going to the store-room on the quiet and eating and eating it! So I said to my husband one day, 'What does it mean, Vladimir Mihailitch, that I have such a longing for caviar?' And he smiled and said, 'Why, my dear, you are with child.' And indeed, nine months after that I had Styopka the dolt!"

Porphyry Vladimiritch preserved his enigmatic attitude to Yevpraxeya's pregnancy and never definitely admitted that it had anything to do with him. This naturally made the women feel uncomfortable and prevented their exchange of confidences, and so they kept Iudushka out of it altogether. If in the evening he joined the company in Yevpraxeya's room they drove him away without any ceremony.

"You go, my dear man!" Arina Petrovna said gaily. "You have done your part; now it is our, women's, business! It's our day now!"

Iudushka humbly withdrew, and though he took the

opportunity of reproaching dear friend mamma for being un-
kind to him, at the bottom of his heart he was very glad that
they left him in peace and that Arina Petrovna took genuine
interest in the situation which was distinctly embarrassing for
him. If it had not been for her, heaven only knows what he
would have had to do to hush up the vile affair, the very
thought of which made him squirm and curse. And now he
hoped that, thanks to Arina Petrovna's experience and Ulita's
cleverness, the "trouble" would not lead to any scandal and that
perhaps he would only hear of the event when all was over.

Porphyry Vladimiritch's hopes were not justified. First, there
was the catastrophe with Pètenka and soon after came Arina
Petrovna's death. He had to settle matters personally, and
without the least prospect of arranging some shady transaction. He could not send Yevpraxeya home for "immorality"
because, owing to Arina Petrovna's intervention, things had
gone too far and become common property. It was no use re-
lying on Ulita, for, clever as she was, she might get one into
trouble with the law if one trusted to her. For the first time in
his life Iudushka sincerely and bitterly resented his loneliness, for the first time he vaguely understood that the people
around him were not mere pawns existing for the sole object
of being imposed upon.

"And why couldn't she have waited a bit!" he complained
to himself about dear friend mamma. "She could have
arranged it all cleverly and quietly, and then gone, bless her!
If it's time for one to die, there is nothing for it! I am sorry for
the old lady, but if such be God's will, our tears, and doctors,
and medicines, and ourselves can do nothing against it! The
old lady has had her day and made good use of it! She lived as
befits her station in life and provided for her children. She has
had her day, and that's enough!"

His fussy mind never liked to dwell on matters that presented any practical difficulty, and, as usual, immediately passed on to a more easy subject à propos of which he could chatter endlessly and without hindrance.

"And what a death it was! Truly, it's only the righteous are vouchsafed such an end!" he lied to himself, not knowing whether he was lying or speaking the truth. "No pain, no distress . . . nothing! She heaved a sigh—and behold she was no more! Ah, mamma, mamma! a nice little smile on her face, and her cheeks rosy . . . her hands folded as though in blessing, and her eyes closed . . . adieu!"

And suddenly in the very thick of pathetic words something seemed to prick him. That vile business again . . . curse it! Why couldn't mamma have waited a bit! There was only a month or perhaps less left—and then, she went and died!

For a time he tried to avoid Ulita's questions in the same way as he had done mamma's: "I don't know! I know nothing about it!" But such methods did not answer with Ulita who was an impudent woman, and knew that she had the whip-hand of him.

"Do you suppose I know? Was it I got her into trouble!" she cut him short from the first. He understood that his hopes of happily combining the part of a seducer with that of an outside observer of the results of his sin had been dashed to the ground.

The catastrophe was drawing nearer and nearer, an inevitable, almost tangible catastrophe! It pursued him every moment, and, what was worst of all, it paralyzed his faculty for thinking of nothing in particular. He made every effort to banish the idea of it, to drown it in a torrent of empty words, but he only partly succeeded in this. He tried to take refuge in the immutable laws of Providence, playing with the subject as with a ball of thread that could be unwound indefinitely. He brought in sayings about the hairs of one's head being numbered and about the house that is built on the sand; but just as his idle thoughts began rolling smoothly one after the other down some mysterious abyss and he felt completely confident that he could go on unwinding the ball for ever—one single word suddenly intruded itself upon him, snapping the thread in two. Alas! that word was "fornication" and designated an action which Iudushka did not want to confess even to himself.

And so, when after vain attempts to forget and to banish the thought, he grasped that he had been caught, he felt wretched. He paced up and down the room, thinking of nothing and merely conscious of a sinking, gnawing sensation inside him.

This was the first time in his life that something had happened to check the idle flow of his thoughts. Hitherto, in whatever direction his empty fancy moved, it found nothing but limitless space in which there was room for all sorts of combinations of ideas. Even Volòdenka's and Petenka's tragic fate and Arina Petrovna's death did not cause him any spiritual difficulty. Those were ordinary facts recognized by everyone and could be met in the traditional, generally recognized manner. Requiems, Masses, memorial dinners, etc.—he did all that in accordance with custom and thus justified himself, so to speak, both before men and before Providence. But fornication . . . what was that? That meant showing him up, exposing the falsity of his whole life! True, people had always said he was a backbiter and a "bloodsucker," but these rumors had so little foundation in well-authenticated fact that he had every right to challenge them and demand proofs. And now . . . he had been caught in fornication! Unquestionably, undeniably fornication (he had not even taken any *measures*, thanks to Arina Petrovna—"Ah, mamma, mamma!" —had not even had time to tell a lie) and "on the eve of a fast" too . . . ugh!

These inner deliberations, involved as their subject was, showed something like an awakening of conscience. But the question was, Would Iudushka follow it up, or would his pet-tifogging mind provide him as usual with some way of escape so that he could emerge dry out of water?

While Iudushka was pining under the burden of his own shallowness, an unexpected inner change was gradually taking place in Yevpraxeya. Her approaching motherhood seemed to have loosened the bonds that held her mind captive. So far she had been indifferent to everything and regarded Porphyry Vladimiritch as her "master" whom she was bound to serve. Now for the first time she seemed to grasp that she had her own part in life, a part in which she was the chief person concerned and could not be bullied with impunity. As a result, the very expression of her face, generally dull and ungainly, grew brighter and more intelligent.

Arina Petrovna's death was the first sobering influence in her half-conscious life. The old lady's attitude to Yevpraxeya's expectant motherhood was distinctly peculiar, but there was no doubt of her genuine sympathy as compared with Iudushka's mean and squeamish evasiveness. And so Yevpraxeya began to regard Arina Petrovna as her champion, as though suspecting some attack against herself. Her forebodings were the more persistent as she did not consciously formulate them but merely suffered from a continual vague anxiety. Her intelligence was not sufficient to tell her whence the attack would come and what form it would take; but her instincts were roused so deeply that she felt an unaccountable fear at the very sight of Iudushka. Yes, it would come from there! re-echoed through the inmost recesses of her heart: from there, from this dust-filled coffin which she had been tending as a mere hireling and which, by some miracle, had suddenly become the father and owner of *her* child! The feeling that this thought aroused in her was akin to hatred and would certainly have developed into hatred, had she not found relief in Arina Petrovna's sympathy. Her kindly chatter gave Yevpraxeya no time to think.

But Arina Petrovna first retired to Pogorelka and then faded away altogether. Yevpraxeya felt almost frightened. The stillness into which the Golovlyovo house was plunged was only disturbed by Iudushka walking stealthily along the passage, holding up the skirts of his dressing-gown and listening at doors. Sometimes one of the servants ran in from the yard, banging the maids' room door, and again stillness seemed to creep from every corner—a dead stillness that filled one's heart with a weird painful dejection. And as Yevpraxeya was in the last days of pregnancy she had not even the distraction of housework which in the old days tired her out so thoroughly that towards evening she was only half-awake. She tried being affectionate to Porphyry Vladimiritch, but this merely led to brief but angry scenes that distressed her, insensitive as she was. And so she had to sit with her hands in her lap and think, that is, be a prey to anxiety. Occasions for anxiety increased every day because Arina Petrovna's death untied Ulita's hands and introduced into the Golovlyovo house a new element of gossip which was the only subject of vital interest on which Iudushka's mind could rest.

Ulita understood that Porphyry Vladimiritch was afraid and that in a shallow and mendacious nature like his cowardice came very close to hatred. Besides, she knew very well that Porphyry Vladimiritch was incapable not only of affection but of simple pity, and that he kept Yevpraxeya merely because she was responsible for the smooth running of the household routine. Armed with these simple data Ulita was able to keep continually alive the feeling of hatred that surged in Iudushka's breast the moment anything reminded him of the coming catastrophe. In a short time Yevpraxeya was caught in a regular network of gossip. Ulita was constantly "making reports" to the master. One day she would come and complain of the senseless way household provisions were being used.

"I say, sir, you do get through a lot of food here! I went to the cellar this morning to fetch some salt meat; I thought it wasn't long since a new barrel had been started—and when I looked there wasn't more than two or three pieces left at the bottom!"

"Indeed?" Iudushka stared at her.

"If I hadn't seen it with my own eyes I wouldn't have believed it! It's extraordinary where all the stuff goes to! Butter, corn, cucumbers—everything! On other estates servants have goose-dripping with their porridge—it's good enough for them! —but here they always have butter, and fresh butter at that!"

"Indeed?" Porphyry Vladimiritch was quite alarmed.

Another day she would come in and casually drop a word about the household linen.

"You really ought to pull up Yevpraxeya, master dear. Of course, she is young and not used to things, but take the linen, for instance.... She has used no end of it to make baby's sheets and napkins, and such fine linen, too!"

Porphyry Vladimiritch's eyes gleamed, and though he said nothing, Ulita's words simply wrung his heart.

"Naturally, she feels for her baby," Ulita went on in a honeyed voice. "She thinks the world of him.... She might be expecting a prince! But one would have thought her baby could just as well sleep in hempen sheets ... considering her station in life!"

Sometimes she simply teased Iudushka.

"I meant to ask you, master dear," she began, "what are your intentions about the baby? Will you recognize him as your son, or send him to the Foundling like the others?"

But Porphyry Vladimiritch gave her such a black look that she went no further.

Amidst hatred seething on all sides the moment was drawing closer and closer when the birth of a tiny, weeping "servant of God" would settle one way or another the moral confusion that prevailed in the Golovlyovo household, and at the same time increase the number of other weeping "servants of God" that populate the world.

It was past six o'clock in the evening. Porphyry Vladimiritch had had his afternoon nap and was sitting at his desk covering sheets of paper with figures. He was investigating the question how much money would he have had now if Arina Petrovna had not appropriated the hundred paper rubles which grandpapa Pyotr Ivanitch had given him at his christening, but invested them instead in the name of baby Porphyry. It appeared it would not have been very much: only eight hundred paper rubles.

"It isn't much, of course," Iudushka reflected, "and yet it is nice to know one has something put by for a rainy day. If you need it, you draw it out. You don't have to ask anyone for it, put yourself under no obligation to anyone—you take what is your own, given you by your grandfather! Ah, mamma, mamma! I wonder you could have been so rash!"

Alas, Porphyry Vladimiritch had recovered from anxieties which had so recently paralyzed his idle thinking. The glimpses of something like conscience roused by the difficulties in which Yevpraxeya's pregnancy and Arina Petrovna's sudden death had placed him gradually died down. His habit of thinking of nothing in particular served him as usual and after tremendous efforts he did finally succeed in drowning the idea of his "trouble" in a sea of empty words. It could not be said that he had consciously come to any decision; somehow his favorite old formula to which he had always had recourse in trying circumstances suddenly came into his head of itself: "I know nothing! I permit nothing and I forbid nothing!" It soon put an end to the inner confusion that had distressed him for a time. He now regarded Yevpraxeya's confinement as an event that had nothing to do with him, and consequently his face assumed a dispassionate and impenetrable expression. He almost completely ignored Yevpraxeya and did not even mention her name; when he happened to inquire after her he said: "And is *that woman* still ill?" In short he proved so strong that Ulita, well schooled in the days of serfdom in the science of reading hearts, understood that there was no struggling with a man who was ready to fall in with any situation.

The Golovlyovo house was plunged into darkness; there was a light only in the master's study and in Yevpraxeya's room at the far end of the passage. Stillness reigned in Iudushka's part of the house, interrupted only by the rattle of the counting-beads and the rustle of the pencil with which he was doing his calculations. Suddenly into the midst of general silence a distant but heart-rending moan penetrated to the study. Iudushka started; his lips trembled; his pencil made a zigzag.

"A hundred and twenty-one rubles plus twelve rubles ten kopecks" . . . Porphyry Vladimiritch murmured, trying to forget the unpleasant impression of the moan.

But the moans grew more and more frequent and distressing. It was so difficult to continue work that Iudushka left his desk. At first he walked about the room trying not to listen, but curiosity gradually mastered cowardice. He stealthily opened his study door, thrust his head into the darkness of the adjoining room and listened in an expectant attitude.

"Dear me! I believe they've forgotten to light the sanctuary lamp before Our Lady's image!" flitted through his mind.

Someone's anxious, hurried step was heard in the passage.

Porphyry Vladimiritch hastily drew in his head, shut the study door and ran on tiptoe towards the icon. A second later he was "fully armed," so that when the door flew open and Ulita rushed into the room she found him at prayer, his hands clasped before him.

"I am afraid our Yevpraxeya is breathing her last," said Ulita, without any consideration for Iudushka's devotions.

Porphyry Vladimiritch, however, did not even turn to her but moved his lips more rapidly than usual, and instead of an answer waved one hand in the air as though driving away a persistent fly.

"It's no use your waving your hand! I tell you, Yevpraxeya is in a bad way—she may die any moment!" Ulita insisted rudely.

This time Iudushka did turn to her, but his face looked as calm and serene as though in contemplating the Deity he had left all earthly care behind and simply could not understand why anyone should want to disturb him.

"Though it's a sin to scold when one is at prayers, yet as a man I must point out to you that I've asked you time and again not to disturb me at my devotions!" he said in a voice suitable to the mood of prayer, allowing himself however to shake his head as a sign of Christian reproach. "Well, what is it now?"

"What can it be except that Yevpraxeya is in agony and cannot be delivered! One might think you heard it for the first time! Oh, you.... Come and have a look at her, at least!"

"What is there to see? I am not a doctor. I cannot give any advice. Besides, I know nothing, nothing at all about your affairs. I know there is an invalid in the house, but what her illness is and what caused it, I confess I have never had the interest to inquire. One thing I can advise you is to send for the priest if the invalid is bad! Send for the priest, pray with him, light the sanctuary lamps ... and afterwards the priest and I can have some tea!"

Porphyry Vladimiritch was very pleased to have spoken so plainly at a decisive moment like that. He looked at Ulita bright and confidently as though saying: "You won't catch me now!" Even Ulita was at a loss in the face of such serenity.

"Do come! Have a look at her!" she repeated.

"I won't come because there's no occasion. If there were any need for it I would have gone without your asking. If I had to walk three miles on business I'd go; if I had to walk seven—I'd go just the same! It might be frost or snow-storm but I'd walk on and on! Because I should know that I had business to attend to, that I was bound to go!"

Ulita fancied she was asleep and in her dream saw Satan himself holding forth.

"To send for the priest now, that's a different matter. That would be sensible. Prayer—do you know what it says in the Gospel about prayer? Prayer is *the healing of the sick*—that's what it says. So you had better see to it! Send for the priest, pray together . . . and I'll pray at the same time. You pray in the icon-room, and I'll ask God for grace here, in my study. . . . We'll join forces: you do it there, and I here—and we may find that our prayers have reached God right enough!"

They sent for the priest, but before he had come Yevpraxeya was delivered, in torments and agony, of a child. Porphyry Vladimiritch could guess from the sudden running to and fro and banging of doors at the other end of the house that something decisive had happened. And indeed, a few minutes later, hurried steps were heard in the passage again and Ulita rushed into the study holding in her arms a tiny creature wrapped up in something white.

"Here! Look!" she announced solemnly, bringing the child right up to Porphyry Vladimiritch's face.

Iudushka seemed to hesitate for a moment, his body bent forward and his eyes lit up. But it was only for a moment because he immediately turned away from the baby in disgust and waved both hands in its direction.

"No, no! I am afraid of them. . . . I don't like them! Go . . . go! . . ." he uttered with an expression of unutterable aversion.

"You might ask at least whether it is a boy or a girl!" Ulita admonished him.

"No, no . . . why should I? . . . It's nothing to do with me! It's your affair and I know nothing about it. . . . I know nothing and there's no need for me to know. . . . Go away, for Christ's sake!"

Again it was like a vision of Satan. . . . Ulita could control herself no longer.

"I have a good mind to throw him on the sofa . . . for you to nurse!" she threatened.

But Iudushka was not easily affected. While Ulita was uttering her threat he had already turned to the icon and was modestly lifting his arms to heaven. He was evidently asking God to forgive all: those who sin "in knowledge or in ignorance, by thought, word, or deed," and thanking Him that he was not a thief, or a robber, or an adulterer, and that God in His mercy had firmly planted his feet in the path of righteousness. His very nose quivered with emotion so that after watching him for a time Ulita cursed and went away.

"Here, God has taken away one Volodya and given me another!" suddenly flashed through his mind quite inappropriately but he instantly noticed this unexpected trick of thought and dismissed it in disgust.

The priest came and held a service. Iudushka heard the chorister droning "Mother of God, our defense" and could not resist joining in. Ulita ran up and called in at the door:

"They've christened him Vladimir!"

The strange coincidence of this fact with the aberration of thought that had just made him think of the Volodya who died touched Iudushka. He saw the finger of God in this and said to himself, this time not trying to dismiss the idea:

"Thank heaven! God has taken one Volodya and given me another! That's what God does! One loses something and thinks is never going to recover it, and behold God makes up for it a hundredfold in some other way!"

At last he was told that the samovar was ready, and that the priest was waiting in the dining-room. By now Porphyry Vladimiritch was completely at peace with the world. He found Father Alexander in the dining-room waiting for him. The Golovlyovo priest was a tactful man who tried to maintain a social manner towards Iudushka; but he knew very well that Vigil services were held at the Golovlyovo house every Saturday and also on the eve of great holidays, and a special service on the first of every month—which meant an income of quite a hundred rubles a year for the clergy. He was aware, too, that the church land boundary had not yet been properly fixed and that more than once, driving past the priest's meadow Iudushka had said "a lovely meadow, that!" And so Father Alexander's easy manner was not unmixed with apprehension which forced him to assume whenever he met Porphyry Vladimiritch a serene and joyful expression though he had no reason for it. And when Iudushka developed heretical views with regard to ways of Providence, future life and so on, Father Alexander, though not directly approving of these speculations, did not think them blasphemous or impious, but regarded them merely as daring flights of fancy to which the gentry were prone.

When Iudushka came in, the priest blessed him hastily and still more hastily drew his hand away as though afraid that the bloodsucker would bite him. He was going to congratulate him on the birth of Vladimir but thought better of it, not knowing what Iudushka's attitude to the event might be.

"It is rather misty to-day," the priest began. "The popular belief, in which, however, there is a good deal of superstition, is that such weather is a sign of thaw."

"And maybe there will be a frost; we are thinking of thaw and God will send us frost!" Iudushka responded sitting down busily and almost cheerfully to the tea-table, presided over by the footman Prohor on this occasion.

"It is true that in his dreams man often seeks to attain the unattainable and to approach the unapproachable, and in consequence finds either sorrow or an occasion for repentance."

"And so we ought to steer clear of any omens or predictions, and be content with what God sends us. If He sends us warmth—we shall be glad of warmth; if He sends us frost—we shall welcome frost too! We'll have our stoves heated better than usual, and those who set out on a journey will wrap their fur coats closer round them and so we'll keep nice and warm!"

"That is so!"

"Many people nowadays like to go round a subject, and say this isn't as it should be, and that isn't to their liking, and the other should have been different, but I don't like that. I don't go in for subtleties myself and don't approve of it in others. It's trying to be too clever—that's what I think it is."

"Yes, that is so."

"We are all strangers and pilgrims here; that's how I look upon myself! To have a drink of tea, now, or to take a little light refreshment . . . that is permitted us! Because God has given us a body and other parts. . . . Even the Government doesn't forbid it: eat you may, it says, but you must hold your tongues!"

"You are quite right there, too!" The priest cleared his throat and as a token of inward joy knocked the bottom of his empty glass against the saucer.

"My opinion is that man has been given intelligence not in order to probe the unknown, but to refrain from sin. Suppose, for instance, I feel bodily weakness or confusion and seek my reason's help to overcome the weakness—then I am acting rightly! Because in such cases reason can really be of help!"

"But faith more so," the priest corrected him slightly.

"Faith has its own province, and so has reason. Faith points out the purpose, and reason discovers the means. It knocks at one door, tries another . . . it wanders about and in doing so discovers something useful. Those different medicines, now; herbs, decoctions, plasters, all that has been discovered by our reason. But it must all be in accordance with faith if it is to do us good and not harm."

"I have nothing to say against that either."

"I once read a book, Father, and it said there that one must not despise the services of the intellect if it be directed by faith, for a man without intelligence soon becomes a plaything of passions. I believe, indeed, that the Fall was due to the fact that Satan in the shape of a serpent obscured man's reason."

The priest did not contradict this but expressed no approval, for he did not yet see what Iudushka was driving at.

"We often find that men sin not only in their minds but actually commit crimes—and all through lack of intelligence. The flesh leads one into temptation, and reason is lacking—and so man flies to perdition. He is eager for pleasure and soft living and gaiety, especially if it's a case of the female sex . . . how is one to escape if one isn't intelligent? But if I have intelligence, I take a little camphor or some oil and rub myself here, sprinkle myself there—and behold the temptation is gone!"

Iudushka paused as though waiting to see what the priest would say to it, but Father Alexander, still perplexed as to Iudushka's object, merely cleared his throat and made an utterly irrelevant remark:

"I have some fowls in my yard . . . they are all in a flurry because of the equinox: they run about, scuttle to and fro and don't know what to do with themselves."

"It is all because neither birds nor beasts nor reptiles have intelligence. What sort of creature is a bird, now? It has no troubles, no cares—it just flies about! I looked out of the window this morning: the sparrows were pecking in the manure —that's all they want! But man can't be content with that."

"And yet, in certain cases the Scripture points to the birds of heaven as an example to us!"

"In certain cases—yes. We must imitate the birds in cases when we can be saved by faith alone without intelligence. Praying, for instance, or writing poetry. . . ."

Porphyry Vladimiritch paused. He was a babbler by temperament and longed to discuss the event of the day. But the form in which he could decently put his considerations on the subject was evidently not yet ripe in his mind.

"Hens do not need intelligence," he said at last, "because

they have no temptations. Or, rather, they have temptations but no one expects them to resist them. Everything is natural with them: they have no property to look after, no legal marriages, and consequently no widowhood. They haven't to answer either before God or before their superiors: they have only one superior: the cock!"

"The cock! That's quite true. He is like the Turkish sultan for them."

"But man has so ordered his life that there is nothing natural about it, and so he needs a great deal of intelligence. He must take care not to fall into sin himself and not to lead others into temptation. Isn't it so, Father?"

"It's perfectly true. The Scripture advises us to pluck out the offending eye."

"Yes, if one understands it literally; but one may contrive for the eye not to be tempted even if it isn't plucked out. One must have frequent recourse to prayer, and subdue bodily passions. Take me for instance: I am still in my prime, and fairly strong.... Well, and I have female servants too ... but that doesn't trouble me in the least! I know one cannot do without servants, and so I keep them! I keep men servants and women servants too—all kinds of servants. One needs women servants, you know—to go to the cellar, to pour out tea, to see to the provisions.... Well, bless them! They do their work, I do mine; that's how we get on!"

As he said this Iudushka tried to look the priest in the eyes; the priest, too, for his part, tried to look into Iuduskha's eyes. Fortunately, a candle stood between them so that they could look at each other as much as they liked and see nothing but the flame of the candle.

"And besides, I reason in this way: if one is familiar with servants, they are sure to take liberties. There will be all sort of upsets, rudeness and dissensions: you say a word and they answer back.... And I avoid all that."

The priest had been looking at Iudushka so intently that

everything began to swim before his eyes. Feeling that good manners required one to contribute a word to the general conversation from time to time, he shook his head and said:

"Tsss. . . ."

"But if one behaves as others do . . . for instance as my neighbor Mr. Anpetov or my other neighbor Mr. Utrobin . . . it's easy enough to fall into sin. That Mr. Utrobin has about six of those little horrors playing about in the yard. But I don't want that. What I say is this: if God has taken away my guardian angel, it is His holy Will that I should be a widower. And if by the grace of God I am a widower, I must live in purity and keep my bed undefiled. Isn't it so, Father?"

"It's hard, sir!"

"I know it's hard, but still I carry it out. Some people say 'it's hard' and I say the harder the better, if only God gives one strength. Not everyone can have things sweet and easy— some must endure hardships for God's sake! If you deny yourself *here*—you will be compensated *there*! *Here* we call it hardship, but *there* it is called merit! Is it right, what I say?"

"Couldn't be more so."

"And something must be said about merits too. They are not equal, you know. Some merits are great and others small. Did you know that?"

"Why, of course they are not equal. There's all the difference between great merit and small!"

"That's just what I say. If a man behaves circumspectly: does not indulge in bad language or in empty chatter, does not judge others, never injures or takes away what is theirs . . . and if he is careful, too, about those temptations—such a man will always be at peace with his conscience. And no mud will stick to him! And if someone does speak evil of him behind his back, to my mind he need not even consider such talk. Dismiss it with contempt—that's all."

"In such cases Christian rules recommend forgiveness by preference."

"Well, or forgive it! That's what I always do: if someone speaks evil of me I forgive him and pray for him into the bargain! It's good for him that a prayer about him should reach God, and it's good for me: I have prayed and forgotten all about it!"

"That's right now: nothing relieves one's mind more than prayer. Sorrow and anger, and even disease fly from it like the darkness of night from the sun."

"Well, God be thanked! And one must always behave so that one's life could be seen from all sides like a candle in a lantern. . . . Then there would be less evil spoken of one—for there would be no occasion for it! Take us now, for instance: here we have been sitting and conversing together—who could blame us for that? And now we'll go and say our prayers, and then go bye-byes. And to-morrow we'll get up again . . . isn't it so, Father?"

Iudushka got up and noisily moved back his chair as a sign that the conversation was over. The priest stood up too and raised his hand for blessing; but as a special favor Porphyry Vladimiritch caught his hand and pressed it in both his.

"So you have named him Vladimir, Father?" he asked, sadly shaking his head in the direction of Yevpraxeya's room.

"In honor of the holy prince St. Vladimir, sir."

"Well, thanks be to God. She is a good, faithful servant, but intelligence is not her strong point! That's how it happens that those sort of people commit . . . for-ni-cation!"

All next day Porphyry Vladimiritch sat in his study praying for guidance. The day after he appeared at breakfast not in his dressing-gown as usual, but wearing a frock coat as on a feast day: he always did that when he intended doing something decisive. His face was pale, but shining with spiritual light; a happy smile played about his lips; his eyes had a kindly, forgiving expression; the end of his nose, through excess in devotions was slightly red. He drank in silence his three glasses of tea and in the interval between the gulps moved his lips, clasped his hands and gazed at the icon as though, in spite of his pious exertions the day before, he were still awaiting for help and guidance. After swallowing the last gulp he sent for Ulita and stationed himself before the icon, to fortify himself once more by communing with the Deity, and also to show Ulita that what was going to happen would be not his doing but God's. Ulita, however, understood from the first glance at Iudushka's face that in the depths of his heart he was determined on some perfidy.

"Here I have been praying!" Porphyry Vladimiritch began and as a sign of submission to God's holy Will bent his head and made a gesture of resignation.

"That's excellent," Ulita answered with a note of such unquestionable understanding in her voice that Iudushka looked up.

She was standing before him in her usual attitude leaning her chin in her hand; but her face was alight with laughter. Porphyry Vladimiritch shook his head as a sign of Christian reproach.

"I suppose God has sent you grace?" Ulita continued, unabashed by his warning movement.

"You are always blaspheming!" Iudushka could not resist saying: "the number of times I tried to break you of it by jests and kindness but you are still at it! You have an evil tongue . . . a viper's tongue!"

"I fancy I haven't said anything. . . . It's always said that if you pray, God sends you grace!"

"That's just it, you 'fancy'! But you mustn't babble about all you 'fancy'; you must hold your tongue sometimes. I was going to talk seriously, and she trots out her fancies!"

Instead of answering, Ulita merely shifted from one foot to the other as though meaning by that movement that she

251

knew by heart all that Porphyry Vladimiritch could have to say to her.

"Well, then, listen to me!" Iudushka began. "I prayed yesterday, and again to-day, and what it comes to, is that in any case we must find a home for Volodya."

"Of course! He isn't a puppy—you can't drown him."

"Stay, wait! Let me say a word . . . you viper! Well, so what I say is this: in any case we must find a home for Volodya. In the first place, we must have pity on Yevpraxeya, and secondly—we must make a man of him."

Porphyry Vladimiritch glanced at Ulita, probably hoping that she would have a good chat with him, but she treated the matter simply and even cynically.

"Is it me who is to take him to the Foundling?" she asked, looking him straight in the eyes.

"Oh, oh, oh!" Iudushka exclaimed, "so you've settled it all, have you, Miss Long-tongue? Ah, Ulita, Ulita! You are always on the hop! It's all fuss and chatter with you! But how do you know: maybe I haven't even thought of the Foundling! Maybe I . . . have thought of something else for Volodya?"

"Well, if you have, there's no harm in that."

"So what I say is this: although I am sorry for Volodya, yet, if one considers it and thinks it over, it isn't the thing for us to keep him at home."

"Of course not! What will people say? They'll say: how is it there's a strange baby at Golovlyov's house?"

"Yes, that too, but there's something else as well: it would not be good for him to live at home. His mother is young —she would spoil him; and I, though I am old, and a stranger, yet, because of his mother's faithful service, I shouldn't wonder if I spoiled him too. I am afraid I might be too lenient. Instead of giving the boy a whipping for being naughty I might think of this and that. . . . And there would be no end of tears and crying—so one would simply let it go! Isn't it so?"

"That's true. You would get tired of it."

"And I want everything to be done properly. I want Volodya to grow up into a fine man, a servant to God and a loyal subject to the Tsar. So that if God blesses him to be a peasant, he should know how to work on the land.... To mow, to plow, to chop wood—a little of all that, you know. And if it is his fate to be something else, that he should know a trade or a profession. I hear some come out of there to be teachers!"

"Out of the Foundling? Oh, they make them generals in the Army straight away!"

"Not generals, but still.... Maybe Volodya will turn out to be somebody famous. They do bring them up excellently there, I know that myself. Their little cots are beautifully clean, the wet-nurses are healthy, the babies are dressed in white little shirts, they have feeding-bottles, comforters, napkins ... everything, in short!"

"The best thing possible, of course ... for the illegitimate!"

"And if he is put out to be nursed by a peasant, well, Christ be with him! He will get used to work from childhood, and work, you know, is as good as prayer! We, now—we pray properly: we stand before an icon and make the sign of the cross, and if our prayer finds favor with God, He rewards us for it. But the peasant works. Sometimes he might be glad to pray properly, but he hardly has time for it even on holy days. But, still, God sees his labors and rewards him for his work as He does us for our prayers. Not everyone can live in palaces and skip about at dances—some must live in tiny huts without a chimney and look after our mother-earth! And which is the happier, heaven only knows. One man may live in a palace, in the lap of luxury, but shed tears through gold, and another may have straw for his bed, and bread and kvass for his fare and yet have a paradise in his heart! Isn't it right what I say?"

"What could be better than paradise in one's heart!"

"Well, so that's what we shall do, my dear. You take that

naughty little Volodya, wrap him up warm and snug and drive with him post-haste to Moscow. I'll have a covered sledge rigged out for you, a pair of horses harnessed; the roads are nice and smooth now, no holes or hollows—you just sit in comfort and drive along! But mind that you do the whole thing properly—in my style, as we do it at Golovlyovo, as *I* like it! The feeding-bottle and the teat must be nice and clean . . . and mind you have plenty of nice little shirts and sheets and swaddling clothes and napkins and blankets—everything! Take all you want! Give orders! And if they don't give you things, you get hold of me—appeal to your old master! And when you arrive in Moscow, put up at an inn. Ask anything you want in the way of food or tea! Ah, Volodya, Volodya! What a pity it all is! I am sorry to part from you, but there is nothing for it, my boy! You will see for yourself in time that it was for your good, and thank me!"

Iudushka slightly raised his arms and moved his lips as a sign of inward prayer. This did not prevent him, however, from glancing at Ulita and noticing the mocking expression that flitted over her face.

"What is it? Do you wish to say something?" he asked her.

"No, nothing. Of course he'll be very grateful when he discovers his benefactors."

"Ah, you bad, bad woman! As though we were going to leave him there without a ticket! You must take the ticket with you, and from that we shall find him when the time comes. They'll bring him up and teach him to be a good boy and then we'll come with our ticket and say, 'Give us back our naughty little Volodya!' With a ticket we can fish him out from the bottom of the sea. . . . Isn't it so?"

Ulita made no answer but looked more sarcastic than ever. Porphyry Vladimiritch could contain himself no longer.

"Oh, you viper!" he said. "You've got the devil in you. . . . God bless us! Well, that will do. To-morrow at daybreak you must take Volodya and be quick about it so that Yevpraxeya doesn't hear. Go to Moscow with him, with God's blessing. Do you know the Foundling Hospital?"

"I have taken them there before," Ulita answered shortly, as though hinting at something in the past.

"If so, I have nothing to teach you. You must know your way about. Mind you place him there and bow low to the superiors—like this."

Porphyry Vladimiritch stood up and bowed, touching the ground with his hand.

"Ask them to look after him, to see that he is really comfortable! And be sure you have his ticket given you. Don't forget! With the ticket we can always find him later on. I'll give you two twenty-five-ruble notes for the expenses. I know all about it. You have to tip a man here, grease another's palm there. . . . Ah, sinners, that we are! We are all human, we all want sweets and playthings! Take our Volodya now—he is no bigger than one's thumb and see what a lot of money he costs one already!"

Having said this, Iudushka crossed himself and bowed low to Ulita, silently asking her to take care of the naughty little Volodya. The future of his illegitimate offspring was arranged in the simplest possible way.

The morning after this conversation, while the young mother was tossing about in fever and delirium Porphyry Vladimiritch stood at the dining-room window moving his lips and making the sign of the cross over the glass. A covered sledge carrying away Volodya was leaving the courtyard. It reached the top of the hill beside the church, turned to the left and disappeared in the village. Iudushka made the sign of the cross for the last time and sighed.

"Father Alexander talked of thaw the other day," he said to himself, "and here God has sent us frost instead of thaw!

And such a frost, too! That's how it always is with us. We dream and build castles in the air and try to be clever and outdo God Himself—and God turns all our high-flown ideas to naught in a minute!"

6

THE DERELICT

IUDUSHKA'S DEATH-AGONY dated from the time when the resource of empty talk in which he indulged so readily began to fail him. He was deserted: some had died, others had gone away. Even Anninka, who had nothing but the nomadic life of an actress to look forward to, was not tempted by the Golovlyovo luxuries. There was only Yevpraxeya left, but apart from the fact that that was a very limited resource, something had obviously gone wrong with her, and Iudushka clearly saw that his happy days had gone for ever.

Hitherto Yevpraxeya had been so defenseless that Porphyry Vladimiritch could tyrannize over her without any misgivings. Her mind was so little developed and her nature so yielding that she was not even conscious of this tyranny. While Iudushka was shamelessly babbling away, she looked at him with vacant eyes, thinking of something else. But now she suddenly grasped something, and the immediate result of this awakening of thought was a bitter and invincible, though as yet an unconscious, aversion.

Anninka's visit to Golovlyovo had evidently left an impression on Yevpraxeya's mind. Although she could not clearly say to herself why her casual conversations with Anninka had hurt her, inwardly she was in a state of utter turmoil. It had never entered her head before to ask why, as soon as he met a man, Porphyry Vladimiritch immediately began entangling him in a network of phrases in which there was nothing to take hold of but which made one feel horribly depressed. Now she understood that Iudushka did not really talk about anything in particular but merely "pestered" one, so that it wouldn't be a bad plan to pull him up and make him feel it was time "he drew in his horns." She began listening to his ceaseless flow of words and understood only one thing about it: that Iudushka really did plague one with his buzzing.

"The young lady had said he didn't himself know what he was saying," she reasoned with herself. "Yes he does—it's his spite makes him do it! He knows when one is at his mercy and twists one about as he pleases!"

This, however, was only of secondary importance. The chief effect of Anninka's visit to Golovlyovo was to rouse the instincts of youth in Yevpraxeya. So far those instincts merely smoldered in her; now they flared up into a warm, bright flame. She grasped a great deal of what had left her completely unconcerned before. Take this, for instance: there must have been a reason why Anninka had refused to stay at Golovlyovo and said straight out that it was "terrible." Why was it? Simply because she was young, because she wanted "to live." And she, Yevpraxeya, was young also ... yes, young! One might think her youth was buried under a layer of fat, but no—at times she was keenly aware of it. It seemed to call her, to beckon to her; it died down for a bit and then flared up again. She had thought once that she would be content with Iudushka, but now ... "Ah, you rotten old stump! The way you got round me! But wouldn't it be fine to have a real lover, a young one! We'd lie close together, and he'd kiss and pet me, and whisper nice words into my ear, say I was his soft white dumpling! Ah, you damned scarecrow, to think of your luring me with your old carcass! I expect the Pogorelka young lady has a sweetheart! I am sure she has! No wonder she gathered her skirts and made off. And here I've got to sit within four walls waiting till the old creature's fancy moves him!"

Yevpraxeya did not of course rebel openly straight away, but having once entered that path she went on and on. She searched for grievances, recalled the past, and while Iudushka did not even suspect that a hidden ferment was going on in her, she was silently working herself up to hate him. At first it was a case of general complaints such as "he's ruined my life"; then came comparisons. "There's Pelageya, the Mazulino housekeeper—she sits with her hands folded and wears silk dresses. She hasn't to go to the cattle-sheds or to the cellar but just sits in her room and knits with beads." All these protests and injuries ended in one general outcry:

"How I hate you, you horrid creature! My heart is simply boiling!"

This main reason was reinforced by another, which was particularly valuable as a possible means of attack: namely, the memories of her confinement and the disappearance of her son Volodya. At the time Yevpraxeya did not seem to take it in. Porphyry Vladimiritch merely told her that the baby had been placed in good hands and gave her a new shawl to comfort her. Then the subject was dropped and things went on as before. Indeed, Yevpraxeya threw herself more zealously than ever into the details of housekeeping, as though trying to make up for her disappointed motherhood. Whether the maternal feeling still secretly glowed in Yevpraxeya's heart or it was merely a fancy on her part, but the memory of Volodya suddenly revived in her. And it revived just when Yevpraxeya felt a breath of some new free life, different from the life at Golovlyovo. The pretext naturally was much too good to be ignored.

"To think what he's done!" she egged herself on. "Robbed me of my child. Just like drowning a puppy!"

Gradually this idea gained complete possession of her. She came to believe that she passionately longed to have her child back with her, and the more insistent was her desire, the greater was her anger against Porphyry Vladimiritch.

"I would have had something to cheer me, anyway! Volodya! Volodya darling! My own baby! Where are you, I wonder? I expect they packed you off to some rough peasant woman! Ah, perdition take you, you damned gentry! It's nothing to you to fling your own children into a ditch like puppies; you think no one will call you to task! I had much better have cut my throat there and then than let that filthy beast ruin me!"

She grew to hate him; she longed to vex him, to plague him, to poison his life. She opened the worst kind of war against him—a war of petty bickering, continual pinpricks and taunting. But it was only in a war of that kind Porphyry Vladimiritch could be defeated.

One day at breakfast Porphyry Vladimiritch had a very unpleasant surprise. Usually at that time he poured out floods of his putrid eloquence while Yevpraxeya listened to him in silence holding a saucer of tea in her hand and a lump of sugar between her teeth, and snorting occasionally. That day warm, newly baked bread had been served for breakfast, and he had just begun to develop the idea that there exist two kinds of bread, the visible which we *eat* to sustain our body and the invisible, spiritual bread of which we *partake* to nourish our soul, when Yevpraxeya interrupted him in a most unceremonious way.

"They say Pelageya has a fine time at Mazulino," she began, turning round to the window and swinging one leg.

Iudushka started slightly with surprise, but at first attached no particular importance to the incident.

"And if we go without the visible bread for long," he continued, "we feel bodily hunger; but if for any length of time we are deprived of the spiritual bread ..."

"I hear Pelageya has a fine time at Mazulino," Yevpraxeya interrupted him again, obviously with some object.

Porphyry Vladimiritch glanced at her in amazement, but refrained from pulling her up, as though scenting trouble.

"If Pelageya has a fine time—well and good, bless her," he answered meekly.

"Her master," Yevpraxeya rambled on, "does nothing to annoy her, or force her to work, and he always dresses her in silk."

Porphyry Vladimiritch was more and more amazed. Yevpraxeya's words were so utterly inconsequent that he did not know what to do.

"And she has a different dress every day," Yevpraxeya wandered on, as though in a dream. "To-day it's one dress, to-morrow another, and on holidays a special one. And they drive to church in a coach-and-four, first she, then the gentleman. And the priest has the bells rung as soon as he sees the carriage. And afterwards she sits in her room. If the master wishes to spend his time with her, she receives him and if not she just talks to her maid, or knits beads."

"Well, what of it?" Porphyry Vladimiritch recovered at last.

"Why, that Pelageya has a lovely time."

"And I suppose you think you have a bad time? Oh, oh, oh! What a ... greedy creature you are!"

Had Yevpraxeya said nothing, Porphyry Vladimiritch would of course have poured out a torrent of idle words, completely drowning all the idiotic hints that had disturbed the orderly flow of his eloquence. But Yevpraxeya was evidently in no mood to be silent.

"Of course," she snapped back, "I have a fine time too!

I am not in rags, and that's something to be thankful for! Last year you bought me two cotton dresses . . . forked out ten rubles for them."

"And have you forgotten the woolen dress? And who has just had a new shawl? Aie—aie—aie!"

Instead of answer Yevpraxeya leaned on the table the hand in which she held her saucer of tea and threw at Iudushka a side-glance full of such profound contempt that, not being used to it, he felt quite frightened.

"And do you know how God punishes ingratitude?" he lisped hesitatingly, hoping that perhaps the mention of God would sober the silly woman who had suddenly gone off the lines. But instead of being impressed, Yevpraxeya cut him short at once.

"It's no use trying to bamboozle me! No use bringing in God," she said, "I am not a baby. I've had too much of it. You've bullied me long enough. That will do."

Porphyry Vladimiritch was silent. His glass of tea was almost cold, but he did not touch it. His face was pale, his lips twitched slightly as though vainly trying to smile.

"These are Anna's tricks. She egged you on, the viper!" he said at last, hardly aware of what he was saying.

"What tricks?"

"Why, your beginning to talk to me. . . . She, she taught you that. It couldn't have been anyone else," Porphyry Vladimiritch said in agitation. "Just think of it, suddenly wanting silk dresses! But do you know, you shameless hussy, what women of your class wear silk?"

"Tell me, then I'll know."

"Why, the most . . . the most disreputable ones. Only they dress in silk!"

But even this did not bring Yevpraxeya to her senses. On the contrary, she answered with a kind of impudent reasonableness:

"I don't know why they are disreputable. . . . Naturally, it's what the gentry ask for. . . . If a gentleman makes love to a girl and gets round her . . . she lives with him, of course. I should have thought you and I didn't spend our times at prayers either, but did the same as the Mazulino gentleman."

"Oh, you . . . God bless us!"

Porphyry Vladimiritch turned positively livid with surprise. He looked open-eyed at his rebellious confederate, and a whole mass of idle words surged within him. But for the first time in his life he vaguely suspected that there are cases when even idle words can have no deadly effect.

"Well, my dear, I see it's no use talking to you to-day," he said, getting up from the table.

"It isn't any use to-day, and it won't be to-morrow . . . or ever again. That's the end. You've had your day. I've done my share of listening—now you listen to me."

Porphyry Vladimiritch rushed at her with clenched fists, but she thrust out her breast so resolutely that he was taken aback. Turning to the icon he raised his arms and moved his lips, and then slowly walked to his study.

He felt uncomfortable all that day. He had as yet no definite fears for the future, but he was upset by the mere fact that something quite irregular could have happened with impunity. He did not appear at dinner, pretending to be ill, and modestly asked in a voice of feigned weakness to have his meal brought to the study.

In the evening after tea, which, for the first time in his life passed in perfect silence, he stationed himself as usual before the icon for prayer; but his lips whispered the holy words in vain. His mind was too agitated to follow even superficially the meaning of what he was saying. A kind of petty but persistent restlessness possessed him; in spite of himself he tried to catch the last echoes of the day still audible in the different corners of the Golovlyovo house. When the last desperate yawn resounded somewhere behind the wall, and then all grew suddenly still, as though sinking deep down to the

bottom, he could control himself no longer. Noiselessly stealing along the passage he reached Yevpraxeya's room and put
his ear to the door. Yevpraxeya was alone and all that could
be heard was her saying through her yawns, "O Lord, our
Savior! Mother, Queen of Heaven!" and at the same time
scratching herself. Porphyry Vladimiritch tried the handle
but the door was locked.

"Yevpraxeya, are you there?" he called to her.

"Yes, but not for you!" she snapped back so rudely that Iudushka could do nothing but retire in silence to his study.

The following day there was another conversation. As
though of design, Yevpraxeya chose breakfast time for sting-
ing Porphyry Vladimiritch. She instinctively guessed as it
were that all his idling was timed to a nicety, so that a dis-
turbance in the morning caused him pain and uneasiness for
the rest of the day.

"I wish I could have a look at the way some people live!"
she began enigmatically.

Porphyry Vladimiritch had a twinge.

"She is at it again!" he thought but said nothing, waiting
for developments.

"Just to see how young sweethearts spend their time!
They walk about the rooms together admiring each other. He
never flings a bad word at her, nor she at him. 'My dear' and
'my darling' is all they say. So nice and refined!"

This subject was particularly distasteful to Porphyry Vladimiritch. Although he made allowances for fornication within
the strict limits of necessity, he regarded love-making as a
temptation of the devil. But this time again he had not the
courage of his convictions, especially as he wanted a drink of
tea which had been infusing on the samovar for some minutes,
and Yevpraxeya had apparently no intention of pouring it out.

"Of course, many of us women are just silly," she went on,
rocking herself insolently to and fro on her chair and drum-
ming on the table with her fingers. "Some of us are such nin-

nies that we are ready to do anything for the sake of a cotton frock, or, indeed, lose ourselves for nothing at all! ... 'Have as much kvass and as many cucumbers as you like,' you said. That's something to tempt one, isn't it?"

"But is it only for the sake of gain?" Porphyry Vladimiritch ventured to remark timidly, watching the teapot, which was steaming by now.

"Who says 'Only for the sake of gain'? Do you mean to say I am after gain?" Yevpraxeya went off at a tangent. "You grudge me my keep, do you? You throw that up at me!"

"I don't throw up anything at you, I merely say it isn't only for the sake of gain that people ..."

"You 'merely say'! Well, you must mind what you say! The idea of my serving you for gain! And what gain, may I ask, have I found here? Except kvass and cucumbers ..."

"Come, it's not only kvass and cucumbers ..." Porphyry Vladimiritch could not resist saying, carried away in his turn.

"Well, what else, say? Say, what else?"

"And who sends four sacks of flour to your home every month?"

"Yes, four sacks? Anything else?"

"Corn, Lenten oil ... all sorts of things, in fact."

"Yes, corn, Lenten oil.... So you grudge that to my parents now! Oh, you ..."

Yevpraxeya burst into tears. Meanwhile tea was stewing and stewing on the samovar, so that Porphyry Vladimiritch was seriously alarmed. Controlling himself, he sat down quietly beside Yevpraxeya and patted her on the back.

"Come, come, pour out the tea ... there's nothing to snivel about!"

Yevpraxeya gave two or three more sobs and stared dully in front of her, pouting her lips.

"You were talking of young men just now," he went on, trying to put a caressing note into his voice, "but after all, you know, I also ... I am not too old."

"What next! Leave me alone!"

"I assure you! ... Do you know ... when I was in the Department the head wanted me to marry his daughter."

"She must have been a stale one ... crooked or bandy-legged!"

"No, she was all a young lady should be. ... And the way she sang the *Sarafan*! Simply lovely!"

"She may have sung, but you were no good at seconding."

"Yes, I think I ..."

Porphyry Vladimiritch was perplexed. He was not above the ignominy of showing that he too could be a ladies' man. With this object he began rocking his body in an absurd way, and even tried to put his arm round Yevpraxeya's waist, but she rudely drew away from him and shouted angrily:

"I tell you civilly: leave me alone, you devil. I'll scald you with the boiling water if you don't! I don't want your tea. I don't want anything. Just think of it! Grudging me the food I eat! I won't stay here. Christ is my witness, I'll go!"

And she really did go, banging the door and leaving Porphyry Vladimiritch alone in the dining-room.

Iudushka was completely nonplussed. He began pouring out his tea himself but his hands trembled so that he had to call in the footman to his aid.

"No, this won't do! I must settle it somehow. ... I must think it over!" he whispered, walking up and down the dining-room in agitation.

But the trouble was he was incapable of "settling" or "thinking over" anything. His mind was so accustomed to wander from one fantastic object to another, without meeting any hindrance anywhere, that the simplest occurrence of everyday life caught him unawares. He no sooner began to "think something over" than a whole mass of trifles crowded around him, shutting out every glimpse of real life. He was a prey to a kind of laziness, a moral and intellectual anemia. He longed to turn from actual life to the soft bed of phantoms whom he could shift from place to place and do as he liked with.

Again he spent the whole day in complete solitude because this time Yevpraxeya did not appear either at dinner or at evening tea. She went for a day's visit to the village priest's and returned only late at night. He could not occupy himself with anything because even trifles seemed to have forsaken him for the moment. One relentless thought tormented him: "I must settle it somehow, I must." He could not do his idle calculations or repeat his prayers. He felt as though he were attacked by some disease which he could not as yet define. More than once he stopped before the window trying to fasten his wandering thought on something and to distract himself, but in vain. It was early spring, but the trees were bare and there was not yet any new grass. Black fields stretched in the distance with patches of white snow here and there in the hollows and low-lying places. The road was black with mud and shining with pools. But he saw it all as it were through a mist. The wet outbuildings were completely deserted, and yet all the doors were wide open: in the house too there was no one within call, although the sound as of doors banging was continually heard in the distance. It would be fine to become invisible now and to hear what that brood of Ham was talking about. Did the wretches understand how good he was to them, or were they speaking evil of him in return for his good fare? One might shovel the food down their throats from morning till night and they'd never be satisfied or think anything of it. It wasn't long since they had started a new barrel of cucumbers and already . . . But he no sooner began to forget himself in this thought, reckoning out how many cucumbers there would be in a barrel and what would be a liberal allowance of cucumbers per person, than a gleam of reality flashed through his mind again, upsetting at once all his calculations.

"Fancy her going off, without even asking permission!"

came into his head while his eyes wandered through space trying to make out the priest's house, where at that moment Yevpraxeya was probably pouring out her woes.

Dinner was served. Porphyry Vladimiritch sat at the table alone, listlessly eating clear soup (he could not bear clear soup but *she* had ordered it on purpose that day).

"I expect the priest is pretty sick at her descending upon him like this!" passed through his mind. "It means adding something to their dinner, anyway. Cabbage soup and porridge . . . and perhaps some meat as well because of the visitor."

His imagination began to play again and he forgot himself once more as though he were dropping asleep. How many tablespoonfuls of soup and of porridge would there be? And what are the priest and his wife saying about Yevpraxeya's visit? How they are slanging her to themselves! . . . All this—the food and the conversations—came vividly before his mind.

"I expect they all eat out of the same bowl. . . . She's gone! She could think of no better treat! It's wet and muddy outside, not safe to go out. She'd return with her skirts all bedraggled. Ah, the reptile! Yes, that's just what she is. Yes, I must, I must think of something . . ."

His thoughts invariably broke off at that point. After dinner he lay down to have a sleep as usual but merely wore himself out turning over from side to side. Yevpraxeya came home after dark and stole into her room so quietly that he had not noticed it. He had ordered the servants to be sure and tell him when she returned, but the servants seemed to be in league with her and said nothing. He tried her door but again found it locked.

The following day Yevpraxeya did appear at breakfast, but her talk was more aggressive and menacing than ever.

"I wonder where my Volodya is now?" she began in a tearful voice.

Porphyry Vladimiritch turned livid at the question. "If only I could have a peep at him and see what a hard time he's having there, the darling! And very likely he is already dead.... Yes!..."

Iudushka moved his lips in agitation, whispering a prayer.

"We never do things like other people! Pelageya bore a daughter to the Mazulino gentleman and they at once dressed her up in finest cambric and rigged up a pink little cot for her... And the wet-nurse had no end of *sarafans* and head-dresses given her! But with us... o-oh... you!"

Yevpraxeya turned sharply to the window and sighed noisily.

"It's true what they say, that the gentry is a cursed lot! They bring children in the world and throw them away like puppies. And they don't care a bit! They don't answer to any-one for it, God is nothing to them. Not even a wolf would behave like that!"

Porphyry Vladimiritch was simply boiling inwardly. He tried to control himself but at last could not resist saying through his teeth:

"I must say... you've started a new fashion! It's the third day I am listening to your talk!"

"Well, it is a new fashion! Call it that if you like. You aren't the only one to do all the talking—other people too can put in a word! Yes, indeed! You gave me a child and what have you done to it? I expect it's rotting away at some peasant woman's. No one to look after him, no food, no clothes.... He lies in the dirt, I expect, sucking a filthy comforter."

She shed a tear and wiped her eyes with a corner of the kerchief round her neck.

"The Pogorelka young lady was right when she said that it's fearful to be with you. Fearful it is. No joy, no pleasure, nothing but mean tricks.... Convicts in prison live better. If at least I had my baby now, I should have had something to distract me, anyway. But just think of it! I've had a child and been robbed of it!"

Porphyry Vladimiritch sat still moving his head painfully

as though he were being pushed to the wall. Groans escaped him from time to time.

"Ah, it's hard!" he brought out at last.

"No use saying it's hard! You've brought it on yourself. I really think I'll go to Moscow and have a peep at Volodya. Volodya! Volodya! Da-arling! Hadn't I better go to Moscow, master?"

"No need to," Porphyry Vladimiritch answered dully.

"Yes, I'll go! I won't ask anyone's permission, and no one can forbid me to go! Because I am a mother!"

"A mother, indeed! You are no better than a whore, that's what you are!" Porphyry Vladimiritch broke out at last. "Tell me, what do you want of me?"

Yevpraxeya was evidently not prepared for this question. She stared at Iudushka in silence, as though wondering what it was she really did want.

"So now you call me a whore!" she cried, bursting into tears.

"Yes, a whore! A whore! That's what you are, curse you!"

Losing all self-control, Porphyry Vladimiritch jumped up from his seat and almost ran out of the dining-room.

That was the last outburst of energy that he indulged in. After that he soon went downhill and grew dull and timid, while Yevpraxeya persecuted him as relentlessly as ever. She had the tremendous force of obstinate stupidity at her disposal, and since that force was always applied to one object only—to pester him, to poison his life—it was really terrible at times. She gradually found the arena of the dining-room too small for her, and invaded the study, attacking Iudushka there. (In the old days she would not have dared to think of going there when master was "busy.") She came in, sat down by the window, scratched her shoulder-blades against the window-frame and, staring dully in front of her, meandered on. There was one subject that she liked particularly—conversations about her leaving Golovlyovo. As a matter of fact she had never seriously thought of it and would have been very much surprised had she suddenly been offered to return to her parents; but she guessed that Porphyry Vladimiritch feared her going more than anything. She always approached the subject gradually, by side-tracks. She would be silent for a bit, scratch her ear, and then as it were suddenly recall something.

"I expect they are baking pancakes at home to-day."

This introduction made Porphyry Vladimiritch turn green with malice. He had just begun a very complicated calculation: how many rubles' worth of milk could he sell a year if all the cows in the neighborhood died and only his, with God's help, remained alive, and produced twice as much milk as before. However, in view of Yevpraxeya's coming in and mentioning pancakes, he gave up his work and actually tried to smile.

"Why are they baking pancakes there?" he asked, twisting his face into a smile. "Dear me, yes, of course, it's Commemoration Day. I had quite forgotten, thoughtless me! How dreadful, we'll have nothing to eat in dear mamma's memory!"

"I should like to have some pancakes...my mother's pancakes!"

"Well, why not? Give orders. Tell the cook or Ulita. Ah, Ulita makes excellent pancakes."

"Perhaps she's pleased you about something else as well?" Yevpraxeya said maliciously.

"No, it would be a sin to deny it—Ulita makes excellent pancakes, light and soft. One simply can't stop eating them!"

Porphyry Vladimiritch thought of distracting Yevpraxeya by playful talk and laughter.

"I should like to have some pancakes but at home, not at Golovlyovo!" she went on giving herself airs.

"Well, that's quite feasible too. Get hold of Arhip the coachman, order a pair of horses, and drive there in style."

"No, what's the good! Once the bird is caught in the net . . . It was my own foolishness. Nobody wants a girl like me. You yourself called me a whore the other day. . . . Nothing is any good now."

"Aie-aie-aie! Aren't you ashamed to bring such charges against me? Don't you know how God punishes one for slander?"

"You did call me that! You said so straight out. The icon here is my witness. It was in Our Lord's presence you said so! Oh, I am sick of this Golovlyovo. I'll run away from here, I really will."

Yevpraxeya behaved in a most free and easy manner as she said this. She rocked herself on her chair, scratched herself, picked her nose. She was obviously acting a part, teasing him.

"I wanted to tell you something, Porphyry Vladimiritch," she wandered on. "I must go home, you know."

"Go there on a visit, you mean?"

"No, go for good. I shall stay there."

"Why is that? Are you offended, or what?"

"No, I am not offended, but still . . . I must go sometime . . . and besides it's so dull here . . . it makes me frightened. The house might be dead. The servants have got out of hand, they are always in the kitchens or in their own quarters. I have to sit alone in the house. One might easily be murdered at that rate. When one goes to bed at night whispers seem to creep out of every corner."

Day followed day, however, and Yevpraxeya did not show any sign of carrying out her threats. Nevertheless that threat had a most crushing effect on Porphyry Vladimiritch. He suddenly seemed to understand that, although he slaved away from morning till night at so-called work, he did not really do anything, and could be left without dinner, clean linen, or decent clothes if someone did not watch over the smooth working of his daily routine. So far he had not seemed as it were to be conscious of life or to grasp that it had an external setting which did not come into being of itself. His days had been spent in a way fixed once for all. Everything in the house centered round him and existed for his sake. Everything was done at the appointed time, every object was in its proper place—in short, such unfailing regularity reigned in all things that he practically failed to notice it. Thanks to this established order he could devote himself to his heart's content to idle thinking and idle talk without any fear that the stings of life might one day force him to face reality. True, all this artificial arrangement hung by a thread; but a man entirely self-centered was not likely to be struck by the thought that that thread was very fine and easily broken. He fancied that his life had been regulated once for all.... And suddenly everything was to crumble away at one stupid phrase, "No, what's the good? I'd better go." Iudushka was utterly discomfited. "What if she really does go?" he thought. He began planning all sorts of absurd arrangements in order to retain her somehow, and actually made up his mind to such concessions in favor of Yevpraxeya's rebellious youth as would never have occurred to him before.

"God bless us!" He dismissed the thought in disgust when he pictured to himself with mortifying clearness a possible encounter with Arhip the coachman or Ignat the accountant.

Soon, however, he came to the conclusion that his fears of Yevpraxeya leaving had been unfounded; and after that his life suddenly took a new and completely unexpected turn. Yevpraxeya did not go away, and she no longer pestered him. Instead, she completely neglected Porphyry Vladimiritch. It was May, the weather was lovely, and she was hardly ever in the house now. It was only from the banging of doors that Iudushka guessed she had run into her room for something and immediately disappeared again. Getting up in the morning he failed to find his clothes in the usual place, and had to carry on long negotiations to obtain a change of linen; his tea and dinner were served either too early or too late; the waiting at table was done by the footman Prohor, always slightly tipsy, dressed in a stained coat and smelling of some disgusting mixture of fish and vodka.

But Porphyry Vladimiritch was glad that at any rate Yevpraxeya left him in peace. He did not even mind the disorder so long as he knew that there was someone in the house responsible for it. What he feared was not so much the discomfort as the thought that he might have to take a personal part in the practical details of life. He pictured to himself with horror that a moment might come when he would have to give orders, to superintend, to make arrangements. In the anticipation of that moment he tried to stifle every protest, he closed his eyes to the anarchy that reigned in the house, made himself scarce, said nothing. And meanwhile regular festivals were held every day in the courtyard. With the warm weather Golovlyovo, that had always been sedate and even gloomy, seemed to come to life. In the evening all the servants and their families, old and young, the superannuated and the workers, gathered in the courtyard. They sang, played the accordion, laughed, shrieked, had games. Ignat the accountant wore a flaming red shirt and an extremely narrow jacket that did not meet across his manly chest; Arhip the coachman had taken possession of the driving outfit—the silk shirt and velveteen sleeveless jerkin—and was obviously rivaling Ignat's claims on Yevpraxeya's heart. Yevpraxeya played with them both and dashed like mad from one to the other. Porphyry Vladimiritch was afraid of looking out of the window for fear of witnessing a love-scene. At times his ears caught the sound of a heavy blow: it was Arhip the coachman giving a good smack to Yevpraxeya as he chased her in the *catch who can* (she was not cross but merely winced a little); at times a conversation reached him:

"Yevpraxeya Nikitishna! I say, Yevpraxeya Nikitishna!"
the drunken Prohor was calling from the front steps.

"What is it?"

"Give me, please, the key of the tea-caddy, master asks
for tea."

"He can wait . . . the scarecrow."

In a short time Porphyry Vladimiritch had become a complete recluse. The whole of his daily routine had been upset
but he appeared to take no longer any notice of it. All he
asked of life was that he should not be disturbed in his last
refuge—his study. Just as once he had been tiresome and exacting towards other people, so now he was timid and sullenly submissive. He seemed to have lost all touch with real
life. His one wish was not to hear anything, not to see anyone. Yevpraxeya might not show herself in the house for days
at a time, the servants might take any liberties they liked,
idling in the courtyard—he was as indifferent to it all as
though it did not exist. In the old days had the accountant
been in the least remiss in drawing up reports about the various branches of estate management he would have worn him
out with sermonizing; now he had to sit for weeks without
any reports, and he did not mind except on the rare occasions
when he needed some figures to confirm his fantastic calculations. But when he was by himself in his study he felt perfectly independent and free to indulge in idle thinking to his
heart's content. Both his brothers had died victims of an un-
controllable passion for drink; he too suffered from a similar
disease, but his was a different sort of drunkenness, a mental
intoxication. Shutting himself up in his study and settling
down to his writing-table he toiled away from morning
till night at fantastic work: he made all kinds of impossible

projects, checked his expenditure, talked to imaginary people, and acted whole scenes in which anyone he happened to
think of had a part to play.

The chief element in this whirl of fantastic actions and
images was a morbid passion for gain. Porphyry Vladimiritch
had always been mean and pettifogging, but he derived no
benefit from it because all he did was absurdly impractical.
He pestered, tormented, and oppressed other people (chiefly
the most helpless ones, who, so to speak, invited ill-treatment),
but more often than not he himself was the loser, through
being too clever. Now he entirely transferred his activities to
an abstract fantastic world where there was no one to oppose
or contradict him, where there were no distinctions between
the weak and the strong, no policemen, no justices of peace
(or rather where they existed solely for the sake of defending
his interests), and where, consequently, he was free to entan-
gle the whole world in a network of litigation, oppression,
and trickery.

He enjoyed the thought of tormenting people, ruining
them, spoiling their lives, bleeding them. He went in turn over
the various items of his revenue: timber, cattle, corn meadows, etc., and built round each of them an intricate system of
fantastic extortions accompanied by the most complicated
calculations of profits to be derived from fines, usury, national
calamities, stocks, and shares. In short, he created for himself
a whole complex world made up of all the sterile ideals of a
landowner's idle fancy. And since it all rested upon arbitrary
assumptions with regard to supposed payments, a kopeck too
much or too little provided an opportunity for reconstructing
the whole thing and thus varying it *ad infinitum*. When his
mind was too tired to follow with due attention the details of
his involved financial operations, he occupied it with less exacting fancies. He recalled all the disputes and quarrels he
had had with people, not only of recent years but in his early
youth, and reconstructed them so as to come out victorious

from every conflict. He mentally revenged himself on his former colleagues who had outstripped him in the service and wounded his vanity so deeply that he decided to retire; he revenged himself on his old schoolfellows who had once taken advantage of their strength to tease and bully him; on neighbors who had resisted his encroachments and defended their rights; on servants who had been rude or insufficiently respectful to him; on his mamma for having spent on Pogorelka a great deal of money which "by rights" belonged to him; on his brother Styopka the dolt for having nicknamed him "little Judas"; on his aunt Varvara Mihailovna because, when no one was any longer expecting it, she bore several children of doubtful parentage, and thus caused the Goryushkino estate to be for ever lost to the Golovlyov family. He revenged himself on the living, he revenged himself on the dead.

Indulging his fancy in this way he gradually became as it were drunk; the ground slipped from under his feet, he felt as though he had wings. His eyes glittered, his trembling lips were covered with foam, his face turned pale and looked menacing. And as his imagination grew more active, the air around him became crowded with phantoms that engaged him in an imaginary struggle.

His existence was now so full and self-sufficient that he had nothing more to desire. The whole world was at his feet—that is, the poor and limited world within his narrow field of vision. He could vary endlessly the simplest theme, taking it up again and again, and each time giving it a new form. It was a kind of intoxication, something similar to what happens at spiritualistic seances. Uncontrolled imagination creates an illusory reality which, owing to perpetual mental excitement, becomes concrete, almost tangible. It is not faith, it is not conviction—it is intoxication, spiritual debauchery. Men cease to be human, their faces are distorted, their eyes glitter, their tongues babble incoherently, their bodies make involuntary movements.

Porphyry Vladimiritch was happy. He tightly shut his

windows and doors not to hear and pulled down the blinds not to see. All that was not directly concerned with the world of his fancy he did in a hurry, almost with aversion. When Prohor, always slightly tipsy, knocked at his door to say that dinner was ready he ran impatiently to the dining-room, contrary to all his habits, hurriedly ate his three courses, and disappeared in his study again. When he met people, his manner was both timid and stupidly ironical, as though he were afraid and defiant at the same time. He was in a hurry to get up in the morning so as to set to work as soon as possible. He spent less time at his devotions; he uttered the words of the prayers indifferently, without attending to their meaning; he crossed himself and raised his arms carelessly, mechanically. Even the thought of hell and its tortures (with special punishments for each sin) had apparently left him.

Yevpraxeya meanwhile was languishing in the throes of fleshly lust. Prancing in indecision between Ignat the accountant and Arhip the coachman, and casting sidelong glances at the red-faced carpenter Ilusha, who had contracted with his men to repair the cellar, she noticed nothing of what was going on in the house. She thought that the master was playing "some new trick," and many cheerful remarks had been passed about it in the friendly company of flunkeys, who had lost all sense of restraint. But one day she happened to come into the dining-room while Iudushka was hastily finishing a piece of roast goose, and she suddenly felt frightened.

Porphyry Vladimiritch was wearing a greasy dressing-gown with pieces of the quilted lining showing in places; he was pale, disheveled, and had several days' growth on his cheeks and chin.

"Master dear! What is it? What has happened?" she rushed to him in alarm.

But Porphyry Vladimiritch merely smiled a stupidly sardonic smile by way of answer, as though to say, "You try and see if you can wound me now!"

"But what is it, master dear? Tell me, what has happened?" she repeated.

He stood up, and fixing upon her a glance full of hatred, said deliberately:

"If you ever dare, you whore, to go into my study again, I'll . . . kill you!"

As a result of this encounter Porphyry Vladimiritch's domestic arrangements changed for the better. With no material cares to hinder him, he wholly abandoned himself to solitude and did not even notice the summer pass. It was the end of August; the days had grown shorter; there was a continual drizzle outside; it was wet underfoot; the trees stood dejectedly, dropping their yellow leaves on the ground. Unbroken stillness reigned in the yard and outside the kitchens; the servants kept to their own quarters, partly because of the bad weather and partly because they guessed that something had gone wrong with their master. Yevpraxeya had completely recovered and thought no more of sweethearts and silk dresses; she sat for hours on the box in the maids' room not knowing what to do or to decide. Prohor taunted her by saying that she had poisoned the master and would be sure to be sent to Siberia for it.

Iudushka meanwhile sat shut up in his study, lost in dreams. He liked it all the better that the weather had turned cold; the rain ceaselessly pattering on his windows made him drowsy, and his imagination had all the more scope and freedom. He fancied that he was invisible, and in that guise was inspecting his possessions accompanied by old Ilya, who was bailiff in his papa's, Vladimir Mihailitch's, time, and had been dead and buried years ago.

"A sensible peasant, that Ilya! An old-fashioned servant! Such men are rare nowadays. The people to-day are ready enough with their tongues, but as soon as it's a question of work, there's no one to be had!" Porphyry Vladimiritch reasoned with himself, very pleased that Ilya had risen from the dead.

Without haste or bustle, unseen by anyone, they leisurely made their way over fields and ravines, across meadows and dales to the Uhovshchina wood—and could not believe their eyes. A huge forest rose before them like a wall, with the tree-tops murmuring overhead. They were splendid trees, red pines that two or even three men could not clasp round; the trunks were straight and bare and the tops huge and bushy—that meant the forest had still a long life before it!

"Now this is something like a forest!" Iudushka exclaimed in delight.

"It's been preserved," old Ilya explained, "it had been blessed with icons in your grandfather's, Mihail Vassilyevitch's, time—and see how it's grown!"

"How many acres is it, do you think?"

"At that time it measured just two hundred and ten, but now . . . the acre in those days meant about an acre and a half at the present reckoning."

"And how many trees do you think there are to an acre?"

"God only knows! He alone counted them."

"I think there is sure to be about two hundred to an acre. Not by the old reckoning but by the present. Wait a minute. If it's two hundred . . . or, say, two hundred and fifteen to an acre—how much will it be on three hundred and fifteen acres?

Porphyry Vladimiritch took a piece of paper and multiplied 215 by 315; it proved to be 67,725 trees.

"If now we were to sell all this forest . . . for timber . . . do you think each tree would fetch ten rubles?"

Old Ilya shook his head.

"That's not enough!" he said. "Just see what trees they are! Each tree would make two mill-shafts, and a good beam for any purpose, and two smaller ones, and then there are the branches. . . . What do you imagine a mill-shaft costs?"

Porphyry Vladimiritch pretended not to know, though in truth he had calculated it all down to the last farthing long ago.

"In these parts the shaft alone is worth ten rubles, and in Moscow it would be simply priceless. Think what a shaft that would make! Three horses could only just draw it. And then another smaller shaft and a beam, and another beam, and logs, and twigs. . . . A tree would fetch twenty rubles at the lowest."

Porphyry Vladimiritch could go on listening to Ilya for ever. That Ilya was a sensible man, a faithful servant! And indeed he was very lucky with his servants altogether. Ilya's assistant was old Vavilo (he too had long been dead and buried) —he was a staunch one! His accountant was Filka, whom mamma had brought from the Vologda estate some sixty years ago; the foresters were experienced, trusty men; the dogs by the granaries were fierce. Both the men and the dogs were ready to seize the devil himself by the throat in defending their master's property!

"Now, let us see, brother, what will it come to if we sell the whole forest for timber."

Porphyry Vladimiritch calculated once more in his mind the price of the mill-shaft, of the smaller shaft, of the beam, of the smaller beam, of the logs and twigs. He added the figures together, and multiplied them, leaving out the fractions in one place and adding them in another. The piece of paper was covered with figures.

"Look, brother, see what it comes to!" Iudushka showed the imaginary Ilya such an unheard-of figure that Ilya, who was by no means averse to increasing his master's property, seemed taken aback.

"It seems too much, you know!" he said hesitatingly, shrugging his shoulders.

But Porphyry Vladimiritch had thrown away all doubts and was chuckling gaily.

"You queer fellow! That's not my doing, it's what the figures say.... There's a science, brother, called arithmetic ... you may be sure it won't deceive you! Well, now we have finished here; let's go to the Fox's Pits, I haven't been there for ages. I have an idea that the peasants are up to mischief there, I very much fear they are! And Garanka the watchman ... I know, I know! He is a good servant, trusty and hardworking—there's no gainsaying that! And yet ... he seems to have got a bit slack lately."

Unseen and unheard they made their way through the thicket of birches, and suddenly stopped with bated breath. A peasant's cart lay upturned on the road, and the peasant stood by, looking ruefully at the broken axle. After grieving over it he swore at the axle and at himself, and gave his horse a cut with the whip ("Oh, you doodle!"); but something had to be done—he could not spend the night there! The thievish peasant looked round and listened if anyone was coming; then he selected a birch-tree and pulled out his ax.... Iudushka stood by, not stirring a limb. The birch-tree shuddered, waved, and suddenly fell on the ground. The peasant was just going to cut off the thick end a piece big enough for the axle when Iudushka decided that the moment for action had come. He stole up to the peasant and instantly snatched the ax out of his hands....

"Oh!" cried the thief caught unawares.

"Oh!" Porphyry Vladimiritch mimicked him, "and is it allowed to steal other people's wood? Oh, indeed! And was it your own birch you've just cut down?"

"Forgive me, sir!"

"I've forgiven everyone long ago, brother! I am a sinner myself and dare not condemn others. It's not I but the law condemns you. Take to my house the birch you've cut down for the axle, and you may as well bring a ruble's fine with you; and meanwhile I'll keep your ax! Don't be uneasy, I'll take care of it!"

Pleased to have proved to Ilya how right he was about Garanka, Porphyry Vladimiritch went in his mind from the spot of the crime to the forester's hut and reprimanded him as befitted the occasion. Then he went home, and on the way caught in his oats three fowls belonging to the peasants. Returning to his study he set to work again, and suddenly a new economic system came into his mind. He thought of all that grew on his land, whether sown by him or not, in terms of prices it could fetch in the market or of damages that could be claimed for it. The peasants did nothing but cut down his wood and spoil his corn and meadows, and instead of being grieved by it he actually rubbed his hands with pleasure.

"Do as much damage as you like, my dears, it's all the better for me!" he repeated with satisfaction.

And he immediately took up a new sheet of paper and began reckoning and calculating.

How much oats could be grown on an acre, and how much would it fetch if the peasants' fowls trampled it down and he received damages for it all?

"And though the oats were trampled down the crop recovered after rain, thank heaven!" Iudushka added mentally.

How many birches grew in Fox's Pits, and how much would they fetch if the peasants cut them down and paid damages for all they had tried to steal?

"And the birches that had been cut down will serve me as fuel, so I won't have to spend anything on firewood," Iudushka added in his mind again.

The paper was covered with huge columns of figures—rubles, tens, hundreds, thousands of rubles. Iudushka was so exhausted by his work and so agitated by it that he got up from the table bathed in perspiration and lay down on the sofa to rest. But his turbulent imagination refused to stop working and merely selected another and an easier subject.

"Mamma was a clever woman," Porphyry Vladimiritch rambled on. "She was exacting but she knew how to be kind also, and that's why people liked working for her. But she too had her weaknesses! The old lady has many sins on her conscience!"

No sooner had Iudushka mentioned Arina Petrovna than she appeared before him; her heart must have told her that she had to give an answer and she came from her grave to her dear son.

"I don't know, dear, I really don't know what wrong I have done you," she said despondently. "I believe, I . . ."

"Tut—tut—tut, my dear! Don't you pretend!" Iudushka pulled her up unceremoniously. "If it's come to that, I'll put it all plainly to you! Why, for instance, didn't you stop Auntie Varvara Mihailovna at that time?"

"But how could I! She was of age and could do what she pleased with herself!"

"Oh no, allow me! What sort of husband had she? Old and drunken . . . the very useless sort, that is! And yet she had four children. . . . Where did those children come from, I ask you?"

"How strangely you talk, my dear! As though I were the cause of it!"

"Not the cause, but still you might have influenced her! Had you tried joking her and being nice to her, she might have had qualms about it—but you were always against her! Always riding the high horse. It was nothing but 'that horrid woman,' that 'shameless Varka'! You made out all the neighbors were her lovers! And so naturally . . . it put her back up. Pity! Goryushkino would have been ours now!"

"You are always after that Goryushkino," said Arina Petrovna, evidently nonplussed by her son's accusations.

"Oh, I don't care about Goryushkino! I don't want anything for myself, really. If I have enough to buy a votive candle and lamp oil, I am content. But speaking generally, and considering the justice of it . . . Yes, mamma, I don't like talking about it but I can't help saying it's a sin on your conscience, a great sin!"

Arina Petrovna made no answer and merely threw up her hands in distress or perplexity.

"Or take another thing," Iudushka went on, enjoying his mother's discomfiture. "Why did you buy that house in Moscow for my brother Stepan?"

"I had to, my dear! I had to chuck him a piece," said Arina Petrovna justifying herself.

"And he went and squandered it! As though you didn't know him: he was rowdy, disrespectful, and foul-tongued—and yet you did it! And you wanted to give him papa's Vologda estate too! A lovely little estate! All in one piece, with a nice little wood and a lake, no neighbors, no other people's land intervening . . . all trim and neat, like a shelled egg, bless it! Good thing I happened to be present and stopped you. . . . Ah, mamma, aren't you ashamed of yourself?"

"But after all he was my son. . . . Don't you understand? My son!"

"I know and I understand very well! But still you shouldn't have done it. No, you shouldn't. The house cost twelve thousand silver rubles—and where are they now? That's twelve thousand gone, and Auntie Varvara Mihailovna's Goryushkino, poor as it is, must be worth at least fifteen thousand. . . . So it comes to a lot altogether."

"Come, come, that will do. Don't be cross, for heaven's sake!"

"I am not cross, mamma, I am only considering the justice of it. . . . What is true is true—I can't bear lies! Truthful I was born, truthful I have lived, and truthful I will die! God loves truth and tells us to love it too. Or take Pogorelka now—I will always say you wasted a lot of money on improving it."

"But I lived there myself."

Iudushka read in his mother's face the words, "You ridiculous bloodsucker!" but pretended not to see.

"Never mind that you lived there, it was a waste all the same. . . . The icon-stand is at Pogorelka to this day, and whose is it? And that little horse too; and the tea-caddy. . . . I saw it with my own eyes at Golovlyovo while papa was still living. And a very pretty caddy it is!"

"Oh, that's nothing!"

"No, mamma, don't say that! One doesn't see it at once, of course, but when it's a ruble here, and fifty kopecks there, and twenty-five there . . . If one looks at it and considers . . . Allow me, though, I'll work it all out in figures. There's nothing better than figures—they never deceive one."

Porphyry Vladimiritch rushed to his desk once more in order to make quite clear at last what losses his kind friend mamma had brought upon him. He rattled the counting-beads, wrote down columns of figures—in short, made ready to convince Arina Petrovna of her misdeeds. Fortunately for her, his wandering thought could not dwell on any subject for long. A new object of gain unnoticeably came into his mind and, as though by magic, gave quite a new turn to his thoughts. Arina Petrovna, whom he had seen so vividly only a minute before, suddenly dropped into the well of forgetfulness. The figures grew muddled.

Porphyry Vladimiritch had long been meaning to calculate how much he could make by farming his land, and now was precisely the moment for it. He knew that the peasants were always in need, always wanting to borrow, and always paying their debts with interest. The peasants were particularly lavish about their labor, which "cost nothing," and in settling their accounts was just thrown in, for love. There are many needy people in Russia. Oh, how many! Many do not know to-day what awaits them to-morrow. Many look round despondently and see nothing but a hopeless void, hear nothing but the words "pay back." It is those despairing people, those poor starvelings that Iudushka entangled in his web, going off sometimes into the wildest flights of fancy.

It was April and the peasants as usual had no corn left. "They've eaten all they had, idling all the winter, and so in the spring they have to tighten their belts!" Iudushka reflected. As it happened, he had just put his accounts of last year's farming into perfect order. In February the last stacks of corn had been thrashed, in March the grain was stored away, and the other day he put it all down in the appropriate columns of his account books. Iudushka was standing at the window waiting. In the distance, the peasant Foka appeared on the bridge in his old cart. At the cross-roads to Golovlyovo he hurriedly pulled at the reins, and for lack of whip, brandished his arm at the horse, that could scarcely move its legs.

"He's coming here!" Iudushka whispered. "The state his horse is in! Why, it's barely alive! But if it were fed for a month or two it wouldn't be a bad beast. It would be worth a good twenty-five rubles, perhaps thirty."

Meanwhile Foka had driven up to the servants' cottage, tied his horse to the fence, gave it some small hay, and a minute later was shifting from one foot to the other in the maids' room, where Porphyry Vladimiritch generally received petitioners.

"Well, my friend, what have you to tell me?"

"I have come to ask you for some rye, sir."

"How so? So you've eaten all you had? Dear me, what a pity! If now you drank less vodka and worked more, and gave more time to prayer, the earth would feel that, you know! Where you now gather one grain you would gather two or three—and you wouldn't have to borrow!"

Foka smiled irresolutely by way of an answer.

"You imagine God is far off and so He doesn't see?" Porphyry Vladimiritch went on moralizing. "Oh no, God is near enough. Here and there and everywhere—with us now while we are talking. And He sees and hears everything, He only makes it appear as though He didn't. Let men live by their own devices, He thinks, We'll see if they'll remember Me! And we take

287

advantage of this, and instead of sparing some of our earnings
for a votive candle we take it all to the pot-house! And that's
why God doesn't give us a good harvest. Isn't that so, friend?"

"There's no gainsaying that. That's true enough!"

"There, you see, now you have grasped it too. And why
have you grasped it? Because God has taken His favor from
you. If you had had a good harvest, you would be giving yourselves airs again! But now that God . . ."

"That's right. If now we . . ."

"Wait, let me have my say! God always sends a reminder,
my man, to those who forget Him. And we mustn't murmur
against Him because of it but understand that it's done for
our own good. Had we remembered God, He wouldn't have
forgotten us either. He would have given us everything: lovely
rye, and fine oats, and delicious potatoes—there, have as
much as you like! And He would have looked after your ani-
mals too—and now, see, your horse is almost at its last gasp!
And He would have given a good start to your poultry, if you
have any!"

"You are right there, Porphyry Vladimiritch."

"To honor God—that's the first thing, and then to honor
your superiors, who have received distinction from the Tsars
. . . the landed gentry, for instance . . ."

"But Porphyry Vladimiritch, I believe we . . ."

"You 'believe,' but if you think about it you'll find it's not
so. Now that you've come to ask me for some rye, there's no
denying you are very nice and respectful; but the year before
last, you remember, when I wanted hands for the harvest and
had to ask a favor from you peasants, saying, 'Please help me,
brothers,' what did you answer? 'We have our own harvest
to see to,' you said. 'We needn't work for the gentry like in
the old days, now we are free,' you said. You are free, but you
have no rye!"

Porphyry Vladimiritch looked admonishingly at Foka, who
stood stock-still.

"You are too proud, that's why you have no luck! Take me, for instance. One would have thought God has given me grace and the Tsar his favor, and yet I am not proud. How could I be? What am I? A worm! A midge! Nothing! And here God has blessed me for my humility. He's bestowed grace upon me Himself, and inspired the Tsar to show me favor!"

"I reckon we had a far better time in the old days, Porphyry Vladimiritch, when we had masters," said Foka to flatter him.

"Yes, brother, you have had your good times. You had a fine time of it. You had everything—rye, and hay, and potatoes! Well, it's no use remembering old scores, I am not one to do that. I had forgotten all about those harvest hands, brother, and merely recalled it by the way. And so you say you want some rye?"

"Yes please, sir."

"Do you want to buy some?"

"No chance of that! Perhaps you would lend me some till the new harvest."

"Dear, dear! Rye is worth a good deal nowadays. I don't know what I'd better do about it. . . ."

Porphyry Vladimiritch sunk into thought for a moment, as though really not knowing what to do: "I should like to help the man, but rye is very dear. . . ."

"Very well, my friend, I can lend you some rye," he said at last, "and, to tell you the truth, I haven't any for sale. I can't bear to deal in God's gifts. But to lend it—that's another matter, and I shall be pleased to do it. I never forget, you know, that to-day you borrow from me, the next day I may have to borrow from you. To-day I have plenty—take it, borrow as much as you like. If you want six bushels—take six. If you want three—help yourself to three. And to-morrow it may come to pass that I'll have to knock at your window and say, 'Lend me a little rye, Foka, I have nothing to eat.'"

"Is it likely, sir!"

"Of course not, but I give it as an instance.... Worse changes than that happen in the world, my man! Here they write in the papers that Napoleon, high and mighty as he was, has come to grief—not good enough, it appears. So that's that, brother. How much rye do you want?"

"Six bushels, if you are so kind."

"Very well, six bushels. Only I warn you, rye is very dear nowadays, my man, frightfully dear! So I'll tell you what we'll do: I'll give you four and a half bushels, and in eight months' time you bring me back six—that will be just right. I don't charge interest but take it back in kind, out of your plenty...."

Iudushka's offer took Foka's breath away. He said nothing for a time and merely wriggled his shoulders.

"Isn't that too much, sir?" he brought out timidly at last.

"If it's too much—ask someone else! I don't force you, friend, but offer it you in all kindness. I didn't send for you, you came to me yourself. You ask me a question and I give you an answer. So that's that, my friend."

"That is so, but it seems a great deal to pay back."

"Aie—aie—aie! And I thought you were a steady, fair-minded man! And what do you expect *me* to live on? How am I to provide for my expenses? Do you know what my expenses are? There is simply no end to them. I have to give to that one, and to satisfy another, and to produce something for a third. Everyone needs something, everyone goes for Porphyry Vladimiritch, and Porphyry Vladimiritch has to answer for all! Then there's another thing: had I sold my rye to a corn-dealer I should have had the money there and then. There's nothing like money, brother. With the money I can buy securities, keep them in a safe place and receive the interest! No fuss, no worry: I cut off the coupon and present it to be paid. But if I have rye I have to look after it, and take no end of trouble. So much must be lost through its drying, and being split, and eaten by mice. No, my man, money is very much better. I ought to have done the sensible thing long ago, converted all I have into money and left you."

"No, you stay with us, Porphyry Vladimiritch!"

"I should like to, my dear, but it's too much for me. If I still had the strength of course I should stay and put up a good fight. But no, it's time, high time, I had a rest. I'll go to St. Sergius's and take shelter under the saint's wing, and there will be no sight or sound of me. And it will be simply lovely: peaceful, quiet, decorous, no noise, no quarrels, no shouting—like heaven!"

In short, in spite of all Foka's efforts, the matter was settled as Porphyry Vladimiritch wished. But more than this. When Foka had already agreed to his terms, Porphyry Vladimiritch suddenly thought of a waste piece of ground he had, some three acres of meadow-land, or perhaps less.... It would be a good thing if ...

"I am doing a favor to you, and you do a favor to me!" he said. "That's not by way of interest but just as a favor. God helps us all, and we help each other. It will be nothing to you to mow those three acres, and I'll remember it in the future. I am a simple-hearted man, you know. You'll do a ruble's worth of work for me, and I ..."

Porphyry Vladimiritch stood up and crossed himself looking at the church, to show that the affair was settled. Following his example Foka crossed himself too.

Foka disappeared. Porphyry Vladimiritch took up a piece of paper, armed himself with the reckoning frame, and the beads jumped up and down under his nimble fingers.... It was a regular orgy of figures. A kind of mist seemed to hide the rest of the world from Iudushka. With feverish haste he passed from the beads to the paper, from the paper to the beads. The rows of figures grew longer and longer....

7

THE RECKONING

IT WAS THE middle of December; the country-side, wrapped in an endless winding sheet of snow, seemed spell-bound. During the night such snowdrifts had formed in the road that the peasants' horses struggled hard, dragging empty sledges out of them. There was hardly a track leading to Go-lovlyovo. Porphyry Vladimiritch never had any visitors, and when autumn came he had the main gate and the front door nailed up, letting his household communicate with the out-side world by means of the maids' door and the side gate.

It was eleven in the morning. Iudushka stood by the win-dow in his dressing-gown looking aimlessly before him. He had been walking up and down his study since early morning, thinking of something and reckoning up imaginary sources of income till at last he grew muddled and tired of figures. The orchard in front of the house and the village hidden away behind it were buried in snow. After the snow-storm of the day before, the weather was bright and frosty and the snow glittered in the sun with millions of sparks so that Porphyry Vladimiritch could not help screwing up his eyes.

The courtyard was deserted and still; no one was stirring near the servants' hall or the cattle-shed, and even the village was so quiet that it might have been dead. Lilac smoke rising over the priest's house attracted Iudushka's attention.

"It has struck eleven and the priest's wife hasn't finished cooking yet!" he thought. "They guzzle away all day long, those priests!"

Taking this for his starting-point, he went on to consider whether it was a week-day, a holiday, or a fast, and what the priest's wife could be cooking—when his attention was suddenly distracted. A black speck appeared on the top of the hill, just outside the Naglovka village, and gradually grew bigger and nearer; as Porphyry Vladimiritch watched it he began of course asking himself a number of idle questions. Who was it coming, a peasant or somebody else? But it could not be anyone else, so it must be a peasant . . . yes, it was! What was he coming for? If it was for firewood, the Naglovka wood lay on the other side of the village . . . the rascal was probably going to steal some wood belonging to Golovlyovo! If he were going to the mill, he would have turned to the right. . . . Perhaps he was coming for the priest. Someone might be dying or have died already. . . . Or perhaps a child was born. Which woman could have a baby? Nenila was in the family way in the autumn, but one would have thought it was too soon for her. . . . If the child was a boy he would be included in the census presently—let's see, how many souls were there in Naglovka by the last census? But if it was a girl she wouldn't be registered, and altogether. . . . And yet one cannot manage without the female sex . . . ugh!

Iudushka spat and looked at the icon as though seeking its defense against evil.

His thoughts would probably have gone on wandering had the black dot that came into sight by Naglovka flitted past and disappeared as usual, but it grew and grew and at last turned towards the dam leading to the church. Then Iudushka clearly saw that it was a small covered sledge drawn by a pair of horses. It climbed up the hill, drove past the church ("Can it be the Father Superintendent," flashed through his mind; "that's why they haven't finished cooking at the priest's!"), turned to the right and came straight towards his house. "Yes, it's coming here!" Porphyry Vladimiritch instinctively wrapped his dressing-gown round him and hastily drew away from the window as though afraid that the visitor might notice him.

He was right: the sledge drove up to the house and stopped at the side gate. A young woman hastily jumped out of it. She was dressed, not at all seasonably, in a quilted town coat trimmed with astrakhan, for appearance' sake rather than for warmth, and was evidently stiff with cold. Nobody came out to meet her; she skipped up the side-door steps and a few seconds later the maids' room door banged, then another door, and there were sounds of banging, footsteps, and general commotion in all the adjoining rooms. Porphyry Vladimiritch stood at the door of his study listening. It was so long since he had seen any strangers or been in company that he was quite alarmed. A quarter of an hour passed; the banging and walking about still went on, but no one came to tell him who had arrived. This agitated him all the more. The visitor obviously belonged to the family and had an unquestionable right to his hospitality; but what relatives had he? He tried to think, but his memory did not help him much. He once had a son Volòdenka and a son Pètenka, and he had a mother, Arina Petrovna . . . but that was long, long ago! Last autumn Nadya Galkin, a daughter of his late aunt Varvara Mihailovna, had settled at Goryushkino—could it be she? It couldn't! She did try once to force an entrance into Golovlyovo, but had to beat an ignominious retreat. "She daren't! She won't venture!" Iudushka repeated to himself, indignant at the very thought that Nadya Galkin might come. But who else could it be?

While he was thus reflecting, Yevpraxeya cautiously came to the door and announced:

"The Pogorelka young lady, Anna Semyonovna, has come."

It really was Anninka. But she was so changed that it was almost impossible to recognize her. She was no longer the handsome, lively girl, brimming over with youthful vitality, with rosy cheeks, prominent gray eyes, high bosom and heavy blond tresses, who came to Golovlyovo shortly after Arina Petrovna's death. She was a feeble, broken creature, with a flat chest, sunken cheeks, a hectic color, and languid movements; she seemed round-shouldered, almost stooping. Even her splendid hair somehow seemed pitiful, and only her eyes, burning with a feverish light, looked larger on her thin face. Yevpraxeya gazed at her for some time as at a stranger but recognized her at last.

"Is it really you, miss?" she cried, clasping her hands.

"Yes. Why?"

Saying this, Anninka laughed softly, as though wishing to add, "Yes, I've had a fine time of it!"

"Is my uncle well?" she asked.

"He is and he isn't. . . . He is alive, that's all one can say, but we hardly ever see him."

"What's the matter with him?"

"I don't know. . . . I expect it's with being bored."

"Do you mean to say he doesn't talk by the hour any more?"

"No, miss, he doesn't. He always used to talk, and all of a sudden he's grown silent. We sometimes hear him talk to himself in the study, and laugh as it were, but he doesn't speak when he comes out. They say it was the same trouble with his brother Stepan Vladimiritch. . . . He had always been cheerful—and suddenly ceased to speak. But what about you, miss—how are you?"

Anninka made a gesture of despair.

"And how is your sister?"

"She lies buried by the roadside at Kretchetov."

"God bless us, how do you mean, by the roadside?"

"Why, you know how they bury suicides."

"Good heavens! She had always been a lady and suddenly she laid hands on herself. . . . How was that?"

"Yes, first 'she was a lady,' and then poisoned herself—that's all! And I was a coward, I wanted to live, and here I have come to you! Not for long, don't be alarmed. . . . I shall soon be dead."

Yevpraxeya stared at her open-eyed, as though not taking it in.

"Why do you stare at me? A pretty sight, am I not? Well, there it is. . . . But we'll talk of that presently . . . not now. . . . Now tell them to settle with the driver and warn my uncle."

Saying this she pulled an old purse out of her pocket and took out of it two yellow notes.

"And here are my belongings!" she added, pointing to a half-empty suitcase. "All my property is here—both hereditary and acquired! I am cold, Yevpraxeya, very cold! I am ill through and through, not a single bone in me is sound, and then this awful weather into the bargain. As I drove along I kept thinking: if I get to Golovlyovo, at any rate I'll die where it's warm! I should like some vodka . . . Have you any?"

"Hadn't you better have some tea, miss? The samovar will be ready in a minute."

"No, I'll have tea later. I'd like some vodka first. Don't tell my uncle about the vodka, though. . . . He will see for himself presently."

While the table was being set for tea, Porphyry Vladimiritch came into the dining-room. It was Anninka's turn to be surprised—he had grown so thin, faded, and queer. He greeted Anninka rather peculiarly: not with any direct coldness but with a curious unconcern. He spoke little and with constraint, like an actor recalling with difficulty bits out of the parts he used to play. Altogether he seemed absent-minded, as though thinking all the time of some important subject from which he had been, most annoyingly, called away for no reason at all.

"Well, so you have come!" he said. "What will you have? Tea? Coffee? Order what you like."

In the old days it was Iudushka who generally acted the emotional part at family meetings, but this time it was Anninka, and she was genuinely moved too. Her heart must have been very sore, for she threw her arms round Porphyry Vladimiritch's neck and hugged him.

"Uncle, I have come to you!" she cried, suddenly bursting into tears.

"Well, you are welcome! There's plenty of room. You can live here."

"I am ill, uncle darling! I am very, very ill!"

"And if you are ill, you must pray! When I am ill, I always cure myself by prayer."

"I have come to you to die, uncle!"

Porphyry Vladimiritch looked at her critically and a hardly perceptible smile flitted over his lips.

"Played out, are you?"

"Yes, I am. Lubinka was 'played out,' and died, and I . . . am still alive, you see!"

Hearing about Lubinka's death, Iudushka crossed himself devoutly and murmured a prayer. Anninka meanwhile sat down at the table, leaned her elbow on it, and looking in the direction of the church, wept bitterly.

"Now, weeping and despairing is a sin!" Porphyry Vladimiritch remarked admonishingly. "Do you know what a Christian's duty is? Not to weep, but to submit and trust—that's what a Christian should do!"

But Anninka threw herself back in her chair and repeated, dropping her arms despondently:

"Oh, I don't know! I don't know! I don't know!"

"If you are distressing yourself about your sister, that too is a sin!" Iudushka went on sermonizing. "For although it is praiseworthy to love one's brothers and sisters, yet if it pleases God to call one or even several of them to Himself . . ."

"Oh, no, no! Uncle, you are good, aren't you? Tell me!"

Anninka rushed to him again and put her arms round him.

"Yes, yes, I am! Now, is there anything you would like? Something to eat, some tea or coffee? Ask, tell them to bring it you!"

Anninka suddenly recalled how on her first visit to Golovlyovo her uncle had asked her, "Would you like to have some veal? A suckling pig? Some potatoes?"—and she understood that she would find no other comfort here.

"Thank you, uncle," she said sitting down to the table again. "I don't want anything special. I am sure I shall be quite satisfied with everything."

"Well, if you will be satisfied, so much the better. Will you go to Pogorelka?"

"No, uncle, I'll stay with you for the present. You have nothing against it, have you?"

"Of course not, bless you! I only asked about Pogorelka because if you think of going there I must give orders about the sledge and horses."

"No, later on, not now!"

"Excellent. You can go there some time later, and now stay with us. You can help with the housekeeping—I am alone, you know! That beauty"—Iudushka pointed almost with hatred to Yevpraxeya, who was pouring out tea—"goes traipsing about most of the day, so at times I can't make anyone hear. The whole house is deserted! Well, good-bye for the present. I'll go to my room. I'll say my prayers and see to my work, and pray again. . . . So that's how it is, my dear! How long is it since Lubinka died?"

"About a month, uncle."

"Then we'll go to early Mass to-morrow and have a requiem said for her. . . . Well, good-bye for the present! Drink your tea, and if you are hungry after your journey, tell them to bring you something. We shall see each other at dinner again. We'll have a talk, and if there's anything to see to, we'll see to it, and if not—we'll just sit quietly!"

Such was their first meeting. When it was over Anninka began her new existence at Golovlyovo that she had hated so much and had twice been so anxious to leave in the course of her short life.

Anninka had gone downhill very quickly. Her visit to Go-lovlyovo after her grandmother's death had made her feel that she was a "young lady" with a home and family graves of her own, that her life was not confined to the smelly and noisy inns and hotels, that she had a refuge where the foul breaths reeking of vodka and the stables could not reach her, and where she was safe from that man with a big mustache, red eyes, and a voice hoarse with drink (Oh, what he had said to her! What gestures he had made in her presence!); but that consciousness had disappeared almost as soon as she lost sight of Golovlyovo.

Anninka had then gone straight to Moscow to try if she and Lubinka could be taken on at one of the State theaters. She went to see, among other people, the head mistress of the boarding school where she had been brought up, and some of her school friends. The head mistress, who received her gra-ciously at first, grew cold and distant as soon as she heard that Anninka was a provincial actress; and her friends, married women most of them, looked at her with such impudent sur-prise that she simply lost her nerve. One, more kind-hearted than the others, asked her by way of being sympathetic:

"Tell me, dear, is it true that when you actresses dress for the stage, officers tighten your corsets for you?"

All her attempts to establish herself in Moscow came to nothing. It is only fair to say, however, that she was not good enough for the Moscow stage. Both she and Lubinka were of the type of those lively but not very talented actresses who play one and the same part all their lives. Anninka was good in *Perichole* and Lubinka in *Pansies* and the *Old-fashioned Colonel*. Whatever else they attempted it seemed always like *Perichole* and *Pansies* again, and very often, indeed, like nothing at all. In the course of her duties Anninka often had to act the *Belle Hélène*; she put a fiery red wig over her ash-blond hair, slit her tunic open right down to the waist, but with all that, her performance was dull, mediocre, and not even improper. From *Hélène* she passed to the *Grand-Duchess of Gerolstein*, but her colorless acting, combined with the absurd production, made the whole performance downright silly. At last she attempted Clairette in *La Fille de Madame Angot*, and in trying to warm up the audience overacted to such an extent that even the uncritical provincial public was repelled by the indecency of the performance. Generally speaking Anninka had the reputation of a lively actress with quite a good voice, and as she was pretty into the bargain, she could be fairly certain of a full house in the provinces. But that was all. She could not make a name for herself and there was nothing individual about her acting. Even in the provinces her admirers were chiefly men belonging to the Army, whose main ambition was to have free access behind the scenes. She could have only been tolerated on the Moscow stage if she had had very strong backing, and even then she would certainly have received from the public the unflattering title of a "street-singer."

She had to return to the provinces. In Moscow she received a letter from Lubinka saying that their company had moved to Samovarnov, of which Lubinka was very glad, for she had made friends with a member of the local Rural Board. He was so infatuated with her that he seemed "ready to steal public money" to satisfy all her whims. And indeed, arriving at Samovarnov, Anninka found that her sister had thought-

lessly given up the stage and was living in comparative luxury. When Anninka came, Lubinka's "friend," Gavrilo Stepan-
itch Lyulkin, was with her. He was a retired captain of the
Hussars, once a handsome man but now distinctly heavy. He
had a noble expression, noble manners, a noble way of thinking, and yet all of it taken together made one feel confident
that that man was not likely to beat a retreat before the Rural
Board money-box. Lubinka received her sister with open arms
and said that she had a room ready for her at her flat.

But Anninka, still under the influence of her recent visit
to "her own home," grew angry. The sisters had a heated conversation which ended in a quarrel; and Anninka could not
help recalling how the Voplino priest had said that it was difficult for an actress to keep her "treasure."

Anninka settled at an hotel and broke off all relations with
her sister. Easter came. In the week after Easter theaters re-
opened and Anninka learned that a Miss Nalimov from Kazan
had been engaged in her sister's place—a poor actress but with
no compunctions with regard to decency. Anninka appeared
in *Perichole* as usual and delighted the Samovarnov audience.
Returning to her hotel she found in her room an envelope
containing a hundred rubles and a short note saying, "And
in case of anything, as much again. Fancy-draper Kukishev."
Anninka was angry and complained to the hotel-keeper, who
explained that it was Kukishev's habit to congratulate all actresses on arrival, but that he was a harmless man and there
was no need to take offense. Following his advice Anninka
put the money and the note into an envelope and returning it
to the sender the following day, troubled no more about it.

But Kukishev proved to be more persistent than the hotel-
keeper had said. He considered himself to be one of Lyulkin's
friends and was on good terms with Lubinka. He was a man
of property and as a member of the municipal council was,
like Lyulkin, most favorably placed with regard to the municipal funds. And, like Lyulkin, he had no scruples in this

respect. His appearance, from the shop-walkers' point of view, was most seductive; he reminded one of that beetle which, in the words of the song, Masha found in the meadow instead of wild strawberries:

> A dark beetle with a mustache,
> And a head of curly hair.
> His eyebrows were coal-black
> Like the man's for whom I care.

Considering his looks and the fact that Lubinka had pro-promised him her help, he considered that he had every right to presume.

Altogether Lubinka had evidently burnt her boats, and the rumors about her were by no means gratifying to her sister's pride. It was said that every evening a merry company gathered in her flat and sat at supper from midnight till morning; that Lubinka, in the role of a gypsy, presided over these parties half-clad, while Lyulkin exclaimed, addressing his drunken friends, "There's a bosom for you!," she had her hair down and sang, with a guitar in her hands:

> "Oh, what a lovely time I've had
> With that young and handsome man!"

Anninka listened to these stories with agitation. What surprised her most was that Lubinka should sing in the gypsy style, like the Moscow Matryosha! Anninka always did justice to her sister, and had she been told that Lubinka sang "inimitably" the couplets out of the *Old-fashioned Colonel*, she would have thought this perfectly natural and believed it readily. She could not help believing it in fact because the Kursk and the Tambov and the Penza audiences still remembered with what inimitable naïveté Lubinka declared in her sweet little voice that she would like to be *under* the

Colonel.... But that Lubinka could sing in the gypsy style, like Matryosha—certainly not! It wasn't true! Now she, Anninka, *could* sing like that, there was no doubt of it. It was her *genre*, and the whole Kursk that had seen her in the "Impersonations of Russian Songs" could bear witness to it.

And Anninka took a guitar, flung a striped scarf over her shoulder, sat down crossing her legs, and began: "Eee-eh! eee-ah!" And she really did it exactly like the gypsy Matryosha.

But however that might be Lubinka was living in luxury, and Lyulkin, anxious not to dim their drunken bliss by any refusals, had obviously begun helping himself to municipal money. To say nothing of the champagne drunk and spilt on the floor every night in Lubinka's flat, she herself grew more capricious and exacting every day. First it was a case of dresses from Madame Minangoua in Moscow, and then of diamonds from Foulde. Lubinka was practical and did not despise valuables. Drinking was one thing, and jewels and State lottery tickets another. In any case her life, if not really gay, was a perpetual round of reckless, rowdy festivities. The only unpleasant thing about it was that she had to keep on good terms with the captain of police, who, though a friend of Lyulkin, liked to assert his authority at times. Lubinka always knew when he was dissatisfied with her suppers, for in that case a police inspector called on her the following morning demanding her passport. She had to give in; in the morning she offered vodka and something to eat to the inspector, and in the evening mixed for the police captain some special "Swedish" punch which he particularly liked.

Kukishev saw this sea of drink and burned with envy. He wanted at all costs to have a place exactly like Lyulkin's and a "lady" exactly like his. One could then spend one's time with greater variety too; one night at Lyulkin's "lady's" and another at his, Kukishev's. This was his cherished dream, the cherished dream of a stupid man—and the more stupid a man is, the more obstinate in achieving his ends. And

Anninka seemed to him the most suitable person for realizing that dream.

Anninka would not give in, however. So far she had not yet felt any stirrings of passion, though she had many admirers and was very free in her manners. There was a moment when she fancied she might fall in love with the local tragic actor Miloslavsky, who was obviously burning with passion for her. But Miloslavsky was permanently tipsy, and so stupid that he never declared himself and did nothing but stare at her and hiccup in an absurd kind of way when she went past him. So her love for him never came to anything. As to her other admirers, Anninka regarded them merely as an inevitable part of the conditions in which she had to carry on her trade as a provincial actress. She put up with those conditions, took advantage of the small privileges they gave her (applause, bouquets, troika drives, picnics, etc.), but went no further than, so to speak, this show of immorality.

She behaved in the same way now. During the whole summer she steadily trod in the path of virtue, jealously guarding her "treasure," as though wishing to prove to the Voplino priest that heroic characters could be found even among actresses. Once she actually decided to complain of Kukishev to the governor of the province, who heard her graciously and praised her fortitude, advising her to keep it up. But regarding her complaint merely as a pretext for an indirect attack upon his own person, he added that, having spent his energies in the struggle with internal enemies, he thought he could not be useful to her in the way she wished. Hearing this, Anninka blushed and went away.

Kukishev meanwhile was acting so cleverly that he succeeded in getting the general public interested in his suit. The public seemed to have suddenly grasped that Kukishev was right and that Miss Pogorelsky 1st (that was Anninka's stage name) was not anybody very grand and had no business to act a *sainte nitouche.*

A whole party was formed whose object was to teach the rebellious upstart a lesson. The assiduous visitors of the actresses' dressing-rooms deserted her for her neighbor, Miss Nalimov. Then, without doing anything definitely hostile, they began receiving her when she appeared on the stage with such deadly coldness that one might think she were some wretched chorus girl and not the leading lady. At last they insisted on the manager taking away some of Anninka's parts and giving them to Miss Nalimov. The most curious thing of all was that Lubinka took a very active part in this underhand intrigue and had Miss Nalimov for her bosom friend.

At the end of August Anninka saw with surprise that she had to play the part of Orestes in the *Belle Hélène* and that Perichole was the only one of her old parts still left her—and that solely because Miss Nalimov did not venture to compete with her in it. Besides, the manager informed her that in view of her losing her popularity her salary would be reduced to seventy-five rubles a month and one-half benefit performance a year.

Anninka was alarmed because with such a salary she would have to move from the hotel to an inn. She wrote to two or three theatrical managers offering her services, but they all wrote in reply that there were too many Pericholes on the market already and there was no chance for her, especially as they had heard from trustworthy sources that she was difficult to deal with.

Anninka was spending her last savings. Another week—and she would have had to move to the inn in company with Miss Horoshavin, who acted Parthenis and enjoyed the patronage of the police sergeant. She began to feel something like despair, all the more so because every day some mysterious hand left in her room a note with the words: "Perichole, submit! Your Kukishev." One day when she was feeling particularly depressed Lubinka suddenly burst in upon her.

"Tell me, please, for what prince are you saving your treasure?" she asked briefly.

Anninka was completely taken aback. The first thing that struck her was that the Voplino priest and Lubinka used the word "treasure" in exactly the same sense. The only difference was that the priest thought it all-important while Lubinka regarded it as a thing of no consequence, though it could drive "those beastly men" to frenzy.

Then she could not help asking herself what, after all, was this "treasure"? Was it really precious and worth keeping? —and, alas, found no satisfactory answer to that question. On the one hand it seemed rather a shame to be left without it, and on the other . . . hang it all, surely the whole meaning of life could not be reduced to a mere struggle for one's "treasure"?

"I have put by thirty lottery tickets in six months," Lubinka went on, "and no end of trinkets . . . see what a dress I have on!"

Lubinka turned round, pulled her dress straight in front and behind, and let Anninka examine her on all sides. The dress really was expensive and marvelously made: straight from Madame Minangoua in Moscow.

"Kukishev is kind," Lubinka began again. "He'll dress you up like a doll and give you some money too. You can give up the stage then. . . . You've had enough of it!"

"Never!" Anninka exclaimed warmly; she had not yet forgotten the words "holy art"!

"You can stay on if you like. You'll have the highest salary again and play the leading parts instead of the Nalimov girl."

Anninka said nothing.

"Well, good-bye. My friends are waiting for me downstairs. Kukishev is there too. Won't you come?"

Anninka was still silent.

"Well, think it over, if there's anything to think about. And when you've made up your mind, come. Good-bye."

On September 17th, Lubinka's name-day, the poster of the Samovarnov theater announced a *special* performance. Anninka appeared again in the part of the *Belle Hélène* and the part of Orestes was played "just for this once" by Miss Pogorelsky 2nd, that is, Lubinka. To crown the occasion Miss Nalimov, "also for this evening only," took the part of the smith, Cleon, dressed in tights and a short jacket, her face slightly blackened with soot, and a sheet of iron in her hands. In view of all this the audience was distinctly enthusiastic. The moment Anninka appeared on the stage she was met with such a storm of applause that, having lost the habit of it, she felt like bursting into tears. When, in act three, in the night scene, she got up from the couch almost naked, there was quite an uproar in the house and one member of the audience was so electrified that he shouted at Menelaus as he appeared at the door, "Go out, you tiresome man!" Anninka understood that the audience had forgiven her.

Kukishev, meanwhile, in evening dress, white tie, and white gloves, announced his triumph with dignity, treating friends and strangers to champagne in the buffet during the entr'actes. Finally, the theater manager appeared, jubilant, in Anninka's dressing-room and said, kneeling before her:

"Now you are a good girl, miss! And so from to-night onwards you'll receive the same salary as before and have the old number of benefits!"

In short, all praised her, congratulated her, expressed their sympathy, and she who had been afraid and so wretched that she did not know what to do with herself, suddenly grew convinced that she had . . . fulfilled her mission in life!

After the theater all went to Lubinka's flat and congratulations were redoubled. Such a crowd gathered there, immediately beginning to smoke, that one could hardly breathe. They all sat down to supper, and champagne flowed in streams. Kukishev kept close to Anninka, who was evidently rather embarrassed, but no longer resented his attentions. She was slightly amused and also flattered at having so easily gained possession of this big strong creature who thought nothing of bending or unbending a horseshoe but was like wax in her hands, ready to do anything she pleased. There was much merriment at supper—that drunken, rowdy merriment which does not appeal either to the heart or to the mind and results in headache and sickness next day. Only one of the company, the tragedian Miloslavsky, looked gloomy, and refusing champagne swallowed glass after glass of plain vodka. Anninka refrained from drinking for a time, but Kukishev was so insistent and implored her so pitifully, kneeling before her: "Anna Semyonovna! You are in arrears! Please allow me to beg you! Drink to your bliss and our love and concord! Do me the favor!"—that though his stupid face and silly words annoyed her she could not refuse, and very soon began to feel giddy. Lubinka was so generous that she actually asked Anninka to sing, "Ah, the lovely time I had with that young and handsome man," and Anninka did it to such perfection that everyone cried, "Now, that's the thing . . . just like Matryosha!" Lubinka sang instead the couplets about being *under* the Colonel so admirably as to convince everyone that this was her true *genre* in which she had no rivals, just as Anninka had none in the gypsy songs. In conclusion Miloslavsky and Miss Nalimov acted a "masquerade" in which the tragedian recited verses out of *Ugolino* (tragedy in five acts by N. Polevoy), and Miss Nalimov replied with bits from an unpublished play by Barkov. The result was so unexpected that Miss Nalimov very nearly carried the day, almost eclipsing the Misses Pogorelsky.

It was daylight when Kukishev helped Anninka into a carriage. Pious townspeople coming back from matins looked at Anninka in her gorgeous dress, hardly able to stand on her feet, and murmured crossly:

"Good people are returning from church while they are guzzling wine . . . damnation take them!"

Anninka went from her sister's, not to the hotel, but to her own flat, small but cozy and very nicely furnished. Kukishev followed her in.

The winter passed in a continuous whirl of revelry. Anninka completely lost her head, and if she ever thought of the "treasure" it was only to say to herself, "What a fool I was though!" Kukishev, proud of the fact that his dream about having a "lady" as good as Lubinka had been realized, spared no expense, and from the spirit of rivalry bought two dresses when Lyulkin bought one and ordered two dozen of champagne when Lyulkin ordered one. Lubinka actually began to envy her sister because in the course of the winter Anninka acquired forty State lottery tickets and a number of gold trinkets with and without stones. The sisters had again made friends, however, and decided to pool all their savings. Anninka still had dreams about the future and said to her sister in intimate conversation:

"When all *this* is over we'll go to Pogorelka. We shall have money and we'll start farming."

To which Lubinka very cynically replied:

"Do you imagine *this* will ever end . . . you fool!"

Unluckily for Anninka, Kukishev conceived a new idea which he began pursuing with his usual obstinacy. Being an uneducated and unquestionably a stupid man, he fancied that he would attain the height of bliss if his "beauty" learned to drink vodka with him.

"Let's toss off a glass together, dear lady!" he pestered her continually. He always addressed Anninka rather formally, valuing the fact that she was a born lady and wishing to prove that it was not for nothing he had served in a Moscow shop.

Anninka refused for a time, saying that Lyulkin never forced Lubinka to drink vodka with him.

"And yet she does take it out of love for Mr. Lyulkin!" Kukishev replied. "And allow me to point out to you, my beauty, there's no need for us to copy the Lyulkins! They are the

Lyulkins and you and I are the Kukishevs! That's why we'll toss a glass in our own, Kukishev, style!"

Kukishev prevailed at last. One day Anninka took from her lover's hands a glass filled with a greenish liquid and poured it down her throat. Of course it simply took her breath away, she gasped, coughed, wheeled round, and Kukishev was wildly delighted.

"Allow me to inform you, my beauty, you don't do it properly! You are too quick!" he instructed her when she calmed down a little. "That's how you must hold the glass in your little hand! Then raise it to your lips and, without any hurry: one, two, three . . . here goes!"

Calmly and seriously he poured the vodka down his throat as though down a sink. He did not even wince, but, taking a tiny piece of black bread from the plate dipped it into the salt-cellar and chewed it.

In this way Kukishev realized his second "dream" and began wondering what he could do next to impress the Lyulkins. And of course he did think of something.

"Do you know what?" he announced suddenly. "When summer comes let us go with the Lyulkins to my water-mill, take a hamper with food and drinks and bathe in the river by common consent!"

"Never! Certainly not!" Anninka answered indignantly.

"Why not? We'll bathe first, then toss off a glass or two, then have a little rest, and bathe again! That will be fine!"

History does not say whether this new idea of Kukishev's was realized, but in any case all this drunken revelry continued for a whole year, during which the municipal and the rural councils did not manifest the slightest uneasiness about Lyulkin and Kukishev. For appearance' sake Lyulkin did go to Moscow, however, and said on returning that he had sold some of his forest for timber; and when he was reminded that he had sold it four years ago, while he was living with the gypsy Domashka, he replied that on that occasion he sold the

310

Drygalovsky forest and this time—the forest called Dashka's Shame. To make his story more convincing he added that the forest received that name because in times of serfdom a girl called Dashka was "surprised" there and whipped on the spot. As to Kukishev, in order to throw people off the scent, he spread the rumor that he had smuggled in a quantity of foreign lace free of duty and made good profits on the transaction.

Nevertheless, in September of the following year the police captain asked Kukishev to lend him a thousand rubles, and Kukishev was foolish enough to refuse. Then the police captain began whispering together with the assistant prosecutor. ("They both swilled champagne at my house every evening!" Kukishev said at the trial afterwards.) On September 17th, the anniversary of Kukishev's "love," when he, together with the others, was again celebrating Lubinka's name-day, a member of the Municipal Council rushed in and told Kukishev that the Council committee had met at the Town Hall and were drawing up a protocol.

"So they've found a deficit, have they?" Kukishev exclaimed, quite unabashed, and without further ado followed the man to the Town Hall, and from there to prison.

The next day the Rural Council too was all agog. The members assembled and sent to the treasury for the money-box; they counted the money over and over again, but, reckon it as they would, there proved to be a deficit in their case also. Lyulkin was present at the auditing, pale, gloomy, but... noble! When the deficit was established beyond a shadow of doubt and the members were debating in their own minds which forest plot each of them would have to sell in order to cover it, Lyulkin went up to the window, pulled a revolver out of his pocket, and shot himself in the temple.

This caused a great deal of talk in the town. People discussed the two men and compared them. They were sorry for Lyulkin and remarked, "At any rate he died like an honorable man," and of Kukishev they said, "A money-grubber, that's all he is." Of Anninka and Lubinka people said straight out that "it was their doing," "it was all because of them," and that "it would not be a bad plan to put them in prison too, as a warning to hussies like them."

The investigating magistrate did not put them into prison but frightened them so thoroughly that they completely lost their heads. There were friends of course who advised them to put away their valuables but they listened without taking it in. In consequence, the prosecuting counsel, an enterprising young man, came, accompanied by a sheriff, to the two sisters, and in order to secure the plaintiffs' claims sequestered all he found, leaving the girls only their clothes and such gold and silver things that, to judge from inscriptions engraved on them, were gifts from delighted audiences. Lubinka managed, however, to secure a packet of notes that had been given her the day before, and hid it in her corsets. There proved to be a thousand rubles in that packet—all that the sisters had to live on for an indefinite time to come.

They were kept for about four months at Samovarnov awaiting the trial. Then came the trial which was perfect torture to them, especially to Anninka. Kukishev was horribly cynical; there was not any need for the details he supplied, but he evidently wanted to show off before the Samovarnov ladies and told absolutely everything. The public prosecutor and the counsel for the plaintiffs, both of them young men and also anxious to please the Samovarnov ladies, took advantage of this to give the case a scabrous character. Anninka fainted more than once but the counsel, bent on securing the plaintiffs' claims, took no notice of it and went on asking question after question. At last the preliminary investigation was over, and the case for the plaintiffs and the defendant was stated by their respective counsels. Late at night the jury returned a verdict of "guilty" against Kukishev, but with extenuating circumstances, in view of which he was sentenced there and then to be banished to Western Siberia.

When the trial was over the sisters were able to leave Samovarnov. It was high time because their thousand rubles were coming to an end. Besides, the manager of the Kretchetov theater, who had provisionally engaged them, requested them to come to Kretchetov at once, threatening to break off the agreement if they did not. Of the money, jewelry, and securities sequestered at the prosecuting counsel's request, nothing more was heard...

Such were the consequences of being careless of the "treasure." Wretched, worn out, crushed by the general contempt, the sisters lost all self-confidence, all hope of a better future. They grew thin, frightened, careless of their appearance. And, to crown it all, Anninka, having been through Kukishev's training, had learnt to drink.

Things went from bad to worse. No sooner had the sisters arrived at Kretchetov than they were taken possession of— Lubinka by Captain Papkov and Anninka by Zabvenny, a tradesman. But they no longer had a gay time of it. Papkov and Zabvenny were coarse bullies, by no means liberal with money (as Zabvenny put it, "It depended upon the goods"), and in three or four months' time they cooled considerably. To make matters worse the sisters had as little success on the stage as in their love-affairs. The theater manager who had engaged them, hoping that the Samovarnov scandal would make them popular, proved to have made a bad mistake. The very first time that the Misses Pogorelsky were on the stage somebody called from the gallery, "Ah, you jail birds!"—and this nickname stuck to the sisters, damning their theatrical career once for all.

Dull, colorless days followed, devoid of any intellectual interest. The audience was cold, the theater manager bore them a grudge, their patrons did not stand up for them. Zabvenny had dreamed, like Kukishev, of how he would insist on his "lady" taking a drop of vodka with him, of her being shy about it at first and gradually giving in to him; and he was quite aggrieved when he found that the lesson had been learnt already so that there was nothing left him but the comfort of inviting his friends "to see the hussy swill down vodka." Papkov too was dissatisfied because Lubinka had grown thinner.

"There used to be some flesh on you, what have you done with it, tell me?" he questioned her.

In consequence he did not stand on ceremony with her; indeed, when drunk he often beat her.

By the spring the sisters had neither "regular" patrons nor a "definite position." They still held on to the theater, but it was no longer a question of taking the leading parts. Lubinka looked rather the better of the two; Anninka, being more sensitive, broke down altogether; she seemed to have forgotten her past, and not to be aware of the present. Besides, she developed a suspicious cough; some mysterious disease was evidently threatening her.

The following summer was dreadful. The sisters were gradually reduced to being hauled round from hotel to hotel to visit gentlemen staying in the town, and came to have a definite market price. There were perpetual rows and fights, but the sisters seemed to have nine lives and desperately clung to existence. They reminded one of miserable little dogs, lamed, wounded, and squealing, that insist on going to their favorite spot in spite of having hot water thrown over them. The theater manager found it impossible to keep such women in his company.

Only once during that awful year a ray of light broke in upon Anninka's existence: the tragedian Miloslavsky sent her a letter from Samovarnov, urgently begging her to accept his hand and his heart. Anninka read the letter and wept. She tossed about all night, beside herself with agitation, but in the morning she sent him a brief reply: "What for? To drink vodka together?"

After that the darkness grew denser than ever and she was caught once more in the hideous, unending whirl.

Lubinka was the first to come to her senses, or, rather, instinctively to feel that she had had enough of life. They had no prospect of work: youth and beauty, and glimmerings of talent—all seemed to have suddenly disappeared. The thought that they had a home at Pogorelka had not once occurred to her. It all seemed so vague and distant that she scarcely remembered it. Pogorelka had had no attraction for her before and now less than ever. Yes, now, when they were almost starving, she least of all wanted to return there. With what face would she look at the people there? With a face branded with degradation by innumerable drunken breaths? She seemed to feel those vile breaths all over her body, to be conscious of them at all times. And, the most awful part of it was, both she and Anninka had grown so used to all this vileness that it had imperceptibly become a part of their very life. They were not disgusted by the stinking hotels, by the rowdy inns, by the shameless drunken speeches, and if they settled at Pogorelka they would be sure to miss all that. And, besides, at Pogorelka too they would have to live on something. It seemed many years since they were knocking about the world but nothing had been heard about any income from Pogorelka. Perhaps it was only a myth. Perhaps everyone there was dead—all those witnesses of their far off and memorable childhood when grandmamma Arina Petrovna brought them up on sour milk and putrid salt meat.... Oh, what a childhood it was! What a life it was ... all life in general! All life ... all, all!

It was clear that they ought to die. Once this thought lights upon one's conscience there is no getting rid of it. Both sisters often woke up from the drunken nightmare in which they lived; with Anninka these awakenings were accompanied by hysterical sobbing and tears and passed off more quickly; Lubinka was colder by nature, and so she did not weep or curse but merely went on obstinately remembering that she was "vile." Besides, Lubinka was sensible and argued it out quite clearly that there was simply no point in living.

There was nothing to look forward to except shame, destitution, and the streets. Shame was a matter of habit and one could endure that, but destitution—never! Better put an end to it all.

"We must die," she said one day to Anninka in the same coldly reasonable tone in which two years ago she had asked her for whom she was guarding her "treasure."

"Why?" Anninka asked in fear.

"I tell you seriously; we must die!" Lubinka repeated. "Come to your senses, try to understand!"

"Well . . . let's die then!" Anninka agreed, though probably she scarcely grasped the stern significance of that decision.

That very day Lubinka broke off the heads of some sulphur matches and prepared two glassfuls of the solution. She drank one and gave the other to her sister. But Anninka instantly lost courage and refused to drink.

"Drink . . . you vile creature!" Lubinka shouted at her. "Sister, darling, dearest, drink!"

Beside herself with fear, Anninka screamed and rushed about the room, and at the same time instinctively clutched at her throat as though trying to strangle herself.

"Drink, drink . . . you vile creature!"

The artistic career of the Misses Pogorelsky was over. That same evening Lubinka's body was carted out into the fields and buried by the roadside. Anninka remained alive.

Arriving at Golovlyovo, Anninka soon introduced a hopelessly Bohemian atmosphere into Iudushka's old nest. She got up late and without dressing or doing her hair slouched about the rooms till dinner-time, coughing so dreadfully that Porphyry Vladimiritch in his study started in alarm each time he heard her. Her room was always untidy; her bed remained unmade and various articles of clothing lay scattered about the chairs and on the floor. At first she used to see her uncle only at dinner and at evening tea. The lord of Golovlyovo came out of his study dressed all in black, spoke little, and ate wearisomely-slowly, as before. He was evidently taking stock of Anninka, as she guessed from his slanting glances at her.

Soon after dinner came the early dusk of a December afternoon, and Anninka began desolately pacing up and down the long enfilade of the reception-rooms. She liked to watch the last glimmer of a gray winter day dying out, to see the twilight gathering, the rooms being filled with shadows, and then the whole house plunging suddenly into impenetrable darkness. She felt better in that darkness and hardly ever lighted the candles. Only one cheap little palm candle spluttered at the end of the large drawing-room, making a small circle of light with its flame. For a time the usual after-dinner sounds were heard in the house: the clatter of crockery and the noise of drawers being opened and shut; then came the sound of retreating steps, and a dead stillness followed. Porphyry Vladimiritch lay down to have a nap, Yevpraxeya buried herself in the feather-bed in her room, Prohor went to the servants' hall, and Anninka was left quite alone. She walked up and down, singing in an undertone and trying to tire herself out and, above all, not to think. As she walked towards the drawing-room she gazed at the bright circle made by the candle-flame; as she walked back she tried to distinguish some point in the gathering darkness. But in spite of her efforts memories crowded around her. Here was her dressing-room with cheap wall-paper on the wooden partition walls, the inevitable long mirror and no less inevitable bouquet from Sub-lieutenant Papkov 2nd, here was the stage with smoky, begrimed scenery, slimy with the damp; here was she herself, skipping about the stage—skipping about, that was just it, though she had imagined she was acting; here was the house that from the stage seemed so smart, almost brilliant, but was really poor and dark, with odd chairs and boxes upholstered in worn magenta velveteen. And finally—officers, officers, no end of officers. Then the hotel with a smelly corridor dimly lighted by a smoking oil-lamp, her room into which she ran hastily when the performance was over to dress for further triumphs—a room with a bed that had not been made all day, with a washing-stand full of dirty water, a sheet on the floor, and a pair of drawers forgotten on the back of a chair; then the common-room reeking with kitchen smells, with a table in the middle; supper, cutlets and peas, tobacco smoke, shouting, pushing, drunken gaiety.... And again officers, officers, no end of officers. . . .

Such were her memories of the time that she had once called the time of her success, her triumphs, her prosperity.

These memories were followed by others. The most vivid thing about them was a stinking inn, with walls frozen through in winter, with rickety floors and a wooden partition in the cracks of which could be seen the shiny bellies of bugs. Drunken and rowdy nights; gentlemen visitors hastily pulling a three-ruble note out of their thin pocket-books; jaunty tradesmen "livening up the actresses" almost with a whip. And in the morning—headache, sickness and misery, hopeless misery. And in the end—Golovlyovo.

Golovlyovo—that was death itself, cruel, greedy death, that is for ever stalking a fresh victim. Two of her uncles had died here; two cousins had received here "serious wounds" that resulted in death; and, then Lubinka too. . . . It seemed as though she had died at Kretchetov, "for reasons of her own," but the beginning of the "serious wounds" lay certainly here, at Golovlyovo. All deaths, all poison, all sickness—all came from here. It was here they had been fed on putrid meat; it was here that the orphans had heard for the first time the words, "hateful children, beggars, greedy mouths to feed, useless creatures," and so on; nothing remained unpunished here, nothing escaped the keen eye of the hard and capricious old woman; not an extra piece of food, not a broken penny doll, not a torn rag, not a worn shoe. Every infringement of law was immediately punished by a slap or a scolding. And so when at last they were free to dispose of themselves and understood that they could escape from all this meanness, they did escape . . . *there*! No one had stopped them, and indeed no one could have done so, because they felt that nothing could be worse and more hateful than Golovlyovo.

Oh, if one could forget it all and create, if only in a dream, something different, some beautiful world of fancy, that would blot out both the past and the present! But, alas! the crushing experiences she had been through were so overwhelmingly real that they extinguished the slightest glimmer of imagination. In vain she tried to dream of angels with silver wings—Kukishevs, Lyulkins, Zabvennys, Papkovs, pitilessly peeped out from behind the angels. . . . Good God, could she really have lost it all? Could her very powers of self-deception have been destroyed by the night revelries, drink and debauchery? But she had to kill her past somehow so that it should not poison her blood and wring her heart! She wanted something to fall upon it like a dead weight, crushing it, destroying it utterly!

And how strange and cruel it all was! She could not even imagine that there was any future before her, that there were any means of escape, that anything could possibly happen. Nothing could happen. And the most unbearable of all was that she was really dead and yet all the outer signs of life were there. She ought to have ended it *then*, together with Lubinka, but somehow she had remained alive. How was it she had not been crushed by the terrible load of shame that fell upon her then? And what a miserable worm she must be to have crawled out from under the mass of stones that had been hurled at her!

She moaned at the thought of it. She ran about the drawing-room, whirling round and round, trying to stifle her memories. But they all floated up to meet her: the Grand-Duchess of Gerolstein shaking her hussar cloak, Clairette Angot in a wedding dress cut as low as the waist in front, the Belle Hélène in a dress cut in front and behind and at the sides. . . . Nothing but shame and nakedness . . . that's how her life had been spent. Could it all have really happened?

About seven o'clock the house began to wake up again. Preparations for tea were heard, and at last Porphyry Vladimiritch's voice. The uncle and the niece sat down to the tea-table and exchanged remarks about the day; but since the day had been poor in events, their conversation was as poor. Having finished tea and performed the rite of kissing good-night, Iudushka crept into his hole for the night and Anninka went to Yevpraxeya's room to play cards.

At eleven o'clock the night-orgy began. After making certain that Porphyry Vladimiritch had gone to bed, Yevpraxeya put on the table all sorts of home-made pickles and a decanter of vodka. Anninka recalled shameless and senseless songs, played the guitar, and, in the intervals between singing and indecent conversation, drank glass after glass of vodka. At first she drank calmly in Kukishev's style, "Here goes," but gradually she grew tragic and began to curse and to moan. Yevpraxeya looked on and pitied her.

"I look at you, miss, and I feel so sorry for you, so sorry!"

"Have a drink too—then you won't be sorry!" Anninka replied.

"No, I couldn't! As it is I'm hardly respectable because of your uncle and if I take to drink . . ."

"Well, then, it's no use your talking. Better let me sing the 'Handsome Man' for you."

Again there was the strumming of the guitar and the shrieks, "Ee-ah! ee-oh!" In the small hours of the morning sleep heavy as a stone overpowered Anninka at last. That welcome stone killed her past for a few hours and kept her disease at bay. But next day she crept out from under it, half-dazed and shattered and again began to live.

On one of those nights when Anninka was jauntily singing to Yevpraxeya her repertory of vile songs, Iudushka's emaciated figure suddenly appeared in the doorway. He was deadly pale; his lips were trembling; in the dim flicker of a palm candle his sunken eyes looked like blind hollows; his hands were folded as for prayer. He stood for a few seconds before the dumbfoundered women and, turning slowly, walked out of the room.

A kind of doom seems to hang over some families. One notices it particularly among the class of small landowners scattered all over Russia who, having no work, no connection with public life, and no political importance, were at one time sheltered by serfdom, but now, with nothing to shelter them, are spending the remainder of their lives in their tumble-down country houses. Everything in those pitiful families' existence—both success and failure—is blind, unexpected, haphazard.

Sometimes such a family is suddenly caught up as it were by a wave of success. Some humble retired lieutenant and his wife vegetating in the wilds of the country suddenly produce a whole bevy of spruce, alert, sturdy children who show a wonderful aptitude for mastering the essentials of life. They are "clever" children, all of them, both boys and girls. The young men do excellently at school and, while still there, form good social connections and find patrons. They know when to behave modestly ("*J'aime cette modestie,*" their superiors say) and when to be independent ("*J'aime cette indépendence!*"), are very sensitive to every wind that blows and never break with any new movement without leaving a safe loophole through which they can creep back. In consequence they are able all their life long to change their skin at any time without creating scandal, and, in case of emergency, to change back again. In short they are true children of the age who always begin by seeking favors and *almost always* end by perfidy. As to the girls, they too further the family fortunes in their special line, that is, they make successful marriages and afterwards show so much tact in bestowing their charms that they easily win prominent positions in so-called society.

Thanks to all these chance circumstances, luck simply pours upon the humble family. Its first successful members having won their way bring up another spruce generation who find life easier because the road has already been made for them. That generation will be followed by others until at last the family naturally becomes one of those which regard a life of continual jubilation as their birthright.

Instances of such lucky families have been fairly frequent of late, owing to the growing demand for "fresh" men—a demand due to the gradual degeneration of the "stale ones." In the old days too a "new star" appeared occasionally on the horizon, but that was a rare occurrence. The wall round the blissful domain the gates of which bear the inscription, "Meat pies eaten here at all times," had in those days hardly any cracks in it, and, besides, a "new" man could only penetrate there if he really were worth his salt. But now there are a great many more cracks, and the business of penetration is not so hard as it used to be, since the newcomer is not expected to have any sterling qualities—"freshness" is enough.

Side by side with those successful families, however, there exist a great number of others upon whom their household gods seem to shower nothing but ill-luck. The family is attacked as by vermin by misfortune or vice that steadily gnaws away at it, gradually creeping to its very core and undermining generation after generation. There appears a whole crop of weaklings, drunkards, debauchees, idlers, and good-for-nothing men generally. As time goes on the family degenerates more and more till at last it produces such miserable weaklings as the Golovlyovs I have described in an earlier chapter*—weaklings who cannot resist the impact of life and perish at its first thrust.

It was precisely this kind of doom that hung over the Golovlyov family. Three characteristics had marked its history in the course of several generations: love of idleness, incapacity for any kind of work, and passion for drink. The first two characteristics resulted in moral shallowness, empty talk, and idle fancies; the third was as it were the inevitable conclusion of their failure in life. Porphyry Vladimiritch had seen several victims of this evil fate perish before his eyes, and there was the tradition that the same thing had happened to his grandparents and great-grandparents. They were all rowdy, empty-headed, and good-for-nothing drunkards, so that the Golovlyov family would certainly have come to grief altogether had not Arina Petrovna appeared like a bright meteor amidst this drunken disorder. By her personal efforts and energy that woman built up the family's prosperity, but her labor was wasted because her children did not inherit her qualities and she herself died entangled in the meshes of idleness, empty talk, and petty feelings.

So far, however, Porphyry Vladimiritch had restrained himself. Perhaps he consciously avoided drink in view of his family's past, or maybe he had been satisfied with mental drunkenness. It was not for nothing, however, that the neighbors predicted that he too would be the victim of drink. He himself felt at times as though there were some blank in his life, as though the play of empty thought, enjoyable as it was, were not enough. He seemed to feel the lack of something pungent and overpowering that would finally banish all idea of reality and plunge him into emptiness once and for all.

The longed-for moment came of itself. For some weeks after Anninka's arrival Porphyry Vladimiritch, shut up in his

---

*The Family Tribunal.

study, listened to the vague noises that reached him from the other end of the house; for weeks he tried to guess what it meant and wondered. . . . At last he scented it out.

The following day Anninka expected a reprimand but there was none. As usual Porphyry Vladimiritch spent the whole morning in his study, but when he came out to dinner he poured out two glasses of vodka instead of one for himself, and with a stupid smile silently pointed out one of them to Anninka. It was, so to speak, a silent invitation which Anninka accepted.

"So you say that Lubinka died?" Iudushka bethought himself half-way through dinner.

"Yes, uncle."

"Well, the Kingdom of Heaven be hers! It's a sin to repine, but we ought to remember her. Shall we drink to her memory?"

"Let us, uncle."

They had another glass each and Iudushka said nothing more: he had evidently not quite recovered after his long spell of solitude. But after dinner, when Anninka, carrying out the family ritual, went up to kiss and thank him, he patted her on the cheek and said:

"So that's what you are!"

That same evening at tea, which lasted longer than usual, Porphyry Vladimiritch kept glancing at Anninka with an enigmatic smile and said at last:

"Shall I tell them to bring a decanter and something to eat?"

"Well . . . do!"

"That's right; better do it in your uncle's presence than in hiding. . . . At any rate your uncle . . ."

Iudushka did not finish his sentence. He probably meant to say, "At any rate your uncle would restrain you," but somehow could not bring it off.

After that, every evening a decanter of vodka and various

324

pickles appeared on the dining-room table. The window-shutters were closed, the servants went to bed, and the uncle and niece remained alone. At first Iudushka lagged behind as it were, but after a little practice he quite caught up with Anninka. They sat there, drinking without haste, and, in the intervals between glasses, talked and recalled the past. At first their conversation was dull and listless, but as their heads grew hotter it became more and more lively and at last inevitably turned into an inconsequent quarrel based upon memories of all the deadly injuries suffered and inflicted at Golovlyovo.

Anninka was always the one to begin those quarrels. With pitiless insistence she went through the family history, and particularly enjoyed taunting Iudushka by proving to him that he and his mother were responsible for all the wrongs. Every word she uttered breathed of such burning hatred that one wondered how a creature so feeble and worn out could have preserved so much vital energy. Her jeering wounded Iudushka inexpressibly, but as a rule, though angered, he defended himself feebly; only when Anninka went too far with her bitter taunts, he began to curse and shout.

Such scenes took place every day without fail. Though the details of the tragic family history were soon exhausted, the memory of it haunted their minds so persistently that all their powers of thought were completely absorbed by it. Every episode, every reminiscence disturbed some old sore and brought back to mind some new series of Golovlyovo wrongs. Anninka found a bitter vindictive pleasure in bringing them to light, in condemning and even exaggerating them. Not a single moral principle to stand by could she find in the whole of the Golovlyovo past and present. Nothing but wretched miserliness and empty talk, stones instead of bread, slaps instead of advice, or—by way of a change—horrid reminders about eating the bread of others, being a hanger-on, a beggar, a greedy mouth to feed. . . . That was all the answer given to a young heart that was yearning for love, warmth, kindness. And to think of it! Through a bitter irony of fate this cruel bringing up resulted not in a Spartan attitude to life but in a passionate desire to enjoy its poisonous delights. Youth worked the miracle of forgetfulness: it did not let her heart grow hard, did not allow the hatred to develop in it but filled it with an overwhelming thirst for life. That was why the reckless excitement of stage life held her under its spell for years, thrusting all the Golovlyovo memories far into the background. Only now, when the end was in sight, a gnawing pain invaded her heart; only now Anninka thoroughly understood her past and began to hate it bitterly. Those drunken conversations continued long after midnight, and had not their sting been softened by drunken incoherence of thought and of speech they might have soon led to something dreadful. Fortunately, however, while drink opened up an inexhaustible source of pain in their aching hearts, it also gave them peace. As night advanced their words grew more and more confused and their hatred less virulent. In the end all sense of pain disappeared and both the past and the present were obliterated by a luminous void. Their tongues hardly obeyed them, their eyes refused to keep open, their movements grew stiff. Uncle and niece got up heavily from their chairs and staggered to their lairs.

These night-orgies could not of course remain a secret. Their character was so obvious that no one thought it strange when some member of the household said it might soon end in crime. The Golovlyovo house grew stiller than ever; even in the mornings there was no sign of life in it. The uncle and niece woke up late and then till dinner-time Anninka's heart-rending cough, accompanied by continual cursing, resounded through the rooms. Iudushka listened in fear to the terrible sounds, feeling that he too was heading for a catastrophe that would make an end of him.

Death seemed creeping out of every corner of that hateful house. Whichever way one looked, in whatever direction one turned, gray ghosts were stirring everywhere. There was his father Vladimir Mihailitch in a white cap, putting out his tongue and quoting Barkov; there was his brother, Styopka the dolt and beside him his other brother, the dull and quiet Pavel; there was Lubinka and there were the last scions of the Golovlyovo house, Volòdenka and Pètenka. All of them drunken, lecherous, tortured and bleeding. . . . And a living ghost was hovering above all those shadows—he himself, Porphyry Vladimiritch Golovlyov, the last representative of the dying family.

Constant reminders of old wrongs were bound to produce an effect at last. The past had been laid bare so completely that the least touch made it hurt. The natural consequence of this was something like fear or an awakening of conscience—the second rather than the first. Surprisingly enough it appeared that conscience had not been altogether absent, but merely pushed far back and as it were forgotten—losing in consequence the acute sensitiveness that always reminds one of its existence.

Such awakenings of a neglected conscience are extremely painful. When a man's moral sense has not been trained it does not reconcile him to himself, does not reveal to him the possibility of a new life but merely tortures him endlessly and vainly, giving him no hope for the future. A man feels as though he were in a stone well, pitilessly condemned to suffer the agonies of remorse without any chance of ever returning to life. And the only means of stilling the pain that wears him away to no purpose is to take advantage of a moment of gloomy resolve and break his head against the walls of stone.

In the course of his long and empty life it had never occurred to Iudushka that living souls were being stifled all round him. He thought he lived soberly and piously, without rush or hurry and never supposed that this was spoiling other people's lives and, still less, that he was responsible for their coming to grief.

And suddenly the awful truth dawned upon his conscience —dawned too late, for there was no revoking or remedying the past. Here he was old, solitary, with one foot in the grave, and there was not a single creature in the whole world who would go near him and pity him. Why was he alone? Why did he meet with nothing but indifference and hatred? Why did all that had anything to do with him perish? Here at that very Golovlyovo there had once been quite a human nest—how was it that not a feather was left of it? The only fledgling that had survived was his niece, but she had come back merely to mock him, to hound him to death. Even Yevpraxeya, simple as she was, hated him. She lived at Golovlyovo because he sent a monthly supply of food to her father, the sexton, but she certainly lived there hating him. And he, the Judas, had done her the greatest wrong of all—he had put out the light of her life, taking away her son and casting him out, as into some bottomless pit. What did all his life come to? Why had he lied, babbled, clung to his possessions, injured other people? Even from the material point of view, from the point of view of "legacy"—who would profit by the result of it all? Who?

I repeat, his conscience woke up at last but to no purpose. Iudushka groaned and, consumed with anger and restlessness, with feverish impatience waited for the evening, not only to get drunk like a brute but to drown his conscience in the vodka. He hated "the wench" who so coldly and impudently probed his wounds but he was irresistibly drawn to her as though something still remained unsaid between them and there were more wounds to be probed. Every evening he made Anninka repeat the story of Lubinka's death and every evening the idea of self-destruction gained greater hold on him. At first it flashed through his mind accidentally, but as the wrongs of the past grew clearer it began to take root and at last became the only point of light in the blackness of the future.

His physical health was shattered as well. He had a bad cough and suffered from horrible attacks of asthma, which are enough to make one's life a perfect agony apart from any moral tortures. All the symptoms of the typical Golovlyovo poisoning were present and the death-bed groans of his brother Pavel gasping for breath in the upper rooms of the Dubrovino house were already echoing in his ears. And yet his flat sunken chest, that seemed ready to split any moment, proved extraordinarily strong. Every day it went through more and more physical agony and yet it did not give in. It was as though his body too were avenging the old wrongs by refusing to die. "Surely this is the end!" Iudushka said hopefully as the attack came on; but the end did not come. Evidently violence was needed to hurry it.

In short, from whatever angle one looked at it, all his accounts with life were done with. There was nothing to live for and it was torture to go on; what he needed most was death, but the trouble was that death would not come. There is something mean and perfidious in this insulting delay, when one's whole being longs for death, but death merely taunts one and lures one on. . . .

It was the end of March, and Holy Week was nearly over. Slack as Porphyry Vladimiritch had grown of late, he too could not help feeling the holiness of those days which he had been taught to revere as a child. His thoughts unconsciously turned to solemn matters; his heart longed for nothing but perfect peace. Under the influence of this mood the evenings were now spent in silence and melancholy abstinence.

Iudushka and Anninka were alone in the dining-room. The

Vigil service with the reading of "twelve Gospels"* finished about an hour before and there still was a strong smell of incense in the room. The clock struck ten; the servants had gone to their quarters and a profound silence reigned in the house. Anninka, resting her head on her hands, leant on the table, lost in thought; Porphyry Vladimiritch, sad and silent, sat facing her.

Anninka had always been deeply moved by this service. While still a child she wept bitterly when the priest read out, "And when they had plaited a crown of thorns, they put it upon His head, and a reed in His right hand," and in a thin little voice breaking with sobs seconded the choristers singing, "Glory to Thy long suffering, O Lord! Glory to Thee!" After the service, still shaken with emotion, she ran to the maids' room and there, in the gathering twilight (Arina Petrovna gave the maids no candles when there was no work to do), told the serf-girls the story of Our Lord's Passion. The serf-girls shed quiet tears, heaved profound sighs. In their bondage they felt that their Lord and Redeemer was near, they believed that He would rise from the dead in very truth. And Anninka too felt it and believed. Beyond the dark night of scourging, vile jeers, and wagging of heads all those poor in spirit saw the kingdom of light and liberty. Arina Petrovna herself, usually so stern, grew gentle during those days, did not scold, did not reproach Anninka with being an orphan but stroked her hair and begged her not to be distressed. But Anninka could not calm herself even after going to bed, tossed about, jumped up several times in the night, and talked in her sleep.

Then followed the years at school and the years of wandering. The first were without any interest, the second—full of horrible vulgarity. Even then, however, in the hideous

---

*Twelve selections from the Gospels, beginning with St. John xiii and ending with Matt. xxvii. —Translator's note.

strolling life of an actress, Anninka jealously guarded "the holy days," calling up the echoes of the past that helped her to sigh and weep like a child. But now, when all her life down to the smallest detail was bared before her, when a curse lay on her past and the future held neither repentance nor forgiveness, when her heart could no longer be melted and she had no more tears to shed—the impression produced on her by the sorrowful story to which she had just listened was truly overwhelming. In her childhood too dark night was all around her, but beyond the darkness there was a hope of dawn. And now there was nothing to hope for, nothing to expect: nothing but an eternal and unchanging night. Anninka did not sigh or distress herself or even think of anything; a kind of numbness possessed her.

Porphyry Vladimiritch from early youth had also held "the holy days" in reverence, but solely as a matter of form, like a true idolater. Every year on the eve of Good Friday he invited the priest, listened to the Gospel story, sighed, raised his arms, bowed down to the ground, marked on his candle* the number of Gospels read, but never understood anything. And only now, when Anninka had roused in him a sense of guilt, he grasped for the first time that the Gospel story told of a terrible, cruel wrong that had been done to Truth. . . .

Of course it would be an exaggeration to say that this discovery made him draw any practical comparisons, but there is no doubt that a confusion akin to despair possessed his mind. That confusion was all the more painful because he had been so unconscious of the past which brought it upon him. There was something dreadful in that past, but what it was he could not remember clearly. And yet he could not forget it either. Something huge that had so far stood motionless, covered with an impenetrable veil, suddenly seemed to

---

*While the Gospels are being read the people stand with lighted wax candles in their hands. —Translator's note.

have moved towards him, threatening to crush him any moment. If it really crushed him, that would be best of all; but he was not easily killed—he might crawl out from under it after all. No, there was no certainty that the natural course of events would bring any solution with it; he ought to discover the solution for himself and thus put an end to this unbearable confusion. There was a solution, he knew. He had been considering it for the last month and he thought that this time he would not fail. "We shall be going to Communion on Saturday," flashed suddenly through his mind. "I must go to mamma's grave to ask her forgiveness."

"Shall we?" he asked Anninka, having told her of his plan.

"Perhaps . . . let's drive there."

"No, not drive there, but . . ." Porphyry Vladimiritch began and broke off suddenly, as though grasping that Anninka might hinder him.

"I have wronged mamma . . . it was I brought her to her death . . . I!" wandered through his mind, and his longing "to ask her forgiveness" grew stronger and stronger every minute —not to do it in the ordinary, traditional way but to fall moaning at her grave, transfixed with grief and pain.

"So you say Lubinka died of her own will?" he asked suddenly, as though to give himself courage.

At first Anninka did not seem to have heard her uncle's question, but it had evidently reached her because in another two or three minutes she too felt an irresistible desire to return to that death and torture herself with the memories of it.

"She really said, 'Drink . . . you vile creature'?" he asked when she had repeated her story.

"Yes . . . she did."

"And you remained alive. . . . You didn't drink?"

"No, I am living."

He got up and walked up and down the room in obvious agitation. At last he came up to Anninka and stroked her hair.

"You poor, poor child!" he said quietly.

Something unexpected happened to her at that touch. At first she was amazed, but then her face began to work and suddenly a storm of horrible, hysterical sobs broke from her breast.

"Uncle, you are good, aren't you? Tell me!" she almost screamed.

In a breaking voice, with sobs and tears, she kept repeating the question to which he had given such an absurd answer on the day when she returned from her wanderings to settle at Golovlyovo.

"You are good? Tell me, answer me, you are good, aren't you?"

"Have you heard what the priest read to-night?" he said when she had quieted down at last. "Ah, what suffering that was! It's only by suffering like Him that one can . . . And He forgave, He forgave all and for ever!"

In distress and misery he began pacing up and down the room again, not noticing that beads of perspiration covered his face.

"He forgave them all!" he said, speaking aloud to himself. "Not merely those who at that time gave Him vinegar and gall to drink but also those who afterwards, now and for ever and ever, will go on putting vinegar mingled with gall to His lips. . . . It's terrible! Ah, it's terrible!"

And stopping in front of her he asked suddenly:

"And you . . . have you forgiven?"

Instead of an answer she rushed to him and flung her arms round his neck.

"I need forgiving!" he went on, "for everyone . . . and for yourself . . . and for those who are no more. . . . How is it? What has happened?" he cried almost distractedly, looking round him. "Where are . . . *they all?*"

333

They went to their rooms feeling utterly shattered. But Porphyry Vladimiritch could not sleep. He turned from side to side in his bed trying to think what it was he had to do. And suddenly the words that had casually flitted through his mind a couple of hours before appeared quite clearly in his memory: "I must go to mamma's grave and ask her forgiveness." At this reminder a terrible, restless anxiety possessed him. . . .

At last he could stand it no longer. He got out of bed and put on his dressing-gown. It was still dark out of doors and not the faintest rustle could be heard anywhere. Porphyry Vladimiritch walked up and down the room for some time, stopping to gaze at the icon of the Redeemer in a crown of thorns lighted by a sanctuary lamp. At last he made up his mind. It is hard to say to what extent he was conscious of his own decision, but a few minutes later he stealthily walked to the hall and undid the front-door latch.

A wind was howling outside and a March snow-storm blinded the eyes with whirling masses of sleet. But Porphyry Vladimiritch walked along the road, stepping in the puddles, noticing neither the wind nor the snow and only instinctively wrapping his dressing-gown closer about him.

Early next morning a messenger on horseback galloped up from the village nearest to the churchyard where Arina Petrovna was buried and said that Porphyry Vladimiritch's frozen corpse had been found within a few steps of the road. They rushed to Anninka, but she lay in bed unconscious, with all the symptoms of a brain-fever. Then another messenger was dispatched to Goryushkino, to Nadya Galkin (daughter of Auntie Varvara Mihailovna), who ever since the autumn had kept close watch on all that was going on at Golovlyovo.

TITLES IN SERIES

For a complete list of titles, visit www.nyrb.com or write to:
Catalog Requests, NYRB, 435 Hudson Street, New York, NY 10014

* *Also available as an electronic book.*